DEBBIE MACOMBER

A Country Affair

2 Great Stories
A Little Bit Country and *Country Bride*

ISBN-13: 978-0-7783-11124-9

9 780778 311249

50899

EAN

DEBBIE MACOMBER

A Country Affair

A Little Bit Country and *Country Bride*

mira

Recycling programs for this product may not exist in your area.

ISBN-13: 978-0-7783-1124-9

A Country Affair

Copyright © 2021 by Harlequin Books S.A.

A Little Bit Country
First published in 1990. This edition published in 2021.
Copyright © 1990 by Debbie Macomber

Country Bride
First published in 1990. This edition published in 2021.
Copyright © 1990 by Debbie Macomber

This edition published by arrangement with Harlequin Books S.A.

For questions and comments about the quality of this book, please contact us at CustomerService@Harlequin.com.

Mira
22 Adelaide St. West, 40th Floor
Toronto, Ontario M5H 4E3, Canada
www.Harlequin.com

Printed in U.S.A.

Also available from Debbie Macomber and MIRA

CONTENTS

A LITTLE BIT COUNTRY

One

"**H**elp! Fire!" Rorie Campbell cried as she leaped out of the small foreign car. Smoke billowed from beneath the hood, rising like a burnt offering to a disgruntled god. Rorie ran across the road, and a black-and-white cow ambled through the pasture toward her, stopping at the split-rail fence. Soulful brown eyes studied her, as if the cow wondered what all the commotion was about.

"It's not even my car," Rorie said, pointing in the direction of the vehicle. "All of a sudden smoke started coming out."

The cow regarded her blankly, chewing its cud, then returned lazily to the shade of a huge oak tree.

"I think it's on fire. Dan's going to kill me for this," Rorie muttered as she watched the uninterested animal saunter away. "I don't know what to do." There was no water in sight and even if there had been, Rorie didn't have any way of hauling it to the car. She was so desperate, she was talking to a cow—and she'd almost expected the creature to advise her.

"Howdy."

Rorie whirled around to discover a man astride a

chestnut stallion. Silhouetted against the warm afternoon sun, he looked like an apparition smiling down at her from the side of the hill opposite Dan's car.

"Hello." Rorie's faith in a benign destiny increased tenfold in that moment. "Boy, am I glad to see another human being." She'd been on this road for the past two hours and hadn't encountered another car in either direction.

"What seems to be the problem?" Leather creaked as the man swung out of the saddle with an ease that bespoke years of experience.

"I… I don't know," Rorie said, flapping her hands in frustration. "Everything was going just great when all of a sudden the car started smoking like crazy."

"That's steam."

"Steam! You mean the car isn't on fire?"

The man flipped the reins over his horse's head and walked toward the hood of the sports car. It was then that Rorie realized the man wasn't a man at all, but a boy. Sixteen, or possibly a little older. Not that Rorie was particular. She was just grateful someone had stopped. "A friend of mine insisted I drive his MGB up to Seattle." She sighed. "I should've known that if anything went wrong, I'd be at a total loss about what to do. I should've known…"

The boy whipped a large blue-starred hankie from the hip pocket of his faded jeans and used it to protect his hand while he raised the hood of her car. The instant he did, a great white cloud of steam swirled up like mist from a graveyard in a horror movie.

"I…thought I'd take the scenic route," Rorie explained, frantically waving her hand in front of her face to dispel the vapor. "The man at the gas station a hundred miles back said this is beautiful country. He said I'd miss some of the best scenery in Oregon if I stuck to the freeway." Rorie knew she was chattering, but she'd never experienced this type of situation before or felt quite so helpless.

"It's not only the best scenery in the state, it tops the whole country, if you ask me," the boy murmured absently while he examined several black hoses beneath the raised hood.

Rorie looked at her watch and moaned. If she wasn't in Seattle before six, she'd lose her hotel reservation. This vacation wasn't starting out well—not at all. And she'd had such high expectations for the next two weeks.

"I think you've got a leak in your water pump," the teenager stated, sounding as though he knew what he was talking about. "But it's hard to tell with all that fancy stuff they got in these foreign cars. Clay can tell you for sure."

"Clay?"

"My brother."

"Is he a mechanic?" Rorie's hopes soared.

"He's done his share of working on cars, but he's not a mechanic."

Rorie gnawed on her lower lip as her spirits plummeted again. Her first concern was getting to a phone. She'd make the necessary arrangements to have the car repaired and then call the hotel to ask if they'd hold her room. Depending on how close she was to the nearest town, Rorie figured it would take an hour for a tow truck to arrive and then another for it to get her car to a garage. Once there, the repairs shouldn't take too long. Just how hard could it be to fix a water pump?

"How far is it to a phone?"

The young man grinned and pointed toward his horse. "Just over that ridge…"

Rorie relaxed. At least that part wasn't going to be much of a problem.

"…about ten miles," he finished.

"Ten miles?" Rorie leaned her weight against the side of the car. This was the last time she'd ever take the scenic route and the last time she'd ever let Dan talk her into borrowing his car!

"Don't worry, you won't have to walk. Venture can handle both of us. You don't look like you weigh much."

"Venture?" Rorie was beginning to feel like an echo.

"My horse."

Rorie's gaze shifted to the stallion, who had lowered his head to sample the tall hillside grass. Now that she had a chance to study him, she realized what an extraordinarily large animal he was. Rorie hadn't been on the back of a horse since she was a child. Somehow, the experience of riding a pony in a slow circle with a bunch of other six-year-olds didn't lend her much confidence now.

"You…you want me to ride double with you?" She was wearing a summer dress and mounting a horse might prove…interesting. She eyed the stallion, wondering how she could manage to climb into the saddle and still maintain her dignity.

"You wearing a dress and all could make that difficult." The boy rubbed the side of his jaw, frowning doubtfully.

"I could wait here until someone else comes along," she offered.

He used his index finger to set his snap-brim hat further back on his head. "You might do that," he drawled, "but it could be another day or so—if you're lucky."

"Oh, dear!"

"I suppose I could head back to the house and grab the pickup," he suggested.

It sounded like a stroke of genius to Rorie. "Would you? Listen, I'd be more than happy to pay you for your time."

He gave her an odd look. "Why would you want to do that? I'm only doing the neighborly thing."

Rorie smiled at him. She'd lived in San Francisco most of her life. She loved everything about the City by the Bay, but she couldn't have named the couple in the apartment next door had her life depended on it. People in the city kept to themselves.

"By the way," he said, wiping his hands with the bright blue handkerchief, "the name's Skip. Skip Franklin."

Rorie eagerly shook his hand, overwhelmingly grateful that he'd happened along when he did. "Rorie Campbell."

"Pleased to meet you, ma'am."

"Me too, Skip."

The teenager grinned. "Now you stay right here and I'll be back before you know it." He paused, apparently considering something else. "You'll be all right by yourself, won't you?"

"Oh, sure, don't worry about me." She braced her feet wide apart and held up her hands in the classic karate position. "I can take care of myself. I've had three self-defence lessons."

Skip chuckled, ambled toward Venture and swung

up into the saddle. Within minutes he'd disappeared over the ridge.

Rorie watched him until he was out of sight, then walked over to the grassy hillside and sat down, arranging her dress carefully around her knees. The cow she'd been conversing with earlier glanced in her direction and Rorie felt obliged to explain. "He's gone for help," she called out. "Said it was the neighborly thing to do."

The animal mooed loudly.

Rorie smiled. "I thought so, too."

An hour passed, and it seemed the longest of Rorie's life. With the sun out in full force now, she felt as if she was wilting more by the minute. Just when she began to suspect that Skip Franklin had been a figment of her overwrought imagination, she heard a loud chugging sound. She leaped to her feet and, shading her eyes with her hand, looked down the road. It was Skip, sitting on a huge piece of farm equipment, heading straight toward her.

Rorie gulped. Her gallant rescuer had come to get her on a tractor!

Skip removed his hat and waved it. Even from this distance, she could see his grin.

Rorie feebly returned the gesture, but her smile felt brittle. Of the two modes of transportation, she would have preferred the stallion. Good grief, there was only one seat on the tractor. Where exactly did Skip plan for her to sit? On the engine?

Once he'd reached the car, he parked the tractor directly in front of it. "Clay said we should tow the car to our place instead of leaving it on the road. You don't mind, do you?"

"Whatever he thinks is best."

"He'll be along any minute," Skip explained, jumping down from his perch. He used a hook and chain to connect the sports car to the tractor. "Clay had a couple of things he needed to do first."

Rorie nodded, grateful her options weren't so limited, after all.

A few minutes later, she heard the sound of another vehicle. This time it was a late-model truck in critical need of a paint job. Rust showed through on the left front fender, which had been badly dented.

"That's Clay now," Skip announced, nodding toward the winding road.

Rorie busied herself brushing bits of grass from the skirt of her dress. When she'd finished, she looked up to see a tall muscular man sliding from the driver's side of the pickup. He was dressed in jeans and a denim shirt, and his hat was pulled low over his forehead, shading his eyes. Rorie's breath caught in her throat as she noticed his grace of movement—a thoroughly masculine grace. Something about Clay Franklin grabbed her imagination. He embodied everything she'd ever linked with the idea of an outdoorsman, a man's man. She could imagine him taming a wilderness or forging an empire. In his clearly defined features she sensed a strength that reminded her of the land itself. The spellbinding quality of his steel-gray eyes drew her own and held them for a long moment. His nose had a slight curve, as though it had been broken once. He smiled, and a tingling sensation Rorie couldn't explain skittered down her spine.

His eyes still looked straight into hers and his hands rested on his lean hips. "Looks as if you've got yourself

into a predicament here." His voice was low, husky—
and slightly amused.

His words seemed to wrap themselves around Rorie's throat, choking off any intelligent reply. Her lips
parted, but to her embarrassment nothing came out.

Clay smiled and the fine lines that fanned out from
the corners of his eyes crinkled appealingly.

"Skip thinks it might be the water pump," she said,
pointing at the MGB. The words came out weak and
rusty and Rorie felt even more foolish. She'd never had
a man affect her this way. He wasn't really even handsome. Not like Dan Rogers. No, Clay wasn't the least
bit like Dan, who was urbane and polished—and very
proud of his little MGB.

"From the sounds of it, Skip's probably right." Clay
walked over to the car, which his brother had connected
to the tractor. He twisted the same black hose Skip had
earlier and shook his head. Next he checked to see that
the bumper of Dan's car was securely fastened to the
chain. He nodded, lightly slapping his brother's back
in approval. "Nice work."

Skip beamed under his praise.

"I assume you're interested in finding a phone.
There's one at the house you're welcome to use," Clay
said, looking at Rorie.

"Thank you." Her heart pounded in her ears and
her stomach felt queasy. This reaction was so unusual
for her. Normally she was a calm, levelheaded twenty-
four-year-old, not a flighty teenager who didn't know
how to act when an attractive male happened to glance
in her direction.

Clay walked around to the passenger side of the
pickup and held open the door. He waited for Rorie,

then gave her his hand to help her climb inside. The simple action touched her; it had been a long time since anyone had shown her such unselfconscious courtesy.

Then Clay walked to the driver's side and hoisted himself in. He started the engine, which roared to life immediately, and shifted gears.

"I apologize for any inconvenience I've caused you," Rorie said stiffly, after several moments of silence.

"It's no problem," Clay murmured, concentrating on his driving, doing just the speed limit and not a fraction more.

They'd been driving for about ten minutes when Clay turned off the road and through a huge log archway with ELK RUN lettered across the top. Lush green pastures flanked the private road, and several horses were grazing calmly in one of them. Rorie knew next to nothing about horse breeds, but whatever these were revealed a grace and beauty that was apparent even to her untrained eye.

The next thing Rorie noticed was the large two-story house with a wide wraparound veranda on which a white wicker swing swayed gently. Budding rosebushes lined the meandering brick walkway.

"It's beautiful," she said softly. Rorie would have expected something like this in the bluegrass hills of Kentucky, not on the back roads of Oregon.

Clay made no comment.

He drove past the house and around the back toward the largest stable Rorie had ever seen. The sprawling wood structure must have had room for thirty or more horses.

"You raise horses?" she said.

A smile moved through his eyes like distant light. "That's one way of putting it. Elk Run is a stud farm."

"Quarter horses?"

That was the only breed that came to mind.

"No. American Saddlebreds."

"I don't think I've ever heard of them before."

"Probably not," Clay said, not unkindly.

He parked the truck, helped Rorie down and led her toward the back of the house.

"Mary," he called, holding the screen door for Rorie to precede him into the large country kitchen. She was met with the smell of cinnamon and apples. The delectable aroma came from a freshly baked pie, cooling on the counter. A black Labrador retriever slept on a braided rug. He raised his head and thumped his tail gently when Clay stepped over to him and bent down to scratch the dog's ears. "This is Blue."

"Hi, Blue," Rorie said, realizing the dog had probably been a childhood pet. He looked well advanced in years.

"Mary doesn't seem to be around."

"Mary's your wife?"

"Housekeeper," Clay informed her. "I'm not married."

That small piece of information gladdened Rorie's heart and she instantly felt foolish. Okay, so she was attracted to this man with eyes as gray as a San Francisco sky, but that didn't change a thing. If her plans went according to schedule, she'd be in and out of his life within hours.

"Mary's probably upstairs," Clay said when the housekeeper didn't answer. "There's a phone on the wall." He pointed to the other side of the kitchen.

While Rorie retrieved her AT&T card from her eelskin wallet, Clay crossed to the refrigerator and took out a brightly colored ceramic pitcher.

"Iced tea?" he asked.

"Please." Her throat felt parched. She had to swallow several times before she could make her call.

As she spoke on the phone, Clay took two tall glasses from a cupboard and half filled them with ice cubes. He poured in the tea, then added thin slices of lemon.

Rorie finished her conversation and walked over to the table. Sitting opposite Clay, she reached for the drink he'd prepared. "That was my hotel in Seattle. They won't be able to hold the room past six."

"I'm sure there'll be space in another," he said confidently.

Rorie nodded, although she thought that was unlikely. She was on her way to a writers' conference, one for which she'd paid a hefty fee, and she hated to miss one minute of it. Every hotel in the city was said to be filled.

"I'll call the garage in Nightingale for you," Clay offered.

"Is that close by?"

"About five miles down the road."

Rorie was relieved. She'd never heard of Nightingale and was grateful to learn it had a garage. After all, the place was barely large enough to rate a mention on the road map.

"Old Joe's been working on cars most of his life. He'll do a good job for you."

Rorie nodded again, not knowing how else to respond.

Clay quickly strode to the phone, punched out the number and talked for a few minutes. He was frowning when he replaced the receiver. Rorie wanted to question him, but before she could, he grabbed an impossibly thin phone book and dialed a second number. His frown was deeper by the time he'd completed the call.

"I've got more bad news for you."

"Oh?" Rorie's heart had planted itself somewhere between her chest and her throat. She didn't like the way Clay was frowning, or the concern she heard in his voice. "What's wrong now?"

"Old Joe's gone fishing and isn't expected back this month. The mechanic in Riversdale, which is about sixty miles south of here, says that if it is your pump it'll take at least four days to ship a replacement."

Two

"Four days!" Rorie felt the color drain from her face. "But that's impossible! I can't possibly wait that long."

"Seems to me," Clay said in his smooth drawl, "you don't have much choice. George tells me he could have the water pump within a day if you weren't driving a foreign job."

"Surely there's someone else I could call."

Clay seemed to mull that over; then he shrugged. "Go ahead and give it a try if you like, but it isn't going to do you any good. If the shop in Riversdale can't get the part until Saturday, what makes you think someone else can do it any faster?"

Clay's calm acceptance of the situation infuriated Rorie. If she stayed here four days, in the middle of nowhere, she'd completely miss the writers' conference, which she'd been planning to attend for months. She'd scheduled her entire vacation around it. She'd made arrangements to travel to Victoria on British Columbia's Vancouver Island after the conference and on the way home take a leisurely trip down the coast.

Clay handed her the phone book, and feeling defeated Rorie thumbed through the brief yellow pages until she came to the section headed Automobile Repair. Only a handful were listed and none of them promised quick service, she noted.

"Yes, well," she muttered, expelling her breath, "there doesn't seem to be any other option." Discouraged, she set the directory back on the counter. "You and your brother have been most helpful and I want you to know how much I appreciate everything you've done. Now if you could recommend a hotel in…what was the name of the town again?"

"Nightingale."

"Right," she said, with a wobbly smile, which was the best she could do at the moment. "Actually, anyplace that's clean will be fine."

Clay rubbed the side of his jaw. "I'm afraid that's going to present another problem."

"Now what? Has the manager gone fishing with Old Joe?" Rorie did her best to keep the sarcasm out of her voice, but it was difficult. Obviously the people in the community of… Nightingale didn't take their responsibilities too seriously. If they were on the job when someone happened to need them, it was probably by coincidence.

"A fishing trip isn't the problem this time," Clay explained, his expression thoughtful. "Nightingale doesn't have a hotel."

"What?" Rorie exploded. "No hotel…but there must be."

"We don't get much traffic through here. People usually stick to the freeway."

If he was implying that *she* should have done so, Rorie couldn't have agreed with him more. She might have seen some lovely scenery, but look where this little side trip had taken her! Her entire vacation was about to be ruined. She slowly released her breath, trying hard to maintain her composure, which was cracking more with every passing minute.

"What about Riversdale? Surely they have a hotel?"

Clay nodded. "They do. It's a real nice one, but I suspect it's full."

"Full? I thought you just told me people don't often take this route."

"Tourists don't."

"Then how could the hotel possibly be full?"

"The Jerome family."

"I beg your pardon?"

"The Jerome family is having a big reunion. People are coming from all over the country. Jed was telling me the other day that a cousin of his is driving out from Boston. The overflow will more than likely fill up Riversdale's only hotel."

One phone call confirmed Clay's suspicion.

"Terrific," Rorie murmured, her hand still on the receiver. The way things were beginning to look, she'd end up sleeping on a park bench—if Nightingale even had a park.

The back door opened and Skip wandered in, obviously pleased about something. He poured himself a glass of iced tea and leaned against the counter, glancing from Rorie to Clay and then back again.

"What's happening?" he asked, when no one volunteered any information.

"Nothing much," Rorie said. "Getting the water pump for my car is going to take four days and it seems the only hotel within a sixty-mile radius is booked full for the next two weeks and—"

"That's no problem. You can stay here," Skip inserted quickly, his blue eyes flashing with eagerness. "We'd love to have you, wouldn't we, Clay?"

Rorie spoke before the elder Franklin had an opportunity to answer. "No, really, I appreciate the offer, but I can't inconvenience you any more than I already have."

"She wouldn't be an inconvenience, would she?" Once more Skip directed the question to his older brother. "Tell her she wouldn't, Clay."

"I can't stay here," she returned, without giving Clay the chance to echo his brother's invitation. She didn't know these people. And, more important, they didn't know her and Rorie refused to impose on them further.

Clay gazed into her eyes and a slow smile turned up the edges of his mouth. "It's up to you, Rorie. You're welcome on Elk Run if you want to stay."

"But you've done so much. I really couldn't—"

"There's plenty of room," Skip announced ardently.

Those baby-blue eyes of his would melt the strongest resolve, Rorie mused.

"There's three bedrooms upstairs that are sitting empty. And you wouldn't need to worry about staying with two bachelors, because Mary's here—she has a cottage across the way."

It seemed inconceivable to Rorie that this family would take her in just like that. But, given her options, her arguments for refusing their offer were weak, to say the least. "You don't even know me."

"We know all we need to, don't we, Clay?" Skip glanced at his older brother, seeking his support.

"You're welcome to stay here, if you like," Clay repeated, his gaze continuing to hold Rorie's.

Again she was struck by the compelling quality of this man. He had a stubborn jaw and she doubted there were many confrontations where he walked away a loser. She'd always prided herself on her ability to read people. And her instincts told her firmly that Clay Franklin could be trusted. She sensed he was scrupulously honest, utterly dependable—and she already knew he was generous to a fault.

"I'd be most grateful," she said, swallowing a surge of tears at the Franklins' uncomplicated kindness to a complete stranger. "But, please, let me do something to make up for all the trouble I've caused you."

"It's no trouble," Skip said, looking as if he wanted to jump up and click his heels in jubilation.

Clay frowned as he watched his younger brother.

"Really," Rorie stressed. "If there's anything I can do, I'd be more than happy to lend a hand."

"Do you know anything about computers?"

"A little," she said. "We use them at the library."

"You're a librarian?"

Rorie nodded and brushed a stray dark curl from her forehead. "I specialize in children's literature." Someday she hoped to have her own work published. That had been her reason for attending the conference in Seattle. Three of the top children's authors in the country were slated to speak. "If you have a computer system, I'd be happy to do whatever I can…"

"Clay bought a new one last winter," Skip informed her proudly. "He has a program that records horse breeding and pedigrees up to the fourth and fifth generation."

A heavyset woman Rorie assumed was the house-keeper entered the kitchen, hauling a mop and bucket. She inspected Rorie with a measuring glance and seemed to find her lacking. She grumbled something about city girls as she sidled past Skip.

"Didn't know you'd decided to hold a convention right in the middle of my kitchen."

"Mary," Clay said, "this is Rorie Campbell, from San Francisco. Her car broke down, so she'll be staying with us for the next few days. Could you see that a bed is made up for her?"

The older woman's wide face broke into a network of frown lines.

"Oh, please, I can do that myself," Rorie said quickly.

Mary nodded. "Sheets are in the closet at the top of the stairs."

"Rorie is our guest." Clay didn't raise his voice, but his displeasure was evident in every syllable.

Mary shrugged, muttering, "I got my own things to do. If the girl claims she can make a bed, then let her."

Rorie couldn't contain her smile.

"You want to invite some city slicker to stay, then fine, but I got more important matters to attend to before I make up a bed for her." With that, Mary marched out of the kitchen.

"Mary's like family," Skip explained. "It's just her way to be sassy. She doesn't mean anything by it."

"I'm sure she doesn't," Rorie said, smiling so Clay and Skip would know she wasn't offended. She gathered that the Franklins' housekeeper didn't hold a high opinion of anyone from the city and briefly wondered why.

"I'll get your suitcase from the car," Skip said, heading for the door.

Clay finished his drink and set the glass on the counter. "I've got to get back to work," he told her, pausing for a moment before he added, "You won't be bored by yourself, will you?"

"Not at all. Don't worry about me."

Clay nodded. "Dinner's at six."

"I'll be ready."

Rorie picked up the empty glasses and put them by the sink. While she waited for Skip to carry in her luggage, she phoned Dan. Unfortunately he was in a meeting and couldn't be reached, so she left a message, explaining that she'd been delayed and would call again. She felt strangely reluctant to give him the Franklins' phone number, but decided there was no reason not to do so. She also decided not to examine that feeling too closely.

Skip had returned by the time she'd hung up. "Clay says you can have Mom and Dad's old room," the teenager announced on his way through the door. He hauled her large suitcase in one hand and her flight bag was slung over his shoulder. "Their room's at the other end of the house. They were killed in an accident five years ago."

"But—"

"Their room's got the best view."

"Skip, really, any bedroom will do... I don't want your parents' room."

"But that's the one Clay wants for you." He bounded up the curving stairway with the energy reserved for the young.

Rorie followed him more slowly. She slid her hand along the polished banister and glanced into the living room. A large natural-rock fireplace dominated one wall. The furniture was built of solid oak, made comfortable with thick chintz-covered cushions. Several braided rugs were placed here and there on the polished wood floor. A piano with well-worn ivory keys stood to one side. The collection of family photographs displayed on top of it immediately caught her eye. She recognized a much younger Clay in what had to be his high-school graduation photo. The largest picture in an ornate brass frame was of a middle-aged couple, obviously Clay and Skip's parents.

Skip paused at the top of the stairway and looked over his shoulder. "My grandfather built this house more than fifty years ago."

"It's magnificent."

"We think so," he admitted, eyes shining with pride.

The master bedroom, which was at the end of the hallway, opened onto a balcony that presented an unobstructed panorama of the entire valley. Rolling green pastures stretched as far as the eye could see. Rorie felt instantly drawn to this unfamiliar rural beauty. She drew a deep breath, and the thought flashed through her mind that it must be comforting to wake up to this serene landscape day after day.

"Everyone loves it here," Skip said from behind her.

"I can understand why."

"Well, I suppose I should get back to work," he said regretfully, setting her suitcases on the double bed. A colorful quilt lay folded at its foot.

Rorie turned toward him, smiling. "Thank you, Skip. I hate to think what would've happened to me if you hadn't come along when you did."

He blushed and started backing out of the room, taking small steps as though he was loath to leave her. "I'll see you at dinner, okay?"

Rorie smiled again. "I'll look forward to it."

"Bye for now." He raised his right hand in a farewell gesture, then whirled around and dashed down the hallway. She could hear his feet pounding on the stairs.

It took Rorie only a few minutes to hang her things in the bare closet. When she'd finished, she went back to the kitchen, where Mary was busy peeling potatoes at the stainless steel sink.

"I'd like to help, if I could."

"Fine," the housekeeper answered gruffly. She took another potato peeler out of a nearby drawer, slapping it down on the counter. "I suppose that's your fancy sports car in the yard."

"The water pump has to be replaced... I think," Rorie answered, not bothering to mention that the MGB wasn't actually hers.

"Humph," was Mary's only response.

Rorie sighed and reached for a large potato. "The mechanic in Riversdale said it would take until Saturday to get a replacement part."

For the second time, Mary answered her with a gruff-sounding *humph*. "If then! Saturday or next Thursday or a month from now, it's all the same to George. Fact is, you could end up staying here all summer."

Three

Mary's words echoed in Rorie's head as she joined Clay and Skip at the dinner table that evening. She stood just inside the dining room, dressed in a summer skirt and a cotton-knit cream-colored sweater, and announced, "I can't stay any longer than four days."

Clay regarded her blankly. "I have no intention of holding you prisoner, Rorie."

"I know, but Mary told me that if I'm counting on George what's-his-name to fix the MG, I could end up spending the summer here. I've got to get back to San Francisco—I have a job there." She realized how nonsensical her little speech sounded, as if that last bit about having a job explained everything.

"If you want, I'll keep after George to make sure he doesn't forget about it."

"Please." Rorie felt a little better for having spoken her mind.

"And the Greyhound bus comes through on Mondays," Skip said reassuringly. "If you had to, you could take that back to California and return later for your friend's car."

"The bus," she repeated. "I *could* take the bus." As it was, the first half of her vacation was ruined, but it'd be nice to salvage what she could of the rest.

Both men were seated, but as Rorie approached the table Skip rose noisily to his feet, rushed around to the opposite side and pulled out a chair for her.

"Thank you," she said, smiling up at him. His dark hair was wet and slicked down close to his head. He'd changed out of his work clothes and into what appeared to be his Sunday best—a dress shirt, tie and pearl-gray slacks. With a good deal of ceremony, he pushed in her chair. As he leaned toward her, it was all Rorie could do to keep from grimacing at the overpowering scent of his spicy aftershave. He must have drenched himself in the stuff.

Clay's gaze seemed to tug at hers and when Rorie glanced in his direction, she saw that he was doing his utmost not to laugh. He clearly found his brother's antics amusing, though he took pains not to hurt Skip's feelings, but Rorie wasn't sure how she should react. Skip was only in his teens, and she didn't want to encourage any romantic fantasies he might have.

"I hope you're hungry," Skip said, once he'd reclaimed his chair. "Mary puts on a good feed."

"I'm starved," Rorie admitted, eyeing the numerous serving dishes spread out on the table.

Clay handed her a large platter of fried chicken. That was followed by mashed potatoes, gravy, rolls, fresh green beans, a mixed green salad, milk and a variety of preserves. By the time they'd finished passing around the food, there wasn't any space left on Rorie's oversize plate.

"Don't forget to leave room for dessert," Clay commented, again with that slow, easy drawl of his. Here Skip was practically doing cartwheels to attract her attention and all Clay needed to do was look at her and she became light-headed. Rorie couldn't understand it. From the moment Clay Franklin had stepped down from his pickup, she hadn't been the same.

"After dinner I thought I'd take you up to the stable and introduce you to King Genius," Skip said, waving a chicken leg.

"I'd be happy to meet him."

"Once you do, you'll feel like you did when you stood on the balcony in the big bedroom and looked at the valley."

Obviously this King wasn't a foreman, as Rorie had first assumed. More than likely, he was one of the horses she'd seen earlier grazing on the pasture in front of the house.

"I don't think it would be a good idea to take Rorie around Hercules," Clay warned his younger brother.

"Of course not." But it looked as if Skip wanted to argue.

"Who's Hercules?"

"Clay's stallion," Skip explained. "He has a tendency to act up if Clay isn't around."

Rorie could only guess what "act up" meant, but even if Skip didn't intend to heed Clay's advice, she gladly would. Other than that pony ride when she was six, Rorie hadn't been near a horse. One thing was certain; she planned to steer a wide path around the creature, no matter how much Skip encouraged her. The largest pet she'd ever owned had been a guinea pig.

"When Hercules first came to Elk Run, the man who brought him said he was mean-spirited and untrainable.

He wanted him destroyed, but Clay insisted on working with the stallion."

"Now he's your own personal horse?" Rorie asked Clay.

He nodded. "We've got an understanding."

"But it's only between them," Skip added. "Hercules doesn't like anyone else getting close."

"He doesn't have anything to worry about as far as I'm concerned," Rorie was quick to assure both brothers. "I'll give him as much space as he needs."

Clay grinned, and once again she felt her heart turn over. This strange affinity with Clay was affirmed in the look he gave her. Unexpected thoughts of Dan Rogers sprang to mind. Dan was a divorced stockbroker she'd been seeing steadily for the past few months. Rorie enjoyed Dan's company and had recently come to believe she was falling in love with him. Now she knew differently. She couldn't be this powerfully drawn to Clay Franklin if Dan was anything more than a good friend. One of the reasons Rorie had decided on this vacation was to test her feelings for Dan. Two days out of San Francisco, and she had her answer.

Deliberately Rorie pulled her gaze from Clay, wanting to attribute everything she was experiencing to the clean scent of country air.

Skip's deep blue eyes sparkled with pride as he started to tell Rorie about Elk Run's other champion horses. "But you'll love the King best. He was the five-gaited world champion four years running. Clay put him out to stud four years ago. National Show Horses are commanding top dollar and we've produced three of the best. King's the sire, naturally."

"Do all the horses I saw in the pasture belong to you?"

"We board several," Skip answered. "Some of the others are brought here from around the country for Clay to break and train."

"You break horses?" She couldn't conceal her sudden alarm. The image of Clay sitting on a wild bronco that bucked and heaved in a furious effort to unseat him did funny things to Rorie's stomach.

"Breaking horses isn't exactly the way Hollywood pictures show it," Clay explained.

Rorie was about to ask him more when Skip planted his elbows on the table and leaned forward. Once again Rorie was assaulted by the overpowering scent of his aftershave. She did her best to smile, but if he remained in that position much longer, her eyes would start watering. Already she could feel a sneeze tickling her nose.

"How old are you, Rorie?" he asked.

The question was so unexpected that she was too surprised to answer immediately. Then she said, "Twenty-four."

"And you live in San Francisco. Is your family there, too?"

"No. My parents moved to Arizona and my brother's going to school back east."

"And you're not engaged or anything?"

As Rorie shook her head, Clay shot his brother an exasperated look. "Are you interviewing Rorie for the *Independent?*"

"No. I was just curious."

"She's too old for you, little brother."

"I don't know about that," Skip returned fervently.

"I've always liked my women more mature. Besides, Rorie's kind of cute."

"Kind of?"

Skip shrugged. "You know what I mean. She doesn't act like a city girl…much."

Rorie's eyes flew from one brother to the next. They were talking as if she wasn't even in the room, and that annoyed her—especially since she was the main topic of conversation.

Unaware of her reaction, Skip helped himself to another roll. "Actually, I thought she might be closer to twenty. With some women it's hard to tell."

"I'll take that as a compliment," Rorie muttered to no one in particular.

"My apologies, Rorie," Clay said contritely. "We were being rude."

She took time buttering her biscuit. "Apology accepted."

"How old do you think I am?" Skip asked her, his eyes wide and hopeful.

It was Rorie's nature to be kind, and besides, Skip had saved her from an unknown fate. "Twenty," she answered with barely a pause.

The younger Franklin straightened and sent his brother a smirk. "I was seventeen last week."

"That surprises me," Rorie continued, setting aside her butter knife and swallowing a smile. "I could've sworn you were much older."

Looking even more pleased with himself, Skip cleared his throat. "Lots of girls think that."

"Don't I remember you telling me you're helping Luke Rivers tonight?" Clay reminded his brother.

Skip's face fell. "I guess I did."

"If Rorie doesn't mind, I'll introduce her to King."

Clay's offer appeared to surprise Skip, and Rorie studied the boy, a little worried now about causing problems between the two brothers. Nor did she want to disappoint Skip, who had offered first.

"But I thought…" Skip began, then swallowed. "You want to take Rorie?"

Clay's eyes narrowed, and when he spoke, his voice was cool. "That's what I just said. Is there a problem?"

"No…of course not." Skip stuffed half a biscuit in his mouth and shook his head vigorously. After a moment of chewing, he said, "Clay will show you around the stable." His words were measured and even, but his gaze held his brother's.

"I heard," Rorie said gently. She could only speculate on what was going on between them, but obviously something was amiss. There'd been more than a hint of surprise in Skip's eyes at Clay's offer. She noticed that the younger Franklin seemed angry. Because his vanity was bruised? Rorie supposed so. "I could wait until tomorrow if you want, Skip," she suggested.

"No, that's all right," he answered, lowering his eyes. "Clay can do it, since that's what he seems to want."

When they finished the meal, Rorie cleared the table, but Mary refused to let her help with cleaning up the kitchen.

"You'd just be in the way," she grumbled, though her eyes weren't unfriendly. "Besides, I heard the boys were showing you the barn."

"I'll do the dishes tomorrow night then."

Mary murmured a response, then asked brusquely, "How was the apple pie?"

"Absolutely delicious."

A satisfied smile touched the edges of the woman's mouth. "Good. I did things a little differently this time, and I was just wondering."

Clay led Rorie out the back door and across the yard toward the barn. The minute Rorie walked through the enormous double doors she felt she'd entered another world. The wonderful smells of leather and liniments and saddle soap mingled with the fragrance of fresh hay and the pungent odor of the horses themselves. Rorie found it surprisingly pleasant. Flashes of bright color from halters and blankets captured her attention, as did the gleam of steel bits against the far wall.

"King's over here," Clay said, guiding her with a firm hand beneath her elbow.

When Clay opened the top of the stall door, the most magnificent creature Rorie had ever seen turned to face them. He was a deep chestnut color, so sleek and powerful it took her breath away. This splendid horse seemed to know he was royalty. He regarded Rorie with a keen eye, as though he expected her to show him the proper respect and curtsy. For a wild moment, Rorie was tempted to do exactly that.

"I brought a young lady for you to impress," Clay told the stallion.

King took a couple of steps back and pawed the ground.

"He really is something," Rorie whispered, once she'd found her voice. "Did you raise him from a colt?"

Clay nodded.

Rorie was about to ask him more when they heard frantic whinnying from the other side of the aisle.

Clay looked almost apologetic. "If you haven't already guessed, that's Hercules. He doesn't like being ignored." He walked to the stall opposite King's and opened the upper half of the door. Instantly the black stallion stuck his head out and complained about the lack of attention in a loud snort, which brought an involuntary smile to Rorie's mouth. "I was bringing Rorie over to meet you, too, so don't get your nose out of joint," Clay chastised.

"Hi," Rorie said, and raised her right hand in a stiff greeting. It amused her that Clay talked to his animals as if he honestly expected them to understand his remarks and join in the conversation. But then who was she to criticize? Only a few hours earlier, she'd been conversing with a cow.

"You don't need to be frightened of him," Clay told her when she stood, unmoving, a good distance from the stall. Taking into consideration what Skip had mentioned earlier about the moody stallion, Rorie decided to stay where she was.

Clay ran his hand down the side of Hercules's neck, and his touch seemed to appease the stallion's obviously delicate ego.

Looking around her, Rorie was impressed by the size of the barn. "How many stalls are there altogether?"

"Thirty-six regular and four foaling. But this is only a small part of Elk Run." He led her outside to a large arena and pointed at a building on the opposite side. "My office is over there, if you'd like to see it."

Rorie nodded, and they crossed to the office. Clay opened the door for her. Inside, the first thing she noticed was the collection of championship ribbons and photographs displayed on the walls. A large trophy case was filled with a variety of awards. When he saw her interest in the computer, Clay explained the system he'd had installed and how it would aid him in the future.

"This looks pretty straightforward," Rorie told him.

"I've been meaning to hire a high-school kid to enter the data for me so I can get started, but I haven't got around to it yet."

Rorie sorted through the file folders. There were only a few hours of work and her typing skills were good. "There's no need to pay anyone. If I'm going to be imposing on your hospitality, the least I can do is enter this into the computer for you."

"Rorie, that isn't necessary. I don't want you to spend your time stuck here in the office doing all that tedious typing."

"It'll give me something productive to do instead of fretting over how long it's taking to get the MG repaired."

He glanced at her, his expression concerned. "All right, if you insist, but it really isn't necessary, you know."

"I do insist." Rorie clasped her hands behind her back and decided to change the subject. "What's that?" she asked, gesturing toward a large room off the office. Floor-to-ceiling windows looked out over the arena.

"The observation room."

"So you can have your own private shows?"

"In a manner of speaking. Would you like to go down there?"

"Oh, yes!"

Inside the arena, Rorie saw that it was much bigger than it had appeared from above. They'd been walking around for several minutes when Clay checked his watch and frowned. "I hate to cut this short, but I've got a meeting in town. Normally I wouldn't leave company."

"Oh, please," she said hurriedly, "don't worry about it. I mean, it's not as though I was expected or anything. I hardly consider myself company."

Still Clay seemed regretful. "I'll walk you back to the house."

He left in the pickup a couple of minutes later. The place was quiet; Mary had apparently finished in the kitchen and retired to her own quarters, a cottage not far from the main house. Skip, who had returned from helping his friend, was busy talking on the phone. He smiled when he saw Rorie, without interrupting his conversation.

Rorie moved into the living room and idly picked up a magazine, leafing through it. Restless and bored, she read a heated article on the pros and cons of a new medication used for equine worming, although she couldn't have described what it said.

When Skip was finished on the phone, he suggested they play cribbage. Not until after ten did Rorie realize she was unconsciously waiting for Clay's return. But she wasn't quite sure why.

Skip yawned rather pointedly and Rorie took the hint.

"I suppose I should think about heading up to bed," she said, putting down the deck of playing cards.

"Yeah, it seems to be that time," he answered, yawning again.

"I didn't intend to keep you up so late."

"Oh, that's no problem. It's just that we start our days early around here. But you sleep in. We don't expect you to get up before the sun just because we do."

By Rorie's rough calculation, getting up before the sun meant Clay and Skip started their workday between four-thirty and five in the morning.

Skip must have read the look in her eyes, because he chuckled and said, "You get used to it."

Rorie followed him up the stairs, and they said their good-nights. But even after a warm bath, she couldn't sleep. Wearing her flower-sprigged cotton pajamas, she sat on the bed with the light still on and thought about how different everything was from what she'd planned. She was supposed to be in Seattle now, at a cocktail party arranged for the first night of the conference; she'd hoped to talk to several of the authors there. But she'd missed that, and the likelihood of attending even one workshop was dim. Instead she'd made an unscheduled detour onto a stud farm and stumbled upon a handsome rancher.

She grinned. Things could be worse. Much worse.

An hour later, Rorie heard a noise outside, behind the house. Clay must be home. She smiled, oddly pleased that he was back. Yawning, she reached for the lamp on the bedside table and turned it off.

The discordant noise came again.

Rorie frowned. This time, whatever was making the racket didn't sound the least bit like a pickup truck parking, or anything else she could readily identify. The dog was barking intermittently.

Grabbing her housecoat from the foot of the bed and tucking her feet into fuzzy slippers, Rorie went downstairs to investigate.

As she stood in the kitchen, she could tell that the clamor was coming from the barn. A problem with the horses?

Not knowing what else to do, she scrambled up the stairs and hurried from room to room until she found Skip's bedroom.

The teenager lay sprawled across his bed, snoring loudly.

"Skip," she cried, "something's wrong with the horses!"

He continued to snore.

"Skip," she cried, louder this time. "Wake up!"

He remained deep in sleep.

"Skip, please, oh, please, wake up!" Rorie pleaded, shaking him so hard he'd probably have bruises in the morning. "I'm from the city. Remember? I don't know what to do."

The thumps and bangs coming from the barn were growing fiercer and Blue's barking more frantic. Perhaps there was a fire. Oh, dear Lord, she prayed, not that. Rorie raced halfway down the stairs, paused and then reversed her direction.

"Skip," she yelled. "Skip!" Rorie heard the panic in her own voice. "Someone's got to do something!"

No one else seemed to think so.

Nearly frantic now, Rorie dashed back down the stairs and across the yard. Trembling, she entered the barn. A lone electric light shone from the ceiling, dimly illuminating the area.

Several of the stalls' upper doors were open and Rorie could sense the horses becoming increasingly restless. Walking on tiptoe, she moved slowly toward the source of the noise, somewhere in the middle of the stable. The horses were curious and their cries brought Rorie's heart straight to her throat.

"Nice horsey, nice horsey," she repeated soothingly

over and over until she reached the stall those unearthly sounds were coming from.

The upper half of the door was open and Rorie flattened herself against it before daring to peek inside. She saw a speckled gray mare, head thrown back and teeth bared, neighing loudly, ceaselessly. Rorie quickly jerked away and resumed her position against the outside of the door. She didn't know much about horses, but she knew this one was in dire trouble.

Running out of the stable, Rorie picked up the hem of her robe and sprinted toward the house. She'd find a way to wake Skip or die trying.

She was breathless by the time she got to the yard. That was when she saw Clay's battered blue truck.

"Clay," she screamed, halting in the middle of the moonlit yard. "Oh, Clay."

He was at her side instantly, his hands roughly gripping her shoulders. "Rorie, what is it?"

She was so glad to see him, she hugged his waist and only just resisted bursting into tears. Her shoulders were heaving and her voice shook uncontrollably. "There's trouble in the barn...."

Four

Clay ran toward the barn with Rorie right behind him. He paused to flip a switch, flooding the interior with bright light.

The gray mare in the center stall continued to neigh and thrash around. Rorie found it astonishing that the walls had remained intact. The noise of the animal's pain echoed through the stable, reflected by the rising anxiety of the other horses.

Clay took one look at the mare and released a low groan, then muttered something under his breath.

"What's wrong?" Rorie cried.

"It seems Star Bright is about to become a mother."

"But why isn't she in one of the foaling stalls?"

"Because two different vets palpated her and said she wasn't in foal."

"But…"

"She's already had six foals and her stomach's so stretched she looks pregnant even when she isn't." Clay opened the stall door and entered. Rorie's hand flew to her heart. Good grief, he could get killed in there!

"What do you want me to do?" she said.

Clay shook his head. "This is no place for you. Get back to the house and stay there." His brow furrowed, every line a testament to his hard, outdoor life.

"But shouldn't I be phoning a vet?"

"It's too late for that."

"Boiling water—I could get that for you." She wanted to help; she just had no idea how.

"Boiling water?" he repeated. "What the hell would I need that for?"

"I don't know," she confessed with a shrug, "but they always seem to need it in the movies."

Clay gave an exasperated sigh. "Rorie, please, just go to the house."

She made it all the way to the barn door, then abruptly turned back. If anyone had asked why she felt it so necessary to remain with Clay, she wouldn't have been able to answer. But something kept her there, something far stronger than the threat of Clay's temper.

She marched to the center stall, her head and shoulders held stiff and straight. She stood with her feet braced, prepared for an argument.

"Clay," she said, "I'm not leaving."

"Listen, Rorie, you're a city girl. This isn't going to be pretty."

"I'm a woman, too. The sight of a little blood isn't enough to make me faint."

Clay was doing his best to calm the frightened mare, but without much success. The tension in the air seemed to crackle like static electricity.

"I haven't got time to argue with you," he said through clenched teeth.

"Good."

Star Bright heaved her neck backward and gave a

deep groan that seemed to reverberate in the stall like the boom of a cannon.

"Poor little mother," Rorie whispered in a soothing voice. Led by instinct, she carefully unlatched the stall door and slipped inside.

Clay sent her a look hot enough to peel paint. "Get out of here before you get hurt." His voice was low and urgent.

Star Bright reacted to his tension immediately, jerking about, her body twitching convulsively. One of her hooves caught Clay in the forearm and, almost immediately, blood seeped through his sleeve. Rorie bit her lip to suppress a cry of alarm, but if Clay felt any pain he didn't show it.

"Hold her head," Clay said sharply.

Somehow Rorie found the courage to do as he asked. Star Bright groaned once more and her pleading eyes looked directly into Rorie's, seeming to beg for help. The mare's lips pulled back from her teeth as she flailed her head to and fro, shaking Rorie in the process.

"Whoa, girl," Rorie said softly, gaining control. "It's painful, isn't it, but soon you'll have a beautiful baby to show off to the world."

"Foal," Clay corrected from behind the mare.

"A beautiful foal." Rorie stroked the sweat-dampened neck, doing what she could to reassure the frightened horse.

"Keep talking to her," Clay whispered.

Rorie kept up a running dialogue for several tense minutes, but there was only so much she could find to say on such short acquaintance. When she ran out of ideas, she started to sing in a soft, lilting voice. She began with lullabies her mother had once sung to her, then followed those with a few childhood ditties. Her singing lasted only minutes, but Rorie's lungs felt close to collapse.

Suddenly the mare's water broke. Clay wasn't saying much, but he began to work quickly, although she couldn't see what he was doing. Star Bright tossed her neck in the final throes of birth and Rorie watched, fascinated, as two hooves and front legs emerged, followed by a white nose.

The mare lifted her head, eager to see. Clay tugged gently, and within seconds, the foal was free. Rorie's heart pounded like a locomotive struggling up a steep hill as Clay's strong hands completed the task.

"A filly," he announced, a smile lighting his face. He reached for a rag and wiped his hands and arms.

Star Bright turned her head to view her offspring. "See?" Rorie told the mare, her eyes moist with relief. "Didn't I tell you it would all be worth it?"

The mare nickered. Her newborn filly was gray, like her mother, and finely marked with white streaks on her nose, mane and tail. Rorie was touched to her very soul by the sight. Tears blurred her vision and ran down her flushed cheeks. She blotted them with her sleeve so Clay couldn't see them, and silently chided herself for being such a sentimental fool.

It was almost another hour before they left Star Bright's stall. The mare, who stood guard over her long-legged baby, seemed content and utterly pleased with herself. As they prepared to leave, Rorie whispered in her ear.

"What was that all about?" Clay wanted to know, latching the stall door.

"I just told her she'd done a good job."

"That she did," Clay whispered. A moment later, he added, "And so did you, Rorie. I was grateful for your help."

Once more tears sprang to her eyes. She responded with a nod, unable to trust her voice. Her heart was racing with exhilaration. She couldn't remember a time she'd felt more excited. It was well past midnight, but she'd never felt less sleepy.

"Rorie?" He was staring at her, his eyes bright with concern.

She owed him an explanation, although she couldn't fully explain this sudden burst of emotion. "It was so... beautiful." She brushed the hair from her face and smiled up at him, hoping he wouldn't think she was just a foolish city girl. She wasn't sure why it mattered, but she doubted that any man had seen her looking worse, although Rorie was well aware that she didn't possess a classic beauty. She was usually referred to as cute, with her slightly turned-up nose and dark brown eyes.

"I understand." He walked to the sink against the barn's opposite wall and busily washed his hands, then splashed water on his face. When he'd finished, Rorie handed him a towel hanging on a nearby hook.

"Thanks."

"I don't know how to describe it," she said, after a fruitless effort to find the words to explain all the feeling that had surged up inside her.

"It's the same for me every time I witness a birth," Clay told her. He looked at her then and gently touched her face, letting his finger glide along her jaw. All the world went still as his eyes caressed hers. There was a primitive wonder in the experience of birth, a wonder that struck deep within the soul. For the first time,

Rorie understood this. And sharing it with Clay seemed to intensify the attraction she already felt for him. During that brief time in the stall, just before Star Bright delivered her foal, Rorie had felt closer to Clay than she ever had to any other man. It was as though her heart had taken flight and joined his in a moment of sheer challenge and joy. That was a silly romantic thought, she realized. But it seemed so incredible to her that she could feel anything this strong for a man she'd known for mere hours.

"I've got a name for her," Clay said, hanging up the towel. "What do you think of Nightsong?"

"Nightsong," Rorie repeated softly. "I like it."

"In honor of the woman who sang to her mother."

Rorie nodded as emotion clogged her throat. "Does this mean I did all right for a city slicker?"

"You did more than all right."

"Thanks for not sending me away... I probably would've gone if you'd insisted."

They left the barn, and Clay draped his arm across her shoulders as though he'd been doing it for years. Rorie was grateful for his touch because, somehow, it helped ground the unfamiliar feelings and sensations.

As they strolled across the yard, she noticed that the sky was filled with a thousand glittering stars, brighter than any she'd ever seen in the city. She paused midstep to gaze up at them.

Clay's quiet voice didn't dispel the serenity. "It's a lovely night, isn't it?"

Rorie wanted to hold on to each exquisite minute and make it last a lifetime. A nod was all she could manage as she reminded herself that this time with Clay was about to end. They would walk into the house and

Clay would probably thank her again. Then she'd climb the stairs to her room and that would be all there was.

"How about some coffee?" he asked once they'd entered the kitchen. Blue left his rug and wandered over to Clay. "The way I feel now, it would be a waste of time to go to bed."

"Me, too." Rorie leaped at the suggestion, pleased that he wanted to delay their parting, too. And when she did return to her room, she knew the adrenaline in her system would make sleep impossible, anyway.

Clay was reaching up for the canister of coffee, when Rorie suddenly noticed the bloodstain on his sleeve and remembered Star Bright's kick.

"Clay, you need to take care of that cut."

From the surprised way he glanced at his arm, she guessed that he, too, had forgotten about the injury. "Yes, I suppose I should." Then he calmly returned to his task.

"Let me clean it for you," Rorie offered, joining him at the kitchen counter.

"If you like." He led her into the bathroom down the hall and took a variety of medical supplies from the cabinet above the sink. "Do you want to do it here or in the kitchen?"

"Here is fine."

Clay sat on the edge of the bath and unfastened the cuff, then rolled back his sleeve.

"Oh, Clay," Rorie whispered when she saw the angry torn flesh just above his elbow. Gently her fingers tested the edges, wondering if he needed stitches. He winced slightly at her probing fingers.

"Sorry."

"Just put some antiseptic on it and it'll be all right."

"But this is really deep—you should probably have a doctor look at it."

"Rorie, I'm as tough as old leather. This kind of thing happens all the time. I'll recover."

"I don't doubt that," she said primly.

"Then put on a bandage and be done with it."

"But—"

"I've been injured often enough to know when a cut needs a doctor's attention."

She hesitated, then conceded that he was probably right. She filled the sink with warm tap water and took care to clean the wound thoroughly. All the while, Rorie was conscious of Clay's eyes moving over her face, solemnly perusing the chin-length, dark brown hair and the big dark eyes that—judging by a glance in the mirror—still displayed a hint of vulnerability. She was tall, almost five-eight, her figure willowy. But if Clay found anything attractive about her, he didn't mention it. Her throat muscles squeezed shut, and, although she was grateful for the silence between them, it confused her.

"You missed your vocation," he told her as she rinsed the bloody cloth. "You should've been a nurse."

"I toyed with the idea when I was ten, but decided I liked books better."

His shoulders were tense, Rorie noted, and she tried to be as gentle as possible. A muscle leaped in his jaw.

"Am I…hurting you?"

"No," he answered, his voice curt.

After that, he was an excellent patient. He didn't complain when she dabbed on the antiseptic, although she was sure it must have stung like crazy. He cooperated when she wrapped the gauze around his arm, lifting and lowering it when she asked him to. The silence continued as she secured the bandage with adhesive tape. Rorie had the feeling that he wanted to escape the close confines of the bathroom as quickly as possible.

"I hope that stays."

He stood up and flexed his elbow a couple of times. "It's fine. You do good work."

"I'm glad you think so."

"The coffee's probably ready by now." He spoke quickly, as if eager to be gone.

She sighed. "I could use a cup."

She put the medical supplies neatly back inside the cabinet, while Clay returned to the kitchen. Rorie could smell the freshly made coffee even before she entered the room.

He was leaning against the counter, sipping a cup of the fragrant coffee, waiting for her.

"It's been quite a night, hasn't it?" she murmured, adding cream and sugar to the mug he'd poured for her.

A certain tension hung in the air, and Rorie couldn't explain or understand it. Only ten minutes earlier, they'd walked across the yard, spellbound by the stars, and Clay had laid his arm across her shoulders. He'd smiled down on her so tenderly. Now he looked as if he couldn't wait to get away from her.

"Have I done anything wrong?" she asked outright.

"Rorie, no." He set his mug aside and gripped her shoulders with both hands. "There's something so intimate and…earthy in what we shared." His eyes were intense, strangely darker. "Wanting you this way isn't right."

Rorie felt a tremor work through him as he lifted his hands to her face. His callused thumbs lightly caressed her cheeks.

"I feel like I've known you all my life," he whispered hoarsely, his expression uncertain.

"It's...been the same for me, from the moment you stepped out of the truck."

Clay smiled, and Rorie thought her knees would melt. She put her coffee down and as soon as she did Clay eased her into his arms, his hands on her shoulders. Her heart stopped, then jolted back to frenzied life.

"I'm going to kiss you...."

He made the statement almost a question. "Yes," she whispered, letting him know she'd welcome his touch. Her stomach fluttered as he slowly lowered his mouth to hers.

Rorie had never wanted a man's kiss more. His moist lips glided over hers in a series of gentle explorations. He drew her closer until their bodies were pressed tight.

"Oh, Rorie," he breathed, dragging his mouth from hers. "You taste so good... I was afraid of that." His mouth found the pulse in her throat and lingered there.

"This afternoon I thought I'd cry when the car broke down and now...now I'm glad...so glad," she said.

He kissed her again, nibbling on her lower lip, gently drawing it between his teeth. Rorie could hardly breathe, her heart was pounding so hard. She slumped against him, delighting in the rise and fall of his broad chest. His hands moved down her back with slow restraint, but paused when he reached the curve of her hips.

He tensed. "I think we should say good-night."

A protest sprang to her lips, but before she could voice it, Clay said, "Now."

She looked at him, dazed. The last thing she wanted to do was leave him. "What about my coffee?"

"That was just an excuse and we both know it."

Rorie said nothing.

The silence between them seemed to throb for endless minutes.

"Good night, Clay," she finally whispered. She broke away, but his hand caught her fingers, and with a groan he pulled her back into his arms.

"What the hell," he muttered fiercely, "sending you upstairs isn't going to help. Nothing's going to change."

His words brought confusion, but Rorie didn't question him, didn't want to. What she longed for was the warmth and security she'd discovered in his arms.

"Come on," he whispered, after he'd kissed her once more. He led her through the living room and outside to the porch, where the swing moved gently in the night breeze.

Rorie sat beside him and he wrapped his arm around her. She nestled her head against his shoulder, savoring these precious moments.

"I'll never forget this night."

"Neither will I," Clay promised, kissing her again.

Rorie awoke when the sun settled on her face and refused to leave her alone. Keeping her eyes closed, she smiled contentedly, basking in the memory of her night with Clay. They'd sat on the swing and talked for hours. Talked and kissed and laughed and touched...

Sitting up, Rorie raised her hands high above her head and stretched, arching her spine. She looked at her watch on the nightstand and was shocked to see that it was after eleven. By the time she'd climbed the stairs for bed the sky had been dappled with faint shreds of light. She suspected Clay hadn't even bothered to sleep.

Tossing aside the blankets, Rorie slid to the floor, anxious to shower and dress. Anxious to see him again. Fifteen minutes later, she was on her way down the stairs.

Mary, who was dusting in the living room, nodded when she saw Rorie. Then the housekeeper resumed her task, but not before she'd muttered something about how city folks were prone to sleeping their lives away.

"Good morning, Mary," Rorie greeted her cheerfully.

"'Mornin'."

"Where is everyone?"

"Where they ought to be this time of day. Working."

"Yes, I know, but where?"

"Outside."

Rorie had trouble hiding her smile.

"I heard about you helping last night," Mary added gruffly. "Seems you did all right for a city girl."

"Thank you, Mary. You don't do half bad for a country girl, either."

The housekeeper seemed uncomfortable with the praise, despite the lightness of Rorie's tone. "I suppose you want me to cook you some fancy breakfast."

"Good heavens, no, you're busy. I'll just make myself some toast."

"That's hardly enough to fill a growing girl," Mary complained.

"It'll suit me fine."

Once her toast was ready, Rorie carried it outside. If she couldn't find Clay, she wanted to check on Nightsong.

"Rorie."

She turned to discover Skip walking toward her, in animated conversation with a blonde. His girlfriend, she guessed. He waved and Rorie returned the gesture, smiling. The sun was glorious and the day held marvelous promise.

"I didn't think you were ever going to wake up," Skip said.

"I'm sorry—I don't usually sleep this late."

"Clay told me how you helped him deliver Star Bright's filly. You could've knocked me over with a feather when I heard."

Rorie nodded, her heart warming with the memory. "Well, I tried to get you up. It would've been easier to wake a dead man than to get you out of bed last night."

Skip looked slightly embarrassed. "Sorry about that, but I generally don't wake up too easily once I'm asleep." As he spoke, he slipped his arm around the blonde girl's shoulders. "Rorie, I want you to meet Kate Logan."

"Hello, Kate." Rorie held out a hand and Kate shook it politely.

"Hello, Rorie," she said. "Clay and Skip told me about your car troubles. I hope everything turns out all right for you."

"I'm sure it will. Do you live around here?" Rorie already knew she was going to like her. At a closer glance, she saw that Kate was older than she'd first assumed. Maybe her own age, which gave credence to Skip's comment about liking older, more mature women.

"I don't live far," Kate said. "The Circle L is down the road, only a few miles from here."

"She's going to be living *with* us in the near future," Skip put in, gazing fondly at Kate.

The young woman's cheeks reddened and she smiled shyly.

"Oh?" Skip couldn't possibly mean he planned to marry her, Rorie thought. Good heavens, he was still in high school.

He must have seen Rorie's puzzled frown, and hurried to explain. "Not me," he said with a short laugh. "Kate is Clay's fiancée."

Five

"You and Clay are…engaged," Rorie murmured as shock waves coursed through her blood. They stopped with a thud at her heart and spread out in ripples of dismay.

Somehow Rorie managed a smile, her outward composure unbroken. She was even able to offer her congratulations. To all appearances, nothing was wrong. No one would've known that those few simple words had destroyed a night she'd planned to treasure all her life.

"I hope you and Clay will be very happy," Rorie said—and she meant it. She'd just been introduced to Kate Logan, but already Rorie knew that this sweet, friendly woman was exactly the kind of wife a man like Clay would need.

"Skip's rushing things a little," Kate pointed out, but the glint of love in her eyes contradicted her words. "Clay hasn't even given me an engagement ring yet."

"But you and Clay have been talking about getting married, haven't you?" Skip pressed. "And you're crazy about him."

Kate blushed prettily. "I've loved Clay from the time

I was in fifth grade. I wrote his name all over my books. Of course, Clay wouldn't have anything to do with me, not when he was a big important high-schooler and I was just the pesky little girl next door. It took a while for him to notice me—like ten years." She gave a small laugh. "We've been dating steadily for the past two."

"But you and Clay *are* going to get married, right?" Skip continued, clearly wanting to prove his point.

"Eventually, but we haven't set a date, although I'm sure it'll be soon," Kate answered, casting a sharp look at Rorie.

The tightness that had gripped Rorie's throat eased and she struggled to keep her smile intact. It was impossible not to like Kate, but that didn't lessen the ache in Rorie's heart.

"The wedding's inevitable," Skip said offhandedly, "so I wasn't exaggerating when I said you were Clay's fiancée, now was I?"

Kate smiled. "I suppose not. We love each other, and have for years. We're just waiting for the right time." Her eyes held Rorie's, assessing her, but she didn't seem worried about competition.

Rorie supposed she should be pleased about that, at least.

"I was taking Kate over to see Nightsong," Skip explained to Rorie.

"I actually came to Elk Run to meet you," the other woman said. "Clay stopped by last night and told me about your car. I felt terrible for you. Your whole vacation's been ruined. You must be awfully upset."

"These things happen," Rorie said with a shrug. "Being upset isn't going to ship that part any faster. All I can do is accept the facts."

Kate nodded sympathetically. "Skip was about to show me the filly. You'll come with us, won't you?"

Rorie nodded, unable to excuse herself without sounding rude. If there'd been a way, she would have retreated, wanting only to lick her wounds in private. Instead, hoping she sounded more enthusiastic than she felt, she mumbled, "I was headed in that direction myself."

Skip led the way to the barn, which was alive with activity. Clay had explained that Elk Run employed five men full-time, none of whom lived on the premises. Two men mucking out stalls paused when Skip and the women entered the building. Skip introduced Rorie and they touched the tips of their hats in greeting.

"I don't understand Clay," Skip said as they approached the mare's stall. "When we bought Star Bright a few years back, all Clay could do was complain about that silly name. He even talked about getting her registration changed."

"Star Bright's a perfectly good name," Kate insisted, her sunny blue eyes intent on the newborn foal.

Nightsong was standing now on knobby, skinny legs that threatened to buckle, greedily feasting from her mother.

"Oh, she really is lovely, isn't she?" Kate whispered.

Rorie hadn't been able to stop looking at the filly from the moment they'd reached the stall. Finished with her breakfast, Nightsong gazed around, fascinated by everything she surveyed. She returned Rorie's look, not vacantly, but as though she recognized the woman who'd been there at her birth.

Rorie couldn't even identify all the emotions she suddenly felt. Some of these feelings were so new she couldn't put a name to them, but they gripped her heart and squeezed tight.

"What I can't understand," Skip muttered, "is why Clay would go and call her Nightsong when he hates the name Star Bright. It doesn't sound like anything he'd ever come up with on his own, yet he says he did."

"I know," Kate agreed, "but I'm glad, because the name suits her." She sighed. "Clay's always been so practical when it comes to names for his horses, but Nightsong has such a romantic flavor, don't you think?"

Skip chuckled. "You know what Clay thinks about romance, and that makes it even more confusing. But Nightsong she is, and she's bound to bring us a pretty penny in a year or two. Her father was a Polish Arabian, and with Star Bright's bloodlines Nightsong will command big bucks as a National Show Horse."

"Skip." Clay's curt voice interrupted them. He strode from the arena leading a bay mare. The horse's coat gleamed with sweat, turning its color the shade of an oak leaf in autumn. One of the stablemen approached to take the reins. Then Clay removed his hat, wiping his brow with his forearm, and Rorie noticed the now-grimy bandage she'd applied last night. No, this morning.

She stared hungrily at his sun-bronzed face, a face that revealed more than a hint of impatience. The lines around his mouth were etched deep with poorly disguised regrets. Rorie recognized them, even if the others didn't.

Clay stopped short when he saw Kate, his eyes narrowing.

"'Morning, Kate."

"Hello, Clay."

Then his gaze moved, slowly and reluctantly, to Rorie. The remorse she'd already sensed in him seemed unmistakable.

"I hope you slept well," was all he said to her.

"Fine." She detected a tautness along his jawline and decided he was probably concerned that she'd say or do something to embarrass him in front of his fiancée. Rorie wouldn't, but not because she was worried about him. Her sense of fair play wouldn't allow her to hurt Kate, who so obviously adored this man.

"We're just admiring Nightsong," Kate explained, her expression tender as she smiled up at him.

"I can't understand why you'd name her that," Skip said, his mouth twitching with barely suppressed laughter. "You always pick names like Brutus and Firepower, but Nightsong? I think you're going soft on us." Considering himself particularly funny, Skip chuckled and added, "I suppose that's what love does to a man."

Kate's lashes brushed against the high arch of her cheek and she smiled, her pleasure so keen it was like a physical touch.

"Didn't I ask you to water the horses several hours ago?" Clay asked in a tone that could have chipped rock.

"Yes, but—"

"Then kindly see to it. The farrier will be here any minute."

The humor left Skip's eyes; he was clearly upset by Clay's anger. He looked from his brother to the two women and then back at Clay again. Hot color rose into his neck and invaded his face. "All right," he muttered. "Excuse me for living." Then he stormed out of the barn, slapping his hat against his thigh in an outburst of anger.

Kate waited until Skip was out of the barn. "Clay, what's wrong?"

"He should've done what I told him long before now. Those horses in the pasture are thirsty because of his neglect."

"I'm the one you should be angry with, not Skip." Kate's voice was contrite. "I should never have stopped in without calling first, but I...wanted to meet Rorie."

"You've only been here a few minutes," Clay insisted, his anger in check now. "Skip had plenty of time to complete his chores before you arrived."

Rorie tossed invisible daggers at Clay, annoyed with him for taking his irritation out on his younger brother. Skip had introduced her to Clay's fiancée. *That* was what really bothered him if he'd been willing to admit it—which he clearly wasn't.

"We came here to see Nightsong," Kate said again. "I'm glad you named her that, no matter what Skip thinks." She wrapped her arm around his waist, and rested her head against his broad chest. "He was just teasing you and you know how he loves to do that."

Clay gave her an absent smile, but his gaze settled with disturbing ease on Rorie. She met his eyes boldly, denying the emotions churning furiously inside her. The plea for patience and understanding he sent her was so obvious that Rorie wondered how anyone seeing it wouldn't know what was happening.

As though she'd suddenly remembered something, Kate dropped her arm and glanced hurriedly at her watch. She groaned. "I promised Dad I'd meet him for lunch today. He's getting together with the other Town Council members in one of those horribly boring meetings. He needs me as an excuse to get away." She stopped abruptly, a chagrined expression on her face. "I guess that tells you how informal everything is in Nightingale, doesn't it, Rorie?"

"The town seems to be doing very well." She didn't know if that was true or not, but it sounded polite.

"He just hates these things, but he likes the prestige of being a Council member—something I tease him about."

"I'll walk you to your car," Clay offered.

"Oh, there's no need. You're busy. Besides, I wanted to talk to Rorie and arrange to meet her tomorrow and show her around town. I certainly hope you remembered to invite her to the Grange dance tomorrow night. I'm sure Luke would be willing to escort her."

"Oh, I couldn't possibly intrude," Rorie blurted.

"Nonsense, you'd be more than welcome. And don't worry about having the right kind of clothes for a square dance, either, because I've got more outfits than I know what to do with. We're about the same size," Kate said, eyeing her. "Perhaps you're a little taller, but not so much that you couldn't wear my skirts."

Rorie smiled blandly, realizing it wouldn't do any good to decline the invitation. But good heavens, square dancing? Her?

"Knowing you and Skip," Kate chastised Clay, "poor Rorie will be stuck on Elk Run for the next four days bored out of her mind. The least I can do is see that she's entertained."

"That's thoughtful of you," Rorie said. The sooner she got back on the road, the safer her heart would be, and if Kate Logan was willing to help her kill time, then all the better.

"I thought I'd give you a tour of our little town in

the morning," Kate went on. "It's small, but the people are friendly."

"I'd love to see Nightingale."

"Clay." The brusque voice of a farmhand interrupted them. "Could you come here a minute?"

Clay turned to the man and nodded. "I have to find out what Don needs," he said quietly. As he met Rorie's eyes, a speculative look flashed into his own.

She nearly flinched, wondering what emotion her face had betrayed. From the minute Clay had walked into the barn, she'd been careful to school her expression, not wanting him to read anything into her words or actions. She'd tried to look cool and unconcerned, as if the night they'd shared had never happened.

"You two will have to excuse me." Weary amusement turned up the corners of his mouth and Rorie realized he'd readily seen through her guise.

"Of course," Kate said. "I'll see you later, sweetheart."

Clay nodded abruptly and departed with firm purposeful strides.

Kate started walking toward the yard. Rorie followed, eager to escape the barn and all the memories associated with it.

"Clay told us you're a librarian," Kate said when she reached the Ford parked in the curving driveway. "If you want, I can take you to our library. We built a new one last year and we're rather proud of it. I know it's small compared to where you probably work, but I think you'll like what we've done."

"I'd love to see it." Libraries were often the heart of a community, and if the citizens of Nightingale had seen fit to upgrade theirs, it was apparent they shared Rorie's love of books.

"I'll pick you up around ten tomorrow, if that's convenient?"

"That'd be fine."

"Plan on spending the afternoon with me and we'll meet Clay and Skip at the dance later."

Rorie agreed, although her enthusiasm was decidedly low. The last thing she wanted was to be at some social event with Clay. Never mind how Dan would tease her if he ever discovered she'd spent part of her vacation square dancing with the folks at the Grange.

"Bye for now," Kate said.

"Bye," Rorie murmured, waving. She stood in the yard until Kate's car was out of sight. Not sure what else to do, she wandered back into the house, where Mary was busy with preparations for lunch.

"Can I help?" she asked.

In response, Mary scurried to a drawer and once again handed her a peeler. Rorie started carefully whittling away at a firm red apple she'd scooped from a large bowlful of them.

"I don't suppose you know anything about cooking?" Mary demanded, pointing her own peeler at Rorie.

"I've managed to keep from starving for the last few years," she retorted idly.

The merest hint of amusement flashed into the older woman's weathered face. "If I was judging your talents in the kitchen on looks alone, I think you'd starve a man to death within a week."

Despite her glum spirits, Rorie laughed. "If you're telling me you think I'm thin, watch out, Mary, because I'm likely to throw my arms around your neck and kiss you."

The other woman threw her a grin. Several peaceful minutes passed while they peeled apple after apple.

"I got a call from my sister," Mary said hesitantly, her eyes darting to Rorie, then back to her task. "She's coming to Riversdale and wants to know if I can drive over and see her. She's only going to be in Oregon one day."

This was the most Mary had said to Rorie since her arrival. It pleased her that the older woman was lowering her guard and extending a friendly hand.

"I'd like to visit with my sister."

"I certainly think you should." It took Rorie another minute to figure out where Mary was heading with this meandering conversation. Then suddenly she understood. "Oh, you're looking for someone to do the cooking while you're away."

Mary shrugged as if it didn't concern her one way or the other. "Just for the evening meal, two nights from now. I could manage lunch for the hands before I leave. It's supper I'm worried about. There's only Clay and Skip who need to be fed—the other men go home in the evenings."

"Well, relax, because I'm sure I can manage one dinner without killing off the menfolk."

"You're sure?"

Mary was so completely serious that Rorie laughed outright. "Since my abilities do seem to worry you, how would you feel if I invited Kate Logan over to help?"

Mary nodded and sighed. "I'd rest easier."

Rorie stayed in the kitchen until the lunch dishes had been put away. Mary thanked her for helping, then went home to watch her daily soap operas.

Feeling a little lost, Rorie wandered outside and into

the stable. Since Clay had already shown her the computer, she decided to spend the afternoon working in his office.

The area was deserted, which went some distance toward reassuring her—but then, she'd assumed it would be. From what she'd observed, a stud farm was a busy place and Clay was bound to be occupied elsewhere. That suited Rorie just fine. She hoped to avoid him as much as possible. In three days she'd be out of his life, leaving hardly a trace, and that was the way she wanted it.

Rorie sat typing in data for about an hour before her neck and shoulders began to cramp. She paused, flexing her muscles, then rotated her head to relieve the building tightness.

"How long have you been here?"

The rough male voice behind her startled Rorie. Her hand flew to her heart and she expelled a shaky breath. "Clay! You frightened me."

"How long?" he repeated.

"An hour or so." She glanced at her watch and nodded.

Clay advanced a step toward her, his mouth a thin line of impatience. "I suppose you're looking for an apology."

Rorie didn't answer. She'd learned not to expect anything from him.

"I'll tell you right now that you're not going to get one," he finished gruffly.

Six

"You don't owe me anything, Clay," Rorie said, struggling to make her voice light. Clay looked driven to the limits of exhaustion. Dark shadows had formed beneath his eyes and fatigue lines fanned out from their corners. His shoulders sagged slightly, as if the weight he carried was more than he could bear. He studied her wearily, then turned away, stalking to the other side of the office. His shoulders heaved as he drew in a shuddering breath.

"I know I should feel some regrets, but God help me, Rorie, I don't."

"Clay, listen…"

He turned to face her then, and drove his fingers into his hair with such force Rorie winced. "I'd like to explain about Kate and me."

"No." Under no circumstances did Rorie want to listen to his explanations or excuses. She didn't have a lot of room to be judgmental herself. She had, after all, been dating a man steadily for the past few months. "Don't. Please don't say anything. It isn't necessary."

He ignored her request. "Kate and I have known each other all our lives."

"Clay, stop." She pushed out the chair and stood up, wanting only to escape.

"For the last two years, it's been understood by everyone around us that Kate and I would eventually get married. I didn't even question the right or wrong of it, just calmly accepted the fact. A man needs someone to share his life."

"Kate will make you a wonderful wife," she said, feeling both disillusioned and indignant, but she refused to let him know how much his indiscretion had hurt her. "If you owe anyone an apology, it's Kate, not me."

His responding frown was brooding and dark. "I know." He drew his fingers across his eyes, and she could feel his exhaustion. "The last thing in the world I want is to hurt Kate."

"Then don't."

He stared at her, and Rorie made herself send him a smile, although she feared it was more flippant than reassuring. "There's no reason for Kate to find out. What good would it do? She'd only end up feeling betrayed. Last night was a tiny impropriety and best forgotten, don't you agree?" Walking seemed to help, and Rorie paced the office, her fingers brushing the stack of books and papers on his cluttered desk.

"I don't know what's best anymore," Clay admitted quietly.

"I do," Rorie said with unwavering confidence, still struggling to make light of the incident. "Think about it, Clay. We were alone together for hours—we shared something beautiful with Star Bright and…her foal. And we shared a few stolen kisses under the stars. If anything's to blame, it's the moonlight. We're strangers, Clay. You don't know me and I don't know you." Afraid to look him directly in the eye, Rorie lowered her gaze and waited, breathless, for his next words.

"So it was the moonlight?" His voice was hoarse and painfully raw.

"Of course," she lied. "What else could it have been?"

"Yes, what else could it have been?" he echoed, then turned and walked out of the office.

It suddenly seemed as though the room's light had dimmed. Rorie felt so weak, she sank into the chair, shocked by how deeply the encounter had disturbed her.

Typing proved to be a distraction and Rorie left the office a couple of hours later with a feeling of accomplishment. She'd been able to enter several time-consuming pages of data into the computer. The routine work was a relief because it meant she had no time to think.

The kitchen smelled of roasting beef and simmering apple crisp when Rorie let herself in the back door. It was an oddly pleasant combination of scents. Mary was nowhere to be seen.

While she thought of it, Rorie reached for the telephone book and called the number listed for the garage in Riversdale.

"Hello," she said when a gruff male voice answered. "This is Rorie Campbell...the woman with the broken water pump. The one in Nightingale."

"Yeah, Miss Campbell, what can I do for you?"

"I just wanted to be sure there wasn't any problem in ordering the part. I don't know if Clay... Mr. Franklin told you, but I'm more or less stuck here until the car's repaired. I'd like to get back on the road as soon as possible—I'm sure you understand."

"Lady, I can't make that pump come any faster than what it already is."

"Well, I just wanted to check that you'd been able to order one."

"It's on its way, at least that's what the guy in Los Angeles told me. They're shipping it by overnight freight to Portland. I've arranged for a man to pick it up the following day, but it's going to take him some time to get it to me."

"But that's only three days."

"You called too late yesterday for me to phone the order in. Lady, there's only so much I can do."

"I know. I'm sorry if I sound impatient."

"The whole world's impatient. Listen, I'll call you the minute it arrives."

She sighed. "Thanks, I'd appreciate it."

"Clay got your car here without a hitch, so don't worry about that—he saved you a bundle on towing charges. Shipping costs and long-distance phone bills are going to be plenty high, though."

Rorie hadn't even noticed that Dan's shiny sports car wasn't in the yard where Skip had originally left it. "So you'll be calling me within the next day or two?" she asked, trying to hide the anxiety in her voice. And trying not to consider the state of her finances, already depleted by this disastrous vacation.

"Right. I'll call as soon as it comes in."

"Thank you. I appreciate it," she said again.

"No problem," the mechanic muttered, obviously eager to end their conversation.

When the call was finished, Rorie toyed with the

idea of phoning Dan next. She'd been half expecting to hear from him, since she'd left the Franklins' number with his secretary the day before. He hadn't phoned her back. But there was nothing new to tell him, so she decided not to call a second time.

Hesitantly Rorie replaced the telephone receiver, pleased that everything was under control—everything except her heart.

Dinner that evening was a strained affair. If it hadn't been for Skip, who seemed oblivious to the tension between her and Clay, Rorie didn't think she could have endured it. Clay hardly said a word throughout the meal. But Skip seemed more than eager to carry the conversation and Rorie did her best to lighten the mood, wondering all the time whether Clay saw through her facade.

"While you're here, Rorie," Skip said with a sudden burst of enthusiasm, "you should learn how to ride."

"No, thank you," she said pointedly, holding up her hand, as though fending off the suggestion. An introduction to King and Hercules was as far as she was willing to go.

"Rain Magic would suit you nicely."

"Rain Magic?"

"That's a silly name Kate thought up, and Clay went along with it," Skip explained. "He's gentle, but smart—the gelding I mean, not Clay." The younger Franklin laughed heartily at his own attempt at humor.

Clay smiled, but Rorie wasn't fooled; he hadn't been amused by the joke, nor, she suspected, was he pleased by the reference to Kate.

"No, thanks, Skip," she said, hoping to bring the subject to a close. "I'm really not interested." There, that said it plainly enough.

"Are you afraid?"

"A little," she admitted truthfully. "I prefer my horses on a merry-go-round. I'm a city girl, remember?"

"But even girls from San Francisco have been known to climb on the back of a horse. It'll be good for you, Rorie. Trust me—it's time to broaden your horizons."

"Thanks, but no thanks," she told him, emphasizing her point by biting down on a crisp carrot stick with a loud crunch.

"Rorie, I insist. You aren't going to get hurt—I wouldn't let that happen, and Rain Magic is as gentle as they come. In fact—" he wiggled his eyebrows up and down "—if you want, we can ride double until you feel more secure."

Rorie laughed. "Skip, honestly."

"All right, you can ride alone, and I'll lead you around in a circle. For as long as you want."

Rorie shook her head and, amused at the mental picture that scenario presented, laughed again.

"Leave it," Clay said with sudden sharpness. "If Rorie doesn't want to ride, drop it, okay?"

Skip's shocked gaze flew from Rorie to his brother. "I was just having fun, Clay."

His older brother gripped his water goblet so hard Rorie thought the glass might shatter. "Enough is enough. She said she wasn't interested and that should be the end of it."

The astounded look left Skip's features, but his eyes narrowed and he stiffened his shoulders in a display of righteous indignation. "What's with you, Clay?" he shouted. "You've been acting like a wounded bear all day, growling at everyone. Who made *you* king of the universe all of a sudden?"

"If you'll excuse me, I'll bring in the apple crisp," Rorie said, and hurriedly rose to her feet, not wanting to be caught in the cross fire between the two brothers. Whatever they had to say wasn't meant for her ears.

The exchange that followed ended quickly, Rorie noted gratefully from inside the kitchen. Their voices were raised and then there was a hush followed by laughter. Rorie relaxed and picked up the dessert, carrying it into the dining room along with a carton of vanilla ice cream.

"I apologize, Rorie," Clay said soberly when she reentered the room. "Skip's right, I've been cross and unreasonable all day. I hope my sour mood hasn't ruined your dinner."

"Of course not," she murmured, giving him a smile.

Clay stood up to serve the dessert, spooning generous helpings of apple crisp and ice cream into each bowl.

Skip chattered aimlessly, commenting on one subject and then bouncing to another without any logical connection, his thoughts darting this way and that.

"What time are you going over to Kate's tonight?" he casually asked Clay.

"I won't be. She's got some meeting with the women's group from the Grange. They're decorating for the dance tomorrow night."

"Now that you mention it, I seem to remember Kate saying something about being busy tonight." Without a pause he turned to Rorie. "You'll be coming, I hope. The Grange is putting on a square dance—the biggest one of the year, and they usually do it up good."

"Kate already invited me. I'll be going with her," Rorie explained, although she hadn't the slightest idea how to square dance. Generally she enjoyed dancing, although she hadn't gone for several months because Dan wasn't keen on it.

"You could drive there with us if you wanted," Skip offered. "I'd kinda like to walk in there with you on my arm. You'd cause quite a stir with the men, especially Luke Rivers—he's the foreman at the Logan place. Most girls go all goo-goo-eyed over him."

Clay's spoon clanged loudly against the side of his glass dish and he murmured an apology.

"I'm sorry, Skip," Rorie said gently. "I told Kate I'd drive over with her."

"Darn," Skip muttered.

The meal was completed in silence. Once, when Rorie happened to glance up, her eyes met Clay's. Her heart felt as though it might hammer its way out of her chest. She was oppressively aware of the chemistry between them. It simmered in Rorie's veins and she could tell that Clay felt everything she did. Throughout dinner, she'd been all too conscious of the swift stolen glances Clay had sent in her direction. She'd sent a few of her own, though she'd tried hard not to. But it was impossible to be in the same room with this man and not react to him.

A thousand times in the next couple of hours, Rorie told herself that everything would be fine as soon as she could leave. Life would return to normal then.

When the dishes were finished, Skip challenged her to a game of cribbage, and grateful for the escape Rorie accepted. Skip sat with his back to his brother, and every time Rorie played her hand, she found her eyes wandering across the room to where Clay sat reading. To all outward appearances, he was relaxed and comfortable, but she knew he felt as tense as she did. She knew he was equally aware of the electricity that sparked between them.

Rorie's fingers shook as she counted out her cards.

"Fifteen eight," Skip corrected. "You forgot two points."

Her eyes fell to the extra ten, and she blinked. "I guess I did."

Skip heaved a sigh. "I don't think your mind's on the game tonight."

"I guess not," she admitted wryly. "If you'll excuse me, I think I'll go up to bed." She threw him an apologetic smile and reached for her coffee cup. Skip was right; her mind hadn't been on the game at all. Instead, her thoughts had been on a man who owed his loyalties to another woman—a woman whose roots were intricately bound with his. A woman Rorie had liked and respected from the moment they met.

Feeling depressed, she bade the two men good-night and carried her cup to the kitchen. Dutifully, she rinsed it out and set it beside the sink, but when she turned around Clay was standing in the doorway, blocking her exit.

"Where's Skip?" she asked a little breathlessly. Heat seemed to throb between them and she retreated a step in a futile effort to escape.

"He went upstairs."

She blinked and faked a yawn. "I was headed in that direction myself."

Clay buried one hand in his jeans pocket. "Do you know what happened tonight at dinner?"

Not finding her voice, Rorie shook her head.

"I was jealous," he said from between clenched teeth. "You were laughing and joking with Skip and I wanted it to be *me* your eyes were shining for. Me. No one else." He stopped abruptly and shook his head. "Jealous of a seventeen-year-old boy... I can't believe it myself."

Seven

Rorie decided to wear a dress for her outing with Kate Logan. Although she rose early, both Skip and Clay had eaten breakfast and left the house by the time she came downstairs. Which was just as well, Rorie thought.

Mary stood at the stove, frying chunks of beef for a luncheon stew. "I spoke to Clay about your cooking dinner later this week. He says that'll be fine if you're still around, but the way he sees it, you'll be on your way in a day or two."

Rorie poured herself a cup of coffee. "I'll be happy to do it if I'm here. Otherwise, I'm sure Kate Logan would be more than pleased."

Mary turned to face her, mouth open as if to comment. Instead her eyes widened in appreciation. "My, my, you look pretty enough to hog-tie a man's heart."

"Thank you, Mary," Rorie answered, grinning.

"I suppose you got yourself a sweetheart back there in San Francisco?" she asked, watching her closely. "A pretty girl like you is bound to attract plenty of men."

Rorie paused to think about her answer. She briefly considered mentioning Dan, but decided against it.

She'd planned this separation to gain a perspective on their relationship. And within hours of arriving at Elk Run, Rorie had found her answer. Dan would always be a special friend—but nothing more.

"The question shouldn't require a week's thought," Mary grumbled, stirring the large pot of simmering beef.

"Sorry... I was mulling something over."

"Then there is someone?"

She shook her head. "No."

The answer didn't seem to please Mary, because she frowned. "When did you say that fancy car of yours was going to be fixed?"

The abrupt question caught Rorie by surprise. Mary was openly concerned about the attraction between her and Clay. The housekeeper, who probably knew Clay as well as anyone did, clearly wasn't blind to what had been happening—and just as clearly didn't like it.

"The mechanic in Riversdale said it should be finished the day after tomorrow if all goes well."

"Good!" Mary proclaimed with a fierce nod, then turned back to her stew.

Rorie couldn't help smiling at the older woman's astuteness. Mary was telling her that the sooner she was off Elk Run the better for everyone concerned. Rorie had to agree.

Kate Logan arrived promptly at ten. She wore tight-fitting jeans, red checkered western shirt and a white silk scarf knotted at her throat. Her long honey-colored hair was woven into thick braids that fell over her shoulders. At first glance, Kate looked closer to sixteen than the twenty-four Rorie knew her to be.

Kate greeted her with a warm smile. "Rorie, there

wasn't any need to wear something so nice. I should've told you to dress casually."

Rorie's shoulders slumped. "I brought along more dresses than jeans. Am I overdressed? I could change," she said hesitantly.

"Oh, no, you look lovely…" But for the first time, Kate seemed worried. The doubt that played across her features would have been amusing if Rorie hadn't already been suffering from such a potent bout of guilt. It was all too obvious that Kate viewed Rorie as a threat.

If Clay Franklin had chosen that moment to walk into the kitchen, Rorie would've called him every foul name she could think of. She was furious with him for doing this to her—and to Kate.

"I wear a lot of dresses because of my job at the library," Rorie rushed to explain. "I also date quite a bit. I've been seeing someone—Dan Rogers—for a while now. In fact, it's his car I was driving."

"You're dating someone special?" Kate asked, sounding relieved.

"Yes, Dan and I've been going out for several months."

Mary coughed noisily and sent Rorie an accusing glare; Rorie ignored her. "Shouldn't we be leaving?"

"Oh, sure, any time you're ready." When they were outside, Kate turned to face Rorie. Looking uncomfortable, she slipped her hands into the back pockets of her jeans. "I've embarrassed you and I'm sorry. I didn't mean to imply that I didn't trust you and Clay."

"There's no need for an apology. I'm sure I wouldn't react any differently if Clay was *my* fiancé."

Kate shook her head. "But I feel as if I *should* apologize. I'm not going to be the kind of wife Clay wants if I can't trust him around a pretty girl once in a while."

Had the earth cracked open just then, Rorie would gladly have fallen in. That had to be preferable to looking at Kate and feeling the things she did about Clay Franklin.

"Don't have any worries about me," she said, dismissing the issue as nonchalantly as she could. "I'll be out of everyone's hair in a day or two."

"Oh, Rorie, please, I don't want you to rush off because I had a silly attack of jealousy. Now I feel terrible."

"Don't, please. I have to leave... I want to leave. My vacation's on hold until I can get my car repaired and there's so much I'd planned to see and do." She dug in her bag for a brochure. "Have you ever been up to Victoria on Vancouver Island?"

"Once, but I was only five, too young to remember much of anything," Kate told her, scanning the pamphlet. "This does sound like fun. Maybe this is where Clay and I should have our honeymoon."

"It'd be perfect for that," Rorie murmured. Her heart constricted with a sudden flash of pain, but she ruthlessly forced down her emotions, praying Kate hadn't noticed. "I'm looking forward to visiting Canada. By the way, Mary's driving to Riversdale to visit her sister later in the week. She's asked me to take charge of cooking dinner if I'm still here. Would you like to help? We could have a good time and really get to know each other."

"Oh, that would be great." Kate slipped her arm around Rorie's waist and gave her an enthusiastic squeeze. "Thank you, Rorie. I know you're trying to reassure me, and I appreciate it."

That had been exactly Rorie's intent.

"It probably sounds selfish," Kate continued, "but I'm glad your car broke down when it did. Without any difficulty at all, I can see us becoming the best of friends."

Rorie could, too, but that only added to her growing sense of uneasiness.

Nightingale was a sleepy kind of town. Businesses lined both sides of Main Street, with a beauty shop, an insurance agency, Nellie's Café and a service station on one side, a grocery store, pharmacy and five-and-dime on the other. Rorie had the impression that things happened in their own time in Nightingale, Oregon. Few places could have been more unlike San Francisco, where people always seemed to be rushing. Here, no one seemed to feel any need to hurry. It was as though this town, with its population of fifteen hundred, existed in a time warp. Rorie found the relaxed pace unexpectedly pleasant.

"The library is across from the high school on Maple Street," Kate explained as she parked her Ford on Main. "That way, students have easy access."

Rorie climbed out of the car, automatically pressing down the door lock.

"You don't have to do that here. There hasn't been a vehicle stolen in...oh, at least twenty years."

Rorie's eyes must have revealed her surprise, because Kate went on, "Actually, we had trouble passing our last bond issue for a new patrol car. People couldn't see the need since there hasn't been a felony committed in over two years. About the worst thing that goes on is when Harry Ackerman gets drunk. That happens once or twice a year and he's arrested for disturbing the peace." She grinned sheepishly. "He sings old love songs to Nellie at the top of his lungs in front of the café. They were apparently sweet on each other a long time back. Nellie married someone else and Harry never got over the loss of his one true love."

Looping the strap of her bag over her shoulder, Rorie looked around the quiet streets.

"The fire and police station are in the same building," Kate pointed out next. "And there's a really nice restaurant on Oak. If you want, we could have lunch there."

"Only if you let me treat."

"I wouldn't hear of it," Kate said with a shake of her head that sent her braids flying. "You're my guest."

Rorie decided not to argue, asking another question instead. "Where do the ranchers get their supplies?" It seemed to her that type of store would do a thriving business, yet she hadn't seen one.

"At Garner's Feed and Supply. It's on the outskirts of town—I'll take you past on the way out. In fact, we should take a driving tour so you can see a little more of Nightingale. Main Street is only a small part of it."

By the time Kate and Rorie walked over to Maple and the library, Rorie's head was swimming with the names of all the people Kate had insisted on introducing. It seemed everyone had heard about her car problems and was eager to talk to her. Several mentioned the Grange dance that night and said they'd be looking for her there.

"You're really going to be impressed with the library," Kate promised as they walked the two streets over to Maple. "Dad and the others worked hard to get the levy passed so we could build it. People here tend to be tightfisted. Dad says they squeeze a nickel so hard, the buffalo belches."

Rorie laughed outright at that.

The library was the largest building in town, a sprawling one-story structure with lots of windows. The hours were posted on the double glass doors, and Rorie noted that the library wouldn't open until the middle of the afternoon, still several hours away.

"It doesn't seem to be open," she said, disappointed.

"Oh, don't worry, I've got a key. All the volunteers do." Kate rummaged in her bag and took out a large key ring. She opened the door, pushing it wide for Rorie to enter first.

"Mrs. Halldorfson retired last year, a month after the building was finished," Kate told her, flipping on the lights, "and the town's budget wouldn't stretch to hire a new full-time librarian. So a number of parents and teachers are taking turns volunteering. We've got a workable schedule, unless someone goes on vacation, which, I hate to admit, has been happening all summer."

"You don't have a full-time librarian?" Rorie couldn't disguise her astonishment. "Why go to all the trouble and expense of building a modern facility if you can't afford a librarian?"

"You'll have to ask Town Council that," Kate returned, shrugging. "It doesn't make much sense, does it? But you see, Mrs. Halldorfson was only part-time and the Council seems to think that's what her replacement should be."

"That doesn't make sense, either."

"Especially when you consider that the new library is twice the size of the old one."

Rorie had to bite her tongue to keep from saying

more. But she was appalled at the waste, the missed opportunities.

"We've been advertising for months for a part-time librarian, but so far we haven't found anyone interested. Not that I blame them—one look at the size of the job and no one wants to tackle it alone."

"A library is more than a place to check books in and out," Rorie said, gesturing dramatically. Her voice rose despite herself. This was an issue close to her heart, and polite silence was practically impossible. "A library can be the heart of a community. It can be a place for classes, community services, all kinds of things. Don't non-profit organizations use it for meetings?"

"I'm afraid not," Kate answered. "Everyone gets together at Nellie's when there's any kind of meeting. Nellie serves great pies," she added, as though that explained everything.

Realizing that she'd climbed onto her soapbox, Rorie dropped her hands and shrugged. "It's a very nice building, Kate, and you have every reason to be proud. I didn't mean to sound so righteous."

"But you're absolutely correct," Kate said thoughtfully. "We're not using the library to its full potential, are we? Volunteers can only do so much. As it is, the library's only open three afternoons a week." She sighed expressively. "To be honest, I think Dad and the other members of the Town Council are expecting Mrs. Halldorfson to come back in the fall, but that's unfair to her. She's served the community for over twenty years. She deserves to retire in peace without being blackmailed into coming back because we can't find a replacement."

"Well, I hope you find someone soon."

"I hope so, too," Kate murmured.

They ate a leisurely lunch, and as she'd promised, Kate gave Rorie a tour of the town. After showing her several churches, the elementary school where she taught second grade and some of the nicer homes on the hill, Kate ended the tour on the outskirts of town near Garner's Feed and Supply.

"Luke's here," Kate said, easing into the parking place next to a dusty pickup truck.

"Luke?"

"Our foreman. I don't know what Dad would do without him. He runs the ranch and has for years—ever since I was in high school. Dad's retirement age now, and he's more than willing to let Luke take charge."

Kate got out of the car and leaned against the front fender, crossing her arms over her chest. Rorie joined her.

"He'll be out in a minute," Kate said.

True to her word, a tall, deeply tanned man appeared with a sack of grain slung over his shoulder. His eyes were so dark they gleamed like onyx, taking in everything around him, but revealing little of his own thoughts. His strong square chin was balanced by a high intelligent brow. He was lean and muscular and strikingly handsome.

"Need any help, stranger?" Kate asked with a laugh.

"You offering?"

"Nope."

Luke chuckled. "That's what I figured. You wouldn't want to ruin those pretty nails of yours now, would you?"

"I didn't stop by to be insulted by you," Kate chastised, clearly enjoying the exchange. "I wanted you to meet Rorie Campbell—she's the one Clay was telling us about the other night, whose car broke down."

"I remember." For the first time the foreman's gaze left Kate. He tossed the sack of grain into the back of the truck and used his teeth to tug his glove free from his right hand. Then he presented his long callused fingers to Rorie. "Pleased to meet you, ma'am."

"The pleasure's mine." Rorie remembered where she'd heard the name. Skip had mentioned Luke Rivers when he'd told her about the Grange square dance. He'd said something about all the girls being attracted to the foreman. Rorie could understand why.

They exchanged a brief handshake before Luke's attention slid back to Kate. His eyes softened perceptibly.

"Luke's like a brother to me," Kate said fondly.

He frowned at that, but didn't comment.

"We're going to let you escort us to the dance tonight," she informed him.

"What about Clay?"

"Oh, he'll meet us there. I thought the three of us could go over together."

Rorie wasn't fooled. Kate was setting her up with Luke, who didn't look any too pleased at having his evening arranged for him.

"Kate, listen," she began, "I'd really rather skip the dance tonight. I've never done any square dancing in my life—"

"That doesn't matter," Kate interrupted. "Luke will be glad to show you. Won't you, Luke?"

"Sure," he mumbled, with the enthusiasm of a man offered the choice between hanging and a firing squad.

"Honestly, Luke!" Kate gave an embarrassed laugh.

"Listen," Rorie said quickly. "It's obvious Luke has his own plans for tonight. I don't want to intrude—"

He surprised her by turning toward her, his eyes searching hers. "I'd be happy to escort you, Rorie."

"I'm likely to step all over your toes... I really think I should sit the whole thing out."

"Nonsense," Kate cried. "Luke won't let you do that and neither will I!"

"We'll enjoy ourselves," the foreman said. "Leave everything to me."

Rorie nodded reluctantly.

A moment of awkward silence fell over the trio. "Well, I suppose I should get Rorie back to Circle L and see about finding her a dress," Kate said, smiling. She playfully tossed her car keys in the air and caught them deftly.

Luke tipped his hat when they both returned to the car. Rorie didn't mention his name until they were back on the road.

"Luke really is attractive, isn't he?" she asked, closely watching Kate.

The other woman nodded eagerly. "It surprises me that he's not married. There are plenty of girls around Nightingale who'd be more than willing, believe me. At every Grange dance, the ladies flirt with him like crazy. I love to tease him about it—he really hates that. But I wish Luke *would* get married—I don't like the idea of him living his life alone. It's time he thought about settling down and starting a family. He was thirty last month, but when I said something about it, he nearly bit my head off."

Rorie nibbled on her lower lip. She inhaled a deep breath and released it slowly. Her guess was that Luke

Rivers had his heart set on someone special, and that someone was engaged to another man. God help him, Rorie thought. She knew exactly how he felt.

The music was already playing by the time Luke, Kate and Rorie arrived at the Grange Hall in Luke's ten-year-old four-door sedan. Rorie tried to force some enthusiasm for this outing, but had little success. She hadn't exchanged more than a few words with the foreman during the entire drive. He, apparently, didn't like this arranged-date business any better than she did. But they were stuck with each other, and Rorie at least was determined to make the best of it.

They entered the hall and were greeted by the cheery voice of the male caller:

Rope the cow, brand the calf
Swing your sweetheart, once and a half...

Rorie hadn't known what to expect, but she was surprised by the smooth-stepping, smartly dressed dancers who twirled around the floor following the caller's directions. She felt more daunted than ever by the evening ahead of her. And to worsen matters, Kate had insisted Rorie borrow one of her outfits. Although Rorie liked the bright blue colors, she felt awkward and self-conscious in the billowing skirts.

The Grange itself was bigger than Rorie had anticipated. On the stage stood the caller and several fiddlers. Refreshment tables lined one wall and the polished dance floor was so crowded Rorie wondered how anyone could move without bumping into others. The entire meeting hall was alive with energy and music, and despite herself, she felt her mood lift. Her toes started tapping out rhythms almost of their own accord. Given time, she'd be out there, too, joining the vibrant, laughing dancers. It was unavoidable, anyway. She knew Kate wouldn't allow her to sit sedately in the background and watch. Neither would Clay and Skip, who'd just arrived.

"Oh, my feet are moving already." Kate was squirming with eagerness. Clay smiled indulgently, tucked his arm around her waist and the two of them stepped onto the dance floor. He glanced back once at Rorie, before a circle of eight opened up to admit them.

"Shall we?" Luke asked, eyeing the dance floor.

He didn't sound too enthusiastic and Rorie didn't blame him. "Would it be all right if we sat out the first couple of dances?" she asked. "I'd like to get more into the swing of things."

"No problem."

Luke looked almost grateful for the respite, which didn't lend Rorie much confidence. No doubt he assumed this city slicker was going to make a fool of herself and of him—and she probably would. When he escorted her to the row of chairs, Rorie made the mistake of sitting down. Instantly her skirts leaped up into her face. Embarrassed, she pushed them down, then tucked the material under her thighs in an effort to tame the layers of stiff petticoats.

"Hello, Luke." A pretty blonde with sparkling blue eyes sauntered over. "I didn't know if you'd show tonight or not. Glad you did."

"Beth Hammond, this is Rorie Campbell."

Rorie nodded. "It's nice to meet you, Beth."

"Oh, I heard about you at the drugstore yesterday.

You're the gal with the broken-down sports car, aren't you?"

"That's me." By now it shouldn't have surprised Rorie that everyone knew about her troubles.

"I hope everything turns out okay."

"Thanks." Although Beth was speaking to Rorie, her eyes didn't leave Luke. It was patently obvious that she expected an invitation to dance.

"Luke, why don't you dance with Beth?" Rorie suggested. "That way I'll gather a few pointers from watching the two of you."

"What a good idea," Beth chirped eagerly. "We'll stay on the outskirts of the crowd so you can see how it's done. Be sure and listen to Charlie—he's the caller. Then you'll see what each step is."

Rorie nodded agreeably.

Luke gave Rorie a long sober look. "You're sure?"

"Positive."

All join hands, circle right around
Stop in place at your hometown...

Studying the dancers, Rorie quickly picked up the terms *do se do, allemande left* and *allemande right* and a number of others, which she struggled to keep track of. By the end of the dance, her foot was tapping out the lively beat of the fiddlers' music and a smile formed as she listened to the perfectly rhyming words.

"Rorie," Skip said, suddenly standing in front of her. "May I have the pleasure of this dance?"

"I... I don't think I'm ready yet."

"Nonsense." Without listening to her protest, he grabbed her hand and hauled her to her feet.

"Skip, I'll embarrass you," she protested in a low whisper. "I've never done this before."

"You've got to start sometime." He tucked his arm around her waist and led her close to the stage.

"We got a newcomer, Charlie," Skip called out, "so make this one simple."

Charlie gave Skip a thumbs-up and reached for the microphone. "We'll go a bit slower this time," Charlie announced to his happy audience. "Miss Rorie Campbell from San Francisco has joined us and it's her first time on the floor."

Rorie wanted to curl up and die as a hundred faces turned to stare at her. But the dancers were shouting and cheering their welcome and Rorie shyly raised her hand, smiling into the crowd.

Getting through that first series of steps was the most difficult, but soon Rorie was in the middle of the floor, stepping and twirling—and laughing. Something she'd always assumed to be a silly, outdated activity turned out to be great fun.

By the time Skip led her back to her chair, she was breathless. "Want some punch?" he asked. Rorie nodded eagerly. Her throat felt parched.

When Skip left her, Luke Rivers appeared at her side. "You did just great," he said sincerely.

"For a city girl, you mean," she teased.

"As good as anyone."

"Thanks."

"I suspect I owe you an apology, Rorie."

"Because you didn't want to make a fool of yourself with me on the dance floor?" she asked with a light laugh. "That's understandable. Kate and Clay practically threw me in your lap. I'm sure you had other plans for tonight, and I'm sorry for your sake that we got stuck with each other."

Luke grinned. "Trust me, I've had plenty of envious looks from around the room. Any of a dozen different men would be more than happy to be 'stuck' with you."

That went a long way toward boosting her ego. She would have commented, but Skip came back just then carrying a paper cup filled with bright pink punch. A teenage girl was beside him, clutching his free arm and smiling dreamily up at him.

"I'm going to dance with Caroline now, okay?" he said to Rorie.

"That's fine," she answered, smiling, "and thank you for braving the dance floor with me." Skip blushed as he slipped an arm around Caroline's waist and hurried her off.

"You game?" Luke nodded toward the dancing couples.

Rorie didn't hesitate. She swallowed the punch in three giant gulps, and gave him her hand. Together they moved onto the crowded floor.

By the end of the third set of dances, Rorie had twirled around with so many different partners, she lost track of them. She'd caught sight of Clay only once, and when he saw her he waved. Returning the gesture, she promptly missed her footing and nearly fell into her partner's waiting arms. The tall sheriff's deputy was all too happy to have her throw herself at him and told her as much, to Rorie's embarrassment.

Although it was only ten o'clock, Rorie was exhausted and so warm the perspiration ran in rivulets down her face and neck. She had to escape. Several times, she'd tried to sit out a dance, but no one would listen to her excuses.

In an effort to catch her breath and cool down, Rorie took advantage of a break between sets to wander outside. The night air was refreshing. Quite a few other people had apparently had the same idea; the field that served as a car park was crowded with groups and strolling couples.

As she made her way through the dimly lit field, she saw a handful of men passing around a flask of whiskey and entertaining each other with off-color jokes. She steered a wide circle around them and headed toward Luke's parked car, deciding it was far enough away to discourage anyone from following her. In her eagerness to escape, she nearly stumbled over a couple locked in a passionate embrace against the side of a pickup.

Rorie mumbled an apology when the pair glanced up at her, irritation written all over their young faces. Good grief, she'd only wanted a few minutes alone in order to get a breath of fresh air—she hadn't expected to walk through an obstacle course!

When she finally arrived at Luke Rivers's car, she leaned on the fender and slowly inhaled the clean country air. All her assumptions about this evening had been wrong. She'd been so sure she'd feel lonely and bored and out of place. And she'd felt none of those things. If she were to tell Dan about the Grange dance, he'd laugh at the idea of having such a grand time with a bunch of what he'd refer to as "country bumpkins." The thought annoyed her. These were good, friendly, fun-loving people. They'd taken her under their wing, expressed their welcome without reserve, and now they were showing her an uncomplicated lifestyle that had more appeal than Rorie would have believed possible.

"I thought I'd find you out here."

Rorie's whole body tensed as she recognized the voice of the man who'd joined her.

"Hello, Clay."

Eight

Rorie injected a cheerful note into her voice. She turned around, half expecting Kate to be with him. The two had been inseparable from the minute Clay had arrived. It was just as well that Kate was around, since her presence prevented Clay and Rorie from giving in to any temptation.

Clay's hands settled on her shoulders and Rorie flinched involuntarily at his touch. With noticeable regret, Clay dropped his hands.

"Are you having a good time?" he asked.

She nodded. "I didn't think I would, which tells you how prejudiced I've been about country life, but I've been pleasantly surprised."

"I'm glad." His hands clenched briefly at his sides, then he flexed his fingers a couple of times. "I would've danced with you myself, but—"

She stopped him abruptly. "Clay, no. Don't explain... it isn't necessary. I understand."

His eyes held hers with such tenderness that she had to look away. The magical quality was in the air again—Rorie could feel it as forcefully as if the stars had spelled it out across the heavens.

"I don't think you do understand, Rorie," Clay said, "but it doesn't matter. You'll be gone in a couple of days and both our lives will go back to the way they were meant to be."

Rorie agreed with a quick nod. It was too tempting, standing in the moonlight with Clay. Much too tempting. The memory of another night in which they'd stood and gazed at the stars returned with powerful intensity. Rorie realized that even talking to each other, alone like this, was dangerous.

"Won't Kate be looking for you?" she asked carefully.

"No. Luke Rivers is dancing with her."

For a moment she closed her eyes, not daring to look up at Clay. "I guess I'll be going inside now. I just came out to catch my breath and cool down a little."

"Dance with me first—here in the moonlight."

A protest rose within her, but the instant Clay slid his arms around her waist, Rorie felt herself give in. Kate would have him the rest of her life, but Rorie only had these few hours. Almost against her will, her hands found his shoulders, slipping around his neck with an ease that brought a sigh of pleasure to her lips. Being held by Clay shouldn't feel this good.

"Oh, Rorie," he moaned as she settled into his embrace.

They fitted together as if they'd been created for each other. His chin touched the top of her head and he caressed her hair with his jaw.

"This is a mistake," Rorie murmured, closing her eyes, savoring the warm, secure feel of his arms.

"I know..."

But neither seemed willing to release the other.

His mouth grazed her temple and he kissed her there. "God help me, Rorie, what am I going to do? I haven't been able to stop thinking about you. I can't sleep, I hardly eat…" His voice was raw, almost savage.

"Oh, please," she said with a soft cry. "We can't…we mustn't even talk like this." His gray eyes smoldered above hers, and their breaths merged as his mouth hovered so close to her own.

"I vowed I wouldn't touch you again."

Rorie looked away. She'd made the same promise to herself. But it wasn't in her to deny him now, although her mind searched frantically for the words to convince him how wrong they were to risk hurting Kate—and each other.

His hands drifted up from her shoulders, his fingertips skimming the sides of her neck, trailing over her cheeks and through the softness of her hair. He placed his index finger over her lips, gently stroking them apart.

Rorie moaned. She moistened her lips with the tip of her tongue. Clay's left hand dug into her shoulders as her tongue caressed the length of his finger, drawing it into her mouth and sucking it gently. She needed him so much in that moment, she could have wept.

"Just this once…for these few minutes," he pleaded, "let me pretend you're mine." His hands cupped her face and slowly brought her mouth to his, smothering her whimper of part welcome, part protest.

A long series of kisses followed. Deep, relentless, searching kisses that sent her heart soaring. Kisses that only made the coming loneliness more painful. A sob swelled within her and tears burned her eyes as she twisted away and tore her mouth from his.

"No," she cried, covering her face with her hands and turning her back to him. "Please, Clay. We shouldn't be doing this."

He was silent for so long that Rorie suspected he'd left her. She inhaled a deep, calming breath and dropped her hands limply to her sides.

"It would be so easy to love you, Rorie."

"No," she whispered, shaking her head vigorously as she faced him again. "I'm not the right person for you—it's too late for that. You've got Kate." She couldn't keep the pain out of her voice. Anything between them was hopeless, futile. Within a day or two her car would be repaired and she'd vanish from his life as suddenly as she'd appeared.

Clay fell silent, his shoulders stiff and resolute as he stood silhouetted against the light of the Grange Hall. His face was masked by shadows and Rorie couldn't read his thoughts. He drew in a harsh breath.

"You're right, Rorie. We can't allow this…attraction between us to get out of hand. I promise you, by all I hold dear, that I won't kiss you again."

"I'll…do my part, too," she assured him, feeling better now that they'd made this agreement.

His hand reached for hers and clasped it warmly. "Come on, I'll walk you back to the hall. We're going to be all right. We'll do what we have to do."

Clay's tone told her he meant it. Relieved, Rorie silently made the same promise to herself.

Rorie slept late the next morning, later than she would have thought possible. Mary was busy with lunch preparations by the time she made her way downstairs.

"Did you enjoy yourself last night?" Mary immediately asked.

In response, Rorie curtsied and danced a few steps with an imaginary partner, clapping her hands.

Mary tried to hide a smile at Rorie's antics. "Oh, get away with you now. All I was looking for was a yes or a no."

"I had a great time."

"It was nothing like those city hotspots, I'll wager."

"You're right about that," Rorie told her, pouring herself a cup of coffee.

"You seeing Kate today?"

Rorie shook her head and popped a piece of bread in the toaster. "She's got a doctor's appointment this morning and a teachers' meeting this afternoon. She's going to stop by later if she has a chance, but if not I'll be seeing her for sure tomorrow." Rorie intended to spend as much time as she could with Clay's fiancée. She genuinely enjoyed her company, and being with her served two useful purposes. It helped keep Rorie occupied, and it prevented her from being alone with Clay.

"What are you going to do today, then?" Mary asked, frowning.

Rorie laughed. "Don't worry. Whatever it is, I promise to stay out of your way."

The housekeeper gave a snort of amusement— or was it relief?

"Actually, I thought I'd finish putting the data Clay needs for his pedigree-research program into the computer. There isn't much left and I should be done by this afternoon."

"So if someone comes looking for you, that's where you'll be?"

"That's where I'll be," Rorie echoed. She didn't know who would "come looking for her," as Mary put it. The housekeeper made it sound as though a posse was due to arrive any minute demanding to know where the Franklin men were hiding Rorie Campbell.

Taking her coffee cup with her, Rorie walked across the yard and into the barn. Once more, she was impressed with all the activity that went on there. She'd come to know several of the men by their first names and returned their greetings with a smile and a wave.

As before, she found the office empty. She set down her cup while she turned on the computer and collected Clay's data. She'd just started to type it in when she heard someone enter the room. Pausing, she twisted around.

"Rorie."

"Clay."

They were awkward with each other now. Almost afraid.

"I didn't realize you were here."

She stood abruptly. "I'll leave…"

"No. I came up to get something. I'll be gone in a minute."

She nodded and sat back down. "Okay."

He walked briskly to his desk and sifted through the untidy stacks of paper. His gaze didn't waver from the task, but his jaw was tight, his teeth clenched. Impatience marked his every move. "Kate told me you're involved with a man in San Francisco. I…didn't know."

"I'm not exactly involved with him—at least not in the way you're implying. His name is Dan Rogers, and we've been seeing each other for about six months. He's divorced. The MG is his."

Clay's mouth thinned, but he still didn't look at her. "Are you in love with him?"

"No."

Lowering his head, Clay rubbed his hand over his eyes. "I had no right to ask you that. None. Forgive me, Rorie." Then, clutching his papers, he stalked out of the office without a backward glance.

Rorie was so shaken by the encounter that when she went back to her typing, she made three mistakes in a row and had to stop to regain her composure.

When the phone rang, she ignored it, knowing Mary or one of the men would answer it. Soon afterward, she heard running footsteps behind her and swivelled around in the chair.

A breathless Skip bolted into the room. Shoulders heaving, he pointed in the direction of the telephone. "It's for you," he panted.

"Me?" It could only be Dan.

He nodded several times, his hand braced theatrically against his heart.

She picked up the extension. "Hello," she said, her fingers closing tightly around the receiver. "This is Rorie Campbell."

"Miss Campbell," came the unmistakable voice of George, the mechanic in Riversdale, "let me put it to you like this. I've got good news and bad news."

"Now what?" she cried, pushing her hair off her forehead with an impatient hand. She had to get out of Elk Run.

"My man picked up the water pump for your car in Portland just like we planned."

"Good."

George sighed heavily. "There's a minor problem, though."

"Minor?" she repeated hopefully.

"Well, not that minor actually."

"Oh, great... Listen, George, I'd prefer not to play guessing games with you. Just tell me what happened and how long it's going to be before I can get out of here."

"I'm sorry, Miss Campbell, but they shipped the wrong part. It'll be two, possibly three more days."

Nine

"What's the matter?" Skip asked when Rorie indignantly replaced the receiver.

She crossed her arms over her chest and breathed deeply, battling down the angry frustration that boiled inside her. The problem wasn't George's fault, or Skip's, or Kate's, or anyone else's.

"Rorie?" Skip asked again.

"They shipped the wrong part for the car," she said flatly. "I'm going to be stuck here for another two or possibly three days."

Skip didn't look the least bit perturbed at this information. "Gee, Roric, that's not so terrible. We like having you around—and you like it here, don't you?"

"Yes, but..." How could she explain that her reservations had nothing to do with their company, the farm or even with country life? She couldn't very well blurt out that she was falling in love with his brother, that she had to escape before she ruined their lives.

"But what?" Skip asked.

"My vacation."

"I know you had other plans, but you can relax and enjoy yourself here just as well, can't you?"

She didn't attempt to answer him, but closed her eyes and nodded, faintly.

"Well, listen, I've got to get back to work. Do you need me for anything?"

She shook her head. When the office door closed, Rorie sat down in front of the computer again and poised her fingers over the keyboard. She sat like that, unmoving, for several minutes as her thoughts churned. What was she going to do? Every time she came near Clay the attraction was so strong that trying to ignore it was like swimming upstream. Rorie had planned on leaving Elk Run the following day. Now she was trapped here for God only knew how much longer.

She got up suddenly and started pacing the office floor. Dan hadn't called her, either. She might have vanished from the face of the earth as far as he was concerned. The stupid car was his, after all, and the least he could do was make some effort to find out what had happened. Rorie knew she wasn't being entirely reasonable, but she was caught up in the momentum of her anger and frustration.

Impulsively she snatched up the telephone receiver, had the operator charge the call to her San Francisco number and dialed Dan's office.

"Rorie, thank God you phoned," Dan said.

The worry in his voice appeased her a little. "The least you could've done was call me back," she fumed.

"I tried. My secretary apparently wrote down the wrong number. I've been waiting all this time for you to call me again. Why didn't you? What on earth is going on?"

She told him in detail, from the stalled car to her recent conversation with the mechanic. She didn't tell him about Clay Franklin and the way he made her feel.

"Rorie, baby, I'm so sorry."

She nodded mutely, close to tears. If she wasn't so dangerously close to falling in love with Clay, none of this would seem such a disaster.

The silence lengthened while Dan apparently mulled things over. "Shall I come and get you?" he finally asked.

"With what?" she asked with surprising calm. "My car? You were the one who convinced me it would never make this trip. Besides, how would you get the MG back?"

"I'd figured something out. Listen, I can't let you sit around in some backwoods farm town. I'll borrow a car or rent one." He hesitated, then expelled his breath in a short burst of impatience. "Damn, forget that. I can't come."

"You can't?"

"I've got a meeting tomorrow afternoon. It's important—I can't miss it. I'm sorry, Rorie, I really am, but there's nothing I can do."

"Don't worry about it," she said, defeat causing her voice to dip slightly. "I understand." In a crazy kind of way she did. Dan was a rising stockbroker, so career moves were critical to him, more important than rescuing Rorie, the woman he claimed to love… Somehow Rorie couldn't picture Clay making the same decision. In her heart she knew Clay would come for her the second she asked.

They spoke for a few more minutes before Rorie ended the conversation. She felt trapped, as though the walls were closing in around her. So far she and Clay had managed to disguise their feelings, but they wouldn't be able to keep it up much longer before someone guessed. Kate wasn't blind, and neither was Mary.

"Rorie?" Clay called her name as he burst into the office. "What happened? Skip told me you were all upset—something about the car? What is it?"

"George called." She whirled around and pointed toward the phone. "The water pump arrived just like it was supposed to—but it's the wrong one."

Clay dropped his gaze, then removed his hat and wiped his forehead. "I'm sorry."

"I am, too, but that doesn't help, does it?" The conversation with Dan hadn't improved matters, and taking her frustration out on Clay wasn't going to change anything, either. "I'm stuck here, and this is the last place on earth I want to be."

"Do you think I like it any better?" he challenged.

Rorie blinked wildly at the tears that burned for release.

"I wish to God your car had broken down a hundred miles from Elk Run," he said. "Before you bombarded your way into my home, my life was set. I knew what I wanted, where I was headed. In the course of a few days you've upended my whole world."

Emotion clogged Rorie's throat at the unfairness of his accusations. She hadn't asked for the MGB to break down where it had. The minute she could, she planned to get out of his life and back to her own.

No, she decided, they couldn't wait that long—it was much too painful for them both. She had to leave now. "I'll pack my things and be gone before evening."

"Just where do you plan to go?"

Rorie didn't know. "Somewhere…anywhere." She had to leave for his sake, as well as hers.

"Go back inside the house, Rorie, before I say or do something else I'll regret. You're right—we can't be in the same room together. At least not alone."

She started to walk past him, eyes downcast, her heart heavy with misery. Unexpectedly his hand shot out and caught her fingers, stopping her.

"I didn't mean what I said." His voice rasped, warm and hoarse. "None of it. Forgive me, Rorie."

Her heart raced when his hand touched hers. It took all the restraint Rorie could muster, which at the moment wasn't much, to resist throwing herself into his arms and holding on for the rest of her life.

"Forgive me, too," she whispered.

"Forgive you?" he asked, incredulous. "No, Rorie. I'll thank God every day of my life for having met you." With that, he released her fingers, slowly, reluctantly. "Go now, before I make an even bigger fool of myself."

Rorie ran from the office as though a raging fire were licking at her heels, threatening to consume her.

And in a way, it was.

For two days, Rorie managed to stay completely out of his way. They saw each other only briefly and always in the company of others. Rorie was sure they gave Academy Award performances every time they were together. They laughed and teased and joked and the only one who seemed to suspect things weren't quite right was Mary.

Rorie was grateful the housekeeper didn't question her, but the looks she gave Rorie were frowningly thoughtful.

Three days after the Grange dance, Mary's sister arrived in Riversdale. Revealing more excitement than Rorie had seen in their acquaintance, Mary fussed with her hair and dress, and as soon as she'd finished the lunch dishes she was off.

Putting on Mary's well-worn apron, Rorie looped the long strands around her waist twice and set to work. Kate joined her mid-afternoon, carrying a large bag of ingredients for the dessert she was going to prepare.

"I've been cooking from the moment Mary left," Rorie told Kate, pushing the damp hair from her forehead as she stirred wine into a simmering sauce. Rorie intended to dazzle Clay and Skip with her one speciality—seafood fettuccine. She hadn't admitted to Mary how limited her repertoire of dishes was, although the housekeeper had repeatedly quizzed her about what she planned to make for dinner. Rorie had insisted it was a surprise. She'd decided that this rich and tasty dish stood a good chance of impressing the Franklin men.

"And I'm making Clay his favorite dessert—homemade lemon meringue pie." Kate reached for the grocery bag on the kitchen counter and six bright yellow lemons rolled out.

Rorie was impressed. The one and only time she'd tried to bake a lemon pie, she'd used a pudding mix. Apparently, Kate took the homemade part seriously.

"Whatever you're cooking smells wonderful," Kate said, stepping over to the stove. Crab, large succulent shrimp and small bite-sized pieces of sole were waiting in the refrigerator, to be added to the sauce just before the dish was served.

Kate was busy whipping up a pie crust when the

phone rang several minutes later. She glanced anxiously at the wall, her fingers sticky with flour and lard.

Rorie looked over at her. "Do you suppose I should answer that?"

"You'd better. Clay usually relies on Mary to catch the phone for him."

Rorie lifted the receiver before the next peal. "Elk Run."

"That Miss Campbell?"

Rorie immediately recognized the voice of the mechanic from Riversdale. "Yes, this is Rorie Campbell."

"Remember I promised I'd call you when the part arrived? Well, it's here, all safe and sound, so you can stop fretting. Just came in a few minutes ago—haven't even had a chance to take it out of the box. Thought you'd want to know."

"It's the right one this time?"

"Here, I'll check it now… Yup, this is it."

Rorie wasn't sure what she felt. Relief, yes, but regret, too. "Thank you. Thank you very much."

"It's a little late for me to be starting the job this afternoon. My son's playing a Little League game and I promised him I'd be there. I'll get to this first thing in the morning and should be finished before noon. Give me a call before you head over here and I'll make sure everything's running the way it should."

"Yes, I'll do that. Thanks again." Slowly Rorie replaced the receiver. She leaned against the wall sighing deeply. At Kate's questioning gaze, she smiled weakly and explained, "That was the mechanic. The water pump for my car arrived and he's going to be working on it first thing in the morning."

"Rorie, that's great."

"I think so, too." She did—and she didn't. Part of her longed to flee Elk Run, and another part of her realized that no matter how far she traveled, no matter how many years passed, she'd never forget these days with Clay Franklin.

"Then tonight's going to be your last evening here," Kate murmured. "Selfish as it sounds, I really hate the thought of you leaving."

"We can keep in touch."

"Oh, yes, I'd like that. I'll send you a wedding invitation."

That reminder was the last thing Rorie needed. But once she was on the road again, she could start forgetting, she told herself grimly.

"Since this is going to be your last night, we should make it special," Kate announced brightly. "We're going to use the best china and set out the crystal wineglasses."

Rorie laughed, imagining Mary's face when she heard about it.

Even as she spoke, Kate was walking toward the dining-room china cabinet. In a few minutes, she'd set the table, cooked the sauce for the pie and poured it into the cooling pie shell that sat on the counter. The woman was a marvel!

Rorie was busy adding the final touches to the fettuccine when Clay and Skip came in through the back door.

"When's dinner?" Skip wanted to know. "I'm starved."

"Soon." Rorie tested the boiling noodles to be sure they'd cooked all the way through but weren't overdone.

"Upstairs with the both of you," Kate said, shooing them out of the kitchen. "I want you to change into something nice."

"We're supposed to dress up for dinner?" Skip complained. He'd obviously recovered from any need to impress her with his sartorial elegance, Rorie noted, remembering that he'd worn his Sunday best that first night. "We already washed—what more do you want?"

"For you to change your clothes. We're having a celebration tonight."

"We are?" The boy looked from Kate to Rorie and then back again.

"That's right," Kate continued, undaunted by his lack of enthusiasm. "And when we're through with dinner, there's going to be a farewell party for Rorie. We're going to send her off country-style."

"Rorie's leaving?" Skip sounded shocked. "But she just got here."

"The repair shop from Riversdale called. Her car will be finished tomorrow and she'll be on her way."

Clay's eyes burned into Rorie's. She tried to avoid looking at him, but when she did chance to meet his gaze, she could feel his distress. His jaw went rigid, and his mouth tightened as though he was bracing himself against Kate's words.

"Now hurry up, you two. Dinner's nearly ready," Kate said with a laugh. "Rorie's been cooking her heart out all afternoon."

Both men disappeared and Rorie set out the fresh green salad she'd made earlier, along with the seven-grain dinner rolls she'd warmed in the oven.

Once everyone was seated at the table and waiting, Rorie ceremonially carried in the platter of fettuccine, thick with seafood. She'd spent at least ten minutes arranging it to look as attractive as possible.

"Whatever it is smells good," Skip called out as she

entered the dining room. "I'm so hungry I could eat a horse."

"Funny, Skip, very funny," Kate said.

Rorie set the serving dish in the middle of the table and stepped back, anticipating their praise.

Skip raised himself halfway out of his seat as he glared at her masterpiece. "That's it?" His voice was filled with disappointment.

Rorie blinked, uncertain how she should respond.

"You've been cooking all afternoon and you mean to tell me that's everything?"

"It's seafood fettuccine," she explained.

"It just looks like a bunch of noodles to me."

Ten

"I'll have another piece of lemon pie," Skip said, eagerly extending his plate.

"If you're still hungry, Skip," Clay remarked casually, "there are a few dinner rolls left."

Skip's gaze darted to the small wicker basket and he wrinkled his nose. "No, thanks. Too many seeds in those things. I got one caught in my tooth earlier and spent five minutes trying to suck it out."

Rorie did her best to smile.

Skip must have noticed how miserable she was because he added, "The salad was real good though. What kind of dressing was that?"

"Vinaigrette."

"Really? It tasted fruity."

"It was raspberry flavored."

Skip's eyes widened. "I've never heard of that kind of vinegar. Did you buy it here in Nightingale?"

"Not exactly. I got the ingredients while Kate and I were out the other day and mixed it up last night."

"*That* tasted real good." Which was Skip's less-than-subtle method of telling her nothing else had. He'd barely touched the main course. Clay had made a show of asking for seconds, but Rorie was all too aware that his display of enthusiasm had been an effort to salve her injured ego.

Rorie wasn't fooled—no one had enjoyed her special dinner. Even old Blue had turned his nose up at it when she'd offered him a taste of the leftovers.

Clay and Skip did hard physical work; they didn't sit in an office all day like Dan and the other men she knew. She should have realized that Clay and his brother required a more substantial meal than noodles swimming in a creamy sauce. Rorie wished she'd discussed her menu with either Mary or Kate. A tiny voice inside her suggested that Kate might have said something to warn her...

"Anyone else for more pie?" Kate was asking.

Clay nodded and cast a guilty glance in Rorie's direction. "I could go for a second piece myself."

"The pie was delicious," Rorie told Kate, meaning it. She was willing to admit Kate's dessert had been the highlight of the meal.

"Kate's one of the best cooks in the entire country," Skip announced, licking the back of his fork. "Her lemon pie won a blue ribbon at the county fair last year." He leaned forward, planting his elbows on the table. "She's got a barbecue sauce so tangy and good that when she cooks up spareribs I just can't stop eating 'em." His face fell as though he was thinking about those ribs now and would have gladly traded all of Rorie's fancy city food for a plateful.

"I'd like the fettuccine recipe if you'd give it to me,"

Kate told Rorie, obviously attempting to change the subject and spare Rorie's feelings. Perhaps she felt a little guilty, too, for not giving her any helpful suggestions.

Skip stared at Kate as if she'd volunteered to muck out the stalls.

"I'll write it down before I leave."

"Since Rorie and Kate put so much time and effort into the meal, I think Skip and I could be convinced to do our part and wash the dishes."

"We could?" Skip protested.

"It's the least we can do," Clay returned flatly, frowning at his younger brother.

Rorie was all too aware of Clay's ploy. He wanted to get into the kitchen so they could find something else to eat without being conspicuous about it. Something plain and basic, no doubt, like roast-beef sandwiches.

"Listen, you guys," Rorie said brightly. "I'm sorry about dinner. I can see everyone's still hungry. You're all going out of your way to reassure me, but it isn't necessary."

"I don't know what you're talking about, Rorie. Dinner was excellent," Clay said, patting his stomach.

Rorie nearly laughed out loud. "Why don't we call for a pizza?" she said, pleased with her solution. "I bungled dinner, so that's the least I can do to make it up to you."

Three faces stared at her blankly.

"Rorie," Clay said gently. "The closest pizza parlour is thirty miles from here."

"Oh."

Undeterred, Skip leaped to his feet. "No problem… You phone in the order and I'll go get it."

* * *

Empty pizza boxes littered the living-room floor, along with several abandoned soft-drink cans.

Skip lay on his back staring up at the ceiling. "Anyone for a little music?" he asked lazily.

"Sure." Kate got to her feet and sat down at the piano. As her nimble fingers ran over the keyboard, the rich sounds echoed against the walls. "Some Lee Greenwood?"

"All *right,*" Skip called out with a yell, punching his fist into the air. He thrust two fingers in his mouth and gave a shrill whistle.

"Who?" Rorie asked once the commotion had died down.

"He's a country singer," Clay explained. Blue ambled to his side, settling down at his feet. Clay gently stroked his back.

"I guess I haven't heard of him," Rorie murmured.

Once more she discovered three pairs of eyes studying her curiously.

"What about Johnny Cash?" Kate suggested next. "You probably know who he is."

"Oh, sure." Rorie looped her arms over her bent knees and lowered her voice to a gravelly pitch. "I hear that train a comin'."

Skip let loose with another whistle and Rorie laughed at his boisterous antics. Clay left the room; he returned a moment later with a guitar, then seated himself on the floor again, beside Blue. Skip crawled across the braided rug in the center of the room and retrieved a harmonica from the mantel. Soon Kate and the two men were making their own brand of music—country songs, from the traditional to the more recent. Rorie didn't know a single one, but she clapped her hands and tapped her foot to the lively beat.

"Sing for Rorie," Skip shouted to Clay and Kate. "Let's show her what she's been missing."

Clay's rich baritone joined Kate's lilting soprano, and Rorie's hands and feet stopped moving. Her eyes darted from one to the other in openmouthed wonder at the beautiful harmony of their two voices, male and female. It was as though they'd been singing together all their lives. She realized they probably had.

When they finished, Rorie blinked back tears, too dumbfounded for a moment to speak. "That was wonderful," she told them and her voice caught with emotion.

"Kate and Clay sing duets at church all the time," Skip explained. "They're good, aren't they?"

Rorie nodded, gazing at the two of them. Clay and Kate were right for each other—they belonged together, and once she was gone they would blend their lives as beautifully as they had their voices. Rorie happened to catch Kate's eye. The other woman slipped her arms around Clay's waist and rested her head against his shoulder, laying claim to this man and silently letting Rorie know it. Rorie couldn't blame Kate. In like circumstances she would have done the same.

"Do you sing, Rorie?" Kate asked, leaving Clay and sliding onto the piano bench.

"A little, and I play some piano." Actually her own singing voice wasn't half bad. She'd participated in several singing groups while she was in high school and had taken five years of piano lessons.

"Please sing something for us." Rorie recognized a hint of challenge in the words.

"Okay." She replaced Kate at the piano seat and started out with a little satirical ditty she remembered from her college days. Skip hooted as she knew he would at the clever words, and all three rewarded her with a round of applause.

"Play some more," Kate encouraged. "It's nice to have someone else do the playing for a change." She sat next to Clay on the floor, once again resting her head against his shoulder. If it hadn't been for the guitar in his hands, Rorie knew he would've placed his arm around her and drawn her even closer. It would have been the natural thing to do.

"I don't know the songs you usually sing, though." Rorie was more than a little reluctant now. She'd never heard of this Greenwood person they seemed to like so well.

"Play what you know," Kate said, "and we'll join in."

After a few seconds' thought, Rorie nodded. "This is a song by Billy Joel. I'm sure you've heard of him— his songs are more rock than country, but I think you'll recognize the music." Rorie was only a few measures into the ballad before she realized that Kate, Clay and Skip had never heard this song.

She stopped playing. "What about Whitney Houston?"

Skip repeated the name a couple of times before his eyes lit up with recognition. "Hasn't she done Coke commercials?"

"Right," Rorie said, laughing. "She's had several big hits."

Kate slowly shook her head. "Sorry, I don't think I can remember the words to her songs."

"Barbra Streisand?"

"I thought she was an actress," Skip said with a puzzled frown. "You mean she sings, too?"

Reluctantly Rorie rose from the piano seat. "Kate, you'll have to take over. It seems you three are a whole lot country and I'm a little bit rock and roll."

"We'll make you into a country girl yet!" Skip insisted, sliding the harmonica across his mouth with an ease Rorie envied.

Clay glanced at his watch. "We aren't going to be able to convert Rorie within the next twelve hours."

A gloom settled over them as Kate took Rorie's place at the piano.

"Are you sure we can't talk you into staying a few extra days?" Skip asked. "We're just getting to know each other."

Rorie shook her head, more determined than ever to leave as soon as she could.

"It would be a shame for you to miss the county fair next weekend. Maybe you could stop here on your way back through Oregon, after your trip to Canada," Kate added. "Clay and I are singing, and we're scheduled for the square dance competition, too."

"Yeah," Skip cried. "And we've got pig races planned again this year."

"Pig races?" Rorie echoed faintly.

"I know it sounds silly, but it's really fun. We take the ten fastest pigs in the area and let them race toward a bowl of Oreos. No joke—cookies! Everyone bets on who'll win and we all have a lot of fun." Skip's eyes shone with eagerness. "Please think about it, anyway, Rorie."

"Mary's entering her apple pie again," Clay put in. "She's been after that blue ribbon for six years."

A hundred reasons to fade out of their lives flew across Rorie's mind like particles of dust in the wind. And yet the offer was tempting. She tried, unsuccessfully, to read Clay's eyes, her own filled with a silent appeal. This was a decision she needed help making. But Clay wasn't helping. The thought of never seeing him again was like pouring salt onto an open wound; still, it was a reality she'd have to face sooner or later.

So Rorie volunteered the only excuse she could come up with at the moment. "I don't have the time. I'm sorry, but I'd be cutting it too close to get back to San Francisco for work Monday morning."

"Not if you canceled part of your trip to Canada and came back on Friday," Skip pointed out. "You didn't think you'd have a good time at the square dance, either, but you did, remember?"

It wasn't a matter of having a good time. So much more was involved…though the pig races actually sounded like fun. The very idea of such an activity would have astounded her only a week before, Rorie reflected. She could just imagine what Dan would say.

"Rorie?" Skip pressed. "What do you think?"

"I… I don't know."

"The county fair is about as good as it gets around Nightingale."

"I don't want to impose on your hospitality again." Clay still wasn't giving her any help with this decision.

"But having you stay with us isn't a problem," Skip insisted. "As long as you promise to stay out of the kitchen, you're welcome to stick around all summer. Isn't that right, Clay?"

His hesitation was so slight that Rorie doubted anyone else had noticed it. "Naturally Rorie's welcome to visit us any time she wants."

"If staying with these two drives you crazy," Kate inserted, "you could stay at my house. In fact, I'd love it if you did."

Rorie dropped her gaze, fearing what she might see in Clay's eyes. She sensed his indecision as she struggled with her own. She had to leave. Yet she wanted to stay....

"I think I should take the rest of my vacation in Victoria," she finally told them.

"I know you're worried about getting back in time for work, but Skip's right. If you left Victoria one day early, then you could be here for the fair," Kate suggested again, but her offer didn't sound as sincere as it had earlier.

"Rorie said she doesn't have the time," Clay said after an awkward silence. "I think we should respect her decision."

"You sound as if you don't want her to come back," Skip accused.

"No," Clay murmured, his eyes meeting hers. "I want her here, but Rorie should try to salvage some of the vacation she planned. She has to do what she think's best."

Rorie could feel his eyes moving over her hair and her face in loving appraisal. She tensed and prayed that Kate and Skip weren't aware of it.

During the next hour, Skip tried repeatedly to convince Rorie to visit on her way back or even to stay until the fair. As far as Skip could see, there wasn't much reason to go to Canada now, anyway. But Rorie resisted. Walking away from Clay once was going to be painful enough. Rorie didn't know if she could do it twice.

Skip was yawning by the time they decided to call an end to the evening. With little more than a mumbled good-night, he hurried up the stairs, abandoning the others.

Rorie and Kate took a few extra minutes to straighten the living room, while Clay drove his pickup around to the front of the house. "I'd better burn the evidence before Mary sees these pizza boxes," Rorie joked. "She'll have my hide once she hears about dinner."

Kate laughed good-naturedly as she collected her belongings. When they heard Clay's truck, she put down her bags and ran to Rorie. "You'll call me before you leave tomorrow?"

Rorie nodded and hugged her back.

"If something happens and you change your mind about the fair, please know that you're welcome to stay with me and Dad—we'd enjoy the company."

"Thank you, Kate."

The house felt empty and silent once Kate had left with Clay. Rorie knew it would be useless to go upstairs and try to sleep. Instead she went out to the front porch, where she'd sat in the swing with Clay that first night. She sank down on the steps, one arm wrapped around a post, and gazed upward. The skies were glittered with the light of countless stars—stars that shone with a clarity and brightness one couldn't see in the city.

Clay belonged to this land, this farm, this small town. Rorie was a city girl to the marrow of her bones. This evening had proved the hopelessness of any dream that she and Clay might have of finding happiness together. There was his commitment to Kate. And there was the fact that he and Rorie were too different, their tastes too dissimilar. She certainly couldn't picture him making a life away from Elk Run.

Clay had accepted the hopelessness of it, too. That was the reason he agreed she should travel to Canada. This evening Rorie had sensed a desperation in him that rivaled her own.

It was a night filled with insights. Sitting under the heavens, she was beginning to understand some important things about life. For perhaps the first time, she'd fallen in love. During the past six days she'd tried to deny what she was feeling, but on the eve of her departure it seemed silly to lie to herself any longer. Rorie couldn't believe something like this had actually happened to her. Meeting someone and falling in love with him in the space of a few days was an experience reserved for novels and movies. This wasn't like her normal sane, sensible self at all. Rorie had always thought she was too levelheaded to fall so easily in love.

Until she met Clay Franklin.

On the wings of one soul-searching realization came another. Love wasn't what she'd expected. She'd assumed it meant a strong sensual passion that overwhelmed the lovers and left them powerless before it. But in the past few days, she'd learned that love marked the soul as well as the body.

Clay would forever be a part of her. Since that first night when Nightsong was born, her heart had never felt more alive. Yet within a few hours she would walk away from the man she loved and consider herself blessed to have shared these days with him.

A tear rolled down the side of her face, surprising her. This wasn't a time for sadness, but joy. She'd discovered a deep inner strength she hadn't known she possessed. She wiped the moisture away and rested her head against the post, her eyes fixed on the heavens.

The footsteps behind Rorie didn't startle her. She'd known Clay would come to her this one last time.

Eleven

Clay draped his arm over Rorie's shoulders and joined her in gazing up at the sky. Neither spoke for several minutes, as though they feared words would destroy the tranquil mood. Rorie stared, transfixed by the glittering display. Like her love for this man, the stars would remain forever distant, unattainable, but certain and unchanging.

A ragged sigh escaped her lips. "All my life I've believed that everything that befalls us has a purpose."

"I've always thought that, too," Clay whispered.

"Everything in life is deliberate."

"Our final hours together you're going to become philosophical?" He rested his chin on her head, gently ruffling her hair. "Are you sad, Rorie?"

"Oh, no," she denied quickly. "I can't be… I feel strange, but I don't know if I can find the words to explain it. I'm leaving tomorrow and I realize we'll probably never see each other again. I have no regrets—not a single one—and yet I think my heart is breaking."

His hand tightened on her shoulder in silent protest

as if he found the idea of relinquishing her more than he could bear.

"We can't defy reality," she told him. "Nothing's going to change in the next few hours. The water pump on the car will be replaced, and I'll go back to my life. The way you'll go back to yours."

"I have this gut feeling there's going to be a hole the size of the Grand Canyon in mine the minute you drive away." He dropped his arm and moved away from her. His eyes held a weary sadness, but Rorie found an acceptance there, too.

"I'm an uncomplicated man," he said evenly. "I'm probably nothing like the sophisticated man you're dating in San Francisco."

Her thoughts flew to Dan, so cosmopolitan and… superficial, and she recognized the truth in Clay's words. The two men were poles apart. Dan's interests revolved around his career and his car, but he was genuinely kind, and it was that quality that had attracted Rorie.

"Elk Run's given me a good deal of satisfaction over the years. My life's work is here and, God willing, some day my son will carry on the breeding programs I've started. Everything I've ever dreamed of has always been within my grasp." He paused, holding in a long sigh and releasing it slowly. "And then you came," he whispered, and a brief smile crossed his lips, "and, within a matter of days, I'm reeling from the effects. Suddenly I'm left doubting what's really important in my life."

Rorie lowered her eyes. "Who'd have believed a silly water pump would be responsible for all this wretched soul-searching?"

"I've always been the type of man who's known what he wants, but you make me feel like a schoolboy no older than Skip. I don't know what to do anymore, Rorie. In a few hours, you'll be leaving and part of me says if you do, I'll regret it the rest of my life."

"I can't stay." Their little dinner party had shown her how different their worlds actually were. She wouldn't fit into his life and he'd be an alien in hers. But Kate... Kate belonged to his world.

Clay rubbed his hands across his eyes and harshly drew in a breath. "I know you feel you should leave, but that doesn't mean I have to like it."

"The pull to stay is there for me, too," she whispered. "And it's tearing both of us apart."

Rorie shook her head. "Don't you see? So much good has come out of meeting you, Clay." Her voice was strong. She had to make him understand that she'd always be grateful for the things he'd taught her. "In some ways I grew up tonight. I feel I'm doing what's right for both of us, although it's more painful than anything I've ever known."

He looked at her with such undisguised love that she ached.

"Let me hold you once more," he said softly. "Give me that, at least."

Rorie shook her head. "I can't... I'm sorry, Clay, but this is how it has to be with us. I'm so weak where you're concerned. I couldn't bear to let you touch me now and then leave tomorrow."

His eyes drifted shut as he yielded to her wisdom. "I don't know that I could, either."

They were only a few feet apart, but it seemed vast worlds stood between them.

"More than anything I want you to remember me fondly, without any bitterness," Rorie told him, discovering as she spoke the words how much she meant them.

Clay nodded. "Be happy, Rorie, for my sake."

Rorie realized that contentment would be a long time coming without this man in her life, but she would find it eventually. She prayed that he'd marry Kate the way he'd planned. The other woman was the perfect wife for him—unlike herself. A thread of agony twisted around Rorie's heart.

She turned to leave him, afraid she'd dissolve into tears if she remained much longer. "Goodbye, Clay."

"Goodbye, Rorie."

She rushed past him and hurried up the stairs.

The following morning, both Clay and Skip had left the house by the time Rorie entered the kitchen.

"Good morning, Mary," she said with a note of false cheer in her voice. "How did the visit with your sister go?"

"Fine."

Rorie stepped around the housekeeper to reach the coffeepot and poured herself a cup. A plume of steam rose enticingly to her nostrils and she took a tentative sip.

"I found those pizza boxes you were trying so hard to hide from me," Mary grumbled as she wiped her hands on her apron. "You fed these good men restaurant pizza?"

Unable to stop herself, Rorie chuckled at the housekeeper's indignation. "Guilty as charged. Mary, you should've known better than to leave their fate in my evil hands."

"Near as I can figure, the closest pizza parlour is a half hour away. Did you drive over and get it yourself or did you send Skip?"

"Actually he volunteered," she admitted reluctantly. "Dinner didn't exactly turn out the way I'd hoped."

The housekeeper snickered. "I should've guessed. You city slickers don't know nothing about serving up a decent meal to your menfolk."

Rorie gave a hefty sigh of agreement. "The only thing for me to do is stay on another couple of months and have you teach me." As she expected, the housekeeper opened her mouth to protest. "Unfortunately," Rorie continued, cutting Mary off before she could launch into her arguments, "I'm hoping to be gone by this afternoon."

Mary's response was a surprise. The older woman's expression grew troubled and intense.

"I suspected you'd be going soon enough," she said in a tight voice, pulling out a chair. She sat down heavily and brushed wisps of gray hair from her forehead. Her weathered face was thoughtful. "It's for the best, you know."

"I knew you'd be glad to get rid of me."

Mary shrugged. "It's other reasons that make it right for you to leave. You know what I'm talking about, even if you don't want to admit it to me. As a person you tend to grow on folks. Like I said before, for a city girl, you ain't half bad."

Rorie took a banana from the fruit bowl in the center of the table. "For a stud farm, stuck out here in the middle of nowhere, this place isn't half bad, either," she said, trying to lighten the mood, which had taken an unexpected turn toward the serious. "The people are friendly and the apple pie's been exceptional."

Mary ignored the compliment on her pie. "By people, I suppose you're referring to Clay. You're going to miss him, aren't you, girl?"

The banana found its way back into the bowl and with it went her cheerful facade. "Yes. I'll miss Clay."

The older woman's frown deepened. "From the things I've been noticing, he's going to be yearning for you, as well. But it's for the best," she said again. "For the best."

Rorie nodded and her voice wavered. "Yes...but it isn't easy."

The housekeeper gave her a lopsided smile as she gently patted Rorie's hand. "I know that, too, but you're doing the right thing. You'll forget him soon enough."

A strong protest rose in her breast, closing off her throat. She wouldn't forget Clay. Ever. How could she forget the man who had so unselfishly taught her such valuable lessons about life and love? Lessons about herself.

"Kate Logan's the right woman for Clay," Mary said abruptly.

Those few words cut Rorie to the quick. Hearing another person voice the truth made it almost unbearably painful.

"I...hope they're very happy."

"Kate loves him. She has from the time she was knee-high to a June bug. And there's something you don't know. Years back, when Clay was in college, he fell in love with a girl from Seattle. She'd been born and raised in the city. Clay loved her, wanted to marry her, even brought her to Elk Run to meet the family.

She stayed a couple of days, and the whole time, she was as restless as water on a hot skillet. Apparently she had words with Clay because the next thing I knew, she'd packed her bags and headed home. Clay never said much about her after that, but she hurt him bad. It wasn't until Kate got home from college that Clay thought seriously about marriage again."

Mary's story explained a lot about Clay.

"Now, I know I'm just an old woman who likes her soaps and Saturday-night bingo. Most folks don't think I've got a lick of sense, and that's all right. What others choose to assume don't bother me much." She paused, and shook her head. "But Kate Logan's about the kindest, dearest person this town has ever seen. People like her—they can't help themselves. She's always got a kind word and there's no one in this world she's too good for. She cares about the people in this community. Those kids she teaches over at the grade school love her like nothing you've ever seen. And she loves them. When it came to building that fancy library, it was Kate who worked so hard convincing folks they'd be doing what was best for Nightingale by voting for that bond issue."

Rorie kept her face averted. She didn't need Mary to tell her Kate was a good person; she'd seen the evidence of it herself.

"What most folks don't know is that Kate's seen plenty of pain in her own life. She watched her mother die a slow death from cancer. Took care of her most of the time herself, nursing Nora when she should've been off at college having fun like other nineteen-year-olds. Her family needed her and she was there. Kate gave old man Logan a reason to go on living when Nora passed away. She still lives with him, and it's long past time for her to be a carefree adult on her own. Kate's a good person clean through." Mary hesitated, then drew in a solemn breath. "Now, you may think I'm nothing but a meddling old fool. But I'm saying it's a good thing you're leaving Elk Run before you break that girl's heart. She's got a chance now for some happiness, and God knows she deserves it. If she loses Clay, I can tell you it'd break her heart. She's too good to have that happen to her over some fancy city girl who's only passing through."

Rorie winced at the way Mary described her.

"I'm a plain talker," Mary said on the end of an abrupt laugh. "Always have been, always will be. Knowing Clay—and I do, as well as his mother did, God rest her soul—he'll pine for you awhile, but eventually everything will fall back into place. The way it was before you arrived."

Tears stung Rorie's eyes. She felt miserable as it was, and Mary wasn't helping. She'd already assured the housekeeper she was leaving, but Mary apparently wanted to be damn sure she didn't change her mind. The woman didn't understand…but then again, maybe she did.

"Have you ever been in love, Mary?"

"Once," came the curt reply. "Hurt so much the first time I never chanced it again."

"Are you sorry you lived your life alone now?" That was what Rorie saw for herself. Oh, she knew she was being melodramatic and over-emotional, but she couldn't imagine loving any man as much as she did Clay.

Mary lifted one shoulder in a shrug. "Some days I have plenty of regrets, but then on others it ain't so bad.

I'd like to have had a child, but God saw to it that I was around when Clay and Skip needed someone.... That made up for what I missed."

"They consider you family."

"Yeah, I suppose they do." Mary pushed out her chair and stood up. "Well, I better get back to work. Those men expect a decent lunch. I imagine they're near starved after the dinner you fed them last night."

Despite her heartache, Rorie smiled and finished her coffee. "And I'd better get upstairs and pack the rest of my things. The mechanic said my car would be ready around noon."

On her way to the bedroom, Rorie paused at the framed photograph of Clay's parents that sat on the piano. She'd passed it a number of times and had given it little more than a fleeting glance. Now it suddenly demanded her attention, and she stopped in front of it.

A tremor went through her hand as she lightly ran her finger along the brass frame. Clay's mother smiled serenely into the camera, her gray eyes so like her son's that Rorie felt a knot in her stomach. Those same eyes seemed to reach across eternity and call out to Rorie, plead with her. Rorie's own eyes narrowed, certain her imagination was playing havoc with her troubled mind. She focused her attention on the woman's hair. That, too, was the same dark shade as Clay's, brushed away from her face in a carefully styled chignon. Clay had never mentioned his parents to her, not once, but studying the photograph Rorie knew intuitively that he'd shared a close relationship with his mother. Blue wandered out from the kitchen and stood at Rorie's side as though offering consolation. Grateful, she bent down to pet him.

Looking back at the photograph, Rorie noted that Skip resembled his father, with the same dancing blue eyes that revealed more than a hint of devilry.

Rorie continued to study both parents, but it was Clay's mother who captured her attention over and over again.

The phone ringing in the distance startled her, and her wrist was shaking when she set the picture back on the piano.

"Phone's for you," Mary shouted from the kitchen.

Rorie assumed it was George at the repair shop in Riversdale; she'd been waiting all morning to hear from him.

"Hello," she said, her fingers closing tightly around the receiver. Her biggest fear was that something had happened to delay her departure a second time.

"Miss Campbell," said the mechanic, "everything's fine. I got that part in and working for you without a hitch."

"Thank God," she murmured. Her hold on the telephone receiver relaxed, a little.

"I've got a man I could spare if you'd like to have your car delivered to Elk Run. But you've got to understand fifty miles is a fair distance and I'm afraid I'll have to charge you extra for it."

"That's fine," Rorie said eagerly, not even bothering to ask the amount. "How soon can he be here?"

Twelve

"So you're really going," Skip said as he picked up Rorie's bags. "Somehow I figured I might've talked you into staying on for the county fair."

"You seem intent on bringing me to ruin, Skip Franklin. I'm afraid I'd bet all my hard-earned cash on those pig races you were telling me about," Rorie teased. Standing in the middle of the master bedroom, she surveyed it to be sure she hadn't forgotten anything.

A pang of wistfulness settled over her as she slowly looked around. Not for the first time, Rorie felt the love and warmth emanating from these brightly papered walls. Lazily, almost lovingly, she ran her fingertips along the top of the dresser, letting her hand linger there a moment, unwilling to pull herself away. This bedroom represented so much of what she was leaving behind. It was difficult to walk away.

Skip stood in the doorway impatiently waiting for her. "Kate phoned and said she's coming over. She wants to say goodbye."

"I'll be happy to see her one last time." Rorie wished Skip would leave so she could delay her parting with this room a little longer. Until now, Rorie hadn't realized how much sleeping in Clay's parents' room had meant to her. Her appreciation had come too late.

"Mary's packing a lunch for you," Skip announced with a wry chuckle, "and knowing Mary, it'll be enough to last you a week."

Rorie smiled and reluctantly followed him down the stairs. As Skip had claimed, the housekeeper had pre-pared two large bags, which sat waiting on the kitchen table.

"Might as well take those with you, too," Mary mut-tered gruffly. "I hate the thought of you eating restau-rant food. This, at least, will stick to your ribs."

"Goodbye, Mary," Rorie said softly, touched by the housekeeper's thoughtfulness. On impulse she hugged the older woman. "Thank you for everything—includ-ing our talk this morning." The impromptu embrace surprised Rorie as much as it obviously did Mary.

"You drive careful now, you hear?" the housekeeper responded, squeezing Rorie tightly and patting her back several times.

"I will, I promise."

"A letter now and again wouldn't be amiss."

"All right," Rorie agreed, and used her sleeve to blot tears from the corners of her eyes. These people had touched her in so many ways. Leaving them was even more difficult than she'd imagined.

The housekeeper rubbed the heel of her hand over her right eye. "Time for you to get on the road. What are you doing standing in the kitchen chitchatting with me?" she asked brusquely.

"I'm going, I'm going." Mary's gruff voice didn't fool Rorie. The housekeeper's exterior might be a little crusty, and her tongue a bit surly, but she didn't succeed in disguising a generous, loving heart.

"I don't know where Clay is," Skip complained after he'd loaded the luggage into the MG's trunk. "I thought he'd want to see you before you left. I wonder where he got off to."

"I'm…sure he's got better things to do than say goodbye to me."

"No way," Skip said, frowning. "I'm going to see if I can find him."

Rorie's first reaction was to stop Skip, then she quickly decided against it. If she made too much of a fuss, Skip might suspect something. She understood what had prompted Clay to stay away from the house all morning, and in truth she was grateful. Leaving Elk Run was hard enough without prolonging the agony in lengthy farewells.

Skip hesitated, kicking at the dirt with the pointed toe of his cowboy boot. "You two didn't have a fight or anything, did you?"

"No. What makes you ask?"

Skip shrugged. "Well… It's just that every time I walked into a room with the two of you, I could feel something. If it wasn't for Kate, I'd think my big brother was interested in you."

"I'm sure you're imagining things."

"I suppose so," Skip said with a nod, dismissing the notion. "Ever since you got here, though, Clay's been acting weird."

"How do you mean?"

"Sort of cranky."

"My unexpected arrival added to his problems, don't you think?" In so many ways it was the truth, and she felt guilty about that. The responsibilities for the farm and for raising Skip were sobering enough; he didn't need her there to wreak havoc with his personal life.

"You weren't any problem," Skip answered sharply. "In fact, having you around was fun. The only trouble is you didn't stay long enough."

"Thank you, Skip." Once again she felt her throat clog with tears. She was touched by his sweet, simple hospitality and reminded of how much she'd miss him.

"I still kinda wish you were going to stay for the fair," he mumbled. "You'd have a good time, I guarantee it. We may not have all the fancy entertainment you do in San Francisco, but when we do a county fair, we do it big."

"I'm sure it'll be great fun."

Skip braced his foot against the bumper of the faded blue pickup, apparently forgetting his earlier decision to seek out Clay, which was just as well.

"You don't like the country much, do you, Rorie?"

"Oh, but I do," she said. "It's a different way of life, though. Here on Elk Run, I feel like a duck in a pond full of swans."

Skip laughed. "I suppose folks there in the big city don't think much of the country."

"No one has time to think," Rorie said with a small laugh.

"That doesn't make any sense. Everyone's got thoughts."

Rorie nodded, not knowing how to explain something so complex. When Skip had spent some time in the city, he'd figure out what she meant.

"The one thing I've noticed more than anything is how quiet it is here," she said pensively, looking around, burning into her memory each detail of the farmhouse and the yard.

"I like the quiet. Some places, the noise is so bad I worry about ear damage," Skip said.

"I imagine if I lived here, I'd grow accustomed to the silence, too. But to be honest, I hadn't realized how much I enjoy the sounds of the city. There's something invigorating about the clang of the trolley cars or the foghorn on the Bay early in the morning."

Skip frowned and shook his head. "You honestly like all that racket?"

Rorie nodded. "It's more than that. The city's exciting. I hadn't really known how much living there meant to me before coming to Elk Run." Rorie wasn't sure how to describe the aroma of freshly baked sourdough bread, or the perfumed scent of budding rosebushes in Golden Gate Park, to someone who'd never experienced them. Country life had its appeal, she couldn't deny that, but she belonged to the city. At least, that was what she told herself over and over again.

"Ah," Skip said, and his foot dropped from the bumper with a thud, "here's Clay now."

Rorie tensed, clasping her hands in front of her. Clay's lengthy strides quickly diminished the distance between the barn and the yard. Each stride was filled with purpose, as though he longed to get this polite farewell over with.

Rorie straightened and walked toward him. "I'll be leaving in a couple of minutes," she said softly.

"Kate's coming to say goodbye," Skip added.

Rorie noted how Clay's eyes didn't quite meet her own. He seemed to focus instead on the car behind her.

They'd already said everything there was to say and this final parting only compounded the pain.

"Saying thank you seems so inadequate," Rorie told him in a voice that wasn't entirely steady. "I've appreciated your hospitality more than you'll ever know." Hesitantly she held out her hand to him.

Clay's hard fingers curled around her own, his touch light and impersonal. Rorie swallowed hard, unable to hold back the emotion churning so violently inside her.

His expression was completely impassive, but she sensed that he held on to his self-control with the thinnest of threads. In that moment, Rorie felt the longing in him and knew that he recognized it in her, too.

"Oh, Clay…" she whispered, her eyes brimming with tears. The impulse to move into his arms was like a huge wave, threatening to sweep over her, and she didn't know how much longer she'd have the strength to resist.

"Don't look at me like that," Clay muttered grimly.

"I…can't help it." But he belonged to Kate and nothing was likely to change that.

He took a step toward her and stopped himself, suddenly remembering they weren't alone.

"Skip, go hold Thunder for Don. Don's trying to paste-worm him, and he's getting dragged all over the stall." Clay's words were low-pitched, sharp, full of demand.

"But, Clay, Rorie's about to—"

"Do it."

Mumbling something unintelligible, Skip trudged off to the barn.

The minute his brother was out of sight, Clay caught Rorie's shoulders, his fingers rough and urgent through the thin cotton of her blouse. The next instant, she was locked against him. The kiss was inevitable, Rorie knew, but when his mouth settled over hers she wanted to weep for the joy she found in his arms. He kissed her temple, her cheek, her mouth, until she clung to him with hungry abandon. They were standing in the middle of the yard in full view of farmhands, but Clay didn't seem to care and Rorie wasn't about to object.

"I told myself I wouldn't do this," he whispered huskily.

Rorie's heart constricted.

At the sound of a car in the distance, Clay abruptly dropped his arms, freeing her. His fingers tangled in her hair as if he had to touch her one last time.

"I was a fool to think I could politely shake your hand and let you leave. We're more than casual friends and I can't pretend otherwise—to hell with the consequences."

Tears flooded Rorie's eyes as she stared up at Clay. Then, from behind him, she saw the cloud of dust that announced Kate's arrival. She inhaled a deep breath in an effort to compose herself and, wiping her damp cheeks with the back of one hand, forced a smile.

Clay released a ragged sigh as he trailed a callused hand down the side of her face. "Goodbye, Rorie," he whispered. With that, he turned and walked away.

Thick fog swirled around Rorie as she paused to catch her breath on the path in Golden Gate Park. She bent forward and planted her hands on her knees, driving the oxygen into her heaving lungs. Not once in the two weeks she'd been on vacation had she followed her jogging routine, and now she was paying the penalty. The muscles in her calves and thighs protested the strenuous exercise and her heart seemed about to explode. Her biggest problem was trying to keep up with Dan, who'd run ahead, unwilling to slow his pace to match hers.

"Rorie?"

"Over here." Her voice was barely more than a choked whisper. She meant to raise her hand and signal to him, but even that required more effort than she could manage. Seeing a bench in the distance, she stumbled over and collapsed into it. Leaning back, she stretched out her legs.

"You *are* out of shape," Dan teased, handing her a small towel.

Rorie wiped the perspiration from her face and smiled her appreciation. "I can't believe two weeks would make such a difference." She'd been back in San Francisco only a couple of days. Other than dropping off the MG at Dan's place, this was the first time they'd had a chance to get together.

Dan stood next to her, hardly out of breath—even after a three-mile workout.

"Two weeks *is* a long time," he said with the hint of a smile. "I suppose you didn't keep up with your vitamin program, either," he chastised gently. "Well, Rorie, it's obvious how much you need me."

She chose to ignore that comment. "I used to consider myself in top physical condition. Not anymore. Good grief, I thought my heart was going to give out two miles back."

Dan, blond and debonair, was appealingly handsome in a clean-cut boyish way. He draped the towel around his neck and grasped the ends. Rorie's eyes were drawn to his hands, with their finely manicured nails and long tapered fingers. Stockbroker fingers. Nice hands. Friendly hands.

Still, Rorie couldn't help comparing them with another pair of male hands, darkly tanned from hours in the sun and roughly callused. Gentle hands. Working hands.

"I meant what I said about you needing me," Dan murmured, watching her closely. "It's time we got serious, Rorie. Time we made some important decisions about our future."

When she least expected it, he slid closer on the bench beside her. With his so smooth fingers, he cupped her face, his thumbs stroking her flushed cheeks. "I did a lot of thinking while you were away."

She covered his fingers with her own, praying for an easier way to say what she must. They'd been seeing each other for months and she hated to hurt him, but it would be even crueler to lead him on. When they'd started dating, Dan had been looking for a casual relationship. He'd recently been divorced and wasn't ready for a new emotional commitment.

"Oh, Dan, I think I know what you're going to say. Please don't."

He paused, searching her face intently. "What do you mean?"

"I did some thinking while I was away, too, and I realized that although I'll always treasure your friendship, we can't ever be more than friends."

His dark eyes ignited with resistance. "What happened to you on this vacation, Rorie? You left, and two weeks later you returned a completely different woman."

"You're exaggerating," Rorie objected weakly. She knew she *was* different, from the inside out.

"You've hardly said a word to me about your trip," Dan complained, in a tone that suggested he felt hurt by her reticence. "All you've said is that the car broke down in the Oregon outback and you were stuck on some farm for days until a part could be delivered. You don't blame me for that, do you? I had no idea there was anything wrong with the water pump."

She laughed at his description of Nightingale as the outback.

"You completely missed the writers' conference, didn't you?"

"That couldn't be helped, but I enjoyed the rest of my vacation. Victoria was like stepping into a small piece of England," she said, in an effort to divert his attention from the time she'd spent on the Franklin farm. Victoria had been lovely, but unfortunately she hadn't been in the proper mood to appreciate its special beauty.

"You didn't so much as mail me a postcard."

"I know," she said with a twinge of guilt.

"I was lonesome without you," Dan said slowly, running his hand over her hair. "Nothing felt right with you gone."

Rorie knew it had taken a lot for him to admit that, and it made what she had to tell him all the more difficult.

"Dan, please," she said, breaking away from him and standing. "I... I don't love you."

"But we're friends."

"Of course."

He seemed both pleased and relieved by that. "Good friends?" he coaxed.

Rorie nodded, wondering where this was leading.

"Then there's really no problem, is there?" he asked, his voice gaining enthusiasm. "You went away, and I realized how much I love you, and you came back deciding you value my friendship. That, at least, is a beginning."

"Dan, honestly!"

"Well, isn't it?"

"Our relationship isn't going anywhere," she told him, desperate to clarify the issue. Dan was a good person and he deserved someone who was crazy in love with him. The way she was with Clay.

To Rorie's surprise, Dan drew her forward and kissed her. Startled, she stood placidly in his arms, feeling his warm mouth move over hers. She experienced no feeling, no excitement, nothing. Kissing Dan held all the appeal of drinking flat soda.

Frustrated, he tried to deepen the kiss.

Rorie braced her hands against his chest and tried to pull herself free. He released her immediately, then stepped back, frowning. "Okay, okay, we've got our work cut out for us. But the electricity will come, in time."

Somehow Rorie doubted that.

Dan dropped her off in front of her apartment. "Can I see you soon?" he asked, his hands clenching the steering wheel. He didn't look at her but stared straight ahead as though he feared her answer.

Rorie hesitated. "I'm not going to fall in love with you, Dan, and I don't want to take advantage of your feelings. I think it'd be best if you started seeing someone else."

He appeared to consider that for an awkward moment. "But the decision should be mine, shouldn't it?"

"Yes, but—"

"Then leave everything to me, and stop worrying. If I choose to waste my time on you, that's my problem, not yours. I think you're going to change your mind, Rorie. Because I love you enough for both of us."

"Oh, Dan." Her shoulders sagged with defeat. He hadn't believed a single word she'd said.

"Now don't look so depressed. How about a movie on Sunday? It's been a while since we've done that."

Exhausted, she shook her head. "Dan, no."

"I insist, so stop arguing."

She didn't have the energy to argue. "All right," she murmured. He'd soon learn she meant what she'd said. "All right."

"Good. I'll pick you up at six."

Rorie climbed out of the MG and closed the door, turning to give Dan a limp wave. She paused in the foyer of her apartment building to unlock her mailbox.

There was a handful of envelopes. Absently, she shuffled through a leaflet from a prominent department store, an envelope with a Kentucky postmark and an electric bill. It wasn't until she was inside her apartment that Rorie noticed the letter postmarked Nightingale, Oregon.

Thirteen

Rorie set the letter on her kitchen counter and stared at it for a moment. Her chest felt as if a dead weight were pressing against it. Her heart was pounding and her stomach churned. The post-office box number for the return address didn't tell her much. The letter could as easily be from Kate as Clay. It could even be from Mary.

Taking a deep, calming breath, Rorie reached for the envelope from Kentucky first. The return address told her nothing—she didn't know anyone who lived in that state.

The slip of paper inside confused her, too. She read it several times, not understanding. It appeared to be registration papers for Nightsong, from the National Show Horse Association. Rorie Campbell was listed as owner, with Clay's name as breeder. The date of Nightsong's birth was also recorded. Rorie slumped into a kitchen chair and battled an attack of memories and tears.

Clay was giving her Nightsong.

It was Nightsong who'd brought them together and it was through Nightsong that they'd remain linked. Life would go on; the loss of one couple's love wouldn't alter the course of history. But now there was something—a single piece of paper—that would connect her to Clay, something that gave testimony to their sacrifice.

Rorie had needed that and Clay had apparently known it.

They'd made the right decision, Rorie told herself for the hundredth time. Clay's action confirmed it.

Clay was wide-open spaces and sleek, well-trained horses, while she thrived in the crowded city.

His strength came from his devotion to the land; hers came from the love of children and literature and the desire to create her own stories.

They were dissimilar in every way—and alike. In the most important matters, the most telling, they were actually very much alike. Neither of them was willing to claim happiness at the expense of someone else.

Tears spilled down her cheeks, and sniffling, Rorie wiped them aside. The drops dampened her fingertips as she picked up the second envelope, blurring the return address. But even before she opened it, Rorie realized the letter was from Kate. Clay wouldn't write her, and everything Mary had wanted to say she'd already said the morning Rorie left Elk Run.

Three handwritten sheets slipped easily from the envelope, with Kate's evenly slanted signature at the bottom of the last.

The letter was filled with chatty news about Nightingale and some of the people Rorie had met. There were so many, and connecting names with faces taxed her memory. Kate wrote about the county fair, telling Rorie that she'd missed a very exciting pig race. The biggest news of all was that after years of trying, Mary had finally won a blue ribbon for her apple pie—an honor long overdue in Kate's opinion.

Toward the end of the letter, Clay's fiancée casually mentioned that Clay would be in San Francisco the first week of September for a horse show. The American Saddlebreds from Elk Run were well-known throughout the Pacific coast for their fire and elegance. Clay had high hopes of repeating last year's wins in the Five Gaited and Fine Harness Championships.

Rorie's pulse shifted into overdrive and her fingers tightened on the letter. Clay was coming to San Francisco. He hadn't said anything about the show to Rorie—although he must've known about it long before she'd left Nightingale.

Kate went on to say that she'd asked Clay if he planned to look up Rorie while he was in town, but he'd claimed there wouldn't be time. Kate was sure Rorie would understand and not take offense. She closed by saying that her father might also be attending the horse show and, if he did, Kate would try to talk him into letting her tag along. Kate promised she'd phone Rorie the minute she arrived in town, if she could swing it with her father.

Not until Rorie folded the letter to return it to the envelope did she notice the postscript on the back of the last page. She turned over the sheet of pink stationery. The words seemed to jump off the page: Kate was planning an October wedding and would send Rorie an invitation. She ended with, "Write soon."

Rorie's breath caught in her lungs. An October wedding… In only a few weeks, Kate would belong to Clay. Rorie closed her eyes as her heart squeezed into a knot of pain. It wasn't that she hadn't known this was coming. Kate and Clay's wedding was inevitable, but Rorie hadn't thought Clay would go through with it quite so soon. With trembling hands, she set the letter aside.

"Rorie, love, I can't honestly believe you want to go to a horse show," Dan complained, scanning the entertainment section of the Friday-evening paper. They sat in the minuscule living room in her apartment and sipped their coffee while they tossed around ideas for something to do.

Rorie smiled blandly, praying Dan couldn't read her thoughts. He'd offered several suggestions for the night's amusement, but Rorie had rejected each one. Until she pretended to hit upon the idea of attending the horse show...

"A horse show?" he repeated. "You never told me you were interested in horses."

"It would be fun, don't you think?"

"Not particularly."

"But, Dan, it's time to broaden our horizons—we might learn something."

"Does this mean you're going to insist we attend a demolition derby next weekend?"

"Of course not. I read an article about this horse show and I just thought we'd enjoy the gaited classes and harness competitions. Apparently, lots of Saddlebreds and National Show Horses are going to be performing. Doesn't that interest you?"

"No."

Rorie shrugged, slowly releasing a sigh. "Then a movie's fine," she said, not even trying to hide her disappointment. They'd seen each other only a handful of times since Rorie's return. Rorie wouldn't be going out with him tonight if he hadn't persisted. She hoped he'd get the message and start dating other women, but that didn't seem to be happening.

"I have no idea why you'd want to see a horse show," Dan said once more.

For the past few days the newspapers had been filled with information regarding the country-wide show in which Kate had said several of Elk Run's horses would be participating. In all the years she'd lived in San Francisco, Rorie couldn't remember reading about a single equine exhibition, but then she hadn't exactly been looking for one, either.

If Dan refused to go with her, Rorie was determined to attend the event on her own. She didn't have any intention of seeking out Clay, but the opportunity to see him, even from a distance, was too tempting to let pass. It would probably be the last time she'd ever see him.

"I don't know what's got into you lately, Rorie," Dan muttered. "Just when I think our lives are on track, you throw me for a loop."

"I said a movie was fine." Her tone was testier than she meant it to be, but Dan had been harping on the same subject for weeks and she was tired of it.

If he didn't want her company, he should start dating someone else. She wasn't going to suddenly decide she was madly in love with him, as he seemed to expect. Again and again, Dan phoned to tell her he loved her, that his love was enough for both of them. She always stopped him there, unable to imagine spending the rest of her life with him. If she couldn't have Clay—and she couldn't—then she wasn't willing to settle for anyone else.

"I'm talking about a lot more than seeing a movie."

He laid the newspaper aside and seemed to carefully consider his next words.

"Really, Dan, you're making a mountain out of a molehill," Rorie said. "Just because I wanted to do something a little out of the ordinary..."

"Eating at an Armenian restaurant is a little out of the ordinary," he said, frowning, "but horse shows... I can't even begin to understand why you'd want to watch a bunch of animals running around in circles."

"Well, you keep insisting I've changed," she said flippantly. If she'd known Dan was going to react so strongly to her suggestion, she'd never have made it. "I guess this only goes to prove you're right."

"How much writing have you done in the past month?"

The question was completely unexpected. She answered him with a shrug, hoping he'd drop the subject, knowing he wouldn't.

"None, right? I've seen you sitting at your computer, staring into space with that sad look on your face. I remember how you used to talk about your stories. Your eyes would light up. Enthusiasm would just spill out of you." His hand reached for hers, tightly squeezing her fingers. "What happened to you, Rorie? Where's the joy? Where's the energy?"

"You're imagining things," she said, nearly leaping to her feet in an effort to sidestep the issues he was raising. She grabbed her purse and a light sweater, eager to escape the apartment, which suddenly felt too small. "Are you going to take me to that movie, or are you going to sit here and ask questions I have no intention of answering?"

Dan stood, smiling faintly. "I don't know what happened while you were on vacation, and it's not important that I know, but whatever it was hurt you badly."

Rorie tried to deny it, but couldn't force the lie past her tongue. She swallowed and turned her head away, eyes burning.

"You won't be able to keep pretending forever. Put whatever it is behind you. If you want to talk about it, I've got a sympathetic ear and a sturdy shoulder. I'm your friend, Rorie."

"Dan, please…"

"I know you're not in love with me," he said quietly. "I suspect you met someone else while you were away, but that doesn't matter to me. Whatever happened during those two weeks is over."

"Dan…"

He took her hand, pulling her back onto the sofa, then sitting down beside her. She couldn't look at him.

"Given time, you'll learn to love me," he cajoled, holding her hand, his voice filled with kindness. "We're already good friends, and that's a lot more than some people have when they marry." He raised her fingers to his mouth and kissed them lightly. "I'm not looking for passion. I had that with my first wife. I learned the hard way that desire is a poor foundation for a solid marriage."

"We've talked about this before," Rorie protested. "I can't marry you, Dan, not when I feel the way I do about…someone else." Her mouth trembled with the effort to suppress tears. Dan was right. As much as she hadn't wanted to face the truth, she'd been heartbroken from the moment she'd left Nightingale.

She'd tried to forget Clay, believing that was the best thing for them both, yet she cherished the memories, knowing those few brief days were all she'd ever have of this man she loved.

"You don't have to decide right now," Dan assured her.

"There isn't anything to decide," she persisted.

His fingers continued to caress hers, and when he spoke his voice was thick. "At least you've admitted there is someone else."

"Was," she corrected.

"I take it there isn't any chance the two of you—"

"None," she blurted, unwilling to discuss anything that had to do with Clay.

"I know it's painful for you right now, but all I ask is that you seriously consider my proposal. My only wish is to take care of you and make you smile again. Help you forget."

His mouth sought hers, and though his kiss wasn't unpleasant, it generated no more excitement than before, no rush of adrenaline, no urgency. She hadn't minded Dan's kisses in the past, but until she met Clay she hadn't known the warmth and magic a man's touch could create.

Dan must have read her thoughts, because he said in a soothing voice, "The passion will come in time—you shouldn't even look for it now, but it'll be there. Maybe not this month or the next, but you'll feel it eventually, I promise."

Rorie brushed the hair from her face, confused and uncertain. Clay was marrying Kate in just a few weeks. Her own life stretched before her, lonely and barren—surely she deserved some happiness, too. Beyond a doubt, Rorie knew Clay would want her to build a good life for herself. But if she married Dan, it would be an act of selfishness, and she feared she'd end up hurting him.

"Think about it," Dan urged. "That's all I ask."

"Dan..."

"Just consider it. I know the score and I'm willing to take the risk, so you don't have to worry about me. I'm a big boy." He rubbed his thumb against the inside of her wrist. "Now, promise me you'll think honestly about us getting married."

Rorie nodded, although she already knew what her answer would have to be.

Dan heaved a sigh. "Now, are you really interested in that horse show, or are we going to a movie?"

"The movie." There was no use tormenting herself with thoughts of Clay. He belonged to Kate in the same way that he belonged to the country. Rorie had no claim to either.

The film Dan chose was surprisingly good, a comedy, which was just what Rorie needed to lift her spirits. Afterward, they dined at an Italian restaurant and drank wine and discussed politics. Dan went out of his way to be the perfect companion, making no demands on her, and Rorie was grateful.

It was still relatively early when he drove her back to her apartment, and he eagerly accepted her invitation for coffee. As he eased the MG into a narrow space in front of her building, he suddenly paused, frowning.

"Do you have new neighbors?"

"Not that I know of. Why?"

Dan nodded toward the battered blue pickup across the street. "Whoever drives that piece of junk is about to bring down the neighborhood property values."

Fourteen

"Clay." His name escaped Rorie's lips on a rush of excitement. She jerked open the car door and stepped onto the sidewalk, her legs trembling, her pulse thundering.

"Rorie?" Dan called, agitated. "Who is this man?"

She hardly heard him. A door slammed in the distance and Rorie whirled around and saw that Clay had been sitting inside his truck, apparently waiting for her to return. He'd been parked in the shadows, and she hadn't noticed him.

Dan joined her on the pavement and placed his hand possessively on her shoulder. His grip was the only thing that rooted her in reality, his hand the restraining force that prevented her from flying into Clay's arms.

"Who is this guy?" Dan asked a second time.

Rorie opened her mouth to explain and realized she couldn't, not in a few words. "A…friend," she whispered, but that seemed so inadequate.

"He's a cowboy!" Dan hissed, making it sound as though Clay's close-fitting jeans and jacket were the garb of a man just released from jail.

Clay crossed the street and his long strides made short work of the distance separating him from Rorie.

"Hello, Rorie."

She heard the faint catch in his voice. "Clay."

A muscle moved in his cheek as he looked past her to Dan, who squared the shoulders of his Brooks Brothers suit. No one spoke, until Rorie saw that Clay was waiting for an introduction.

"Clay Franklin, this is Dan Rogers. Dan is the stockbroker I... I mentioned before. It was his sports car I was driving."

Clay nodded. "I remember now." His gaze slid away from Rorie to the man at her side.

Dan stepped around Rorie and accepted Clay's hand. She noticed that when Dan dropped his arm to his side, he flexed his fingers a couple of times, as though to restore the circulation. Rorie smiled to herself. Clay's handshake was the solid one of a man accustomed to working with his hands. When Dan shook hands, it was little more than a polite business greeting, an archaic but necessary exchange.

"Clay and his brother, Skip, were the family who helped me when the MG broke down," Rorie explained to Dan.

"Ah, yes, I remember your saying something about that now."

"I was about to make a pot of coffee," Rorie went on, unable to take her eyes off Clay. She drank in the sight of him, painfully noting the crow's-feet that fanned out from the corners of his eyes. She couldn't remember their being quite so pronounced before.

"Yes, by all means join us." Dan's invitation lacked any real welcome.

Clay said nothing. He just stood there looking at her. Almost no emotion showed in his face, but she could feel the battle that raged inside him. He loved her still, and everything about him told her that.

"Please join us," she whispered.

Any lingering hope that Dan would take the hint and make his excuses faded as he slipped his arm protectively around Rorie's shoulders. "I picked up some Swiss mocha coffee beans earlier," he said, "and Rorie was going to make a pot of that."

"Swiss mocha coffee?" Clay repeated, blinking quizzically.

"Decaffeinated, naturally," Dan hurried to add.

Clay arched his brows expressively, as if to say that made all the difference in the world.

With Dan glued to her side, Rorie reluctantly led the way into her building. "Have you been here long?" she asked Clay while they stood waiting for the elevator.

"About an hour."

"Oh, Clay…" Rorie felt terrible, although it wasn't her fault; she hadn't known he intended to stop by. Perhaps he hadn't known himself and had been lured to her apartment the same way she'd been contemplating the horse show.

"You should have phoned." Dan's comment was casual, but it contained a hint of accusation. "But then, I suppose, you folks tend to drop in on each other all the time. Things are more casual in the country, aren't they?"

Rorie sent Dan a furious glare. He returned her look blankly, as if to say he had no idea what could have angered her. Rorie was grateful that the elevator arrived just then.

Clay didn't comment on Dan's observation and the three stepped inside, facing the doors as they slowly closed.

"When you weren't home, I asked the neighbors if they knew where you'd gone," Clay said.

"The neighbors?" Dan echoed, making no effort to disguise his astonishment.

"What did they tell you?" Rorie asked.

Clay smiled briefly, then sobered when he glanced at Dan. "They said they didn't know *who* lived next door, never mind where you'd gone."

"Frankly, I'm surprised they answered the door at all," Dan said conversationally. "There's a big difference between what goes on in small towns and big cities."

Dan spoke like a teacher to a grade-school pupil. Rorie wanted to kick him, but reacting in anger would only increase the embarrassment. She marveled at Clay's tolerance.

"Things are done differently here," Dan continued. "Few people have anything to do with their neighbors. People prefer to mind their own business. Getting involved leads to problems."

Clay rubbed the side of his face. "It seems to me *not* getting involved would lead to even bigger problems."

"I'm grateful Clay and Skip were there when *your* car broke down," Rorie said to Dan, hoping to put an end to this tiresome discussion. "Otherwise I don't know what would have happened. I could still be on that road waiting for someone to stop and help me," she said, forcing the joke.

"Yes," Dan admitted, clearing his throat. "I suppose I should thank you for assisting Rorie."

"And I suppose I should accept your thanks," Clay returned.

"How's Mary?" Rorie asked, quickly changing the subject as the elevator slid to a stop at her floor.

Humor sparked in Clay's gray eyes. "Mary's strutting around proud as a peacock ever since she won a blue ribbon at the county fair."

"She has reason to be proud." Rorie could just picture her. Knowing Mary, she was probably wearing the ribbon pinned to her apron. "What about Skip?" Rorie asked next, hungry for news about each one. She took the keys from her bag and systematically began unlocking the three bolts on her apartment door.

"Fine. He started school last week—he's a senior this year."

Rorie already knew that, but she nodded.

"Kate sends you her best," Clay said next, his voice carefully nonchalant.

"Tell her I said hello, too."

"She hasn't heard from you. No one has."

"I know. I'm sorry. She wrote after I got home from Canada, but I haven't had a chance to answer." On several occasions, Rorie had tried to make herself sit down and write Kate a letter. But she couldn't. At the end of her second week back home, she'd decided it was better for everyone involved if she didn't keep in touch with Kate. When the wedding invitation came, Rorie planned to mail an appropriate gift, and that would be the end of it.

Once they were inside the apartment, Rorie hung up her sweater and purse and motioned for both men to sit down. "It'll only take a minute to put on the coffee."

"Do you need me to grind the beans?" Dan asked, obviously eager to assist her.

"No, thanks. I don't need any help." His offer was an excuse to question her about Clay, and Rorie wanted to avoid that if she could. At least for now.

Her apartment had never felt more cramped than it did when she rejoined the two men in her tiny living room. Clay rose to his feet as she entered, and the simple courtly gesture made her want to weep. He was telling her that he respected her and that…he cared for her…would always care for her.

The area was just large enough for one sofa and a coffee table. Her desk and computer stood against the other wall. Rorie pulled the chair away from the desk, turned it to face her guests and perched on the edge. Only then did Clay sit back down.

"So," Dan said with a heavy sigh. "Rorie never did tell me what it is you do in…in…"

"Nightingale," Rorie and Clay said together.

"Oh, yes, Nightingale," Dan murmured, clearing his throat. "I take it you're some kind of farmer? Do you grow soybeans or wheat?"

"Clay owns a stud farm, where he raises American Saddlebreds," Rorie said.

Dan looked as if she'd punched him in the stomach. He'd obviously made the connection between Clay and her earlier interest in attending the horse show.

"I see," he breathed, and his voice shook a little. "Horses. So you're involved with horses."

Clay glanced at him curiously.

"How's Nightsong?" Rorie asked, before Dan could say anything else. Just thinking about the foal with her wide curious eyes and long wobbly legs produced a feeling of tenderness in Rorie.

"She's a rare beauty," Clay told her softly, "showing more promise every day."

Rorie longed to tell Clay how much it had meant to her that he'd registered Nightsong in her name, how she cherished that gesture more than anything in her life. She also knew that Clay would never sell the foal, but would keep and love her all her life.

An awkward silence followed, and in an effort to smooth matters over she explained to Dan, "Clay was gone one night when Star Bright—one of the broodmares—went into labor...if that's what they call it in horses?" she asked Clay.

He nodded.

"Anyway, I couldn't wake Skip, and I didn't know where Mary was sleeping and something had to be done—quick."

Dan leaned forward, his eyes revealing his shock. "You don't mean to tell me *you* delivered the foal?"

"Not exactly." Rorie wished now that she hadn't said anything to Dan about that night. No one could possibly understand what she and Clay had shared in those few hours. Trying to convey the experience to someone else only diminished its significance.

"I'll get the coffee," Rorie said, standing. "I'm sure it's ready."

From her kitchen, she could hear Dan and Clay talking, although she couldn't make out their words. She filled three cups and placed them on a tray, together with cream and sugar, then carried it into the living room.

Once more Clay stood. He took the tray out of her

hands and set it on the coffee table. Rorie handed Dan the first cup and saucer and Clay the second. He looked uncomfortable as he accepted it.

"I'm sorry, Clay, you prefer a mug, don't you?" The cup seemed frail and tiny, impractical, cradled in his strong hand.

"It doesn't matter. If I'm going to be drinking Swiss mocha coffee, I might as well do it from a china cup." He smiled into her eyes, and Rorie couldn't help reciprocating.

"Eaten any seafood fettuccine lately?" she teased.

"Can't say I have."

"It's my favorite dinner," Dan inserted, apparently feeling left out of the conversation. "We had linguini tonight, but Rorie's favorite is sushi."

Her eye caught Clay's and she saw that the corner of his mouth quirked with barely restrained humor. She could just imagine what the people of Nightingale would think of a sushi bar. Skip would probably turn up his nose, insisting that the small pieces of seaweed and raw fish looked like bait.

The coffee seemed to command everyone's attention for the next minute or so.

"I'm still reeling from the news of your adventures on this stud farm," Dan commented, laughing lightly. "You could have knocked me over with a feather when you said you'd helped deliver a foal. I would never have believed it of you, Rorie."

"I brought a picture of Nightsong," Clay said, cautiously putting down his coffee cup. He unsnapped the pocket of his wide-yoked shirt and withdrew two color photographs, which he handed to Rorie. "I meant to show these to you earlier…but I got sidetracked."

"Oh, Clay," she breathed, studying the filly with her gleaming chestnut coat. "She's grown so much in just the past month," she said, her voice full of wonder.

"I thought you'd be impressed."

Reluctantly Rorie shared the pictures with Dan, who barely glanced at them before giving them back to Clay.

"Most men carry around pictures of their wife and kids," Dan stated, his eyes darting to Clay and then Rorie.

Rorie supposed this comment was Dan's less-than-subtle attempt to find out if Clay was married. Taking a deep breath, she said, "Clay's engaged to a neighbor—Kate Logan."

"I see." Apparently he did, because he set aside his coffee cup, and got up to stand behind Rorie. Hands resting on her shoulders, he leaned forward and brushed his mouth over her cheek. "Rorie and I have been talking about getting married ourselves, haven't we, darling?"

Fifteen

No emotion revealed itself on Clay's face, but Rorie could sense the tight rein he kept on himself. Dan's words had dismayed him.

"Is that true, Rorie?" he said after a moment.

Dan's fingers tightened almost painfully on her shoulders. "Just tonight we were talking about getting married. Tell him, darling."

Her eyes refused to leave Clay's. She *had* been talking to Dan about marriage, although she had no intention of accepting his offer. Dan knew where he stood, knew she was in love with another man. But nothing would be accomplished by telling Clay that she'd always love him, especially since he was marrying Kate in a few weeks. "Yes, Dan has proposed."

"I'm crazy about Rorie and have been for months," Dan announced, squarely facing his competition. He spoke for a few more minutes, outlining his goals. Within another ten years, he planned to be financially secure and hoped to retire.

"Dan's got a bright future," Rorie echoed.

"I see." Clay replaced his coffee cup on the tray, then

glanced at his watch and rose to his feet. "I suppose I should head back to the Cow Palace."

"How…how are you doing in the show?" Rorie asked, distraught, not wanting him to leave. Kate would have him the rest of their lives; surely a few more minutes with him wouldn't matter. "Kate wrote that you were going after several championships."

"I'm doing exactly as I expected." The words were clipped, as though he was impatient to get away.

Rorie knew she couldn't keep him any longer. Clay's face was stern with purpose—and resignation. "I'll see you out," she told him.

"I'll come with you," Dan said.

She whirled around and glared at him. "No, you won't."

"Good to see you again, Rorie," Clay said, standing just inside her apartment, his hand on the door. His mouth was hard and flat and he held himself rigid, eyes avoiding hers. He stepped forward and shook Dan's hand.

"It was a pleasure," Dan said in a tone that conveyed exactly the opposite.

"Same here." Clay dropped his hand.

"I'm glad you came by," Rorie told him quietly. "It was…nice seeing you." The words sounded inane, meaningless.

He nodded brusquely, opened the door and walked into the hallway.

"Clay," she said, following him out, her heart hammering so loudly it seemed to echo off the walls.

He stopped and slowly turned around.

Now that she had his attention, Rorie didn't know

what to say. "Listen, I'm sorry about the way Dan was acting."

He shook off her apology. "Don't worry about it."

Her fingers tightened on the doorknob, and she wondered if this was really the end. "Will I see you again?" she asked despite herself.

"I don't think so," he answered hoarsely. He looked past her as though he could see through the apartment door and into her living room where Dan was waiting. "Do you honestly love this guy?"

"He's...he's been a good friend."

Clay took two steps toward her, then stopped. As if it was against his better judgment, he raised his hand and lightly drew his finger down the side of her face. Rorie closed her eyes at the wealth of sensation the simple action provoked.

"Be happy, Rorie. That's all I want for you."

The rain hit during the last week of September, and the dreary dark afternoons suited Rorie's mood. Normally autumn was a productive time for her, but she remained tormented with what she felt sure was a terminal case of writer's block. She sat at her desk, her computer humming merrily as she read over the accumulation of an entire weekend's work.

One measly sentence.

There'd been a time when she could write four or five pages a night after coming home from the library. Perhaps the problem was the story she'd chosen. She wanted to write about a filly named Nightsong, but every time she started, her memories of the real Nightsong invaded her thoughts, crippling her imagination.

Here it was Monday night and she sat staring at the

screen, convinced nothing she wrote had any merit. The only reason she kept trying was that Dan had pressured her into it. He seemed to believe her world would right itself once Rorie was back to creating her warm, light-hearted children's stories.

The phone rang and, grateful for a reprieve, Rorie hurried into the kitchen to answer it.

"Is this Miss Rorie Campbell of San Francisco, California?"

"Yes, it is." Her heart tripped with anxiety. In a matter of two seconds, every horrible scenario of what could have happened to her parents or her brother darted through Rorie's mind.

"This is Devin Logan calling."

He paused, as though expecting her to recognize the name. Rorie didn't. "Yes?"

"Devin Logan," he repeated, "from the Nightingale, Oregon, Town Council." He paused. "I believe you're acquainted with my daughter, Kate."

"Yes, I remember Kate." If her heart continued at this pace Rorie thought she'd keel over in a dead faint. Just as her pulse had started to slow, it shot up again. "Has anything happened?"

"The Council meeting adjourned about ten minutes ago. Are you referring to that?"

"No...no, I mean has anything happened to Kate?"

"Not that I'm aware of. Do you know something I don't?"

"I don't think so." This entire conversation was driving her crazy.

Devin Logan cleared his throat, and when he spoke his voice dropped to a deeper pitch. "I'm phoning in an official capacity," he said. "We voted at the Town Council meeting tonight to employ a full-time librarian."

He paused again, and, not knowing what else to say, Rorie murmured, "Congratulations. Kate mentioned that the library was currently being run by part-time volunteers."

"It was decided to offer *you* the position."

Rorie nearly dropped the receiver. "I beg your pardon?"

"My daughter managed to convince the Council that we need a full-time librarian for our new building. She also persuaded us that you're the woman for the job."

"But…" Hardly able to take in what she was hearing, Rorie slumped against the kitchen wall, glad of its support. Logan's next remark was even more surprising.

"We'll match whatever the San Francisco library is paying you and throw in a house in town—rent-free."

"I…" Rorie's mind was buzzing. Kate obviously thought she was doing her a favor, when in fact being so close to Clay would be utter torment.

"Miss Campbell?"

"I'm honored," she said quickly, still reeling with astonishment, "truly honored, but I'm going to have to decline."

A moment of silence followed. "All right… I'm authorized to enhance the offer by ten percent over the amount you're currently earning, but that's our final bid. You'd be making as much money as the fire chief, and he's not about to let the Council pay a librarian more than he's bringing home."

"Mr. Logan, please, the salary isn't the reason I'm turning down your generous offer. I… I want you to know how much I appreciate your offering me the job.

Thank you, and thank Kate on my behalf, but I can't accept."

Another, longer silence vibrated across the line, as though he couldn't believe what she was telling him.

"You're positive you want to refuse? Miss Campbell, we're being more than reasonable…more than generous."

"I realize that. In fact, I'm flattered by your proposal, but I can't possibly accept this position."

"Kate had the feeling you'd leap at the job."

"She was mistaken."

"I see. Well, then, it was good talking to you. I'm sorry we didn't get a chance to meet while you were in Nightingale. Perhaps next time."

"Perhaps." Only there wouldn't be a next time.

Rorie kept her hand on the receiver long after she'd hung up. Her back was pressed against the kitchen wall, her eyes closed.

She'd regained a little of her composure when the doorbell chimed. A glance at the wall clock told her it was Dan, who'd promised to drop by that evening. She straightened, forcing a smile, and slowly walked to the door.

Dan entered with a flourish, handing her a small white bag.

"What's this?" she asked.

"Frozen yogurt. Just the thing for a girl with a hot keyboard. How's the writing going?" He leaned forward to kiss her cheek.

Rorie walked into the kitchen and set the container in the freezer compartment of her refrigerator. "It's not. If you don't mind, I'll eat this later."

"Rorie." Dan caught her by her shoulders and studied her face. "You're as pale as chalk. What's wrong?"

"I… I just got off the phone. I was offered another job—as head librarian…"

"But, darling, that's wonderful!"

"…in Nightingale, Oregon."

The change in Dan's expression was almost comical. "And? What did you tell them?"

"I refused."

He gave a great sigh of relief. His eyes glowed and he hugged her impulsively. "Does this mean what I think it does? Are you finally over that cowpoke, Rorie? Will you finally consent to be my wife?"

Rorie lowered her gaze. "Oh, Dan, don't you understand? I'll never get over Clay. Not next week, not next month, not next year." Her voice was filled with pain, and with conviction. Everyone seemed to assume that, in time, she'd forget about Clay Franklin, but she wouldn't.

Dan's smile faded, and he dropped his arms to his sides. "I see." Leaning against the counter, he sighed pensively and said, "I'd do just about anything in this world for you, Rorie, but I think it's time we faced a few truths."

Rorie had wanted to confront them long before now.

"You're never going to love me the way you do that horseman. We can't go on like this. It isn't doing either of us any good to pretend your feelings are going to change."

He looked so grim and discouraged that she didn't point out that *he* was the one who'd been pretending.

"I'm so sorry to hurt you—it's the last thing I ever wanted to do," she told him sincerely.

"It isn't as if I didn't know," he admitted. "You've been honest with me from the start. I can't be less than honest with you. That country boy loves you. I knew it the minute he walked across the street without even noticing the traffic. The whole world would know," he said ruefully. "All he has to do is look at you and everything about him shouts his feelings. He may be engaged to another woman, but it's you he loves."

"I wouldn't fit into his world."

"But, Rorie, you're lost and confused in your own."

She bit her lower lip and nodded. Until Dan said it, she hadn't recognized how true that was. But it didn't change the fact that Clay belonged to Kate. And she was marrying him within the month.

"I'm sorry," Dan said, completely serious, "but the wedding's off."

She nearly laughed out loud at Dan's announcement. No wedding had ever been planned. He'd asked her to marry him at least ten times since she'd returned from her vacation, and each time she'd refused. Instead of wearing her down as he'd hoped, Dan had finally come to accept her decision. Rorie felt relieved, but she was sorry to lose her friend.

"I didn't mean to lead you on," she told him, genuinely contrite.

He shrugged. "The pain will only last for a while. I'm 'a keeper' as the girls in the office like to tell me. I guess it's time I put out the word that I'm available." He wiggled his eyebrows, striving for some humor.

"You've been such a good friend."

He cupped her face and gently kissed her. "Yes, I know. Now don't let that yogurt go to waste—you're too thin as it is."

She smiled and nodded. When she let him out of the apartment, Rorie bolted the door then leaned against it, feeling drained, but curiously calm.

Dan had been gone only a few minutes when Rorie's phone rang again. She hurried into the kitchen to answer it.

"Rorie? This is Kate Logan."

"Kate! How are you?"

"Rotten, but I didn't call to talk about me. I want to know exactly why you're refusing to be Nightingale's librarian—after everything I went through. I can't believe you, Rorie. How can you do this to Clay? Don't you love him?"

Sixteen

"Kate," Rorie demanded. "What are you talking about?"

"You and Clay," she said sharply, sounding quite unlike her usual self. "Now, do you love him or not? I've got to know."

This day had been sliding steadily downhill from the moment Rorie had climbed out of bed that morning. To admit her feelings for Clay would only hurt Kate, and Rorie had tried so hard to avoid upsetting the other woman.

"Well?" Kate said with a sob. "The least you can do is answer me!"

"Oh, Kate," Rorie said, her heart in her throat, "why are you asking me if I love Clay? He's engaged to you. It shouldn't matter one little bit if I love him or not. I'm out of your lives and I intend to stay out."

"But he loves you."

The tears in Kate's voice tore at Rorie's already battered heart. She would've given anything to spare her friend this pain. "I know," she whispered.

"Doesn't that mean anything to you?"

Only the world and everything in it. "Yes," she murmured, her voice growing stronger.

"Then how could you do this to him?"

"Do what?" Rorie didn't understand.

"Hurt him this way!"

"Kate," Rorie pleaded. "I have no idea what you're talking about—I'd never intentionally hurt Clay. If you insist on knowing, I do love him, with all my heart, but he's your fiancé. You loved him long before I even knew him."

Kate's short laugh was riddled with sarcasm. "What is this? First come, first served?"

"Of course not—"

"For your information, Clay isn't my fiancé anymore," Kate blurted, her voice trembling. "He hasn't been in weeks…since before he went to San Francisco for the horse show."

Rorie's head came up so fast she wondered whether she'd dislocated her neck. "He isn't?"

"That's…that's what I just told you."

"But I thought… I assumed…"

"I know what you assumed—that much is obvious—but it isn't like that now and it hasn't been in a long time."

"But you love Clay," Rorie muttered, feeling lightheaded.

"I've loved him from the time I was in pigtails. I love him enough to want to see him happy. Why…why do you think I talked my fool head off to a bunch of hard-nosed Council members? Why do you think I ranted and raved about what a fantastic librarian you are? I as good as told them you're the only person who could possibly assume full responsibility for the new library. Do you honestly think I did all that for the fun of it?"

"No, but, Kate, surely you understand why I have to refuse. I just couldn't bear to come between you and—"

Kate wouldn't allow her to finish, and when she spoke, her voice was high and almost hysterical. "Well, if you believe that, Rorie Campbell, then you've got a lot to learn about me…and even more about Clay Franklin."

"Kate, I'm sorry. Please listen to me. There's so much I don't understand. We've got to talk, because I can't make head or tail out of what you're telling me and I've got to know—"

"If you have anything to say to me, Rorie Campbell, then you can do it to my face. Now, I'm telling Dad and everyone else on the Council that you've accepted the position we so generously offered you. The job starts in two weeks and you'd damn well better be here. Understand?"

Rorie's car left a dusty trail on the long, curving driveway that led to the Circle L Ranch. It'd been a week since the telephone call from Kate, and Rorie still had trouble assimilating what the other woman had told her. Their conversation repeated itself over and over in her mind, until nothing made sense. But one thing stood out: Kate was no longer engaged to Clay.

Rorie was going to him, running as fast as she could, but first she had to settle matters with his former fiancée.

The sun had begun to descend in an autumn sky when Rorie parked her car at the Logan ranch and climbed out. Rotating her neck and shoulders to relieve some of the tension there, Rorie looked around, wondering if anyone was home. She'd been on the road most of the day, so she was exhausted. And exhilarated.

Luke Rivers strolled out of the barn, and stopped when he saw Rorie. His smile deepened. It could've been Rorie's imagination, but she sensed that the hard edge was missing from his look, as though life had unexpectedly tossed him a good turn.

"So you're back," he said by way of greeting.

Rorie nodded, then reached inside the car for her purse. "Is Kate here?"

"She'll be back any minute. Usually gets home from the school around four. Come inside and I'll get you a cup of coffee."

"Thanks." At the moment, coffee sounded like nectar from the gods.

Luke opened the kitchen door for her. "I understand you're going to be Nightingale's new librarian," he said, following her into the house.

"Yes." But that wasn't the reason she'd come back, and they both knew it.

"Good." Luke took two mugs from the cupboard and filled them from a coffeepot that sat on the stove. He placed Rorie's cup on the table, then pulled out a chair for her.

"Thanks, Luke."

The sound of an approaching vehicle drew his attention. He parted the lace curtain at the kitchen window and looked out.

"That's Kate now," he said, his gaze lingering on the driveway. "Listen, if I don't get a chance to talk to you later, I want you to know I'm glad you're here. I've got a few things to thank you for. If it hadn't been for you, I might've turned into a crotchety old saddle bum."

Before Rorie could ask what he meant, he was gone.

Kate burst into the kitchen a minute later and hugged Rorie as though they were long-lost sisters. "I don't know when I've been happier to see anyone!"

Rorie's face must have shown her surprise because Kate hurried to add, "I suppose you think I'm a crazy woman after the way I talked to you on the phone last week. I don't blame you, but…well, I was upset, to put it mildly, and my thinking was a little confused." She threw her purse on the counter and reached inside the cupboard for a mug. She poured the coffee very slowly, as if she needed time to gather her thoughts.

Rorie's mind was whirling with questions she couldn't wait for Kate to answer. "Did I understand you correctly the other night? Did you tell me you and Clay are no longer engaged?"

Kate wasn't able to disguise the flash of pain that leaped into her deep blue eyes. She dropped her gaze and nodded. "We haven't been in weeks."

"But…"

Kate sat down across the table from Rorie and folded her hands around the mug. "The thing is, Rorie, I knew how you two felt about each other since the night of the Grange dance. A blind man would've known you and Clay had fallen in love, but it was so much easier for me to pretend otherwise." Her finger traced the rim of the mug. "I thought that once you went home, everything would go back to the way it was before…."

"I was hoping for the same thing. Kate, you've got to believe me when I tell you I would've done anything in the world to spare you this. When I learned you and Clay were engaged I wanted to—"

"Die," Kate finished for her. "I know exactly how you must have felt, because that's the way I felt later. The night of the Grange dance, Clay kept looking at you. Every time you danced with a new partner, he scowled. He might have had me at his side, but his eyes followed you all over the hall."

"He loves you, too," Rorie told her. "That's what makes this all so difficult."

"No, he doesn't," Kate answered flatly, without a hint of doubt. "I accepted that a long time before you ever arrived. Oh, he respects and likes me, and to Clay's way of thinking that was enough." She hesitated, frowning. "To my way of thinking, it was, too. We probably would've married and been content. But everything changed when Clay met you. You hit him right between the eyes, Rorie—a direct hit."

"I'm sure he feels more for you than admiration...."

"No." Kate rummaged in her purse for a tissue. "He told me as much himself, but like I said, it wasn't something I didn't already know. You see, I was so crazy about Clay, I was willing to take whatever he offered me, even if it was only second-best." She swabbed at the tears that sprang so readily to her eyes and paused in an effort to gather her composure. "I'm sorry. It's still so painful. But you see, through all of this, I've learned a great deal about what it means to love someone."

Rorie's own eyes welled with involuntary tears, which she hurriedly brushed aside. Then Kate's fingers clasped hers and squeezed tight in a gesture of reassurance.

"I learned that loving people means placing their

happiness before your own. That's the way you love Clay, and it's the way he loves you." Kate squared her shoulders and inhaled a quavery breath.

"Kate, please, this isn't necessary."

"Yes, it is, because what I've got to say next is the hardest part. I need to ask your forgiveness for that terrible letter I wrote after you left Nightingale. I don't have any excuse except that I was insane with jealousy."

"Letter? You wrote me a terrible letter?" The only one Rorie had received was the chatty note that had told her about Mary's prize-winning ribbon and made mention of the upcoming wedding.

"I used a subtle form of viciousness," Kate replied, her voice filled with self-contempt.

Rorie discounted the possibility that Kate could ever be malicious. "The only letter I got from you wasn't the least bit terrible."

Kate lowered her eyes to her hands, neatly folded on the table. Her grip tightened until Rorie was sure her nails would cut her palms.

"I lied in that letter," Kate continued. "When I told you that Clay wouldn't have time for you while he was at the horse show, I was trying to imply that you didn't mean anything to him anymore. I wanted you to think you'd slipped from his mind when nothing could have been further from the truth."

"Don't feel bad about it. I'm not so sure I wouldn't have done the same thing."

"No, Rorie, you wouldn't have. That letter was an underhand attempt to hold on to Clay… I was losing him more and more each day and I thought… I hoped that if you believed we were going to be married in

October, then... Oh, I don't know, my thinking was so warped and desperate."

"Your emotions were running high at the time." Rorie's had been, too; she understood Kate's pain because she'd been in so much pain herself.

"But I was pretending to be your friend when in reality I almost hated you." Kate paused, her shoulders shaking with emotion. "That was the crazy part. I couldn't help liking you and wanting to be your friend, and at the same time I was eaten alive with jealousy and selfish resentment."

"It's not in you to hate anyone, Kate."

"I... I didn't think it was, either, but I was wrong. I can be a terrible person, Rorie. Facing up to that hasn't been easy." She took a deep, shuddering breath.

"Then...a few days after I mailed that letter to you, Clay came over to the house wanting to talk. Almost immediately I realized I'd lost him. Nothing I could say or do would change the way he felt about you. I said some awful things to Clay that night.... He's forgiven me, but I need your forgiveness, too."

"Oh, Kate, of course, but it isn't necessary. I understand. I truly do."

"Thank you," she murmured, dabbing her eyes with the crumpled tissue. "Now I've got that off my chest, I feel a whole lot better."

"But if Clay had broken your engagement when he came to San Francisco, why didn't he say anything to me?"

Kate shrugged. "I don't know what happened while he was gone, but he hasn't been himself since. He never has been a talkative person, but he seemed to draw even further into himself when he came back. He's working himself into an early grave, everyone says. Mary's concerned about him—we all are. Mary said if you didn't come soon, she was going after you herself."

"Mary said that?" The housekeeper had been the very person who'd convinced Rorie she was doing the right thing by getting out of Clay's life.

"Well, are you going to him? Or are you planning to stick around here and listen to me blubber all day? If you give me any more time," she said, forcing a laugh, "I'll manage to make an even bigger fool of myself than I already have." Kate stood abruptly, pushing back the kitchen chair. Her arms were folded around her waist, her eyes bright with tears.

"Kate," Rorie murmured, "you are a dear, dear friend. I owe you more than it's possible to repay."

"The only thing you owe me is one godchild—and about fifty years of happiness with Clay Franklin. Now get out of here before I start weeping in earnest."

Kate opened the kitchen door and Rorie gave her an impulsive hug before hurrying out.

Luke Rivers was standing in the yard, apparently waiting for her. When she came out of the house he sauntered over to her car and held open the driver's door. "Did everything go all right with Kate?"

Rorie nodded.

"Well," he said soberly, "there may be more rough waters ahead for her. She doesn't know it yet, but I'm buying out the Circle L." Then he smiled, his eyes crinkling. "She's going to be fine, though. I'll make sure of that." He extended his hand, gripping hers in a firm handshake. "Let me be the first to welcome you to our community."

"Thank you."

He touched the rim of his hat in farewell, then glanced toward the house. "I think I'll go inside and see how Kate's doing."

Rorie's gaze skipped from the foreman to the house and then back again. "You do that." If Luke Rivers had anything to say about it, Kate wouldn't be suffering from a broken heart for long. Rorie had suspected Luke was in love with Kate. But, like her, he was caught in a trap, unable to reveal his feelings. Perhaps now Kate's eyes would be opened—Rorie fervently hoped so.

The drive from the Logans' place to the Franklins' took no more than a few minutes. Rorie parked her car behind the house, her heart pounding. When she climbed out, the only one there to greet her was Mary.

"About time you got here," the housekeeper complained, marching down the porch steps with a vengeance.

"Could this be the apple-pie blue-ribbon holder of Nightingale, Oregon?"

Mary actually blushed, and Rorie laughed. "I thought you'd never want to see the likes of me again," she teased.

"Fiddlesticks." The weathered face broke into a smile.

"I'm still a city girl," Rorie warned.

"That's fine, 'cause you got the heart of a country girl." Wiping her hands dry on her apron, Mary reached for Rorie and hugged her.

After one brief, bone-crushing squeeze, she set her free. "I'm a meddling old woman, sure enough, and I suspect the good Lord intends to teach me more than one lesson in the next year or two. I'd best tell you that I never should've said those things I did about Kate being the right woman for Clay."

"Mary, you spoke out of concern. I know that."

"Clay doesn't love Kate," she continued undaunted, "but my heavens, he does love you. That boy's been pining his heart out for want of you. He hasn't been the same from the minute you drove out of here all those weeks ago."

Rorie had suffered, too, but she didn't mention that to Mary. Instead, she slipped her arm around the housekeeper's broad waist and together they strolled toward the house.

"Clay's gone for the day, but he'll be back within the hour."

"An hour," Rorie repeated. She'd waited all this time; another sixty minutes shouldn't matter.

"Dinner will be ready then, and it's not like Clay or Skip to miss a meal. Dinner's been at six every night since I've been cooking for this family, and that's a good many years now." Mary's mouth formed a lopsided grin. "Now what we'll do is this. You be in the dining room waiting for him and I'll tell him he's got company."

"But won't he notice my car?" Rorie twisted around, gesturing at her old white Toyota—her own car this time—parked within plain sight.

Mary shook her head. "I doubt it. He's never seen your car, so far as I know, only that fancy sports car. Anyway, the boy's been working himself so hard, he'll be too tired to notice much of anything."

Mary opened the back door and Rorie stepped inside the kitchen. As she did, the house seemed to fold its arms around her in welcome. She paused, breathing in the scent of roast beef and homemade biscuits. It might not be sourdough and Golden Gate Park roses, but it felt right. More than right.

"Do you need me to do anything?" Rorie asked.

Mary frowned, then nodded. "There's just one thing I want you to do—make Clay happy."

"Oh, Mary, I intend to start doing that the second he walks through that door."

An hour later, almost to the minute, Rorie heard Skip and Clay come into the kitchen.

"What's for dinner?" Skip asked immediately.

"It's on the table. Now wash your hands."

Rorie heard the teenager grumble as he headed down the hallway to the bathroom.

"How'd the trip go?" Mary asked Clay.

He mumbled something Rorie couldn't hear.

"The new librarian stopped by to say hello. Old man Logan and Kate sent her over—thought you might like to meet her."

"I don't. I hope you got rid of her. I'm in no mood for company."

"Nope," Mary said. "Fact is, I invited her to stay for dinner. The least you can do is wipe that frown off your face and go introduce yourself."

Rorie stood just inside the dining room, her heart ready to explode. By the time Clay stepped into the room, tears had blurred her vision and she could hardly make out the tall, familiar figure that blocked the doorway.

She heard his swift intake of breath, and the next thing she knew she was crushed in Clay's loving arms.

Seventeen

Rorie was locked so securely in Clay's arms that for a moment she couldn't draw a breath. But that didn't matter. What mattered was that she was being hugged by the man she loved and he was holding on to her as though he didn't plan to ever let her go.

Clay kissed her again and again, the way a starving man took his first bites of food, initially hesitant, then eager. The palms of Rorie's hands were pressed against his chest and she felt the quick surge of his heart. His own hand was gentle on her hair, caressing it, running his fingers through it.

"Rorie… Rorie, I can't believe you're here."

Rorie felt the power of his emotions, and they were strong enough to rock her, body and soul. This man loved her. He was honest and hardworking, she knew all that, but even more, Clay Franklin was *good,* with an unselfishness and a loyalty that had touched her profoundly. In an age of ambitious, hardhearted, vain men, she had inadvertently stumbled on this rare man of character. Her life would never be the same.

Clay exhaled a deep sigh, and his hands framed her

face as he pulled his head back to gaze into her eyes. The lines that marked his face seemed more deeply incised now, and she felt another pang of sorrow for the pain he'd endured.

"Mary wasn't teasing me, was she? You *are* the new librarian?"

Rorie nodded, smiling up at him, her happiness shining from her eyes. "There's no going back for me. I've moved out of my apartment, packed everything I own and quit my job with barely a week's notice."

Rorie had fallen in love with Clay, caught in the magic of one special night when a foal had been born. But her feelings stretched far beyond the events of a single evening and the few short days they'd spent together. Her love for Clay had become an essential part of her. Rorie adored him and would feel that way for as long as her heart continued to beat.

Clay's frown deepened and his features tightened briefly. "What about Dan? I thought you were going to marry him."

"I couldn't," she said, then smiled tenderly, tracing his face with her hands, loving the feel of him beneath her fingertips.

"But—"

"Clay," she interrupted, "why didn't you tell me when I saw you in San Francisco that you'd broken your engagement to Kate?" Her eyes clouded with anguish at the memory, at the anxiety they'd caused each other. It had been such senseless heartache, and they'd wasted precious time. "Couldn't you see how miserable I was?"

A grimace of pain moved across his features. "All I noticed was how right you and that stockbroker looked together. You both kept telling me what a bright future he had. I couldn't begin to offer you the things he could. And if that wasn't enough, it was all too apparent that Dan was in love with you." Gently Clay smoothed her hair away from her temple. "I could understand what it meant to love you, and, between the two of us, he seemed the better man."

Rorie lowered her face, pressing her forehead against the hollow of his shoulder. She groaned in frustration. "How could you even *think* such a thing, when I love you so much?"

Clay moved her face so he could meet her eyes. "But, Rorie…" He stopped and a muscle jerked in his jaw. "Dan can give you far more than I'll ever be able to. He's got connections, background, education. A few years down the road, he's going to be very wealthy— success is written all over him. He may have his faults, but basically he's a fine man."

"He *is* a good person and he's going to make some woman a good husband. But it won't be me."

"He could give you the kinds of things I may never be able to afford…."

"Clay Franklin, do you love me or not?"

Clay exhaled slowly, watching her. "You know the answer to that."

"Then stop arguing with me. I don't love Dan Rogers. I love you."

Still his frown persisted. "You belong in the city."

"I belong with you," she countered.

He said nothing for a long moment. "I can't argue with that," he whispered, his voice husky with emotion. "You do belong here, because God help me, I haven't got the strength to let you walk away a second time."

Clay kissed her again, his mouth sliding over hers as though he still couldn't believe she was in his arms. She held on to him with all her strength, soaking up his love. She was at home in his arms. It was where she belonged and where she planned to stay.

The sound of someone entering the room filtered through to Rorie's consciousness, but she couldn't bring herself to move out of Clay's arms.

"Rorie!" Skip cried, his voice high and excited, "What are you doing here?"

Rorie finally released Clay and turned toward the teenager who had come to her rescue that August afternoon.

"Hello, Skip," she said softly. Clay slipped his arm around her waist and she smiled up at him, needing his touch to anchor her in the reality of their love.

"Are you back for good?" Skip wanted to know.

She nodded, but before she could answer Clay said, "Meet Nightingale's new librarian." His arm tightened around her.

The smile that lit the teenager's eyes was telling. "So you're going to stick around this time." He blew out a gusty sigh. "It's a damn good thing, because since you left, my brother's been as hard to live with as a rattle-snake."

"I'd say that was a bit of an exaggeration," Clay muttered, clearly not approving of his brother's choice of description.

"You shouldn't have gone," Skip said, sighing again. "Especially before the county fair."

Rorie laughed. "You're never going to forgive me for missing that, are you?"

"You should've been here, Rorie. It was great."

"I'll be here next summer," she promised.

"The fact is, Rorie's going to be around for a lifetime of summers," Clay informed his brother. "We're going to be married as soon as we can arrange it." His eyes held hers but they were filled with questions, as if he half expected her, even now, to refuse him.

Rorie swallowed the emotion that bobbed so readily to the surface and nodded wildly, telling him with one look that she'd marry him anytime he wanted.

Skip crossed his arms over his chest and gave them a smug look. "I knew something was going on between the two of you. Every time I was around you guys it was like getting zapped with one of those stun guns."

"We were that obvious?" It still troubled Rorie that Kate had known, especially since both she and Clay had tried so hard to hide their feelings.

Skip's shrug was carefree. "I don't think so, but I don't care about love and all that."

"Give it time, little brother," Clay murmured, "because when it hits, it'll knock you for a loop."

Mary stepped into the room, carrying a platter of meat. "So the two of you are getting hitched?"

Their laughter signaled a welcome release from all the tensions of the past weeks. Clay pulled out Rorie's chair, then sat down beside her. His hand reached for hers, lacing their fingers together. "Yes," he said, still smiling, "we'll be married as soon as we can get the license and talk to the pastor."

Mary pushed the basket of biscuits closer to Skip. "Well, you don't need to fret—I'll stay for a couple more years until I can teach this child the proper way to feed a man. She may be pretty to look at, but she don't know beans about whipping up a decent meal."

"I'd appreciate that, Mary," Rorie said. "I could do with a few cooking lessons."

The housekeeper's smile broadened. "Now, go ahead and eat before the potatoes get cold and the gravy gets lumpy."

Skip didn't need any further inducement. He helped himself to the biscuits, piling three on the edge of his plate.

Mary playfully slapped his hand. "I've got apple pie for dessert, so don't go filling yourselves up on my buttermilk biscuits." Her good humor was evident as she surveyed the table, glancing at everyone's plate, then bustled back to the kitchen.

Rorie did her best to sample a little of everything. Although the meal was delicious, she was too excited to do anything as mundane as eat.

After dinner, Skip made himself scarce. Mary delivered a tray with two coffee cups to the living room, where Clay and Rorie sat close together on the couch. "You two have lots to talk about, so you might as well drink this while you're doing it."

"Thank you, Mary," Clay said, exchanging a smile with Rorie.

The older woman set the tray down, then patted the fine gray hair at the sides of her head. "I want you to know how pleased I am for you both. Have you set the date yet?"

"We're talking about that now," Clay answered. "We're going to call Rorie's family in Arizona this evening and discuss it with them."

Mary nodded. "She's not the woman I would've chosen for you, her being a city girl and all, but she'll make you happy."

Clay's hand clasped Rorie's. "I know."

"She's got a generous soul." The housekeeper looked at Rorie and her gaze softened. "Fill this house with children—and with love. It's been quiet far too long."

The phone rang in the kitchen and, with a regretful glance over her shoulder, Mary hurried to answer it. A moment later, she stuck her head around the kitchen door.

"It's for you, Clay. Long distance."

Clay's grimace was apologetic. "I'd better get it."

"You don't need to worry that I'll leave," Rorie said with a laugh. "You're stuck with me for a lot of years, Clay Franklin."

He kissed her before he stood up, then headed toward the kitchen. Rorie sighed and leaned back, cradling her mug. By chance, her gaze fell on the photograph of Clay's parents, which rested on top of the piano. Once more, Rorie felt the pull of his mother's eyes. She smiled now, understanding so many things. The day she'd planned to leave Elk Run, this same photograph had captured her attention. The moment she'd walked into this house, Rorie had belonged to Clay and he to her. Somehow, looking at his mother's picture, she'd sensed that. She belonged to this home and this family.

Clay returned a few minutes later, with Blue trailing him. "Just a call from the owner of one of the horses I board," he said, as he sat down beside Rorie and placed his arm around her shoulders. His eyes followed hers to the photo. "Mom would have liked you."

Rorie sipped her coffee and smiled. "I know I would have loved her." Setting her cup aside, she reached up and threw both arms around Clay's neck. Gazing into his eyes, she brought his mouth down to hers.

Perhaps it was her imagination or an optical illusion—in fact, Rorie was sure of it. But she could have sworn the elegant woman in the photograph smiled.

* * * * *

COUNTRY BRIDE

One

"I now pronounce you husband and wife."

A burst of organ music crescendoed through the largest church in Nightingale, Oregon, as a murmur of shared happiness rose from the congregation.

Standing at the altar, Clay Franklin claimed his right to kiss Rorie Campbell Franklin, his bride.

Kate Logan did her best to look delighted for her friends, even though she felt as if a giant fist had been slammed into her stomach. Tears gathered in her eyes and she lowered her gaze, unable to watch as the man she'd loved for most of her life wrapped his arm around his new bride's waist.

Clay should be marrying me, Kate cried silently. *I should be the one he's looking at so tenderly. Me!* During the past few weeks, Kate had repeatedly reassured herself that she'd done the right thing in stepping aside to bring Clay and Rorie together. But that fact didn't lessen her pain now. Kate loved Clay, and that wasn't going to change. He was her best friend and confidant, her compass, her North Star. And now Clay was married to another woman—someone he loved far more than he could ever care for Kate.

A clean white handkerchief was thrust into her hand by Luke Rivers, her father's foreman. Kate knew he'd been waiting for this moment, convinced she'd dissolve into a puddle of tears.

She declined the use of his handkerchief by gently shaking her head.

"I'm here," he whispered in her ear.

"So is half of Nightingale," she returned wryly. Luke seemed determined to rescue her from this pain—as if that was possible. All she wanted was to survive this day with her dignity intact, and his open sympathy threatened the composure she'd painfully mustered.

"You're doing fine."

"Luke," she muttered, "stop making a fuss over me. Please." She'd managed to get through the ceremony without breaking down. The last thing she needed now was to have Luke calling attention to her.

It was ironic that Kate had been the one responsible for bringing Clay and Rorie together. She should be feeling noble and jubilant and honorable. But the only emotion she felt was a deep, abiding sense of loss.

Rorie and Clay walked down the center aisle, and from somewhere deep inside her, Kate found the strength to raise her head and smile blindly in their direction. Luke's hands gripped her shoulders as though to lend her strength. His concern should have been a comfort, but it wasn't.

"I'll walk you to the reception hall," Luke said, slipping his arm through hers.

"I'm perfectly capable of making it there on my own," she snapped, not wanting his pity. She would've argued more, but since they were sitting near the front of the church, they were among the first to be ushered out. Holding her head high, Kate walked past her friends and neighbors, doing her best to appear cheerful and serene.

At least she *looked* her best; Kate had made certain of that. She'd curled her thick blond hair until it lightly brushed her shoulders. The style emphasized her blue eyes and sculpted cheekbones. She'd shopped long and hard for the perfect dress and had found one that enhanced her slender waist and outlined her trim figure. The minute she'd tried on the soft blue silk and viewed herself in the mirror, Kate had known this was the dress. Although the lines were simple, the look was both classic and sophisticated, a look she'd never bothered to cultivate before. Too often in the past, she'd been mistaken for a teenager, mostly, she supposed, because she dressed the part. But she was a woman now and she had the broken heart to prove it.

Kate paused in the church vestibule, waiting for her father. Devin was sitting with Dorothea Murphy, his widow friend. Her father's interest in the older woman was something of a mystery to Kate. Tall and plump and outspoken, she was completely unlike Kate's late mother, who'd been delicate and reserved. Kate sometimes wondered what it was about Dorothea that attracted her father. They'd been seeing a lot of each other in recent weeks, but the possibility of their contemplating marriage filled Kate with a sudden, overwhelming sense of alarm. Kate pushed the thought from her mind. Losing Clay was all she could deal with right now.

"Are you all right, Princess?" Devin asked when he joined her.

"I wish everyone would stop worrying about me. I'm fine." It wasn't the truth, but Kate was well aware that she had to put on a breezy, unconcerned front. At least for the next few hours.

Her father patted her hand. "I know how hard this is for you. Do you want to go to the reception or would you prefer to head home?" His eyes were warm and sympathetic, and Kate felt a rush of love for him. A part of her longed to slip away unnoticed, but she couldn't and she knew it.

"Kate's already agreed to accompany me," Luke inserted, daring her to contradict him.

Indignation rose inside her. Instead of helping, Luke was making everything worse. The pain of watching Clay pledge his life to another woman was difficult enough, without Luke's unsought demands.

"I'm glad to hear that," Devin Logan said, clearly relieved. He smiled as he slipped his arm around Dorothea's waist. "Mrs. Murphy invited me to sit with her and, frankly, I was looking forward to doing that." He released Kate's hand, kissed her on the cheek, then strolled nonchalantly away.

"Shall we?" Grinning, Luke reached for Kate's limp hand and tucked it into the crook of his arm. As if they'd been a couple for years, he casually led her out of the church.

The early evening air was crisp and clear. Autumn had crested on an October tide of bronze and gold leaves, huge pumpkins and early twilights. Normally, this time of year invigorated Kate. If she hadn't been fortifying herself against Clay's wedding, she could have appreciated the season more.

The walk across the parking lot to the reception hall

was a short one. Kate didn't say another word to Luke, mentally preparing herself for the coming encounter with Clay and his bride. With each step her heart grew heavier. Rorie had asked her to be a bridesmaid, and although Kate was honored by the request, she'd declined. Rorie understood and hadn't pressured her. Despite the fact that they both loved the same man, Rorie and Kate had become close. Their friendship made everything more difficult for Kate, yet somehow easier, too.

By the time they arrived at the old brick building, Kate's pulse was so loud it echoed like a drum in her ear. Just outside the double doors leading into the hall, she stopped abruptly.

"I can't go in there," she told Luke. Panic had worked its way into her voice, which was low and trembling. "I can't face them and pretend... I just can't do it."

"Yes, you can."

"How could you possibly know what I can and can't do?" she demanded, wanting to bury her face in her hands and weep. These past few hours had taken their toll and she couldn't keep up the charade much longer. Luke gazed down on her and for the briefest of moments his eyes registered sympathy and regret.

"You can go in there and you will," he repeated.

Kate saw determination in his serious dark eyes and swallowed an angry retort, knowing he was right.

At six feet, Luke towered over her, and the hard set of his mouth did more than hint at determination and a will of iron. "If you don't attend the reception, everyone in Nightingale will talk. Is that what you want?"

"Yes," she cried, then lowered her head, battling down wave after wave of depression and self-pity. "No," she said reluctantly, loath to agree with him.

"I'm here for you, Kate. Lean on me for once in your life, and let me help you through the next few hours."

"I'm doing fine. I—"

He wouldn't allow her to finish. "Quit fighting me. I'm your friend, remember?"

His words, hushed and tender, brought a burning to her eyes. Her fingers tightened around his arm and she nodded, calling upon a reserve of strength she didn't know she possessed. "Just don't be so bossy with me. Please. I can bear almost anything but that." She'd made it through the wedding ceremony on her own. Now she needed someone at her side to help her appear strong and steady, in control of her emotions, when she felt as though the entire universe was pitching and heaving.

"Anything you say, Princess."

Although she'd objected earlier, she felt comforted by his strong arm against her. She heard his voice, as if from a distance, too preoccupied with her own pain to respond to his concern. But his presence restored her determination to acquit herself well during the long evening ahead.

"Only Daddy calls me Princess," she said distractedly.

"You mind?"

"I don't know... I suppose it's all right."

"Good." His fingers intertwined with hers as he guided her into the brightly decorated reception hall.

The next half hour was a blur. Drawing upon Luke's silent strength, Kate managed to make it through the reception line without a problem. Still, her knees felt shaky by the time she reached Clay, who kissed her cheek and thanked her for being so wonderful. Kate certainly didn't *feel* wonderful—even particularly admirable—but she smiled. And she was sincere when she offered Clay and Rorie her very best wishes.

Somehow Luke must have known how frail she felt because he took her hand and led her to one of the round lace-covered tables. His fingers were cool and callused, while Kate's were damp with her stubborn resolve to hide her pain.

Wordlessly, she sat beside Luke until the cake had been cut and the first piece ceremonially fed to the bride and groom. The scene before her flickered like an old silent movie. Kate held herself still, trying not to feel anything, but not succeeding.

"Would you like me to get you something to eat?" Luke asked, when a line formed to gather refreshments.

She stared at him, hardly able to comprehend his words. Then she blinked and her eyes traveled across the hall to the three-tiered heart-shaped wedding cake. "No," she said automatically.

"When was the last time you ate?"

Kate didn't remember. She shrugged. "Breakfast, I guess." As she spoke she realized that wasn't true. Dinner the night before was the last time she'd eaten. No wonder she felt so shaky and light-headed.

"I'm getting you some wedding cake," Luke announced grimly

"Don't. I'm—I'm not hungry."

He was doing it again! Taking over, making decisions on her behalf because he felt sorry for her. She would have argued with him, but he was already walking away, blithely unaware of her frustration.

Kate watched him, suddenly seeing him with fresh eyes. Luke Rivers had lived and worked on the Circle L for a decade, but Kate knew next to nothing about his past. His official title was foreman, but he was much more than that. He'd initiated several successful cattle-breeding programs and been involved in a profit-sharing venture with her father almost from the first. Devin had often remarked that Luke was certainly capable of maintaining his own spread. But year after year, he stayed on at the Circle L. This realization—that she knew so little of his past and even less about his thoughts and plans—shocked Kate. He'd always been just plain Luke. And he'd always been around—or so it seemed.

She had to admit that Luke puzzled her. He was handsome enough, but he rarely dated any woman for long, although plenty of Nightingale's finest had made their interest obvious. He was a "catch" who refused to play ball. He could be as tough as leather and mean as a saddle sore when the mood struck him, but it seldom did. Tall, lean and rugged adequately described him on the surface. It was what lay below that piqued her interest now.

Kate's musings about Luke were interrupted by the man himself as he pulled out the chair beside her and sat down. He pushed a delicate china plate filled with cheese and mixed nuts in her direction.

"I thought you were bringing me cake." His own plate was loaded with a huge piece, in addition to a few nuts and pastel mints.

"I brought you some protein instead. Sugar's not a good idea on an empty stomach."

"I don't believe you," she muttered, her sarcasm fuelled by his arrogance. "First you insist on bringing me cake, and then just when I'm looking forward to it, you decide I shouldn't be eating sweets."

Luke ignored her, slicing into his cake. "Just a minute ago, you said it would be a waste of time for me to bring you anything. Fact is, you downright refused to eat."

"That…was before."

He smiled, and that knowing cocky smile of his infuriated her.

"You'll feel sick if you eat sugar," he announced in an authoritative voice.

So much for helping her through the evening! All he seemed to want to do was quarrel. "Apparently you know how my stomach's going to react to various food groups. You amaze me, Luke Rivers. I had no idea you knew so much about my body's metabolism."

"You'd be shocked if I told you all the things I know about you and your body, Princess."

Kate stood abruptly. "I don't think it's a good idea for you to call me that. I'm not your 'Princess.' I'm a woman, not a little girl."

"Honey, you don't need to tell me that. I already know. Now sit down." His tone was brusque, and his smile humorless.

"I'll stand if I choose."

"Fine then. Look like a fool, if that's what you want."

No sooner had the words left his lips than she lowered herself back into the chair. The fight had gone out of her as quickly as it had come. Absently she scooped up a handful of nuts and chewed them vigorously, taking her frustration out on them.

Luke pushed his plate aside and took her hand, squeezing it gently. "I'm your friend. I've always been your friend and I'll continue to be your friend as long as I live. Don't ever doubt that."

Kate's eyes filled and her throat tightened painfully.

"I know. It's just that this is so much more…exhausting than I thought it would be."

Voices drew Kate's eyes to the front of the room, where Clay and Rorie were toasting each other with glasses of sparkling champagne. Soon flutes were being delivered around the room. Kate took one, holding the stem with both hands as if the champagne would lend her strength.

When the newlyweds were toasted, she took a sip. It bubbled and fizzed inside her mouth, then slid easily down her throat.

The soft strains of a violin drifted around the hall, and, mesmerized, Kate watched as Clay claimed his bride and led her onto the dance floor. Just watching the couple, so much in love, with eyes only for each other, heaped an extra burden of pain on Kate's shoulders. She looked away and, when she did, her gaze met Luke's. She tried to smile, to convince him she wasn't feeling a thing, but her effort failed dismally. Ready tears brimmed at the corners of her eyes and she bent her head, not wanting anyone to notice them, least of all Luke. He'd been wonderful; he'd been terrible. Kate couldn't decide which.

Soon others joined Clay and Rorie. First the matron of honor and then the bridesmaids and groomsmen, each couple swirling around the polished floor with practiced ease.

Luke got to his feet, walked to Kate's side and offered her his hand. His eyes held hers, silently demanding that she dance with him. Kate longed to tell him no, but she didn't have the energy to argue. It was simpler to give in than try to explain why she couldn't.

Together they approached the outskirts of the dance floor and Luke skillfully turned her into his arms.

"Everything's going to be all right," he whispered as his hand slid around her waist.

Kate managed a nod, grateful for his concern. She needed Luke this evening more than she'd realized. One thing was clear; she'd never make it through the remainder of the night without him.

During the past few years, Luke had danced with Kate any number of times. She'd never given it a second thought. Now they danced to one song and then another, but when she slipped into his embrace a third time, and his fingers spread across the small of her back, a shiver of unexpected awareness skidded up her spine. Kate paused, confused. Her steps faltered and in what seemed like an attempt to help her, Luke pulled her closer. Soon their bodies were so close together Kate could hear the steady beat of Luke's heart against her own. The quickening rate of his pulse told her he was experiencing the same rush of excitement she was.

Kate felt so light-headed she was almost giddy. Luke's arms were warm and secure, a solid foundation to hold on to when her world had been abruptly kicked off its axis. It might have been selfish, but Kate needed that warmth, that security. Smiling up at him, she closed her eyes and surrendered to the warm sensations carried on the soft, lilting music.

"Kate, there's something I need to tell you about the Circle L—"

She pressed her fingers against his lips, afraid that words would ruin this feeling. Arms twined around his neck, she grazed his jaw with the side of her face, reveling in the feel of him. Male and strong. Lean and hard.

"All right," he whispered, "we'll talk about it later."

They continued dancing and Luke rubbed his face against her hair, mussing it slightly, but Kate didn't mind.

Like a contented cat, she purred softly, the low sound coming from deep in her throat. The music ended all too quickly and with heavy reluctance, she dropped her arms and backed up one small step. Silently they stood an inch or so apart until the music resumed, when they reached for each other once again.

But this time Kate decided to figure out what was happening between them. Knowing how much she loved Clay, Luke was trying to help her through the evening. Yes, that was it. And doing a fine job, too. She felt...marvelous. It didn't make sense to her that she should experience this strong, unexpectedly sensual attraction to Luke, but at the moment she didn't care. He was concerned and gentle and she needed him.

They remained as they were, not speaking, savoring these warm sensations, until Kate lost count of the number of times they'd danced.

When the band took a ten-minute break, Luke released her with an unwillingness that made her heart soar. As though he couldn't bear to be separated from her, he took her hand, lacing her fingers with his.

He was leading her back to their table when they were interrupted by Beth Hammond, a pert blonde, who'd hurried toward them. "Hello, Luke," she said, ignoring Kate.

"Beth." He bowed his head politely, but it was evident that he didn't appreciate the intrusion.

The other woman placed a proprietary hand on his arm. "You promised me a dance, remember?"

Kate's eyes swivelled from Beth, who was pouting prettily, to Luke, who looked testy and impatient.

"If you'll excuse me a minute, I'm going to get a drink," Kate said. Her throat was parched and she didn't want to be left standing alone when the music started and Beth walked off with Luke.

The fruit punch was cold and refreshing, but she still felt warm. Kate decided to walk outside and let the cool night air clear her mind. Try though she might, she didn't really understand what was happening between her and Luke. It probably had to do with the confused state of her emotions, she decided. She'd think about it later.

The stars glittered like frost diamonds against a velvety black sky. Kate stood in the crisp evening air with her arms around her waist, gazing up at the heavens. She didn't hear Luke until he stepped behind her and lightly rested his hands on her shoulders. "I couldn't find you," he said in a voice that was softly accusing.

Kate didn't want to discuss Beth Hammond. For as long as she could remember, the other woman had been going out of her way to attract him.

"It's beautiful out, isn't it?" she asked instead. Instinctively she nestled closer to Luke, reclining against the lean strength of his body, seeking his warmth.

"Beautiful," he repeated, running his hands down her arms.

How content she felt with Luke, how comfortable— the way she imagined people felt when they'd been married for twenty years. But along with this familiar sense of ease, she experienced a prickle of anticipation. Her feelings were contradicting themselves. Secure and steady, and at the same time this growing sense of giddy excitement. It must be that glass of champagne.

The band started playing again and the music wafted outside. Gently Luke turned her to face him, slipping his hands around her as if to dance. Her arms reached for his neck, resuming their earlier position.

"We should talk," he whispered close to her ear.

"No," she murmured with a sigh. It seemed the most natural thing in the world to stand on the tips of her toes and brush her moist lips over his. Then she realized what she'd done. Her eyes widened and she abruptly stepped back, her heart hammering inside her chest.

Neither spoke. In the light that spilled from the hall, they stared at each other. Kate didn't know what her eyes told Luke, but his own were clouded with uncertainty. Kate half expected him to chastise her, or to tease her for behaving like such a flirt. Instead he reached for her once more, his eyes challenging her to stop him.

She couldn't.

The warmth of his mouth on hers produced a small sigh of welcome as her eyes slid languidly shut; she felt transported into a dreamworld, one she'd never visited before. This couldn't actually be happening, she told herself, and yet it felt so real. So right.

Luke's kiss was surprisingly tender, unlike anything she'd expected. "My darling Kate," he breathed against her hair, "I've dreamed of this so often."

"You have?" To her own ears, her voice sounded far, far away. Her head was swimming. If this was a dream, then she didn't want it to end. Sighing, she smiled beguilingly up at him.

"You little tease," he said, and laughed softly. He rained light kisses on her forehead, the corners of her eyes and her cheek, until she interrupted his meandering lips, seeking his mouth with her own.

He seemed to want the kiss as much as she did, but apparently saw no need to rush the experience, as if he feared hurrying would spoil it. Kate's mouth parted, inviting a deeper union. His willing compliance was so effective it buckled her knees.

"Kate?" Still holding her, he drew back, tilting his head to study her. Boldly she met his look, her eyes dancing with mischief. If he'd been kissing her out of pity, she was past caring.

A long moment passed before a slow, thoughtful smile played across his lips. "I think I'd better get you inside."

"No," she said, surprised at how vehement she felt about returning to the reception hall and the newlyweds. "I don't want to go back there."

"But—"

"Stay with me here. Dance with me. Hold me." He'd said he wanted to take care of her. Well, she was giving him the opportunity. She leaned into him and sighed, savoring his strength and support. This was Luke. Luke Rivers. Her trusted friend. Surely he understood; surely he'd help her through this most difficult night of her life. "I want you with me." She couldn't explain what was happening any more than she could deny it.

"You don't know what you're asking me." He stared down at her, searching her features for a long, breathless moment. Then the cool tips of his fingers brushed her face, moving along her cheekbones, stroking her skin as if he expected her to vanish.

Kate caught his hand with her own and gazed into

his dark eyes. They glittered like freshly polished onyx, full of light and a deep inner fire.

"I want you to kiss me. You taste so good." She moistened her lips and leaned closer to him, so close that she could feel the imprint of his buttons against her body. So close that the beat of his heart merged with her own. Excitement shivered through her in tremors so intense they frightened her. But not enough to make her pull away.

Her words spurred Luke into action, and when he kissed her their lips met with hungry insistence. Sensation erupted between them until Kate was weak and dizzy, clinging to him for support, her fingers bunching the material of his jacket. When he lifted his head, ending the kiss, Kate felt nearly faint from the rush of blood to her pounding temples.

There was a look of shock on Luke's face. His eyes questioned her, but Kate's thoughts were as scattered as autumn leaves tossed by the wind.

"How much champagne have you had?" he asked softly.

"One glass," she answered with a sigh, resting her forehead against his heaving chest. Luke hadn't said taking care of her would be this wonderful. Had she known, she wouldn't have resented it quite so much earlier.

Luke expelled a harsh breath. "You've had more than one glass. I doubt you even know who I am."

"Of course I do!" she flared. "You're Luke. Now don't be ridiculous. Only…"

"Only what?"

"Only you never kissed me before. At least not like

that. Why didn't you tell me you were so good at this?" Finding herself exceptionally witty, she began to laugh.

"I'm taking you home," Luke said firmly, grabbing her elbow with such force that she was half lifted from the walkway.

"Luke," she cried. "I don't want to go back yet."

His grip relaxed immediately. "Kate Logan, you're drunk! Except you don't have the sense to know it."

"I most certainly am not!" She waved her index finger at him like a schoolmarm. "I'll have you know that it takes a lot more than one glass of champagne to do me in."

Luke obviously wasn't willing to argue the point. His hand cradling her elbow, he led her toward the parking lot.

"I want to stay," she protested.

He didn't answer. Then it dawned on her that perhaps she'd misread Luke. Maybe he was trying to get rid of her so he could return to Beth.

"Luke?"

"Kate, please, don't argue with me."

"Are you in love with Beth?"

"No." His answer was clipped and impatient.

"Thank heaven." Her hand fluttered over her heart. "I don't think I could bear it if you were."

Luke stopped abruptly and Kate realized they were standing in front of his truck. He opened the passenger door for her, but she had no intention of climbing in. At least not yet. She wanted to spend more time with Luke, their arms wrapped around each other the way they'd been before. The pain that had battered her heart for weeks had vanished the instant she stepped into his arms.

"Kiss me again, okay?"

"Kate, no."

"Please?"

"Kate, you're drunk."

"And I tell you I'm not." The one glass of champagne had been just enough to make her a little...reckless. It felt so good to surrender to these new emotions—to lean on Luke. From the moment they'd arrived at the wedding, he'd been telling her how much she needed him. Maybe he was right. There'd been so much upheaval in her life, and Luke was here, warm and kind and solid.

"I'm going to drive you home," he insisted. From the sound of his voice, Kate could tell he was growing frustrated.

The house would be dark and cold. How Kate feared being alone, and with Clay out of her life, there was only her father. And Luke. If Devin did decide to marry Mrs. Murphy, he might sell the ranch and then Luke would be gone, too. Alarmed at the thought, she placed her hands on his shoulders, her gaze holding his.

"Kate?" Luke coaxed.

"All right, I'll go back to the house, but on one condition."

"Kate, come on, be reasonable."

"I want you to do something for me. You keep telling me you're my friend and how much you want to help...."

"Just get inside the truck, would you, before someone comes along and finds us arguing?"

"I need your promise first."

Luke ignored her. "You've got a reputation to uphold. You can't let people in Nightingale see you tipsy. The school board will hear about this and that'll be the end of your career."

Kate smiled, shaking her head, then impulsively leaned forward and kissed him again. Being with Luke took the hurt away, and she refused to suffer that kind of pain ever again. "Will you please do what I want?"

"All right," he muttered, clearly exasperated. "What is it?"

"Oh, thank you," she murmured, and sighed expressively. This was going to shock him, but no more than it had already shocked her. She didn't know where the idea had come from, but it seemed suddenly, inarguably right.

Kate smiled at him, her heart shining through her eyes. "It's simple really. All I want you to do is marry me."

Two

Early the following day, Devin Logan walked hesitantly into the kitchen where Kate sat drinking her first cup of coffee. She smiled a greeting. "Morning, Dad."

"Morning, Princess." He circled the table twice before he sat down.

Kate watched him curiously, then rose to pour him a cup of coffee and bring it to the table. It was a habit she'd begun after her mother's death several years earlier.

"Did you and Mrs. Murphy have a good time last night?" Kate asked, before her father could comment on the rumors that were sure to be circulating about her and Luke Rivers. She hadn't seen Luke yet, but she would soon enough, and she was mentally bracing herself for the confrontation. What a fool she'd made of herself. She cringed at the thought of her marriage proposal and didn't doubt for a second that Luke was going to take a great deal of delight in tormenting her about it. She suspected it would be a long while before he let her live this one down.

"Looks like rain," Devin mumbled.

Kate grinned good-naturedly, wondering at her father's strange mood. "I asked you about last night, not about the weather."

Devin's eyes flared briefly with some unnamed emotion, which he quickly disguised. His gaze fell to the steaming mug cupped in his hands.

"Dad? Did you and Mrs. Murphy enjoy yourselves?"

"Why, sure, we had a grand time," he said with forced enthusiasm.

Kate waited for him to elaborate. Instead he reached for the sugar bowl and resolutely added three heaping teaspoons to his mug. He stirred it so briskly the coffee threatened to slosh over the edge. All the while, he stared blankly into space.

Kate didn't know what to make of Devin's unusual behavior. "Dad," she said, trying again, "is there something on your mind?"

His eyes darted about the room, reluctantly settling on Kate. "What makes you ask that?"

"You just added sugar to your coffee. You've been drinking it sugarless for forty years."

He glared down at the mug, surprise written on his tanned face. "I did?"

"I saw you myself."

"I did," he repeated firmly, as if that was what he'd intended all along. "I, ah, seem to have developed a sweet tooth lately."

It was becoming apparent to Kate that her father's experience at Clay and Rorie's wedding reception must have rivaled her own. "Instead of beating around the bush all morning, why don't you just tell me what's on your mind?"

Once more, her father lowered his eyes, then nodded

and swallowed tightly. "Dorothea and I had…a long talk last night," he began haltingly. "It all started innocently enough. Then again, I'm sure the wedding and all the good feelings floating around Clay and Rorie probably had a lot to do with it." He paused to take a sip of his coffee, grimacing at its sweetness. "The best I can figure, we started talking seriously after Nellie Jackson came by and told Dorothea and me that we made a handsome couple. At least that's what I remember."

"It's true," Kate said kindly. Personally she would have preferred her father to see someone who resembled her mother a bit more, but Mrs. Murphy was a pleasant, gentle woman and Kate was fond of her.

Her father smiled fleetingly. "Then the champagne was passed around and Dorothea and I helped ourselves." He paused, glancing at Kate as if that explained everything.

"Yes," Kate said, hiding a smile, "go on."

Slowly Devin straightened, and his eyes, forthright and unwavering, held hers. "You know I loved your mother. When Nora died, there was a time I wondered if I could go on living without her, but I have, and so have you."

"Of course you have, Dad." Suddenly it dawned on Kate exactly where this conversation was leading. It shouldn't have surprised her, and yet… Kate's heart was beginning to hammer uncomfortably. Her father didn't need to say another word; she knew what was coming as surely as if he'd already spoken the words aloud. He was going to marry Dorothea Murphy.

"Your mother's been gone nearly five years now and, well, a man gets lonely," her father continued. "I've been thinking about doing some traveling and, frankly, I don't want to do it alone."

"You should've said something earlier, Dad," Kate interjected. "I'd have loved traveling with you. Still would. That's one of the nice things about being a teacher," she rambled on. "My summers are free. And with Luke watching the ranch, you wouldn't have any worries about what's happening at home and—"

"Princess." His spoon made an irritating clicking sound against the sides of the ceramic mug, but he didn't seem to notice. "I asked Dorothea to marry me last night and she's graciously consented."

After only a moment's hesitation, Kate found the strength to smile and murmur, "Why, Dad, that's fantastic."

"I realize it's going to be hard on you, Princess—so soon after Clay's wedding and all. I want you to know I have no intention of abandoning you—you'll always be my little girl."

"Of course you aren't abandoning me." Tears edged their way into the corners of Kate's eyes and a cold numbness moved out from her heart and spread through her body. "I'm happy for you. Really happy." She meant it, too, but she couldn't help feeling a sense of impending loss. All the emotional certainties seemed to be disappearing from her life.

Her father gently squeezed her hand. "There are going to be some other changes, as well, I'm afraid. I'm selling the ranch."

Kate gasped before she could stop herself. He'd just confirmed all her fears. She'd lost Clay to another woman; now she was about to lose her father, and her home, too. Then another thought crystallized in her mind, a thought that had been half formed the night before. If the ranch was sold, Luke would be gone, too.

Clay. Her father. The Circle L. Luke. Everyone and everything she loved, gone in a matter of hours. It was almost more than she could absorb. Pressing her hand over her mouth, she blinked back the tears.

"Now I don't want you to concern yourself," her father hurried to add. "You'll always have a home with me. Dorothea and I talked it over and we both want you to feel free to live with us in town as long as you like. You'll always be my Princess, and Dorothea understands that."

"Dad," Kate muttered, laughing and crying at the same time. "That's ridiculous. I'm twenty-four years old and perfectly capable of living on my own."

"Of course you are, but—"

She stopped him by raising her hand. "There's no need to discuss it further. You and Dorothea Murphy are going to be married, and... I couldn't be happier for you. Don't you worry about me. I'll find a place of my own in town and make arrangements to move as soon as I can."

Her father sighed, clearly relieved by her easy acceptance of his plans. "Well, Princess," he said with a grin, "I can't tell you how pleased I am. Frankly, I was worried you'd be upset."

"Oh, Dad..."

Still grinning broadly, Devin stroked the side of his jaw. "Dorothea isn't a bit like your mother—I don't know if you're aware of that or not. Fact is, the only reason I asked her out that first time was so she'd invite me over for some of her peach cobbler. Then before I knew it, I was making excuses to get into town and it wasn't because of her cobbler, either."

Kate made an appropriate reply, although a minute later she wasn't sure what she'd said. Soon afterward, her father kissed her cheek and then left the house, telling her he'd be back later that afternoon.

She poured herself a second cup of coffee and leaned against the kitchen counter, trying to digest everything that was happening to her well-organized life. She felt as though her whole world had been uprooted and flung about—as though a hurricane had landed in Nightingale.

Wandering aimlessly from room to room, she paused in front of the bookcase, where a photograph of her mother stood. Tears blurred her eyes as she picked it up and clutched it to her chest. Wave upon wave of emotion swept through her, followed by a flood of hot tears.

She relived the overwhelming grief she'd felt at her mother's death, and she was furious with her father for letting another woman take Nora's place in his life. At the same time, she couldn't begrudge him his new happiness.

Mrs. Murphy wasn't the type of woman Kate would have chosen for her father, but then she wasn't doing the choosing. Suddenly resolute, Kate dragged in a deep breath, exhaling the fear and uncertainty and inhaling acceptance of this sudden change in both their lives.

The back door opened and instinctively Kate closed her eyes, mentally composing herself. It could only be Luke, and he was the last person she wanted to see right now.

"Kate?"

With trembling hands, she replaced the faded photograph and wiped the tears from her face. "Good morning, Luke," she said as she entered the kitchen.

Luke had walked over to the cupboard and taken down a mug. "Your father just told me the news about him and Mrs. Murphy," he said carefully. "Are you going to be all right?"

"Of course. It's wonderful for Dad, isn't it?"

"For your father yes, but it must be a shock to you so soon…"

"After Clay and Rorie," she finished for him. Reaching for the coffeepot, she poured his cup and refilled her own. "I'm going to be just fine," she repeated, but Kate didn't know whether she was telling him this for his benefit or her own. "Naturally, the fact that Dad's marrying Dorothea means a few changes in all our lives, but I'll adjust."

"I haven't seen your father this happy in years."

Kate did her best to smile through the pain. "Yes, I know." To her horror tears formed again, and she lowered her eyes and blinked wildly in an effort to hide them.

"Kate?"

She whirled around and set her coffee aside, then started wiping invisible crumbs from the perfectly clean kitchen counter.

Luke's hands settled on her shoulders, and before she knew what was happening, Kate had turned and buried her face against his clean-smelling denim shirt. A single sob shook her shoulders and she gave a quivering sigh, embarrassed to be breaking down in front of him like this.

"Go on, baby," he whispered gently, his hands rubbing her back, "let it out."

She felt like such a weakling to be needing Luke so much, but he was so strong and steady, and Kate felt as helpless as a rowboat tossed in an angry sea. "Did...did you know Dad might sell the ranch?" she asked Luke.

"Yes." His voice was tight. "When did he tell you?"

"This morning, after he said he was marrying Mrs. Murphy."

"You don't have to worry about it."

"But I do," she said, sobbing brokenly. She felt Luke's chin caress the crown of her head and she snuggled into his warm, safe embrace. Luke was her most trusted friend. He'd seen her through the most difficult day of her life.

The thought of Clay and Rorie's wedding flashed into her mind, and with it came the burning memory of her marriage proposal to Luke. She stiffened in his arms, mortified at the blatant way she'd used him, the way she'd practically begged him to take care of her— to marry her. Breaking free of his arms, she straightened and offered him a watery smile.

"What would I do without you, Luke Rivers?"

"You won't ever need to find out." He slid his arms around her waist and gently kissed the tip of her nose. His smile was tender. "There must've been something in the air last night. First us, and now your father and Mrs. Murphy."

"About us," she began carefully. She drew in a steadying breath, but her eyes avoided Luke's. "I hope you realize that when I asked you to marry me I...didn't actually mean it."

He went very still and for a long moment he said nothing. "I took you seriously, Kate."

Kate freed herself from his arms and reached for

her coffee, gripping the mug tightly. "I'd had too much champagne."

"According to you, it was only one glass."

"Yes, but I drank it on an empty stomach, and with all the difficult emotions the wedding brought out, I… I simply wasn't myself."

Luke frowned. "Oh?"

"No, I wasn't," she said, feigning a light laugh. "The way we were dancing and the way I clung to you, and… and kissed you. That's nothing like me. I'm not going to hold you to that promise, Luke."

As if he found it difficult to remain standing, Luke turned a chair around and straddled it with familiar ease. Kate claimed the chair opposite him, grateful to sit down. Her nerves were stretched to the breaking point. Luke draped his forearms over the back of his chair, cupping the hot mug with both hands, and studied Kate with an intensity that made her blush.

"Listen," Kate said hesitantly, "you were the perfect gentleman and I want you to know how much I appreciate everything you did. But… I didn't mean half of what I said."

The sun-marked crow's feet at the corners of his eyes fanned out as Luke smiled slowly, confidently. "Now that raises some interesting questions."

"I don't understand." Surely Luke knew what she was talking about, yet he seemed to enjoy watching her make an even bigger fool of herself by forcing her to explain.

"Well," he said in an easy drawl, "if you only meant half of what you said, then it leads me to wonder what you did mean and what you didn't."

"I can't remember *everything* I said," she murmured,

her cheeks hot enough to pop a batch of corn. "But I do know I'd greatly appreciate it if you'd forget the part about marrying me."

"I don't want to forget it."

"Luke, please," she cried, squeezing her eyes shut. "This is embarrassing me. Could you please drop it?"

Luke rubbed his jaw thoughtfully. "I don't think I can."

So Luke was going to demand his pound of flesh. Kate supposed she shouldn't be surprised. She had, after all, brought this on herself. "You were so kind to me at the reception... After the wedding ceremony you kept saying you wanted to help me and, Luke, you did, you honestly did. I don't think I could've made it through Clay's wedding without you, but..."

"You want to forget the kissing, too?"

"Yes, please." She nodded emphatically.

He frowned. "That's not what you said last night. In fact, you seemed a little stunned at how pleasant it was. As I recall you told me—and I quote—'why didn't you tell me you were so good at this?'"

"I said that?" Kate muttered, already knowing it was true.

"I'm afraid so."

She covered her face with both hands as the hot color mounted in her cheeks.

"And you made me promise to marry you."

She bit down hard on her lower lip. "Anyone else in the world would have mercifully forgotten I said that."

With a certain degree of ceremony, Luke set his hat farther back on his head and folded his arms. His face was a study in concentration. "I have no intention of forgetting it. I'm a man of my word and I never break my promises."

Kate groaned. In light of her father's news this morning, she'd hoped Luke might be a bit more understanding. "It's obvious you're deriving pleasure from this," she muttered angrily, then pressed her lips together to keep from saying more.

"No, not exactly. When would you like to have the wedding? And while we're at it, you might as well learn now that—"

"You can't be serious!" she interrupted, incredulous that he'd suggest they set a date. If this was a joke, he was carrying it too far.

"I'm dead serious. You asked me to marry you, I agreed, and anything less would be a breach of good faith."

"Then I... I absolve you from your promise." She waved her hands as if she was granting some kind of formal dispensation.

He stroked the side of his face, his forehead creased in a contemplative frown. "My word is my word and I stand firm on it."

"I didn't understand what I was saying—well, I did. Sort of. But you know as well as I do that the...heat of the moment was doing most of the talking."

Luke's frown deepened. "I suppose everybody in town will assume you're marrying me on the rebound. Either that, or I'll be the one they gossip about. That doesn't trouble me much, but I don't like the thought of folks saying anything about you."

"Will you stop?" she cried. "I have no intention of marrying anyone! Ever!" She was finished with love, finished with romance. Thirty years from now she'd be living alone with a few cats and her knitting needles.

"That wasn't what you said last night."

"Would you quit saying that? I wasn't myself, for heaven's sake!"

"Well, our getting married sounded like a hell of a good idea to me. Now, I know you've gone through a hard time, but our marriage will end all that."

Kate brushed a shaking hand across her eyes, hoping this was just part of a nightmare and she'd soon wake up. Unfortunately when she lowered her hand, Luke was still sitting there, as arrogant as could be. "I can't believe we're having this discussion. It's totally unreasonable, and if you're trying to improve my mood, you've failed."

"I'm serious, Kate. I told you that."

Keeping her head down, she spoke quickly, urgently. "It's really wonderful of you to even consider going through with the marriage, but it isn't necessary, Luke. More than anyone, you should know that I can't marry you. Not when I love Clay Franklin."

"Hogwash."

Kate's head jerked up. "I beg your pardon?"

"You're in love with me. You just don't know it yet."

It took Kate only half a second to respond. "Of all the egotistical, vain, high-handed…" She paused to suck in a breath. If Luke's intent was to shock her, he'd succeeded. She bolted to her feet and flailed the air with both hands. Unable to stand still, she started pacing the kitchen. "I don't understand you. I've tried, honestly I've tried. One moment you're the Rock of Gibraltar, steady and secure and everything I need, my best friend, and the next moment you're saying the most ridiculous things to me. It never used to be like this! Why have you changed?"

"Is it really that bad?" he cajoled softly, ignoring her question.

"I don't know what happened to you—to us—at the wedding reception, but like you said, something must've been in the air. Let's blame it on the champagne and drop it before one of us gets hurt."

"If you gave the idea of our getting married some serious thought, it might grow on you," he suggested next.

Then he got to his feet and moved purposefully toward her, his mouth twisted in a cocky grin. "Maybe this will help you decide what's best."

"I—"

He laid a finger across her mouth. "It seems to me you've forgotten it's not ladylike to be quite so stubborn." With that, he slipped his arm around her waist and pulled her gently against him.

Knowing what he intended, Kate opened her mouth to protest, but he fastened his lips over hers, sealing off the words, and to her chagrin, soon erasing them altogether. Her fingers gripped the collar of his blue button-snap shirt and against every dictate of her will her mouth parted, welcoming his touch.

When he released her, it was a minor miracle that she didn't collapse on the floor. He paused and a wide grin split his face.

"Yup," he said, looking pleased, "you love me all right."

Three

Kate had never felt more grateful for a Monday morning than she did the following day. At least when she was at school, she had the perfect excuse to avoid another confrontation with Luke. He seemed to believe he was somehow responsible for her and to take that responsibility quite seriously. She had absolutely no intention of holding him to his promise and couldn't understand why he was being so stubborn. To suggest she was in love with him simply because she'd proposed marriage and responded ardently to his kisses revealed how truly irrational Luke Rivers had become.

Kate paused and let that thought run through her mind a second time, then laughed aloud. No wonder Luke insisted on marrying her. Kate had to admit she could see why he might have the wrong impression. Still, she wished she could think of some way to set him straight.

Luke was right about a few things, though. She *did* love him—but not in the way he implied. She felt for him as a sister did toward a special older brother. As a woman did toward a confidant and companion of many years' standing. The feelings she'd experienced when he kissed her were something of a mystery, but could easily be attributed to the heightened emotions following Clay's wedding. There'd been so many changes in Kate's life during the past few months that she barely understood herself anymore.

She could never love Luke the way she'd loved Clay. For as long as Kate could remember, she'd pictured herself as Clay's wife. Joining her life with any other man's seemed not only wrong but completely foreign.

"Good morning, Miss Logan," seven-year-old Taylor Morgenroth said as he walked casually into the classroom. "I saw you at Mr. Franklin's wedding on Saturday."

"You did?" It shouldn't surprise her, since nearly every family in town had been represented at the wedding. Probably more of her students had seen her there.

"You were with Mr. Rivers, weren't you? My mom kept asking my dad who you were dancing with. That was Mr. Rivers, wasn't it?"

"Yes." Kate had to bite her tongue to keep from explaining that she hadn't actually been "with" Luke. He wasn't her official date, although they'd attended the wedding together. But explaining something like that to a second-grader would only confuse the child.

"My dad made me dance with my older sister. It was yucky."

Kate managed some remark about how much of a gentleman Taylor had been, but she doubted that he wanted to hear it.

Before long, the students of Nightingale Elementary were filing into the classroom and rushing toward their desks. From that point on, Kate didn't have time to think about Luke or Saturday night or anything else except her lesson plans for the day.

At noon she took her packed lunch to the staff room. Several of the other teachers were already seated at the circular tables.

"Kate!" Sally Daley, the sixth-grade teacher, waved her hand to gain Kate's attention. She smiled, patting the empty chair beside her.

Reluctantly Kate joined the older woman, sending an apologetic look to her friend Linda Hutton, the third-grade teacher, with whom she usually had lunch. Sally had the reputation of being a busybody, but Kate couldn't think of a way to elude her without being rude.

"We were just talking about you," Sally said warmly, "and we thought it would be nice if you'd sit with us today."

"I'll be happy to," Kate said, feeling a twinge of guilt at the lie. She opened her brown bag, taking out a container of peach-flavored yogurt and two rye crisps.

"Clay's wedding was really lovely, wasn't it?" Sally asked without preamble. "And now I understand your father and Dorothea Murphy are going to be tying the knot?" Her questioning tone indicated she wasn't certain of her facts.

"That's right," Kate said cheerfully.

"Kind of a surprise, wasn't it?"

"Kind of," was all Kate would admit, although she realized she should've known her father was falling in love with Mrs. Murphy. They'd been spending more and more time together since early summer. If Kate hadn't been so blinded by what was happening between her and Clay, she would've noticed how serious her father had become about Dorothea long before now.

"It's going to be difficult for you, isn't it, dear?" Sally asked sympathetically. "Everyone knows how close you and your father have been since Nora died."

"I'm very pleased my father's planning to remarry." And Kate was. The initial shock had worn off; she felt genuinely and completely happy that her father had found someone to love. He'd never complained, but Kate knew he'd been lonely during the past few years.

"Still, it must be a blow," Sally pressed, "especially coming on the heels of Clay and Rorie getting married. It seems your whole life's been turned upside down, doesn't it?"

Kate nodded, keeping her eyes focused on her sparse meal.

"Speaking of Clay and Rorie, their wedding *was* lovely," Susan Weaver, the kindergarten teacher, put in.

"I thought so, too," Kate said, smiling through the pain. "Rorie will be a perfect wife for him." The words nearly stuck in her throat, although she was fully aware of their truth. Rorie was an ideal complement to Clay. From the moment she'd stepped into their lives, she'd obviously belonged with him.

"The new Mrs. Franklin is certainly an ambitious soul. Why, the library hasn't been the same since she took over. There are education programs going on every other week. Displays. Lectures. I tell you, nothing but good has happened since she moved to Nightingale."

"I couldn't agree with you more."

Sally nodded. "You've taken this…disappointment over Clay rather well," she murmured with cloying sympathy. "And now your father remarrying so soon afterward…" She gently patted Kate's hand. "If there's anything I can do for you, Kate, anything at all, during this difficult time, I want you to call me. I know I speak for each and every staff member when I say that. Your father must see what a wonderful daughter you've been, and I'm sorry all of this is being added to your burden just now. But if it's ever more than you can bear, your friends at Nightingale Elementary will be honored to stand by your side. All you have to do is call." The other women nodded.

If Sally was expecting a lengthy response, Kate couldn't manage it. "Thank you. That's…really good to know," she said in a faltering voice. To hear Sally tell it, Kate was close to a nervous breakdown.

"We're prepared to help as you pick up the shattered pieces of your life. And furthermore, I think Luke Rivers is a fine man."

"Luke Rivers?" Kate repeated, nearly choking on her bite of rye crisp. A huge lump formed in her throat at Sally's implication.

"Why, yes." Sally smiled serenely. "Everyone in Nightingale saw how the two of you were gazing into each other's eyes at the dance. It was the most romantic thing I've seen in years."

"Dance?"

"At the wedding-reception dance," Sally elaborated. "From what I understand, Beth Hammond's been so depressed she hasn't left her house since that night."

"Whatever for?"

Sally laughed lightly. "Surely there's no reason to be so reticent—you're among friends. Everyone knows how she's had her eye on Luke for years."

Susan nodded vigorously. "Apparently they dated a few times a year ago, but Luke's kept her dangling ever since."

"I don't have a clue what you mean," Kate said faintly, her heart beating hard enough to pound its way out of her chest. She'd hoped that with her father's engagement, the rumors about her and Luke would naturally fade away. So much for wishful thinking.

Sally exchanged a meaningful look with the other teachers. "Well, I thought that, you know…that you and Luke Rivers were involved."

"Luke and me?" Kate gave a short, almost hysterical laugh. "Nothing could be further from the truth. Luke's a dear friend, and we've known each other for years, but we're not romantically involved. There's nothing going on between us. Absolutely nothing." She spoke more vehemently than necessary, feeling pleased that for once Sally couldn't get a single word in.

After a moment, she made a show of looking at her watch. "Excuse me, ladies, but I've got to get back to my classroom."

As she left the faculty lounge, she heard the whispers start. Groaning inwardly, Kate marched down the hall and into her own room. Sitting at her desk, she snapped the cracker in half and examined it closely before tossing it in the garbage.

"Don't you know it's wrong to waste food?" Linda Hutton said, leaning against the doorjamb, arms folded.

"I wished I'd never talked to that woman," Kate muttered, feeling foolish for allowing herself to be manipulated into conversation with a known busybody.

"Well, then," Linda said, with a grin, "why did you?"

"If I knew the answer to that, I'd be enjoying my lunch instead of worrying about the tales Sally's going to spread about me…and Luke Rivers."

Linda walked into the room.

"The least you could've done was rescue me," Kate complained.

"Hey, I leave that kind of work to the fire department." Linda planted her hands on the edge of Kate's desk. "Besides, I was curious myself."

"Curious about what? Luke and me? All we did was dance a couple of times. I...was feeling warm and went outside for a little bit. Luke met me there and after a few minutes, he...drove me home. What's the big deal, anyway?"

"A couple of dances... I see," Linda said, her words slow and thoughtful.

"I'd be interested in knowing exactly *what* you see. Everyone keeps making an issue of the dancing. Taylor came into class this morning and the first thing he said was that he'd seen me at the wedding. He didn't talk about running into me at the grocery store earlier that day."

"Did you have your arms wrapped around a man there, too?"

"Don't be silly!"

"I wasn't. Honestly, Kate, nearly everyone in Nightingale saw the way you and Luke were dancing. You acted as though there wasn't anyone else at the reception. Needless to say, rumors were floating in every direction. Everyone was watching the two of you, and neither you or Luke even noticed. Or cared. I heard the pastor mumble something about maybe performing another wedding soon, and he wasn't referring to your father and Dorothea Murphy—which is another matter entirely." Linda paused to suck in a deep breath. "Are you sure you're going to be able to handle this on top of—"

"Clay and Rorie? Yes," Kate answered her own question emphatically. "Oh, I had a few bad moments when Dad first told me, but I got over it." The comfort she'd found in Luke's arms had helped her more than she cared to admit. He seemed to be making a habit of helping her through difficult moments.

Linda eyed her sceptically. "There's been so much upheaval in your life these past few weeks. You know, sometimes people go into shock for weeks after a major change in their lives."

"Linda," Kate cried, "everyone keeps looking at me as though they expect me to have a nervous breakdown. What is it with you people?"

"It isn't us, Katie girl, it's you."

Kate pushed her hair off her forehead and kept her hand there. "What do I have to do to convince you that I'm fine? I'm happy for Clay and Rorie. I consider myself resilient and emotionally strong, but this makes me wonder why you and Sally and the others don't."

"I don't think anyone's waiting for you to fall apart," Linda countered. "We all have your best interests at heart. In fact, with one obvious exception, everyone's really pleased you have Luke."

"But I don't *have* him. Luke isn't a possession, he's a man. We're friends. You know that." Kate expected Linda, of all her friends and colleagues, to recognize the truth when she heard it. Instead she'd made it sound as though Kate's dancing with Luke and then letting him take her home meant instant wedding bells.

Linda shook her head. "To be honest, Kate, you're doing a whole lot of denying and I don't understand why. It seems to me that the person you're really trying to convince is yourself."

By the time Kate arrived home that evening, she was in a fine temper. Her father had already left for a meeting at the Eagles Lodge. He'd taped a note to the refrigerator door telling her not to worry about fixing him any dinner because he planned to stop at Dorothea's later for a bite to eat.

Kate read his scrawled note, pulled it off the fridge and crumpled it with both hands. She was angry and impatient for no reason she could identify.

Heating a bowl of soup, Kate stood by the stove stirring it briskly when Luke let himself in the back door. After her encounter with Sally and Linda, Luke was the last person she wanted to see. Nevertheless, her eyes flew anxiously to his.

"Evening, Kate."

"Hi."

He hung his hat on the peg next to the door, then walked to the kitchen counter and examined the empty soup can. "I hope you're going to eat more than this."

"Luke," she said, slowly expelling her breath, "I had a terrible day and I'm rotten company."

"What happened?"

Kate didn't want to talk about it. Dredging up her lunch-hour conversation with Sally Daley would only refuel her unhappiness.

"Kate?" Luke coaxed.

She shrugged. "The other teachers heard about Dad and Dorothea and seemed to think the shock would do me in, if you know what I mean."

"I think I do." As he was speaking, he took two bowls out of the cupboard and set them on the table.

Kate stirred the soup energetically, not looking at

him, almost afraid of his reaction. "In addition, people are talking about us."

When she glanced in his direction, Luke nodded, his eyes twinkling. "I thought they might be."

"I don't like it!" she burst out. The least Luke could do was show the proper amount of concern. "Sally Daley told me how pleased she was with the way I'd rebounded from a broken heart." She paused, waiting for his response. When he didn't give one, she added, "Sally seems to think you and I are perfect together."

Luke grinned. "And that upset you?"

"Yes!" she cried.

"Sally didn't mean anything. She's got a big heart."

"And an even bigger mouth," Kate retorted. "We're in trouble here, Luke Rivers, and I need to know how we're going to get out of it."

"The answer to that is simple. We should get married and put an end to all the speculation."

Kate's shoulders sagged in defeat. "Luke, please, I'm not in the mood for your teasing tonight. We have to get serious about…"

Her voice dwindled away as Luke, standing behind her, placed his hands on her shoulders and nuzzled her neck. "I'm willing."

His touch had a curious effect on Kate's senses, which sprang to sudden life. It took every ounce of fortitude she possessed to resist melting into his arms and accepting his comfort. But that was how they'd got into this mess in the first place.

"The gossips are having a field day and I hate it."

Luke drew her away from the stove and turned her toward him. He searched her face, but his own revealed not a hint of annoyance or distress. "I don't mind if folks talk. It's only natural, don't you think?"

"How can you *say* that?"

"Kate, you're making this out to be some kind of disaster."

"But don't you see? It is! There are people out there who actually believe we're falling in love."

"You do love me. I told you that earlier. Remember?"

"Oh, Luke," she cried, so disheartened she wanted to weep. "I know what you're trying to do and I appreciate it with all my heart, but it isn't necessary. It really isn't."

Luke looked baffled. "I don't understand."

"You've been so sweet." She laid her hand against his clean-shaven cheek. "Any other man would've laughed in my face when I made him promise to marry me, but you agreed and now, out of consideration for *my* pride, *my* feelings, you claim you're going through with it."

"Kate," he said, guiding her to the table and gently pressing her into a chair. "Sit down. I have something important to tell you—something I've been trying to tell you since the night of the wedding."

"What is it?" she asked, once she was seated.

Luke paced the floor directly in front of her chair. "I should've told you much sooner, but with everything else that's going on in your life, finding the right time has been difficult." He paused and frowned at her as though he was having trouble choosing his words.

"Yes?" she coaxed.

"I'm buying the Circle L."

The kitchen started to sway. Kate reached out and gripped the edge of the table. She'd hoped it would be months, at least, before a buyer was found. And it had never occurred to her that Luke might be that buyer.

"I see," she said, smiling through her shock. "I... I'd have thought Dad would've said something himself."

"I asked him not to."

Her troubled gaze clashed with Luke's. Despite her shock she felt curious. How could Luke afford to buy a ranch, especially one as large as this? She knew he'd been raised by an uncle, who had died years before. Had there been an inheritance? "Luke," she ventured shyly, "I know it's none of my business, but..."

"How did I come by the money?" he finished for her. "You have every right to ask. I inherited it from my uncle Dan—I've told you about him. He owned a couple of businesses in Wyoming, where I grew up. There was also a small sum left to me by my grandfather. I invested everything, together with most of what Devin's paid me over the years, and I've got enough now to buy the ranch outright—which'll leave your dad and Dorothea in good financial shape for their retirement. I'll be able to expand the operation, too."

Kate nodded absently. She hadn't known much about Luke's background, apart from the fact that he had very little family, that he'd lost his parents at an early age. She supposed those losses were the reason he'd been so sympathetic, such a comfort to her and Devin, at the time of Nora's death.

It still seemed too much to take in. Her home—it was going to belong to Luke. He'd move his things from the small foreman's house, though she knew he hadn't accumulated many possessions. But it meant that soon she'd be sorting through and packing up the memories of a lifetime.... She bit her lip.

He knelt in front of her, grasping her fingers with

his warm, hard hands. "I realize you've been through a lot of emotional upheaval lately, but this should help."

"Help!" she wailed. "How could it possibly—?"

"There's no reason for you to be uprooted now."

For a stunned second she didn't react. "I don't have the slightest idea what you're talking about."

"Once we're married, we'll live right here."

"Married!" she almost shouted. "I'm beginning to hate the sound of that word."

"You'd better get used to it, because the way I figure, we're going to be husband and wife before Christmas. We'll let Devin and Dorothea take their vows first—I don't want to steal their thunder—and then we'll wait a couple of weeks and have the Reverend Wilkins marry us."

"Luke, this is all very sweet of you, but *it isn't necessary.*" Kate was convinced that this sudden desire to make her his wife was founded in sympathy. He felt sorry for her because of all the unexpected jolts that had hit her recently. Including this latest one.

"I can't understand why you're arguing with me."

Her hand caressed his jaw. How square and strong it was, and the eyes that gazed at her had never seemed darker or more magnetic. She smiled sadly. "Don't you think it's a little…odd to be discussing marriage when you've never once said you love me?"

"I love you."

It should have been a solemn moment, but Kate couldn't help laughing. "Oh, Luke, that was terrible."

"I'm serious. I love you and you love me."

"Of course we love each other, but what we feel is what *friends* feel. The kind of love brothers and sisters share."

Fire leaped into his eyes, unlike anything she'd seen in him before. With any other man, she would have been frightened—but this was Luke....

"Instead of looking at me as if you're tempted to turn me over your knee, you should be grateful I'm not holding you to your word."

"Kate," he said loudly, "we're getting married." He spoke as though he was daring her to disagree with him.

She lowered her head and brushed his lips with her own. "No, we're not. I'll always be grateful to have a friend as good as you, Luke Rivers. Every woman deserves someone just as kind and thoughtful, but we'd be making the biggest mistake of our lives if we went through with this marriage."

"I don't think that's true."

"I'm sane and rational, and I'm not going to disintegrate under the emotional stress of Clay's wedding or my father's remarriage, or the sale of the ranch. Life goes on—I learned that after my mother died. It sounds so clichéd, but it's the truth. I learned to deal with losing her and I'll do the same with everything else."

"Kate, you don't get it. I *want* to marry you."

"Oh, Luke, it's so nice of you. But you don't love me. Not the way you should. Someday, you'll make some lucky woman a fantastic husband." Kate had grown accustomed to his comfortable presence. But while she felt at ease with him, she experienced none of the thrill, the urgent excitement, that being in love entailed. Well, of course, there was her reaction to Luke's kisses—but that was an aberration, she told herself.

With Clay, the intensity of emotion had wrapped itself around her so securely that she'd been sure it would last a lifetime. Kate hadn't fooled herself into believing

Clay felt as strongly for her. He'd been fond of her, and Kate had been willing to settle for that. But it hadn't been enough for him. And she wasn't allowing Luke to settle for second-best, either.

"People are going to talk, so we both have to do our best to put an end to the rumors."

"I don't intend to do any such thing," Luke said, his jaw rigid. His eyes narrowed. "Kate, darling, a marriage between us is inevitable. The sooner you accept that, the better it'll be for everyone involved."

Four

"The way I figure it," Kate said, munching on a carrot stick, "I'm only going to convince Luke I don't intend to marry him by dating someone else."

Linda looked as if she were about to swallow her apple whole. The two were seated in the school lunchroom on Friday afternoon, reviewing plans for the Thanksgiving play their two classes would present the following month.

"Dating someone else?" Linda echoed, still wearing a stunned expression. "A few days ago you said you were finished with love and completely opposed to the idea of men and marriage."

"I'm not expecting to fall in love again," Kate explained impatiently. "That would be ridiculous."

"You talk about being ridiculous?" Linda asked, setting down her half-eaten apple. "We were discussing Pilgrim costumes and suddenly you decide you want to start dating. I take it you're not referring to Miles Standish?"

"Of course not."

"That's what I thought."

Kate supposed she wasn't making a lot of sense to her friend. Luke and the issue of marriage had been on her mind all week, but she'd carefully avoided any mention of the subject. Until now. The rumors regarding her and Luke continued to burn like a forest fire through Nightingale, aided, Kate was sure, by the silly grin Luke wore around town, and the fact that he was buying her father's ranch. True, he hadn't pressured her into setting a wedding date again, but the thought was there, waiting to ambush her every time they were in the same room. She used to be able to laugh and joke with Luke, but lately, the minute they were together, Kate found herself raising protective barriers.

"All right, you've piqued my curiosity," Linda said, her eyes flashing with humor. "Tell me about this sudden interest in the opposite sex."

"I want to stop the rumors, naturally." And convince Luke that her marriage proposal had been rooted in self-pity. He'd been so strong and she'd felt so fragile....

Linda pushed aside the pages of the Thanksgiving project notes. "Have you picked anyone in particular?"

"No," Kate murmured, frowning. "I've been out of circulation for so long, I'm not sure who's available."

"No one," Linda told her in a despondent voice. "And I should know. If you want the truth, I think Nightingale would make an excellent locale for a convent. Have you ever considered the religious life?"

Kate ignored that. "Didn't I hear Sally Daley mention something about a new guy who recently moved to town? She seemed to think he was single."

"Eric Wilson. Attorney, mid-thirties, divorced, with a small mole on his left shoulder."

Kate was astonished. "Good heavens, how did Sally know all that?"

Linda shook her head. "I don't even want to guess."

"Eric Wilson." Kate repeated it slowly, letting each syllable roll off her tongue. She decided the name had a friendly feel, though it didn't really tell her anything about the man himself.

"Have you met him?" Kate asked her friend.

"No, but you're welcome to him, if you want. My track record with divorced men isn't exactly great. The only reason Sally said anything to me was that she assumed you and Luke would be married before the holidays were over." Linda grimaced. "She thought I'd need her help in finding a date for the wedding."

A sense of panic momentarily overtook Kate. This wedding nonsense was completely out of hand, which meant she had to come up with another man *now*.

"There's always Andy Barrett," she murmured. Andy worked at the pharmacy and was single. True, he wasn't exactly a heartthrob, but he was a decent-enough sort.

Linda immediately rejected that possibility. "No one in town would believe you'd choose Andy over Luke." A smile played across her mouth, as if she found the idea of Kate and Andy together somehow comical. "Andy's sweet, don't get me wrong," Linda amended, "but Luke's a real man."

"I'll think of someone," Kate murmured, her determination fierce.

Linda started to gather her Thanksgiving notes. "If you're serious about this, then you may have no choice but to import a man from Portland."

"You're kidding, I hope," Kate groaned.

"Nope. I'm dead serious," Linda said, shoving everything into her briefcase.

Her friend's words echoed depressingly through Kate's mind as she pushed her cart to the frozen-food section of the grocery store later that afternoon. She peered at the TV dinners, trying to choose something for dinner. Her father had dined with Dorothea every night since they'd become engaged, and the wedding was planned for early December.

"The beef burgundy is good," a resonant male voice said from behind her.

Kate turned to face a tall, friendly-looking man with flashing blue eyes and a lazy smile.

"Eric Wilson," he introduced himself, holding out his hand.

"Kate Logan," she said, her heart racing as they exchanged handshakes. It was all Kate could do not to tell him she'd been talking about him only minutes before and that she'd learned he was possibly the only single prospect in town—other than Luke, of course. How bizarre that they should run into each other almost immediately afterward. Perhaps not! Perhaps it was fate.

"The Salisbury steak isn't half-bad, either." As if to prove his point, he deposited both the beef burgundy and the Salisbury steak frozen dinners in his cart.

"You sound as though you know."

"I've discovered frozen entrécs are less trouble than a wife."

He frowned as he spoke, so she guessed that his divorce had been unpleasant. Sally would be able to provide the details, and Kate made a mental note to ask her. She'd do it blatantly, of course, since Sally would spread Kate's interest in the transplanted lawyer all over the county.

"You're new in town, aren't you? An attorney?"

Eric nodded. "At your service."

Kate was thinking fast. It'd been a long time since she'd flirted with a man—if you didn't count the way she'd behaved at the wedding. "Does that mean I can sue you if the beef burgundy isn't to my liking?"

He grinned at that, and although her comment hadn't been especially witty, she felt encouraged by his smile.

"You might have trouble getting the judge to listen to your suit, though," he told her.

"Judge Webster is my uncle," she said, laughing.

"And I suppose you're his favorite niece."

"Naturally."

"In that case, might I suggest we avoid the possibility of a lawsuit and I buy you dinner?"

That was so easy Kate couldn't believe it. She'd been out of the dating game years, and she'd been sure it would take a while to get the hang of it again. "I'd be delighted."

It wasn't until Kate was home, high on her success, that she realized Eric, as a new man in town, was probably starved for companionship. That made her pride sag just a little, but she wasn't about to complain. Within hours of declaring that she wanted to start dating, she'd met a man. An attractive, pleasant man, too. It didn't matter that he'd asked her out because he was lonely or that he was obviously still embittered by his divorce. A date was a date.

Kate showered and changed into a mid-calf burgundy wool skirt and a rose-colored silk blouse. She was putting the last coat of polish on her nails when her father strolled into the kitchen. Even from her position at the far side of the room, Kate caught a strong whiff of his spicy aftershave. She smiled.

"You look nice, Dad."

"Thanks," he said, tugging on the lapels of his tweed jacket, then brushing the sleeves.

"Do you want me to wait up for you?"

A flush worked its way up Devin's neck. "Of course not."

Kate loved teasing him, and as their eyes met, they both started to laugh.

"You're looking awfully pretty yourself," Devin commented. "Are you and Luke going out?"

"Eric Wilson is taking me to dinner."

Devin regarded her quizzically. "Who? You're kidding, aren't you?"

"No." She gave him a warning frown. "Eric's new here. We met in the frozen-food section at the grocery store this afternoon and he asked me to dinner."

"And you accepted?" His eyes were wide with astonishment.

"Of course. It beats sitting around here and watching reruns on television."

"But…but what about Luke?"

"What about him?"

"I thought… I'd hoped after Clay's wedding that the two of you might —"

"Dad, Luke's a dear friend, but we're not in love with each other."

For a moment Devin looked as if he wanted to argue, but apparently decided against it. "He's a good man, Princess."

"Trust me, I know that. If it wasn't for Luke, I wouldn't have survived the last couple of months."

"Folks in town have the impression that you two might be falling in love, and I can't say I blame them after watching you at the wedding."

Kate focused her attention on polishing her nails, knowing that an identical shade of red had crept into her cheeks.

"Luke and I are friends, Dad, nothing more," she repeated.

"I don't mind letting you know, Kate, that I think very highly of Luke. If I were to handpick a husband for you, it would be him."

"I...think Luke's wonderful, too," she said, her words faltering.

"Now that he's buying the ranch, well, it seems natural that the two of you—"

"Dad, please," she whispered. "I'm not in love with Luke, and he doesn't love me."

"That's a real pity," came Devin's softly drawled response. He reached for his hat, then paused by the door. "I don't suppose Luke knows you're going out tonight, does he?"

"There isn't any reason to tell him." She tried to act nonchalant. But she desperately wanted to avoid another showdown with Luke. Pleadingly, she raised her eyes to her father. "You aren't going to tell him, are you?"

"I won't lie to him."

"Oh, I wouldn't expect you to do that," Kate murmured. She blew at the dark-red polish on her nails, trying to dry them quickly. With luck, Eric would arrive soon and she could make her escape before she encountered Luke.

Kate should have known that was asking too much. She was standing at the kitchen window beside the oak table, waiting for Eric's headlights to come down the long drive, when Luke walked into the house.

Kate groaned inwardly, but said nothing. Her fingers tightened on the curtain as she changed her silent entreaty. Now she prayed that Eric would be late.

"You've got your coat on," Luke observed as he poured a mug of coffee.

"I'll be leaving in a couple of minutes," she said, hoping she didn't sound as tense as she felt. Then, a little guiltily, she added, "I baked some oatmeal cookies yesterday. The cookie jar's full, so help yourself."

He did exactly that, then sat down at the table. "If I didn't know better, I'd think you were waiting for someone."

"I am."

"Who?"

"A...friend." Her back was to him, but Kate could feel the tension between them.

"Are you upset about something?"

"No. Should I be?" she asked in an offhand manner.

"You've been avoiding me all week," he said.

He was sitting almost directly behind her and Kate felt his presence acutely. Her knees were shaking, her breath coming in short, uneven gulps. She felt lightheaded. It had to be nerves. If Luke discovered she was going to dinner with Eric, there could be trouble. Yes, she told herself, that explained the strange physical reaction she was experiencing.

"Kate, love—"

"Please," she implored, "don't call me that." She released the curtain and turned to face him. "I made a mistake, and considering the circumstances, it was understandable. Please, Luke, can't you drop this whole marriage business? Please?"

His look of shocked surprise didn't do anything to settle her nerves. A strained moment passed before Luke relaxed, chuckling. "I've broken stallions who've given me less trouble than you."

"I'm no stallion."

Luke chuckled again, and before she could move, his arms reached out and circled her waist to pull her onto his lap.

Kate was so astonished that for a crazy moment she didn't react at all. "Let me go," she said stiffly, holding her chin at a regal angle.

He ignored her demand and lightly ran the tips of his fingers along the side of her jaw, stroking downward to cup her chin. "I've missed you this week, Princess."

A trail of warmth followed his cool fingers, and a foreign sensation nibbled at her stomach. Kate didn't know what was wrong with her—and she didn't *want* to know.

"I've decided to give you a chance to think everything through before we contact Pastor Wilkins—"

"Before we what?" she flared.

"Before we're married," he explained patiently, his voice much too low and seductive to suit her. "But every time we're together, you run away like a frightened kitten."

"Did you stop to think there might be a perfectly logical reason for that?" She'd told him repeatedly that she wasn't going to marry him, but it didn't seem to make any differences. "I'm sorry, I truly am, but I just don't see you that way."

"Oh?"

He raised his hand and threaded his fingers through her hair. She tried to pull away, to thwart him, with no effect.

"That's not the feeling I get when I kiss you."

She braced her hands against his shoulders. "I apologize if I've given you the wrong impression," she said, her voice feeble.

He cocked his eyebrows at her statement, and his lips quivered with the effort to suppress a smile. That infuriated Kate, but she held on to her temper, knowing an argument would be pointless.

"It seems to me," he continued, "that we need some time alone to explore what's happening between us."

Alarm rose in Kate's throat as she struggled to hide her response to him. The last thing she wanted was "time alone" with Luke.

"I'm afraid that's impossible tonight," she said hastily.

"Why's that?"

He was so close that his breath fanned her flushed face. It was all Kate could do to keep from closing her eyes and surrendering to the sensations that encircled her, like lazy curls of smoke from a campfire.

His mouth found her neck and he placed a series of kisses there, each one a small dart of pleasure that robbed her of clear thought. For a wild moment, she couldn't catch her breath. His hands were in her hair, and his mouth was working its magic....

"No," she breathed, her voice low and trembling. Any resistance she'd managed to rally had vanished.

"Yes, my darlin', Kate?"

He sought her mouth then, and excitement erupted

inside her. She clung to him, arms around his neck as his lips returned again and again to taste and tantalize her.

When he buried his face in the hollow of her throat, Kate moaned softly. She felt nearly faint from the rush of pleasure.

"Call Linda and cancel whatever plans you've made," he whispered.

Kate froze. "I can't."

"Yes, you can. I'll talk to her, if you want."

"I'm not going out with Linda."

"Then call whoever it is and cancel."

"No..."

A flash of headlights through the kitchen window announced Eric's arrival. With a burst of frantic energy, Kate leaped off Luke's lap, feeling disoriented and bewildered. She rubbed her hands over her face, realizing she'd probably smudged her makeup, but that didn't concern her as much as the unreserved way she'd submitted to Luke's touch. He'd kissed her before and it had been wonderful—more than wonderful. But in those brief moments when he'd held her, at the wedding and then again the next day, she hadn't experienced this burning *need.* It terrified her.

"Kate?"

She looked at Luke without really seeing him. "I've got to go," she insisted.

"There's a man here."

Kate opened the door for Eric. "Hi," she greeted him, doing her best to appear cheerful and animated, but suspecting that she looked and sounded as though she was coming down with a bad case of flu. "I see you found the place without a problem."

"Actually, I had one hell of a time," he said, glancing at his watch. "Didn't you notice I'm fifteen minutes late?"

Well, no, she hadn't. Not really.

"Kate, who is this man?" Luke demanded in a steely voice.

"Eric Wilson, this is Luke Rivers. Luke is buying the Circle L," she said breathlessly.

The two men exchanged the briefest of handshakes.

Kate didn't dare look in Luke's direction. She didn't need to; she could feel the resentment and annoyance that emanated from him like waves of heat. "Well, I suppose we should be on our way," Kate said to Eric, throwing him a tight, nervous smile.

"Yes, I suppose we should." Eric's gaze traveled from Kate to Luke, then back again. He seemed equally eager to escape.

"I'll say good-night, Luke," she said pointedly, her hand on the back door.

He didn't respond, which was just as well.

Once they were outside, Eric opened his car door for her. "You said Luke is buying the ranch?"

"Yes," she answered brightly.

"And nothing else?" he pressed, frowning. "The look he was giving me seemed to say you came with the property."

"That's not true." Even if Luke chose to believe otherwise. After tonight, she couldn't deny that they shared a strong physical attraction, but that was nothing on which to base a life together. She didn't *love* Luke; how could she, when she was still in love with Clay? She'd been crazy about Clay Franklin most of her life, and feelings that intense didn't change overnight simply because he'd married another woman.

When Clay and Rorie had announced their engagement, Kate had known with desolate certainty that she'd never love again. If she couldn't have Clay, then she would live the remainder of her life alone, treasuring the time they'd had together.

"You're absolutely certain Rivers has no claim on you?"

"None," Kate assured him.

"That's funny," Eric said with a humorless chuckle. "From the way he glared at me, I feel lucky to have walked away with my head still attached."

Kate forced a laugh. "I'm sure you're mistaken."

Eric didn't comment further, but she could tell he didn't believe her.

After their shaky beginning, dinner turned out to be a pleasant affair. Eric took Kate to the Red Bull, the one fancy restaurant in Nightingale, a steak house that specialized in thick T-bones and fat baked potatoes. A country-and-western band played local favorites in the lounge, which was a popular Friday-night attraction. The music drifted into the dining-room, creating a festive atmosphere.

Eric studied the menu, then requested a bottle of wine with their meal.

When the waitress had taken their order, he placed his elbows on the table and smiled at Kate. "Your eyes are lovely," he said, his voice a little too enthusiastic.

Despite herself, Kate blushed. "Thank you."

"They're the same color as my ex-wife's." He said this in bitter tones, as if he wished Kate's were any color other than blue. "I'm sorry," he added, looking chagrined. "I've got to stop thinking about Lonni. It's over. Finished. Kaput."

"I take it you didn't want the divorce."

"Do you mind if we don't talk about it?"

Kate felt foolish for bringing up the subject, especially since it was obviously so painful for him. "I'm sorry, that was thoughtless. You're trying to let go of the past."

The bottle of wine arrived and when Eric had sampled and approved it the waitress filled their glasses.

"Actually you remind me of Lonni," he said, after taking a sip of the chardonnay. "We met when we were both in college."

Kate looked down at her wineglass, twirling the delicate stem between her fingers. Eric was so clearly in love with his ex-wife that she wondered what had torn them apart.

"You were asking about the divorce?" He replenished his wine with a lavish hand.

"If it's too difficult, you don't need to talk about it."

"I don't think either Lonni or I ever intended to let it go this far," he said, and Kate was sure he hadn't even heard her. "I certainly didn't, but before I knew what was happening, the whole thing blew up in my face. There wasn't another man—I would've staked my life on that."

Their dinner salads were served and, picking up her fork, Kate asked, "What brought you to Nightingale?"

Eric drank his wine as if he were gulping cool water on a summer afternoon. "Lonni, of course."

"I beg your pardon?"

"Lonni. I decided I needed to make a clean break. Get a fresh start and all that."

"I see."

"You have to understand that when Lonni first suggested we should separate, I thought it was the right thing to do. We hadn't been getting along and, frankly, if she wanted out of the relationship, I wasn't going to stand in her way. It's best to discover these things before you have children, don't you agree?"

"Oh, yes." Kate nibbled at her salad, wondering what she could say that would help or comfort Eric.

An hour and another bottle of wine later, Kate realized he'd drunk the better part of both bottles and was in no condition to drive home. Now she had to tactfully make *him* realize that.

"Do you dance?" she asked, as he paid the dinner bill.

He frowned slightly. "This country-and-western stuff doesn't usually appeal to me, but I'm willing to give it a whirl, if you are."

Kate assumed all the wine he'd been drinking had quelled his reservations. When the band began a lively melody, Eric led Kate onto the crowded dance floor.

Kate was breathless by the time the song ended. To her relief, the next number was a much slower one. She recognized her mistake the minute Eric locked her in his embrace. His hands fastened at the small of her back, forcing her close. She tried to put some space between them, but Eric didn't seem to notice her efforts. His eyes were shut as he swayed to the leisurely beat. Kate wasn't fooled; her newfound friend was pretending he had Lonni in his arms. It was a good thing her ego wasn't riding on this date.

"I need a little more room," she whispered.

He loosened his grip for a moment, but as the song

continued, his hold gradually tightened again. Kate edged her forearms up and braced them on his chest, easing herself back an inch or two.

"Excuse me, please." A harsh male voice that was all too familiar came from behind Eric. Kate wished she could crawl into a hole and die the instant she heard it.

"I'm cutting in," Luke informed the other man, who turned his head and looked at the intruder incredulously.

Without a word of protest Eric dropped his arms and took a step in retreat. Neither man bothered to ask Kate what *she* wanted. She was about to complain when Luke reached for her hand and with a natural flair swept her into his arms. The immediate sense of welcome she experienced made her want to weep with frustration.

"Why did you cut in like that?" she demanded. She felt disheartened and irritable. Everything she'd worked for this evening was about to be undone.

"Did you mean for that city slicker to hold you so close?"

"How Eric holds me isn't any of your business."

"I'm making it my business."

His face was contorted with anger. His arms were so tight that Kate couldn't have escaped him if she'd tried. Judging by the looks they were receiving from the couples around them, they were quickly becoming the main attraction.

The instant the music ended, Kate abruptly left Luke's arms and returned to Eric. Her date stood in the corner of the room, nursing a shot glass filled with amber liquid. Kate groaned and hid her displeasure. Eric had already had enough wine without adding hard liquor.

"I thought you said there was nothing between you and Luke Rivers," he muttered, when she joined him.

"There isn't. We're just good friends."

"That's not the impression I'm getting."

Kate didn't know how to respond. "I apologize for the interruption. Do you want to dance?"

"Not if it's going to cost me my neck."

"It isn't," she promised.

Another lively song erupted from the band. Eric took her hand and she smiled encouragingly up at him. As they headed for the dance floor, Kate tried to ignore Luke's chilly glare.

Midway through the song, Eric stopped dancing. "I'm not very good at this fancy footwork," he declared. With that, he pulled her into his arms, tucking her securely against him.

"This is much better," he whispered, his mouth close to her ear. Once more his hold tightened.

"Eric, please. I'm having trouble breathing," Kate told him in a strangled voice.

"Oh, sorry." He relaxed his grip. "Lonni and I used to dance like this all the time."

Kate had guessed as much. It was on the tip of her tongue to remind him that she wasn't his ex-wife, but she doubted it would make any difference. Eric had spent much of the evening pretending she was.

At the moment, however, her date and his ex-wife were the least of Kate's problems. Tiny pinpricks moved up and down her spine, telling her that Luke was still glaring at her from the other side of the room. She did her best to act as though he wasn't there.

She smiled up at Eric, she laughed, she talked, but

with each breath she drew she could feel Luke's eyes on her, scrutinizing every move she made.

When the music stopped, Eric returned to their table and his drink, swallowing the remainder of it in one gulp. The music started again and he pulled Kate toward him.

"I think I'll sit this one out." She hoped that would appease Luke, who looked as if he were about to rip Eric in two.

Her gaze fell to her lap and she folded her hands, concentrating on not letting him know how much a single glance from him affected her.

"How much have you had to drink, Wilson?"

While her eyes were lowered, Luke had come over to their table. His voice was controlled but unmistakably furious.

"I can't say that's any of your concern, Rivers." For his part, Eric seemed nervous. He leaned back in his chair, balancing on two legs, and raised his empty shot glass.

"I don't agree," Luke countered, moving closer. "From what I can see, you've had plenty. I'm taking Kate home with me."

"Luke," she protested, "please don't do this."

"Your date's in no condition to drive."

It was all Kate could do not to stand up and defend Eric. Unfortunately Luke was right. She'd known it even before they'd finished dinner, but she wanted to handle things her own way.

"I can hold my liquor as well as the next man," Eric said, daring to wave his glass under Luke's nose. It was apparent to everyone that his courage had been fortified by whiskey. Few men would have taunted Luke in his present mood.

Luke turned to Kate. "You've got better sense than this, Kate."

Kate did. But she had no intention of telling him so. "I think Eric knows his own limit," she returned.

"Then you plan to ride home with him?"

"I'm not sure yet." She wouldn't, but she wasn't about to give Luke an armful of ammunition to use against her.

Luke scowled at her with such fury it was difficult for Kate to swallow normally.

Slowly he turned to Eric. "If you value your teeth, I suggest you stay exactly where you are. Bob," Luke called to the sheriff's deputy across the room, "would you see that this newcomer gets home without a problem?"

"Sure thing, Luke."

"Kate," he said, addressing her next, "you're coming with me."

"I most certainly am not."

Luke didn't leave her any option. He leaned forward and pulled her upright, as if she weighed no more than a bag of popcorn.

She struggled briefly but knew it was useless. "Luke, don't do this. Please, don't do this," she pleaded through clenched teeth, humiliated to the very roots of her hair.

"Either you come with me willingly or I carry you out of here." Luke's composure didn't falter. When she resisted, he swept his arms behind her legs and lifted her from the floor.

"Luke," Kate cried, "put me down this instant. I *demand* that you put me down."

He completely ignored her threat as he strode toward the door, his gaze focused impassively ahead of them. The waitress who'd served her dinner came running up to hand Kate her coat and bag. Her eyes were flashing with humor.

"Stick by your man, honey," she advised. "That city slicker can't hold a candle to Luke Rivers."

"Luke's the man for you," someone else shouted.

"When you gonna tie the knot?"

Two men were holding open the lounge door for them. The last thing Kate heard as Luke carried her into the cold night air was a robust round of applause from inside the lounge.

Five

"I have never been so embarrassed in my life," Kate stormed as Luke parked his pickup outside the house. "How could you *do* that to me? How could you?"

During the entire ride home, Luke hadn't spoken a word, nor had he even glanced at her. He'd held himself stiff, staring straight ahead. For all his concern about her riding with Eric, he drove as if the very devil were on their tail. Only when they entered the long, winding drive that led to the house had he reduced his speed.

"I'll never forgive you for this," she told him, grabbing the door handle and vaulting out of the truck. She couldn't get away from him fast enough. By morning every tongue in Nightingale would be wagging, telling how Luke Rivers had hauled Kate Logan out of the Red Bull.

To her dismay Luke followed her into the house.

"I couldn't care less if you forgive me or not," he said darkly.

"The women were laughing and the men snickering.... I won't be able to show my face in this town again."

"As far as I'm concerned, the problem is one of your own making."

"That's not true!" She'd had no way of knowing that Eric was going to start downing wine like soda pop. And she did *not* need a lecture from Luke Rivers. All she wanted him to do was leave, so she could lick her wounds in private and figure out how long it would be before she dared go out in public again.

Luke started pacing the kitchen floor. Each step was measured and precise. Clipped, like his voice.

"Please go," she beseeched wearily.

"I'm not leaving until I get some answers from you."

Gathering what remained of her dignity, which at this point wasn't much, Kate sank onto a chair. She wouldn't argue with Luke. Every time she tried, she came out the loser. Better to get this over with now rather than wait for morning. She sighed deeply.

"Who the hell is Eric Wilson and why were you having dinner with him?" Luke's heavy boots clicked against the kitchen floor as he paced.

Instead of answering, Kate asked, "What's happened to us?" She gazed sorrowfully up at Luke. "Do you remember how much fun we used to have together? Tonight wasn't fun, Luke. Just a few weeks ago I could laugh with you and cry with you. You were my friend and I was yours. Suddenly nothing's the same, and I don't understand why." Her voice quavered slightly. She fought an overwhelming desire to hide her face in her hands and weep.

She didn't win. Tears of pride and anguish spilled on to her cheeks. She brought her hands up, trying to hide her distress.

Luke knelt in front of her and pried her hands away.

His fingers tenderly caressed her face. "Everything has changed, hasn't it, Princess?"

She sucked in a shaky breath and nodded.

"You're confused, aren't you?" His hands cradled her face and he eased forward to press his warm mouth over hers. Even as she kissed him back, her confusion grew. He'd been so angry with her, more furious than she'd ever seen him. Yet, when he kissed her, he was achingly gentle.

Luke seemed to believe that her ready response to his kiss would answer the questions that haunted her. Instead it raised *more* questions, more qualms.

"Do you understand now?" he asked, his voice a husky murmur, his eyes closed.

How Kate wished she did. She shook her head, bewildered and still uncertain.

Luke stroked her lips with his index finger. His most innocent touches brought her nerves to life with a prickling, wary excitement. Refusing to think about her own impulse, she held his hand to her mouth and brushed her lips across his callused fingertips.

"Oh, love," he moaned, and bent forward, caressing her mouth with his once more. "We've got to put an end to this madness before I go insane."

"How?" she gasped, as she braced her hands against his broad chest. He felt so good, hard muscle and warm flesh, and so strong, as if nothing could stand in his way once he determined a course. Not heaven. Not hell. And not anything in between.

"How?" He repeated her question, then chuckled, the sound rumbling from deep within his chest. "We'll have to do what you suggested."

"What I suggested?"

His mouth continued to tease hers with a series of small, nibbling kisses that seemed to pluck at her soul. "There's only one way to cure what's between us, Kate."

"One way," she echoed weakly.

"You'll have to marry me. There's no help for it and, considering how I feel right now, the sooner the better."

Kate felt as if he'd dumped a bucket of ice water over her head. "Marry you," she shrieked, pushing him away so quickly that he nearly toppled backward. "Your answer to all this confusion is for us to get married?"

"Kate, don't be unreasonable. We're perfect for each other. You need me now more than at any time in your life and I'm here for you."

"Luke, please—"

"No." He stopped her with a look. "You're about to lose everything in life that you thought was secure— your father and your home. I don't have any intention of taking over Devin's role, but the way I figure it, I'd make you a decent husband."

"What about *love?*" Kate cried.

Luke sighed in frustration. "We've gone over that ten times. You already love me—"

"Like a brother."

"Princess, sisters don't kiss their brothers the way you just kissed me."

He apparently believed that was argument enough. Not knowing how else to respond, she shook her head. "I love Clay! You keep ignoring that or insisting I don't —but I do. I have for as long as I can remember. I can't marry you. I won't!"

"For heaven's sake, forget Clay."

"It's not so easy!" she shouted.

"It would be if you'd try a little harder," Luke muttered, obviously losing patience. "I'm asking you to marry me, Kate Logan, and a smart woman like you should know a good offer when she hears one."

So much for love. So much for romance. Luke wasn't even listening to her, and Kate doubted he'd understood a single thing she'd said. "This conversation isn't getting us anywhere."

"Kate—"

"I think you should leave."

"Kate," he said, firmly gripping her shoulders, "how long is it going to take you to realize that I love you and you love me?"

"Love you? How can you say that? Until a few weeks ago I was engaged to marry Clay Franklin!" Angrily she pushed away his hands and sprang to her feet.

"Yes. And all that time you were going to marry the wrong man."

Luke didn't seem to find that statement the least bit odd, as if women regularly chose to marry one man when they were really in love with another. Kate shook her head, releasing a harsh breath.

"It's the truth," he said calmly.

She glared at him. Reasoning with Luke was a waste of time. He repeated the same nonsensical statements over and over, as if his few words were explanation enough.

"I'm going to bed," she said, turning abruptly away from him. "You can do as you like."

A moment of stunned silence followed her words before he chuckled softly, seductively. "I'm sure you don't mean that the way it sounds."

As Kate expected, the small community buzzed with the news of her fiasco with Eric Wilson. Neighbor delighted in telling neighbor how Luke Rivers had swooped her into his arms and how the entire Friday-night crowd at the Red Bull had cheered as he'd carried her off the dance floor.

Kate needed every ounce of courage she possessed just to walk down Main Street. Her smile felt stiff and false and she was convinced she had the beginnings of an ulcer.

To worsen matters, all the townsfolk seemed to believe it was their place to offer her free advice.

"You stick with Luke Rivers. He's a far better man than that city slicker," the butcher told her Saturday afternoon.

Blushing heatedly, she ordered a pork roast and left as soon as she'd paid.

"I understand you and Luke Rivers caused quite a ruckus the other night at the steak house," the church secretary said Sunday morning after the service. "I heard about the romantic way Luke carried you outside."

Kate hadn't found being carried off the least bit romantic but she smiled kindly, made no comment and returned home without a word.

"What's this I hear about you and Luke Rivers?" The moment Kate entered her classroom Monday morning, Sally Daley appeared.

"Whatever you heard, I'm sure it was vastly exaggerated," Kate said hurriedly.

"That could be," Sally admitted with a delicate laugh. "You certainly know how to keep this town talking. First Clay's wedding reception, and now this. By the way, Clay and Rorie are back from Hawaii, and I heard they both have marvelous tans."

"That often happens in Hawaii," Kate said, sarcastically, barely holding on to her composure.

No sooner had Sally left than Linda showed up. "Is it true?" she demanded, her eyes as round as quarters.

Kate shrugged. "Probably."

"Oh, good grief, the whole thing about squelching rumors backfired, didn't it?"

Miserably Kate nodded. She was afraid she'd dissolve in a puddle of tears the next time someone mentioned Luke's name. "After what happened to me Friday night, well... I just don't think it's possible to feel any more humiliated."

"I thought you said you hadn't met Eric," Linda said, clearly puzzled.

"I hadn't when you and I talked. Eric and I ran into each other at the grocery not ten minutes after you mentioned his name."

Linda slumped against the side of Kate's desk. "I try for months to meet a new man and nothing happens. It doesn't make sense. A few minutes after you decide to look, one pops up in front of you like a bird in a turkey shoot!"

"Beginner's luck." Except that Friday night could in no way be classified as lucky.

"Oh, Kate, you've really done it now."

"I know," she whispered in a tone of defeat.

Kate's day ended much as it had begun, which meant that by four o'clock she had a headache to rival all headaches. After school, she stopped at the pharmacy and bought a bottle of double-strength aspirin and some antacid tablets.

When she left the pharmacy, she headed for the library, wondering if Rorie would be back at work so soon after her honeymoon. Her friend's smiling face greeted Kate the instant she walked through the doors.

"Kate, it's so good to see you."

"Hi, Rorie." Kate still felt a little awkward with Clay's bride. She suffered no regrets about bringing them together, though it had been the most painful decision of her life.

"Sally Daley's right," Kate said with a light laugh as she kissed Rorie's cheek. "You're so tanned. You look wonderful."

Rorie accepted the praise with a smile that shone from her dark brown eyes. "To be honest, I never thought I'd get Clay to laze away seven whole days on the beach, but he did. Oh, Kate, we had the most wonderful time."

"I'm glad." And she was. Rorie radiated happiness, and the glow of it warmed Kate's numb heart.

"I was just about to go on my coffee break. Have you got time to join me?" Rorie invited, glancing at her watch.

"I'd love to." Kate crossed her fingers. She hoped Rorie hadn't heard any of the gossip—no doubt colorfully embroidered by now—about what had happened Friday night. At the moment, Kate needed a friend, a good friend, someone she could trust to be objective.

While Rorie arranged to leave the library in the hands of a volunteer assistant, Kate walked over to Nellie's Café, across the street from the pharmacy. She'd already ordered their coffee when Rorie slipped into the red upholstered booth across from her.

"What's this I've been hearing all day about you and Luke? Honestly, Kate, you know how to live dangerously, don't you? And now Luke's buying the Circle L and your father's marrying Mrs. Murphy. We were only gone seven days, but I swear it felt like a year with everything Mary had to tell us once we got home."

Kate tried to maintain a stoic expression, although the acid in her stomach seemed to be burning a hole straight through her. There were no secrets in this town.

"To tell you the truth, Luke and I haven't been getting along very well lately," she admitted, keeping her eyes lowered so as not to meet her friend's questioning gaze.

Rorie took a tentative sip of coffee. "Do you want to talk about it?"

Kate nodded. She felt embarrassingly close to tears and paid careful attention to the silverware, repositioning the fork and the spoon several times.

"Luke was so good to me after you and Clay became engaged. He couldn't have been a better friend. Then… after the wedding I was feeling lost and alone. Luke had been dancing with me and I felt so…secure in his arms, and I'm afraid I suggested something foolish…. And now Luke keeps reminding me of it."

"That doesn't sound like Luke." Rorie frowned in puzzlement. "Nor does suggesting 'something foolish' sound like you."

"I had a glass of champagne on an empty stomach," Kate offered as an excuse.

"What about Luke?"

"I don't know, but I swear, he's become so unreasonable about everything, and he keeps saying the most ridiculous things."

"Give me an example," Rorie said.

Kate shrugged. "He claims I love him."

Her remark was followed by a short silence. "What *do* you feel for Luke?" Rorie asked.

"I care about him, but not in the way he assumes." Her finger idly circled the rim of the coffee cup while she composed her thoughts. "What irritates me most is that Luke discounts everything I felt for Clay, as if my love for him was nothing more than wasted emotion." Kate felt awkward explaining this to her ex-fiancé's wife, but Rorie was the one person who'd understand.

"And now that Clay's married to me," Rorie said, "Luke seems to think some lightbulb has snapped on inside your brain."

"Exactly."

"He thinks you should have no hesitation about throwing yourself into *his* loving arms?"

"Yes!" Rorie explained it far better than Kate had. "He keeps insisting I need him and that if I thought about it I'd realize I do love him. If it was only Luke I could probably deal with it, but everyone in town, including my own father, thinks I should marry him, too."

"That's when you agreed to have dinner with that new attorney. What's his name again?"

"Eric Wilson. Yes, that was exactly the reason I went out with him. Rorie, I tell you I was desperate. Every time I turned around, Luke was there wearing this smug, knowing look and casually announcing that we'd be married before Christmas. He makes the whole thing sound like it's a foregone conclusion and if I resist him I'd be…going against nature or something." She paused and waved her hand dramatically.

Rorie laughed. "Is he really doing that?"

Kate nodded grimly. "Actually there's more." She felt she had to tell Rorie everything. "To be fair, you should know I have no one to blame but myself. Luke may be doing all this talking about us getting married. But I was the one who…suggested it."

"How? When? Oh. The 'something foolish' you mentioned."

Shredding the paper napkin into tiny strips, Kate nodded again, flinching at the memory. "Honestly, Rorie, I didn't mean it. We were standing in the moonlight at your wedding dance and everything was so serene and beautiful. The words just slipped out of my mouth before I stopped to think what I was saying."

"The incident with the attorney didn't help."

Kate sighed. "And now that Dad's marrying Mrs. Murphy and Luke's bought the ranch, everything's getting worse."

"Luke can be a bit overpowering at times, can't he?"

Kate rolled her eyes in agreement. "But you know, what bothers me even more than Luke's cavalier attitude is the way everyone else seems to be siding with him."

"You mean about marrying Luke?"

"Yes." Kate gave another forlorn sigh. "Look at my dad—he's the perfect example. And everyone in town seems to think that if I'm foolish enough to let another good man slip through my fingers, I'll end up thirty and a spinster for sure."

"That's crazy!"

Coming from San Francisco, Rorie couldn't understand how differently people in this small Oregon community viewed life, Kate mused. A woman already thirty years old and unmarried was likely to stay that way—at least in Nightingale. "You haven't lived here long enough to know how folks in this town think."

"Kate, you're over twenty-one. No one can force you to marry Luke. Remember that."

Kate rested her elbows on the table and cradled her coffee cup in both hands. "I feel like I'm caught in a current that's flowing too fast for me. I'm afraid to stand up for fear I'll lose my footing but I can't just allow it to carry me where it will, either."

"No, you can't," Rorie said and her mouth tightened.

"Luke—and practically everyone else—apparently sees me as a poor, spineless soul who can't possibly decide what's best for her own life."

"That's not true at all," Rorie declared. "And don't let anyone tell you you're weak! If that was the case, you would have married Clay yourself, instead of working so hard to make sure we found each other."

Kate dismissed that with a shake of her head. "I did the only thing I could."

"But not everyone would've been so unselfish. Clay and I owe our happiness to you." She clasped Kate's hands with her own. "I wish I knew how to help you. All I can tell you is to listen to your own heart."

"Oh, Rorie, I feel so much better talking to you." She knew her friend was right. She'd faltered for a step or two, but considering everything that had happened in the past little while, that was understandable. Luke might believe she needed him, but she didn't, not really. In the weeks to come, she'd have the opportunity to prove it.

"Before I forget," Rorie said, her voice eager, "Clay and I want to invite you over for dinner one night soon. As I said, we feel deeply indebted to you and want to thank you for what you did."

"Dinner," Kate repeated, suddenly dismayed. She'd

need time to prepare herself before facing Clay again. Here she was reassuring herself in one breath and then doubting herself in the next.

"Would next Tuesday be all right?" Rorie pressed.

"But you've hardly had time to settle in with Clay," Kate said, turning her attention back to her friend. "How about giving it another week or two?"

"Are you worried that I'm going to serve my special seafood fettuccine?" Rorie asked with a laugh. When she'd first been stranded in Nightingale, Rorie had cooked it for Clay and his younger brother, Skip, one night. But, unfortunately, because both men did strenuous physical jobs, they were far more interested in a hearty meat-and-potatoes meal at the end of the day. Neither of them had considered seafood in a cream sauce with fancy noodles a very satisfactory repast, though Clay had politely tried to hide his disappointment. Skip hadn't.

Kate smiled at the memory of that night and slowly shook her head. "You serve whatever you want. I'm much easier to please than Skip."

"Actually Mary will probably do the cooking. She's been the Franklins' housekeeper for so many years that I don't dare invade her kitchen just yet. After the fettuccine disaster, she doesn't trust me around her stove any more than Skip does."

They both laughed, and to Kate, it felt good to forget her troubles, even for a few minutes.

"I should get back to the library," Rorie said reluctantly.

"I need to head home myself." Kate left some change on the table and slid out of the booth. Impulsively she hugged Rorie, grateful for the time they'd spent together and for the other woman's support. "I'm glad you're my friend," she whispered, feeling a little self-conscious.

"I am, too," Rorie said, and hugged her back.

By the time Kate pulled into the Circle L driveway, she was filled with bold resolution. She hurried inside just long enough to set a roast in the oven and change her clothes. Then she went into the yard, intent on confronting Luke. She wanted to get this over with—as soon as possible.

As luck would have it, Luke wasn't in any of the places she normally found him. Bill Schmidt, a long-time ranch hand, was working in the barn by himself.

"Bill, have you seen Luke?" she asked.

Bill straightened and set his hat farther back on his head. "Can't say I have. At least, not in the past couple of hours. Said he was going out to look for strays. I imagine he'll be back pretty soon now."

"I see." Kate gnawed her lower lip, wondering what she should do. Without pausing to question the wisdom of her decision, she reached for a bridle.

"Bill, would you get Nonstop for me?" Nonstop was the fastest horse in their stable. Kate was in the mood for some exercise; if she didn't find Luke, that was fine, too. She could use a good hard ride to vent some of the frustration that had been binding her all week.

"Sure, Miz Logan." Bill left his task and headed for the corral, returning a few minutes later with Nonstop. "Luke seemed to be in the mood to do some riding himself this afternoon," he commented as he helped her cinch the saddle. "Must be the weather."

"Must be," Kate agreed.

Minutes later Nonstop was cantering out of the yard.

Kate hadn't ridden in weeks and she was surprised to realize just how long it had been. When she was engaged to Clay, she'd spent many a summer afternoon in the saddle, many a Saturday or Sunday riding by his side. That had ended about the same time as their wedding plans. She felt a stinging sense of loss but managed to dispel it with the memory of her talk with Rorie.

Bill pointed out the general direction Luke had taken, and Kate followed that course at a gallop. She found it wonderfully invigorating to be in the saddle again.

The afternoon remained mild, but the breeze carried the distinctive scent of autumn. These past few days had been like summer, with rare clement temperatures. Within the hour, the sun would set, bathing the rolling green hills in a golden haze.

"Kate." Her name floated on a whisper of wind.

Pulling back on the reins, Kate halted the mare and turned in the saddle to discover Luke trotting toward her. She raised her hand and waved. Much of her irritation had dissipated, replaced by a newly awakened sense of well-being. No longer did Kate feel her life was roaring out of control; she was in charge, and it exhilarated her.

Luke dismounted as soon as he reached her. "Is everything all right?"

"Of course," she said with a slight laugh. "I hope I didn't frighten you."

"No. I rode into the yard not more than fifteen minutes after you left, according to Bill. I was afraid I wasn't going to catch you. You were riding like a demon."

"I…had some thinking to do."

"Bill said you were looking for me."

"Yes," she agreed. "I wanted to talk to you." There

was no better time than the present. And no better place. They were at the top of a grassy hill that looked out over a lush green valley. Several head of cattle dotted the pasture spread out below them, grazing in the last of the afternoon sun.

Luke lifted his hands to her waist, helping her out of the saddle. His eyes held hers as he lowered her to the ground. Once again, she was aware that his touch had a curious effect on her, but she stringently ignored it.

Still, Kate's knees felt a little shaky and she was more breathless than she should've been after her ride. She watched Luke loop the reins over the horses' heads to dangle on the ground. Both Nonstop and Silver Shadow, Luke's gelding, were content to graze leisurely.

"It's nice out this afternoon, isn't it?" she said, then sank down on the grass and drew up her legs.

Luke sat down beside her, gazing out over the valley. "It's a rare day. I don't expect many more like it."

"Rorie and Clay are back from Hawaii."

Luke had removed his leather work gloves to brush a stray curl from her temple, then stopped abruptly and withdrew his hand. "I take it you saw Rorie?"

She nodded, adding, "We had coffee at Nellie's."

"You're not upset?"

"Not at all."

"I thought you looked more at peace with yourself." He leaned back and rested his weight on the palms of his hands. His long legs were stretched in front of him, crossed at the ankles. "Did you finally recognize that you never did love Clay? That you're in love with me?"

"No," she said vehemently, amazed he could anger her so quickly.

Luke turned away. "I thought… I'd hoped you were willing to discuss a wedding date," he said stiffly.

"Oh, Luke," she whispered and closed her eyes. He was so worried for her, so concerned, and she didn't know how to reassure him.

"Luke," she said softly, "we've been having the same discussion all week, and it's got to come to an end." Luke faced her and their eyes met with an impact that shocked her. "Luke, I think you're a wonderful man—I have for years and years," she continued. "But I don't love you, at least not the way you deserve to be loved."

Luke's eyebrows soared, then his brow furrowed. He seemed about to argue, but Kate stopped him before he had the chance.

"I refuse to be coerced into a wedding simply because *you* feel it's the best thing for me—because you feel I need looking after. Frankly, I don't believe marriage is a good idea for us—at least not to each other."

"Kate, love—"

Lowering her lashes in an effort to disguise her frustration, Kate reminded him for what seemed the thousandth time, "I am not your 'love.'"

His eyes became sharper, more intent. "Then explain," he said slowly, "why it feels so right when I hold you? How do you answer that?"

She avoided his gaze, her eyes focusing a fraction below his. "I can't explain it any more than I can deny it." She'd admit that much. "I do enjoy it when you kiss me, though I don't know why, especially since I'm still in love with Clay. My guess is that we've lived all these years in close proximity and we're such good friends that it was a natural, comforting, thing to do. But I don't think it should continue."

His nostrils flared briefly, and she could tell he was angered by her words.

"I'm begging you, Luke, pleading with you, if you—"

"Kate, would you listen to me for once?"

"No," she said, holding her ground. "I'm asking for only one thing from you. I want you to drop this incessant pressure to marry you."

"But—"

"Give me your word, Luke."

His entire expression changed, and just looking at him told Kate how difficult he was finding this. "All right," he said heavily. "You have my word. I won't mention it again."

Kate sighed shakily and all her muscles seemed to go limp. "Thank you," she whispered. "That's all I want."

Luke lunged to his feet and reached for Silver Shadow's reins. He eased himself back into the saddle, then paused to look down at her, his face dark and brooding. "What about what *I* want, Kate? Did you stop to consider that?"

Six

Kate felt good. The lethargy and depression she'd been feeling since Clay's wedding had started to dissipate. She'd completely adjusted to the idea of her father's impending marriage. And even the sale of the Circle L—to Luke of all people—no longer seemed so devastating. Clearing the air between them had helped, too.

"Evening, Nellie," Kate called as she entered the small, homey café. She'd arrived home from school to discover a message from her father suggesting she meet him for dinner at Nellie's at six sharp.

"Howdy, Kate," Nellie called from behind the counter.

Kate assumed her father would be bringing Dorothea so they could discuss last-minute plans for their wedding, which was scheduled for Friday evening at the parsonage. Minnie Wilkins, Pastor Wilkins's wife, and Dorothea were close friends. Kate would be standing up for Dorothea and Luke for her father in the small, private ceremony.

Carrying a water glass in one hand, a coffeepot in the other and a menu tucked under her arm, Nellie followed Kate to the booth. "I'm expecting my dad and Dorothea Murphy to join me," Kate explained.

"Sure thing," Nellie said. "The special tonight is Yankee pot roast, and when your daddy gets here, you tell him I pulled a rhubarb pie out of the oven no more than fifteen minutes ago."

"I'll tell him."

"Nellie, I could use a refill on my coffee," Fred Garner said. Sitting at the table closest to the window, he nodded politely in Kate's direction. "Good to see you, Kate."

"You, too, Fred." She smiled at the owner of Garner Feed and Supply and the two ranchers who were dining with him. Glancing at her watch, Kate realized her father was a few minutes late, which wasn't like him.

To pass the time she began reading the menu; she was halfway through when the door opened. Smiling automatically, she looked up and saw Luke striding toward her. He slid into the booth across from her.

"Where's your dad?"

"I don't know. He asked me to meet him here for dinner."

"I got the same message."

"I think it has something to do with the wedding."

"No," Luke muttered, frowning. "I've got some bank forms he needs to sign."

Nellie brought another glass of water, then poured coffee for both of them.

"Evening, Nellie."

"Luke Rivers, I don't see near enough of you," the older woman said coyly, giving him a bold wink as she sauntered away with a swish of her hips.

Astonished that Nellie would flirt so openly with

Luke, Kate took a sip of her coffee and nearly scalded her tongue. Why, Nellie had a good fifteen years on Luke!

"Does she do that often?" Kate asked, in a disapproving whisper.

"You jealous?"

"Of course not. It's just that I've never known Nellie to flirt quite so blatantly."

"She's allowed." Luke gazed down at his menu and to all appearances, was soon deep in concentration.

Kate managed to squelch the argument before it reached her lips. There wasn't a single, solitary reason for her to care if a thousand women threw themselves at Luke Rivers. She had no claim on him, and wanted none.

The restaurant telephone pealed, but with four plates balanced on her arms, Nellie let it ring until someone in the kitchen answered it.

A minute later, she approached their table. "That was Devin on the phone. He says he's going to be late and you two should go ahead and order." She pulled a notepad from the pocket of her pink uniform. "Eat hearty since it's on his tab," she said, chuckling amiably.

"The roast-beef sandwich sounds good to me," Kate said. "With a small salad."

"I'll have chicken-fried steak, just so I can taste those biscuits of yours," Luke told the café owner, handing her the menu. "I'll start with a salad, though."

"I got rhubarb pie hot from the oven."

"Give me a piece of that, too," Luke said, grinning up at Nellie.

"Kate?"

"Sure," she said, forcing a smile. "Why not?"

Once Nellie had left, an awkwardness fell between

Kate and Luke. To Kate it felt as though they'd become strangers, standing on uncertain ground.

Luke ventured into conversation first. "So how's school?"

"Fine."

"That's good."

She laughed nervously. "I've started washing down cupboards at the house, clearing out things. I've got two piles. What Dad's going to take with him and what I'll need when I move."

Instead of pleasing Luke, her announcement had the opposite effect. "You're welcome to live on the ranch as long as you want," he said, his dark eyes narrowing. "There's no need to move."

"I know that, but the Circle L belongs to you—or it will soon."

"It's your home."

"It won't be much longer," she felt obliged to remind him. "I'm hoping to find a place in town. In fact, I'm looking forward to the move. You know what the roads are like in the winter. I should have done this years ago."

"You wouldn't have to move if you weren't so damn stubborn," Luke muttered from between clenched teeth. "I swear, Kate, you exasperate me. The last thing I want to do is take your home away from you."

"I know that." She hadn't considered relocating to town earlier for a number of reasons, foremost being that her father had needed her. But he didn't anymore, and it was time to exhibit some independence.

Nellie brought their tossed green dinner salads, lingering at the table to flirt with Luke again. He waited until she'd left before he leaned forward, speaking to Kate in a low, urgent voice. His eyes were filled with regret. "Kate, please stay on at the ranch. Let me at least do this much for you."

She thanked him for his concern with a warm smile, but couldn't resist adding, "People will talk." After all, Luke had pointed that very fact out to her when she'd made her foolish proposal. The night of Clay's wedding...

"Let them talk."

"I'm a schoolteacher, remember?" she whispered. She felt genuinely grateful for his friendship and wanted to assure him that all this worry on her behalf was unnecessary, that she was fully capable of living on her own.

Their dinner arrived before they'd even finished the salads. Another silence fell over them as they ate. Several possible subjects of conversation fluttered in and out of Kate's mind as the meal progressed. Her fear was that Luke would divert the discussion back to the ranch no matter what she said, so she remained silent.

A sudden commotion came from the pavement outside the café.

"It's Harry Ackerman again," Fred Garner shouted to Nellie, who was busy in the kitchen. "You want me to call the sheriff?"

"No, let him sing," Nellie shouted back. "He isn't hurting anyone."

Harry Ackerman was the town drunk. Back in his and Nellie's high-school days, they'd dated seriously, but then Harry went into the military and returned to Nightingale more interested in the bottle than a wife and family. Within six months, Nellie had married a mechanic who'd drifted into town. Problem was, when he drifted out again, he didn't take Nellie or their two children with him. But Nellie hadn't seemed to miss him much, and had supported her family by opening the café, which did a healthy business from the first.

Fifteen years had passed, and Harry was still courting Nellie. Every time he came into town, he took it upon himself to sing love songs from the pavement outside the café. He seemed to believe that would be enough of an inducement for her to forget the past and finally marry him.

"Actually his singing voice isn't that bad," Kate murmured to Luke.

Luke chuckled. "I've heard better."

Fred Garner stood up and strolled toward the cash register. He nodded in Luke's direction and touched the rim of his hat in greeting. "I've been hearing things about the two of you," Fred said, grinning broadly.

Kate concentrated on her sandwich, refusing to look up from her plate.

Luke made some vague reply that had to do with the ranch and not Kate, and she was grateful.

"Be seeing you," Fred said as he headed toward the door. As he opened it, Harry's latest love ballad, sung off-key, could be heard with ear-piercing clarity.

Fred left and soon Harry Ackerman came inside. He stared longingly at Nellie, placed his hand over his heart and started singing again at the top of his lungs.

"You get out of my restaurant," Nellie cried, reaching for the broom. "I don't want you in here bothering my customers." She wielded the broom like a shotgun, and before she could say another word Harry stumbled outside. He pressed his forlorn face to the glass, content to wait until his one true love returned to his waiting arms.

"Sorry, folks," Nellie muttered, replacing the broom.

"No problem," Luke answered, and she threw him a grateful smile, then hurried over to refill their coffee cups.

The disturbance died down when Harry wandered down the street to find a more appreciative audience. Luke sighed as he stirred his coffee. "I don't think your father has any intention of showing up tonight," he began. "In fact—"

"That's ridiculous," Kate said, cutting him off. "Dad wouldn't do that."

"He's trying to tell you something," Luke insisted.

"I can't imagine what." She could, but decided to pretend otherwise.

For a long moment, Luke said nothing. "You're smart enough to figure it out, Kate." He finished off the last bite of his pie and pushed the plate aside. "I've got some things to attend to, so I'd best be leaving." The corners of his eyes crinkled with amusement as he glanced out the café window. "Who knows, you might be singing me love songs in a couple of years if you don't come to your senses soon."

Kate ignored the comment. "My father will be here any minute."

"No, Princess," Luke said, and the smile left his eyes. He leaned across the table to brush his hand gently against her cheek. "But his message is coming across loud and clear."

Kate stayed at the café another half hour after Luke had gone and it took her that long to admit he was right. Her father *had* been giving her a message, this one no more subtle than the rest. Expelling her breath in disgust, Kate dredged up a smile and said goodbye to Nellie.

* * *

Kate didn't see Luke again until Friday evening, when they met at the Wilkins home for her father's wedding. Kate arrived with Devin, and Luke followed a few minutes later. Kate was busy arranging freshly baked cookies on a tray for the small reception to be held after the ceremony, when Luke walked into the dining room. Dorothea was with Minnie Wilkins in the back bedroom, and her father and Pastor Wilkins were talking in the office.

"Hello, Kate," Luke said from behind her.

"Hi," she responded, turning to give him a polite smile. Her breath caught in her throat at the elegant yet virile sight he made. He was dressed in a dark, three-piece suit that did nothing to disguise his strong, well-formed body, and his light blue silk tie enhanced the richness of his tan. Kate suspected that Luke was basking in the wonder she was unable to conceal, and yet she couldn't stop staring at him.

Her heart skipped a beat, then leaped wildly as his penetrating brown eyes looked straight into hers. She felt the tears well up, knowing that only Luke truly understood how difficult this evening was for her.

Many of her emotions tonight were identical to the ones she'd experienced at Clay and Rorie's wedding. All day, she'd worried her stomach into a knot of apprehension. The acceptance and strength of purpose she'd so recently been feeling had fled. Tonight, she was reminded again that everything she loved, everything familiar, had been taken from her life. First the man she'd planned to marry, now her father, and soon, so very soon, her childhood home. It was too much change, too quickly.

Just as she had at Clay's wedding, Kate forced herself to show pleasure, to behave appropriately. She *was* happy for her father and Dorothea—just as she'd been for Clay and Rorie. But why did everyone else's happiness need to cost Kate so much?

Luke must have read the distress in her eyes, because he hurried to her side. "Everything's going to be all right," he told her quietly. He'd said the same thing at Clay's wedding.

"Of course it is," she agreed, braving a smile. She turned back to the flowers, although her fingers were trembling. "I couldn't have chosen a better wife for Dad myself. Dorothea's wonderful."

Luke's hands rested on her shoulders and began to caress them gently. "So are you, Princess."

It demanded every ounce of fortitude Kate possessed not to whirl around and bury her face in Luke's chest, to absorb his strength. But this was exactly how she'd lost control before; she had to remember that.

A sound came from behind them, and Luke released her with a reluctance that echoed her own. She needed Luke now, just as she'd needed him a few weeks before. But this time, she was determined to be stronger.

The ceremony itself was brief. Kate felt almost wooden as she stood next to the woman her father had chosen to replace her mother. Memories of the lovely, soft-spoken Nora, and of their happy, close-knit family, almost overwhelmed Kate. Twice she felt tears threaten, but managed to hold them back. Both times she found Luke's eyes on her, his gaze warm with empathy.

When Pastor Wilkins closed his Bible and announced that Devin and Dorothea were now husband and wife, Devin took his bride in his arms and kissed her. Minnie Wilkins dabbed at her eyes with a lace hankie.

"You look so lovely," the woman murmured, hugging her friend.

Soon they were all hugging each other. When Kate's arms slipped around Luke it felt...comfortable. In fact, it felt *too* comfortable, too familiar, and that frightened her. She stiffened and let her arms drop. Luke would have none of that, however. Locking his hands on her upper arms, he drew her back to him.

"What I wouldn't give for a full moon and some champagne," he whispered in her ear.

Kate could have done without his teasing, but she refused to satisfy him with a response.

The small reception began immediately afterward, and Kate was busy for the next hour, dishing up pieces of wedding cake, passing trays of sugar cookies and pouring coffee.

Her father came to see her in the kitchen, his eyes bright with happiness. "You're going to be fine, aren't you, Princess?"

"You know I am," she said, flashing him a brilliant smile.

"Dorothea and I will be leaving soon." He placed his arm around her shoulders and hugged her. "Don't forget I love you. You'll always be my little girl."

"You'll always be my hero."

Devin chuckled. "I think Luke would like to fill that position and I'd be pleased if he did. He's a good man, sweetheart. You could do a lot worse."

"Dad," she groaned, closing her eyes. "Luke is wonderful, and I understand your concern. You'd like all the loose ends neatly tied up before you leave for your honeymoon, but I'm just not ready for a commitment."

"You'd make a lovely country bride, Princess. I want you to be happy, that's all."

"I will be," she said, standing on the tips of her toes to kiss his cheek.

By the time Devin and Dorothea were ready to leave, more than twenty close friends had gathered at the parsonage. They crowded onto the porch to send the newlyweds off with a flourish of kisses and enthusiastic waves. Almost everyone returned to the warmth of the house but Kate lingered, not wanting to go back inside when tears were blurring her eyes.

Luke joined her, standing silently at her side until she'd composed herself.

"Your father asked me to see you home."

Kate nodded and swallowed a near-hysterical laugh. Despite their conversation Devin was still attempting to throw her together with Luke.

"You mean you aren't going to argue with me?" Luke asked with exaggerated surprise.

"Would it do any good?"

"No," he said and chuckled lightly. Then, suddenly, his strong arms encircled her stiff body. "It's been a long time since you let me kiss you," he said, his warm breath moving closer and closer to her mouth.

Kate stared at his chest, refusing to raise her eyes to his. Gathering her resolve, she snapped her head up to demand he release her. But Luke smothered her words with his mouth. Her hands tightened into fists as soon as the initial shock had subsided and she fully intended to push him away. But once his mouth had settled over hers, he gentled the kiss, and her resolve all but disappeared.

Again and again his mouth sought hers. Luke's sweet, soft kisses seemed to erase all the pain from her heart. Only a moment before, she'd been intent on escaping. Now she clung to him, tilting her face toward him, seeking more. He deepened his kiss, sending jolts of excitement through her.

When he stopped abruptly, Kate moaned her dissatisfaction.

"Kate…" he warned.

"Hmm… Luke, don't stop."

"I'm afraid we've attracted an audience," he returned mildly.

Sucking in her breath, Kate dropped her arms and whirled around so fast she would have stumbled if Luke's arms hadn't caught her. Eyes wide, she stared into the faces of the twenty or so guests who'd stepped outside, preparing to leave.

"I thought Taylor Morgenroth should play the lead Pilgrim," Kate was saying to Linda when Sally Daley walked into the faculty lounge Monday afternoon. The two were discussing the final plans for their Thanksgiving play.

"Taylor's the perfect choice," Linda agreed.

"I see you girls are busy," Sally commented. "This play is such an ambitious project. You two are to be commended."

"Thanks." Linda answered for them both, trying to ignore the other woman as much as possible.

"Wasn't that Rorie Franklin I saw you with the other day, Kate, dear?"

"Yes. We had coffee at Nellie's." She resumed her discussion with Linda, not wanting to be rude to Sally, but at the same time, hoping to dissuade her from further conversation.

But Sally refused to be thwarted. She settled in the chair opposite Kate and said in confidential tones, "You're completely over Clay Franklin now, aren't you, dear?"

Kate shared an exasperated look with Linda and nearly laughed out loud when the third-grade teacher playfully rolled her eyes toward the ceiling. To hear Sally talk, anybody would think Kate had recently recovered from a bad case of the flu.

"Sally!" Kate exclaimed when she realized how avidly the other woman was waiting for her reply. "How am I supposed to answer that?" She covered her heart dramatically with one hand and assumed a look meant to portray misery and anguish. "Do you want me to tell you that my pride's been shattered and I'll never love again?"

Sally shook her head. "I wouldn't believe it, anyway."

"Then why ask?" Linda prompted.

"Well, because we all love Kate. She's such a dear, and she's been through so much lately."

"Thank you," Kate said graciously, then returned her attention to the Thanksgiving project.

"Most of the fuss about you and Eric Wilson and Luke Rivers has died down now," Sally assured her, as if this should lessen the embarrassment of that Friday night.

"I take it you haven't talked to Eric lately?" Linda asked, surprising Kate with her sudden interest. There'd been plenty of opportunity to inquire about him, but Linda hadn't done so until now.

"Talked to him?" Kate echoed with a short, derisive laugh. "I don't even shop at the Safeway store for fear of running into him again."

"I don't think you need to worry," Sally said blandly. "From what I hear, he's avoiding you, too."

Linda snickered softly. "No doubt. I'm sure Luke Rivers put quite a scare into him."

"How do you mean?" Kate demanded, already angry with Luke.

"You don't know?" Sally asked, her eyes sparkling with excitement.

"Know what?" Kate swung her gaze first to Linda, then to Sally. "Did Luke threaten him?" If he had, he was going to hear about it from her.

"I haven't got the foggiest idea what Sally's talking about," Linda said quickly.

"I didn't hear anything specific," Sally confirmed sheepishly. "I thought maybe you..." The older teacher's expression suggested that she hoped Kate would fill in the succulent details herself. "My dear, surely you understand that everyone in town is speculating about you and Luke," she continued.

"Rumors have been floating around since Clay's wedding," Linda added.

"But Sally just finished telling me those were dying down," Kate snapped, irritated with the entire discussion.

"The rumors aren't about you and that Wilson fellow," Sally rushed to explain. "As far as your one date with him is concerned, it's history. He's too smart to cross Luke."

"I'm sure he is," Kate said, anxious to quell the woman's gossip. "Aren't we about finished here, Linda?" she asked pointedly.

"Ah...yes."

"Now folks are talking about seeing you and Luke together at Nellie's last week, just before your father's wedding, and there've been a few rumors flying about the two of you at Pastor Wilkins's, too."

As fast as her hands would cooperate, Kate gathered up their materials. Sally seemed to accept that she was about to lose her audience. If she'd come to pump Kate for information she'd just have to realize Kate wasn't talking. Standing, Sally gave a deep sigh, clearly disappointed. She collected her purse and headed out the door, pausing to look back. "Frankly, I think Fred Garner's carrying this thing about you and Luke a bit too far. I consider what he's doing in poor taste." With that, she left the room.

"Fred Garner?" Linda echoed after a stunned second. "What's that old coot doing now?"

"Fred Garner owns the feed store," Kate said in a puzzled voice.

"Yes, but what's he got to do with anything?"

"Beats me." Still, Kate couldn't help wondering. Fred had seen them at the restaurant, and he'd been at the reception for her father and Dorothea. Although she hadn't seen him on the porch when a number of guests had found her in Luke's arms, she had very little doubt that he was there.

When Kate drove home an hour later, Luke was working in the yard. She climbed out of the car, took two steps toward him and halted abruptly. The lump in her throat was so large she could hardly swallow, let alone speak.

The trembling had started the minute she left Garner Feed and Supply. She'd dropped in at the store following Sally's remark, and from then on everything had grown progressively worse. The way she felt right now, she could slam her bag over Luke's head, or do something equally violent, and feel completely justified.

"Kate?" he asked, looking concerned. "What's wrong?"

She knew her emotions were written on her face. She'd never been more scandalized in her life, which was saying a great deal, considering the fiasco with Eric Wilson.

In fact, the blow her dignity had been dealt by Luke Rivers during that incident paled in comparison with this latest outrage. There was only one thing for her to do. She'd have to move away from Nightingale.

"This is all your doing, isn't it?" she demanded in a shaking voice. She held her head high, although it was a struggle to preserve her composure. Her pride was all she had left, and that was crumbling at her feet.

Luke advanced several steps toward her. "What are you talking about?"

She ground her fist into her hip. "I just got back from the feed store. Does that tell you anything?"

"No."

"I'll bet."

He frowned. "Kate, I swear to you, I don't know what you're talking about."

She made a doubting noise that came out sounding and feeling like a sob. Yet he appeared so bewildered. She didn't know how any man could cause her such life-shattering embarrassment and maintain that look of faithful integrity.

The tears wouldn't be restrained any longer, and they fell from her eyes, running down her face. They felt cool against her flushed cheeks.

"Kate? What's wrong?"

Kate turned and walked rapidly away from Luke rather than allow him to witness her loss of control. She hurried into the house and slumped in a chair, hiding her face in her hands as she battled the terrible urge to weep hysterically. The painful sensation in the pit of her stomach grew more intense every time she took a breath.

The door opened and she said, "Go away."

"Kate?"

"Haven't…you…done…enough?" Each word rolled from her tongue on the end of a hiccuping sob.

He knelt in front of her and wrapped his arms around her, holding her close, but she pushed him away, refusing the comfort he offered.

Kate's shoulders still heaved. With an exasperated sigh, Luke got up. He stood back on his boot heels and buried his hands in his pockets. "All right, tell me about it."

"Pastor… Wilkins…bet…twenty…dollars…on… December," she told him between sobs. Her fingers curled into fists. "Even… Clay…put in a…wager."

Seeing his name on that huge blackboard had hurt more than anything.

"Kate, I swear to you I don't know what you're talking about."

Furiously she wiped the tears from her face and tried to marshal her self-control enough to speak clearly. "The…feed store," she managed.

"What about the feed store?"

"They're taking bets—it's a regular lottery," she cried, all the more furious with him because he was making her spell out this latest humiliation.

"Bets on what?" Luke's frown was growing darker,

and Kate could tell that he was dangerously close to losing his patience.

"On *us!*" she wailed, as if that much, at least, should be obvious.

"For what?"

"When we're going to be married!" she shouted. "What else? Half the town's gambling on the date of our wedding."

Luke moaned, closing his eyes, as if he couldn't quite believe what she was telling him.

"You honestly didn't know?"

"Of course not." He was beginning to look perturbed as only Luke could. His dark eyes took on a cold glare that would intimidate the strongest of men. "How'd you find out?"

"Sally Daley said something about it after school, and then in the school car park one of the mothers told me March is a lovely time of year for a wedding. March sixteenth, she said. Then…then I made the mistake of stopping in at the feed store on my way home to…to check out what was going on."

Luke nodded, but Kate had the impression he was only half listening to her.

"As far as I'm concerned, there's just one thing for me to do," she said, gaining strength from her decision. "I'll offer my resignation to the school board tomorrow morning and leave the district this weekend."

Luke sent her a quick, angry look. "That won't be necessary. I'll take care of this my own way."

Seven

At one time Kate spent as many hours at Elk Run, the Franklin stud farm, as she did at the Circle L. But when she arrived Tuesday night for dinner, Elk Run no longer felt familiar. It seemed like years instead of weeks since her last visit. Kate's enthusiasm for this dinner with Clay and Rorie had never been high, but now she felt decidedly uncomfortable.

"Kate, welcome." Rorie flew out the door the minute Kate pulled into the driveway. She stepped from the car into Rorie's hug.

Clay Franklin followed his wife and briefly held Kate close, smiling down on her the same way he always had from the time she was thirteen. Back then, she'd worshipped him from afar, and she'd worshipped him more with each passing year. Kate paused, waiting for the surge of regret and pain she'd been expecting; to her astonishment, it didn't come.

"We're so glad you could make it," Rorie said as she opened the door.

Recognizing Kate, Clay's old dog, Blue, ambled over

for his usual pat. Kate was more than happy to comply and bent down to scratch his ears.

Mary, the Franklins' housekeeper, bustled about the kitchen, dressed in her bib apron, hair twisted into thick braids and piled on top of her head. Kate could scarcely remember a time she hadn't seen Mary in an apron. The scent of freshly baked pie permeated the room, mingling with the hearty aroma of roast beef and simmering vegetables.

"I hope that's one of your award-winning pies I'm smelling, Mary," Kate said. "I've had my heart set on a piece all day."

"Oh, get away with you," Mary returned gruffly, but the happy light that sparked from her eyes told Kate how gratified the housekeeper was by her request.

"When are you going to give me your recipe?" Kate asked, although she didn't know whom she'd be baking pies for now that her father had remarried. "No one can bake an apple pie like yours."

"Mary won't share her secret with me, either," Rorie said, giving a soft laugh. "I don't think she's willing to trust a city slicker yet."

"I never wrote down any recipe," Mary grumbled, casting Rorie a stern look. "I just make my pies the same way my mother did."

"I wish I could bake like Mary does," Rorie said, slipping her arm around her husband's waist. They exchanged a meaningful glance. Clay's smile showed he couldn't care less whether or not she could bake a pie.

Once more Kate braced herself for the pain of seeing them together, gentle and loving, but to her surprise she didn't feel so much as a pinprick of distress. She relaxed, wondering at what was happening—or rather, wasn't—and why.

"Where's Skip?" she asked suddenly. She missed Clay's younger brother almost as much as she did Clay. They'd been friends for years.

"Football practice," Clay explained. "He's quarterback this year and proud as a peacock. He'll be home later."

"About the time Mary serves her pie," Rorie whispered to Kate. Skip's appetite for sweets was legendary.

The small party headed into the homey living room. The piano stood against one wall, and Kate noted the music on the stand. She'd always been the one who'd played that piano, but it was Rorie who played for Clay now. There'd been a time when Kate and Clay had sung together, their voices blending in a melodious harmony. But Clay sang with Rorie now.

Kate expected the knowledge to claw at her insides, and she did feel a small twinge of regret—but that was all.

"Skip's hoping to catch you later," Rorie said.

"As I recall, you played quarterback your senior year of high school," Kate reminded Clay as she claimed the overstuffed chair. "That was the first year the Nightingale team made it to the state finals."

Rorie smiled delightedly at her husband. "You never told me that."

"There wasn't much to tell," Clay said with a short laugh. "We were eliminated in the first round." He sat beside Rorie and draped his arm around her shoulders, as if he had to keep touching her to believe she was here at his side.

Mary carried in a tray of wineglasses and an unopened bottle of a locally produced sparkling white. "I take it Devin and Dorothea arrived safely in California?" she asked as she uncorked the wine.

"Yes, Dad phoned when they arrived at Dorothea's daughter's house."

"We didn't get a chance to say more than a few words to you at the reception," Rorie apologized. "You were so busy pouring coffee, there wasn't much opportunity to chat."

"I know. It was good of you and Clay to come."

"We wouldn't have missed it for the world," Clay said.

"I wanted to tell you how nice your father and Dorothea looked together. And for that matter, you and Luke, too," Rorie added.

"Thank you," Kate said simply, wondering if her friends had heard about the incident on the Wilkins's front porch. It still embarrassed Kate to think of all her father's friends seeing her and Luke together...like that. "So much has happened in the last month," she said, trying to change the subject before either of them mentioned her father's wedding again. "Who'd ever have believed Luke would end up buying the ranch?"

"It must've come as a shock to you," Clay said evenly, "but I've been after him for years to get his own spread."

"What are your plans now that the Circle L's been sold?" Rorie asked.

"I'm looking for a place in town," she said, and sipped her wine.

"From what Luke told me, he'd rather you continued living on the ranch," Clay said, studying her as though he knew something she didn't.

"I know," Kate admitted. "It's very generous of him, but I'd prefer to get an apartment of my own."

"Good luck finding one," Clay murmured.

They were both aware that a decent apartment might be difficult to locate. Nightingale was a place of family dwellings, not singles' apartments.

They chatted easily as they waited for Mary to announce dinner. Every now and then, Kate saw Clay glance over at Rorie. His look was tender and warm and filled with the deep joy that came from loving completely and knowing that love was returned.

When Rorie Campbell had arrived in their midst, Kate had seen almost immediately that Clay was attracted to her. That was understandable, after all, since Rorie was a beautiful woman. In the beginning, Kate had done everything she could to combat her jealousy. Rorie had been due to leave Elk Run in a few days and once she was gone, Kate had told herself, their lives and feelings would return to normal.

Eventually Rorie did go back to San Francisco, but Clay couldn't forget her. Kate had done her best to pretend; she'd even talked Clay into setting a wedding date, pressuring him in a not-so-subtle way to marry her quickly. They'd been talking about it for years, and Kate wanted the deed done before Rorie realized what she'd given up. Their getting married seemed the perfect solution. Then, if Rorie did come to Nightingale again, it would be too late.

Kate's strategy had been a desperate one, planned by a desperate woman. And as often happened in such cases, her scheme backfired.

Kate didn't think she'd ever forget the day Clay told her he wanted to break their engagement. The words had scarred her soul like lye on tender skin. He'd come to the ranch, and from the minute he'd asked to talk to her, Kate had known something was terribly wrong. She'd tried to ease the tension with talk of bridesmaids' dresses and floral arrangements, but Clay had stopped her.

He'd sat with his hands folded, his eyes regarding her sadly. "I wouldn't hurt you for anything," he'd said, and his words rang with truth and regret.

"Clay, you could never hurt me." Which was a lie, because he was already inflicting pain.

He'd told her then, simply and directly, that it would be wrong for them to marry. Not once did he mention Rorie's name. He didn't need to. Kate had known for weeks that Clay was in love with the other woman. But she'd chosen instead to involve her heart in a painful game of pretend.

Instead of accepting the truth when Clay had come to her with his decision, she'd insisted he was mistaken, that they *were* right for each other and had been all their lives. The memory humbled her now. She'd tried to convince him that all they needed was a little more time. By the next week, or maybe the next month, Clay would understand that he'd made a mistake and he'd want to go through with the wedding. She could afford to be patient because she loved him so much. Kindly, and as gently as possible, Clay had told her time wouldn't alter the way he felt. Then he'd left, although she'd pleaded with him to stay.

In the week that followed, Kate had felt as though she was walking around in a fog. She laughed, she smiled, she slept, she ate. The school year hadn't started yet, so there was little else to occupy her mind. The days bled into each other, one indistinguishable from the next.

Soon after he'd broken their engagement, Clay

headed for San Francisco, purportedly to attend a horse
show. In her heart, she'd expected Clay to return with
Rorie at his side. As hard as it had been, she'd tried to
accept the fact Clay loved Rorie and nothing was ever
going to change that.

To everyone's surprise, Clay came home alone, and
there was no mention of Rorie. Kate didn't know what
had happened between them. Hope stirred in her heart,
and she'd briefly entertained thoughts of Clay resuming their engagement, the two of them marrying and
settling down together, the way she'd always dreamed.

Instead she stood helplessly by as Clay threw himself into his work, making unreasonable demands on
himself and his men. At first she believed the situation
would change. She began stopping off at Elk Run, trying to be the friend she knew Clay needed. But Clay
didn't want her. He didn't want anyone.

Except Rorie.

Only then did Kate recognize that it was in her power
to help this man she loved. She talked over her idea with
Luke, even before she approached her father. Luke, and
Luke alone, had seemed to understand and appreciate
her sacrifice. When she couldn't hold back the tears
any longer, it had been Luke who'd held her in his arms
and who'd beamed with pride over the unselfishness of
what she'd done.

As she sat, listening to the predinner conversation,
even contributing now and then, she reminded herself
that Luke had been the one who'd made it possible to
survive that difficult time.

Luke.

Losing Clay had threatened to destroy her, mentally
and physically. But Luke hadn't allowed that to hap-

pen. It was then he'd started bullying her, she realized. She'd thought of him as a tyrant, with his unreasonable demands and his gentle harassments. Kate had been so furious with him for assuming command of her life that she'd overlooked the obvious. Only now could she understand and appreciate his strategy. Gradually, the fire had returned to her eyes and her life, although it had been fuelled by indignation. Nevertheless it was there, and Luke had been the person responsible.

She'd been furious with him when she should've been grateful. Luke had never stopped being her friend— the best friend she'd ever had. She'd leaned heavily on him in the days and weeks before Clay married Rorie, though she'd never understood how much he'd done for her, how much he cared.

The wineglasses were replenished and Kate proposed a toast. "To your happiness," she said sincerely. It pained her to remember that Clay and Rorie had nearly lost each other. Because of her...

Nightingale had needed a librarian, and with her father's help, Kate had convinced the Town Council to offer the job to Rorie Campbell. When she'd turned them down, Kate herself had called Rorie, and together they'd wept over the phone and later in each other's arms.

So Rorie had returned to Nightingale, and she and Clay had been married. In October. The same month Kate had planned for her own wedding to Clay.

Kate's thoughts were pulled back to the present when Clay said, "Rorie has a piece of good news." He cast a proud look at his wife.

"What's that?" Kate asked.

Rorie blushed becomingly. "Clay shouldn't have said anything. It's not certain yet."

"Rorie," Kate said, studying her carefully, "are you pregnant? Congratulations!"

"No, no." Rorie rushed to correct that impression. "Good grief, we've been married less than a month."

"It's about Rorie's book," Clay explained.

Vaguely Kate recalled that Rorie wrote children's books. In fact, she'd been on her way to a writers' conference when the car she was driving broke down on the road not far from Elk Run.

"Has one of your stories been accepted for publication?" Kate asked eagerly.

"Not exactly," Rorie said.

"An editor from New York phoned and asked for a few revisions, but she sounded enthusiastic about the book and there was talk of a contract once the revisions are done," Clay said. His fingers were twined with his wife's and he looked as excited as if he'd created the story himself.

"Oh, Rorie, that's wonderful." Kate felt pleased and proud for her friend. "What's the book about?"

"Well, the story involves Star Bright and the night we delivered Nightsong, and it's told from the foal's point of view," Rorie said.

"I know I'm her husband," Clay broke in, "but I read it, and I don't mind telling you, the book's gripping. Any editor worth her salt would snap it up in a minute."

"Oh, Clay, honestly!"

"When will you know if it's sold?" Kate asked. "I don't think Nightingale's ever had an author living here before. Dad could convince the Town Council to commission a sign. You might even become a tourist attraction. Who knows where this could go?"

They all laughed, but Rorie cautioned, "It could be months before I hear, so don't go having your father commission any signs."

"You should've seen her after she got the call," Clay said, his eyes twinkling with merriment. "I didn't know what to think. Rorie came running out of the house and started shrieking and jumping up and down."

"So I was a little excited."

Playfully Clay rolled his eyes. "A little! That's got to be the understatement of the year."

"I'd behave the same way," Kate said. "And you seem pretty thrilled about all this yourself, Clay Franklin."

Clay admitted it, and then the discussion turned to the awards Clay had accumulated in several national horse shows in the past year.

A few minutes later, Mary announced that dinner was ready and they moved into the dining room. The meal was lively, and conversation flowed easily around the table.

Kate had been dreading this dinner from the moment Rorie had issued the invitation. Now she was pleasantly surprised by how enjoyable the evening had become. She'd been convinced that seeing Clay and Rorie's happiness would deepen her own pain. It hadn't happened. She'd expected to spend this evening nursing her wounds behind a brave front. Instead she felt giddy with a sense of release.

She *had* loved Clay, loved him with a youthful innocence. But she didn't feel the same way toward him now. Clay belonged to Rorie and Rorie to him. The tender relationship Kate had once shared with him was part of the past. He would always be a special person in her life, but those old feelings, that adulation she'd felt for him, were relegated to her adolescent fantasies.

Kate Logan was a woman now.

She wasn't sure exactly when the transformation had taken place, but it had. She'd struggled with it, fought the metamorphosis, because change, as always, was both painful and difficult. Kate realized for the first time that all the pain, all the uncertainty, had not been for nothing.

"Kate?" Luke called, as he let himself into the kitchen. "You around?"

"Here." She was at the back of the house, packing away the library of books her father kept in his den. Every night she did a little more to get the main house ready for Luke to move in and her to move out.

She straightened and tucked in a few wisps of hair that had escaped the red bandanna. She wore blue jeans and an old gray sweatshirt and no doubt looked terrible. Despite that, she was pleased to see Luke, eager to talk to him. She was wiping her dusty palms on her jeans when he walked in.

"What are you doing?" He stood just inside the door, a frown creasing his forehead.

"What does it look like?" she said. "I'm packing."

He hesitated, then said, "I told you, I want you to live here, at least to the end of the school year. I thought you understood that."

"I do, Luke. It's just that this place is yours now—or will be soon, and there's no reason for me to stay on." For one despairing moment, she was swept away on a crashing wave of disbelief and misery at everything she'd lost in so short a time. She could barely walk through her home and not feel an aching throb at the prospect of leaving it behind. But the sale of the ranch was part of the new reality she was learning to face.

"Of course there's a reason for you to stay here," Luke insisted, his voice sharp with impatience. "It's where you belong—where I want you. Isn't that reason enough?"

Kate forced a laugh. "Come on, Luke, there's no excuse for me to continue living here. You don't need a housekeeper, or a cook or anything else. You're completely self-sufficient. And I could do without all the gossip my living here would start in town." She paused a moment, then added gently, "I really *can* manage on my own, you know. I'm a big girl, Luke, and I don't need anyone to take care of me."

He wanted to argue with her; Kate could sense it with every breath he drew. But when he spoke next, his remarks had nothing to do with her moving.

"I suppose I should tell you about the feed store," he said. His voice was controlled, though Kate heard a hint of anger in his words. He'd been just as incensed as she was over the incident. Once she'd come to grips with her own outrage, she'd seen how furious Luke was.

"No...well, yes, I guess I am curious to hear how you handled that. Would you like some coffee?"

"Please."

Kate led the way into the kitchen and filled two ceramic mugs. After giving Luke his, she walked into the living room and sat on the sofa. Relaxing, she slipped off her shoes and tucked her feet underneath her. It felt good to sit here with Luke—almost like old times. So often over the years, they'd sat and talked like this.

Friends. Confidants. Companions. She cradled the mug in both hands, letting the warmth seep up her arms.

"I had dinner with Clay and Rorie last night," she said, wanting to share with Luke what she'd discovered.

"Yes, I heard. Listen, you can close the door on the situation with Fred Garner. You don't need to worry about it anymore."

Kate lowered her eyes. "Thanks," she murmured. There was so much she wanted to tell Luke. "I had a great time at Elk Run last night, although I honestly didn't expect to."

"I can personally guarantee the matter with Garner is over. If it isn't a dead issue, it soon will be."

Kate would rather not talk about the wedding lottery. The subject had become an embarrassing memory—a very embarrassing one—but as Luke said, it was finished. There were other, more important issues to discuss.

"All day I'd worried about that dinner," she said, starting over. "I wondered how I'd ever be able to sit at a table with Clay, knowing he was married to Rorie. But I did. Oh, Luke, I can't tell you how happy they are. Deep down, I knew they would be, and I had to brace myself for that, expecting to find it unbearably painful. But something incredible happened. During the evening, I learned a valuable lesson about—"

"Good." Luke's response was clipped, detached.

Kate hesitated. From the moment he'd walked into her father's office, she'd felt something was wrong, but she hadn't been able to put her finger on it. "Luke, what is it?"

"Nothing. I'd prefer not talking about Clay and Rorie, all right?"

"I…suppose so," she said, feeling hurt. After an awkward moment, she attempted conversation once more. "You'll never guess who I got a letter from today." If Luke didn't want to talk about Clay and Rorie, then she'd try another topic that was sure to pique his interest. "Eric Wilson. Remember him?"

A slight smile touched Luke's mouth. "I'm not likely to forget him. What'd he have to say?"

"He's moved back to Portland and is talking to his ex-wife. Apparently she's been just as miserable as he has since their divorce. It looks as if they might get back together."

"That's good news."

"He asked me to give you his regards, and sends his thanks." Kate paused. "But he didn't say what I was supposed to thank you for?" She made the statement a question, hoping Luke would supply an answer.

"We talked."

"Oh."

"I told him he was wasting his time on you because you're in love with me."

Kate was outraged. "Luke, you didn't! Please tell me you're joking."

He smiled briefly, then his eyes took on the distant look he'd been wearing a moment earlier. Kate couldn't ignore it any longer. "Luke, please, tell me what's bothering you."

"What makes you think anything is?"

"You don't seem yourself tonight." Something in his voice puzzled her. A reserved quality. It was as if he was distancing himself from her and that was baffling. After Clay's wedding, Luke had actually insisted they get married, and now he was treating her like some casual acquaintance.

Kate took another sip of coffee while she collected her thoughts. Luke was sitting as far away from her as he could. His shoulders were stiff and his dark eyes a shade more intense than usual. Gone was the laughing devilry she adored.

"I'll be out of town for a few days next week," he said abruptly. "I'm hoping to pick up a few pieces of new equipment from a wholesaler in New Mexico."

"When will the bank close the deal on the ranch?"

Luke paused and his eyes pinned hers. "Your father and I signed all the papers the day before he married Dorothea Murphy."

Kate felt like bolting from her chair, the shock was so great. "Why didn't you tell me?" she demanded, her heart racing. "Why didn't my father? I shouldn't even be here now. This is your home. Yours. Bought and paid for and—"

"Kate." He set his mug aside and wearily rubbed the back of his neck. "You're welcome to stay as long as you need. If you insist on leaving, that's fine, too, but there's no rush."

She brought her hands to her cheeks, which were feverishly hot one minute, numb and cold the next. "I'll be out as…as soon as I can find someplace to move."

"Kate, for heaven's sake, why do you persist in being so stubborn?"

She shook her head, hardly understanding it herself. All she knew was that this house, which had been a part of her from the time she was born, no longer belonged to her family. Despite everything Luke said, she couldn't stay on at the Circle L, and she had nowhere else to go.

Eight

Kate had just finished correcting a pile of math papers when her friend Linda Hutton entered her classroom. Linda's third-grade class had been on a field trip and the two friends had missed talking at lunchtime.

"Hi," Kate said, smiling up at her. "How'd the tour of the jail and fire station go?"

Linda pulled up a child-size chair and sank down on it, then started massaging her temples with her fingertips. "Don't ask. By noon I was ready to lock up the entire third-grade class and lose the key."

"It certainly was quiet around school."

Linda gave a soft snicker. "Listen, I didn't come in here to learn what a peaceful day *you* had. The only reason I'm not home in bed curled up with aspirin and a hot-water bottle is so I can tell you I was at Garner Feed and Supply yesterday afternoon."

"Oh?"

"Yes, and you aren't going to like what happened. While I was there, Mr. Garner asked me if I wanted to place a wager on the Rivers-Logan wedding."

Kate's heart stopped cold. "He didn't!"

"I'm afraid so."

"But Luke told me he'd taken care of the problem. He said it was a dead issue and I shouldn't worry about it anymore." It wasn't like Luke to make careless promises.

"I wish I didn't have to tell you this," Linda said, with a sympathetic sigh.

"But Luke told me he'd personally talked to Fred Garner."

"He did. Mr. Garner made a point of telling me that, too," Linda confirmed. "He claimed Luke was hotter than a Mexican chili pepper. Said Luke came into his place, ranted and raved and threatened him within an inch of his life. But, Kate, the whole time old Garner was talking to me, he wore a grin so wide I could've driven a Jeep through it."

Kate sagged against the back of her chair.

"Then Garner told me that the harder a man fights marriage, the faster he falls. Apparently he's taking bets from as far away as Riversdale and south."

Kate pressed a hand over her eyes. "What am I going to do now?"

Linda shook her head. "I don't know. At least Garner's taken it off the blackboard, but when I said something about that, he told me he had to, since half the county wants in on the action. It seems the betting outgrew his blackboard space."

"If nothing else, it proves how desperate this community is for entertainment," Kate muttered. "If the good people of Nightingale have nothing better to do than waste their time and money on something as silly as this, then it's a sad commentary on our lives here."

Kate's friend cleared her throat and looked suspiciously guilty.

Kate hesitated, studying Linda. No, she told herself. Not Linda. Her closest childhood friend wouldn't place a wager. Her expression confirmed that she would.

"You chose a date yourself, didn't you?" Kate demanded.

Linda's gaze darted all over the room, avoiding Kate's completely.

"You did, didn't you?" Kate exclaimed.

Linda's fingers were curling and uncurling in her lap. "You're my oldest, dearest friend. How could I ever do anything like that?" she wailed.

"I don't know, Linda. You tell me."

"All right, all right," Linda confessed. "I did put a wager on June. The first part of summer is such a lovely time of year for a wedding...."

"I can't believe I'm hearing this." Kate had the sinking suspicion that her father had probably gotten in on the action, too, before he left on his honeymoon.

"I had no intention of betting," Linda hurried to explain. "In fact I never would have, but the odds were so good for June. For a five-dollar bet, I could collect as much as five hundred if you were to marry around the middle of the month— say the sixteenth. It's a Saturday. Weekends are always best for weddings, don't you think?"

Kate wasn't about to answer that. "You know, I suspect this whole thing is illegal. Each and every one of you should thank your lucky stars I don't call the sheriff."

"He's betting himself—on March. Said his own wedding anniversary is March tenth and he thinks Luke will be able to persuade you early in the spring. According to Fred, the sheriff figures that once Luke gets you to agree, he won't wait around for a big wedding. He'll want to marry you before you can change your mind."

Kate sent her a furious look. "If you're telling me this to amuse me, you've failed miserably."

"I'm sorry, Kate, I really am. The only reason I went into the feed store was so I could assure you the whole betting thing was over, but I can't and—"

"Instead you placed a bet of your own."

"I feel guilty about that," Linda admitted, her voice subdued.

"Why don't we both forget it and concentrate on the Thanksgiving play?" Instead of upsetting herself with more talk of this wedding lottery, Kate preferred to do something constructive with her time.

"I might be able to make it up to you, though," Linda murmured, fussing with the cuffs of her long-sleeved blouse.

"Whatever it is will have to be good."

"It is." Linda brightened and pulled a slip of paper from her purse. "I got this information from a friend of a friend, so I can't confirm how accurate it is, but I *think* it's pretty much for sure."

"What's for sure?" she asked when Linda handed her the paper. A local phone number was carefully printed on it.

Linda's sheepish look departed. "It's Mrs. Jackson's number—she's the manager of the apartment complex on Spruce Street. They may have a vacancy coming up next week. If you're the first one to apply, you might have a decent chance of getting it."

"Oh, Linda, that's great!"

"Am I forgiven?"

Kate laughed. "This makes up for a multitude of sins."

"I was counting on that."

Kate called five times before she got through. Mrs. Jackson seemed surprised to be hearing from her.

"I thought you were marrying that Rivers chap," the elderly woman said. "Can't understand why you'd want to rent an apartment when you're engaged to that man. The whole town says it's just a matter of time."

"Mrs. Jackson," Kate said loudly, because everyone knew the old woman was hard of hearing, "could I look at the apartment soon?"

"Won't be cleaned up for another day or two. I'll let you know once it's ready to be shown, but I can't help feeling it's a waste of time. Don't know what's wrong with you young women these days. In my day, we'd snap up a good man like Luke Rivers so fast it'd make your head spin."

"I'd still like to see the apartment," Kate said.

"Saturday, I guess. Yes, Saturday. Why don't you plan to come over then? I'll need a deposit if you decide to take the place."

"Will a check be all right?"

"Good as gold when it's got your name on it," Mrs. Jackson said, chuckling. "Don't suppose you have any season or month you're particularly partial to for weddings, would you?"

"No, I can't say I do."

"Well, me and Ethel Martin think you and that Rivers fellow will tie the knot in April. April seems a mighty nice month for a country wedding."

"I'm sure it is," Kate said, clenching her teeth.

"Good. Now listen, soon as the word gets out, someone else'll be wanting that apartment, so if you aren't here by noon Saturday, I'm going to have to give it to whoever shows up. You understand?"

"I'll be there before noon."

"See you then."

"Goodbye, Mrs. Jackson."

"You keep thinking about April, you hear?"

"Yes, I will," Kate murmured, rolling her eyes as she replaced the receiver.

That night, Luke stopped in shortly after Kate had finished dinner, which consisted of a sandwich eaten while she emptied the living-room bookcases. She filled box after box with books, her own and her father's, as well as complete sets of Dickens, Thackeray and George Eliot that had belonged to her mother. The physical activity gave her time to think. She'd realized the night she had dinner at the Franklins' that she wasn't in love with Clay. That same evening, Kate had also realized how much Luke had done for her in the weeks following her broken engagement. It troubled her to acknowledge how unappreciative she'd been of his support.

At Clay's wedding, she'd only added to the problem by asking Luke to marry her. He'd been willing to comply, willing to continue taking care of her through these difficult emotional times. In his own way, he did love her; Kate didn't question that. But he seemed far more concerned with protecting her from the harsh realities of life.

All the talk about weddings had brought the subject to the forefront of Kate's mind. She tried to picture what her life would be like if she were to marry Luke. From the night of Clay's wedding, Luke had been telling her she was in love with him. It came as a shock to realize how right he was. She *did* love him, a thousand times more than she'd ever dreamed.

Luke claimed he loved her, too. If that was true, why was she fighting him so hard? For one thing, Luke had delivered his declaration of love in such a matter-of-fact, unromantic way, it was hard to believe he really meant it. If she could be sure that his feelings were rooted in more than sympathy and physical attraction, she'd feel more confident. But Luke kept trying to shield her, as though she were a child. Now that she was moving into a place of her own, she'd be able to analyze her changing emotions more objectively. She'd be completely independent, away from the environment they'd always shared. Once they were apart, once it was clear that she could manage by herself, Luke would be free to pursue a relationship with her as an equal, an adult woman—not a little girl who needed looking after.

"I see you're at it again," he said, standing in the doorway between the kitchen and the living room.

"Luke—" she slapped her hand over her heart "—you startled me!" Her thoughts had been full of him and then suddenly he was there.

As he did more and more often of late, Luke was frowning, but Kate wasn't going to let that destroy her mood. She was thrilled with the prospect of moving into her own apartment and settling into a different kind of life.

"I have good news. I'm going to look at an apartment on Saturday morning." She dragged a heavy box of books across the carpet. "So," she said, huffing, "I'll probably be out of here sooner than we figured."

Luke interrupted her, effortlessly picking up the cardboard box and depositing it on the growing stack at the far side of the room.

"Thanks," she murmured, grateful for his help.

"You shouldn't be doing this heavy work by yourself."

"It's fine," she said, rubbing the dust from her hands. "The only trouble I'm having is with these books. We've got so many."

"Kate, dammit, I wish you'd listen to reason."

"I'm being reasonable," she said, fixing a reassuring smile on her face. "All I'm doing is giving you what's rightfully yours."

Luke's frown grew darker, and he dragged a hand through his hair. "Listen, I think we may have more of a problem with Fred Garner than I thought."

"Yes, I know," Kate said, already filling the next box. "Linda told me after school that he's doing a thriving business."

Luke knelt on the floor beside her. "You're not upset?"

"Would it do any good? I mean, you obviously did your best and that just seemed to encourage the betting. As far as I can see, the only thing that will resolve this issue is time." She kept her gaze averted and added, "When six months pass and we're still not married, everyone will accept that nothing's going on between us."

"Nothing?" Luke asked bitterly.

Hope stirred briefly within her. "I like to think we'll always be friends." An absent smile touched her lips. "Now that I've decided to distance my emotions from this lottery nonsense, I find it all rather comical. You should do the same."

"This amuses you?"

"The good citizens of Nightingale are amused. Everyone seems to assume that because Clay and Dad both got married and the ranch has been sold, I should swoon into your arms."

"Personally, I don't think that's such a bad idea."

"Oh?" She chuckled and tucked a few more books in the box. Her heart was racing. If Luke was ever really going to declare his love, it would be now. "That wasn't the message I got the other night. I tried to have a serious talk with you about my evening with Clay and Rorie, and all you could do was glower at me." She glanced up, shaking her head. "Like you're doing now."

Luke walked away from her. He stood staring out the window, although Kate suspected the view was of little interest to him. "I just wish you'd be sensible for once in your life," he snapped.

"I didn't know I had a habit of not being sensible," she said conversationally, disheartened by his attitude. She rose and walked over to the larger bookcase, but even standing on her toes, she couldn't quite reach the trophies stored on the top shelf. Not to be defeated, she rolled the ottoman in front of the empty bookcase and climbed onto the thick cushioned seat. She stretched up and her fingers were about to grasp the first trophy when she heard Luke's swift intake of breath.

"Kate!"

Just as he spoke the ottoman started to roll out from under her. She flailed her arms in a desperate effort to maintain her balance.

Kate had never seen Luke move faster. His hands closed around her waist in an iron grip. Her cry of alarm caught in her throat as she was slammed against his solid chest.

"Of all the stupid, idiotic things I've ever seen—"

"I would've been perfectly fine if you hadn't called my name." Her heart was pounding so hard she could barely breathe.

Luke's hold relaxed. "You're all right?"

She nodded.

He closed his eyes, exhaling a ragged sigh. When he opened them, he assessed her carefully; apparently he concluded that she was unhurt because he gave her an impatient little shake. "Whatever possessed you to climb up on that ottoman in the first place?" he demanded.

"I couldn't reach the trophies."

"Couldn't you have asked me to get them for you? Why do you have such a difficult time accepting help from me?"

"I don't know," she admitted softly.

Still he held her and still Kate let him, trying to resist the comfort she felt in his arms. Her hands were braced against his powerful shoulders, but then she relaxed, unconsciously linking her fingers behind his neck.

Neither moved for a long moment.

Slowly Luke ran a provocative finger down the length of her cheek, and Kate's eyes drifted shut. She felt herself drawn inexorably toward him. Her lips parted and trembled, awaiting his kiss. When she realized what she was doing, she opened her eyes and broke away from him so quickly that she would've stumbled had his hands not righted her.

Embarrassed now, she stepped back. Luke brought

down the trophies and handed them to her, but she saw that his eyes had become distant and unreadable.

"That's enough packing for tonight," she murmured, her voice breathless even while she struggled to sound cheerful and bright.

He nodded slightly, then without another word stalked from the room. Kate didn't know what possessed her to follow him, certainly the last thing she should have done.

"Luke?"

He stopped halfway through the kitchen and turned toward her. His eyes were steely and intense, and just seeing that harsh edge drove her to take a step backward in retreat.

"You wanted something?" he asked when she didn't immediately explain.

"Just to say…" She could barely talk coherently. It occurred to her to ask if he loved her the way a man loves his wife, but she lacked the courage. "I thought maybe, I mean, I wanted to know if there was anything I could do for you before I left the house. Paint the living room…or something?"

"No."

Briefly she toyed with the idea of following him outside. For all his words about wanting her to stay, he couldn't seem to get away from her fast enough. The thought of not having Luke for her friend anymore felt crippling. Her pride was the problem. Luke had told her repeatedly that she needed him, and she knew now that she did. But not in the way he meant. Not just as a friend who was willing to offer her the protection and peace of marriage, a friend who felt obliged to take care of her.

"I don't want you to move from the ranch," he said.

Her heart was begging him to give her a reason to
stay—the reason she longed to hear. "Luke, please accept that I'm only doing what I think is best for my life."

"I know that, but dammit, Kate, why are you being
so stubborn? Why do you resist me when all I want is
to make things easier for you? We could be married,
and you could settle down in the house, and nothing
needs to change. Yet you insist on causing all this tur-
moil in your life."

There wasn't anything Kate could say.

"You can't tell me we aren't physically attracted
to each other. The electricity between us is powerful
enough to light up Main Street."

"I...know."

"Say it, Kate. Admit that it felt good when I held
you just now."

"I..."

Luke reached for her then, and Kate felt as if she'd
lost some strategic battle. When his mouth found hers,
her stomach tightened and fluttered wildly. Against her
will, her lips parted, and before she understood what
was happening she slid her arms tightly around his hard,
narrow waist, wanting to hold on to him forever.

Luke moaned, then suddenly tore his lips from hers.
She felt a tremor go through him before he raised his
head and gazed tenderly into her face, his eyes dark
and gentle.

"Is it so difficult to say?" he asked.

Nine

"This is the second bedroom," Mrs. Jackson was saying as she led Kate through the vacant rooms. From the moment she'd walked in the door, Kate had known that this apartment would suit her needs perfectly.

"I can't understand why you'd be wanting a two-bedroom place, but that's none of my business," Mrs. Jackson went on. Her hair was tightly curled in pink plastic rollers. To the best of her ability, Kate couldn't remember ever seeing the woman's hair *without* rollers.

"What did that Rivers fellow say when you told him you were moving into town?" She didn't wait for a response, but cackled delightedly. "Frankly, I wasn't sure you'd show up this morning. My friend Ethel and me talked about it, and we figured Rivers would tie a rope around you and hightail it to Nevada and marry you quick. Offhand, I can't remember who's got money on November."

"You said to be here before noon," she murmured, ignoring the other comments.

"Well, if Luke didn't stop you, I expected that snowstorm would, the one the weatherman's been talking about for the last two days."

"Do you really think it's going to snow?" Kate asked anxiously. The sky had been dark all morning, and the temperature seemed to be dropping steadily. Normally Kate wouldn't have chanced driving into town by herself with weather conditions this uncertain, but if she hadn't come, she might have missed getting the apartment.

"If I was you, I'd stick around town for a while," Mrs. Jackson advised. "I'd hate the thought of you getting trapped on the road in a bad storm."

"I'm sure I'll be all right." She'd driven her father's four-wheel-drive truck, and even if the storm did materialize, she shouldn't have any trouble getting home. The Circle L was only twenty minutes away, and how much snow could fall in that time?

"Would you like me to write you a check now?" Kate asked, eager to be on her way.

"That'd be fine. There's still some cleaning to be done, but it'll be finished before the first of the month. Fact is, you can start moving your things in here next week if you want."

"Thanks, I appreciate that."

Mrs. Jackson bundled her coat around her thin shoulders as they stepped outside. She glanced at the sky and shook her pink-curlered head. "If you are going home, I suggest you do it quick. I don't like the look of them clouds."

"Then I'd better write that check and head out."

No more than five minutes later, Kate was sitting in her father's truck. The sky was an oyster gray and darkening by the minute. Shivering from the cold, she zipped her jacket all the way up to her neck and drew on a pair of fleece-lined leather gloves.

Kate started the engine and shifted the gears. The radio was set on her dad's favorite country station and the music played softly. When she left the outskirts of town, she hit a couple of rough patches in the road and bounced so high her head nearly banged into the roof of the cab. After that she kept her speed down. She drove at a steady pace, her gaze focused on the road ahead, scanning the horizon for any sign of snow.

When she was about ten miles from the ranch, the storm began. Light, fluffy flakes whirled around the windshield. The morning sky darkened until it resembled dusk and Kate was forced to turn on the headlights.

A love song came on the radio, one the band at the Red Bull had played that fateful Friday night. The night Luke had lifted her in his arms and carried her off the dance floor. Embarrassed by the memory, she reached for the radio dial, intending to change the station.

She didn't see the rock that had rolled onto the road, not until she was almost on top of it, and then it was too late. Her instincts took control. She gripped the wheel with both hands, then swerved and slammed into the embankment. The truck stopped with a sudden jerk, and the engine went dead.

For a stunned moment, Kate couldn't breathe. Her heart was in her throat and her hands clenched the steering wheel so tightly her fingers felt numb.

Finally, when she was able to move, Kate released a long, shaky breath, grateful the accident hadn't been worse. She took a moment to compose herself and tried to restart the engine, but nothing happened. Twice more she tried to get the engine to kick over, but it wouldn't even cough or sputter.

Frustrated, she smacked the cushioned seat with her gloved hand and closed her eyes. The snow was coming down thick and fast now.

"Don't worry," she muttered, opening the door and climbing out. "Stay calm." Although everything Kate knew about the internal workings of engines would fit on a Post-It note, she decided to see if she could find the problem.

The snow and wind struck at her viciously, as though to punish her for not listening to Mrs. Jackson and staying in town.

After considerable difficulty locating the latch, Kate raised the hood. With a prayer on her lips, she looked everything over, then touched two or three different parts as if that would repair whatever was broken. Certain that she was destined to sit out the storm huddled in the cab, she returned and tried the key again.

The engine gave one sick cough and promptly died. "Damn!"

Nothing remained but to sit and wait for someone to drive past. Leaving the truck and attempting to make her way to the house would be nearly as insane as driving around in a snowstorm in the first place.

Kate could almost hear Luke's lecture now. It would be hot enough to blister her ears. All she could do was hope her father never found out about this—or she'd get a lecture from him, too.

A half hour passed and, hoping against hope, Kate tried the engine again. Nothing. But it was snowing so hard now that even if the truck had started, she probably wouldn't have been able to drive in these conditions. She tried to warm herself by rubbing her hands and hugging her arms close to her body. It had become cold, the coldest weather she could remember.

With very little to take her mind off the freezing temperature, she laid her head back and closed her eyes, trying to relax. There was nothing to do but sit patiently and wait....

She must have dozed off because the next thing she knew, the truck door was jerked open and her arm gripped in a sudden, painful hold.

"Have you lost your mind?" The fury in Luke's voice was like a slap in the face.

"Luke... Luke." She was so grateful to see him that she didn't question where he'd come from or how he'd found her. It all felt like a dream. Moving was difficult, but she slid her arms around his neck and hugged him, laughing and crying at the same time. "How did you ever find me?"

"Don't you realize I was about to have heart failure worrying about you?"

"You're sick?" Her mind was so muddled. Of course he'd be worried. How had he known where she was? And he seemed so angry, but that was nothing new. For the past few days, he'd been continually upset with her.

Her arms tightened around his neck and she breathed in his fresh, warm scent. When she sat up and looked around, she was shocked by how dark it had become; if it weren't for the blowing, swirling snow, the stars would be twinkling. The storm had abated somewhat, but not by much.

"I can't believe you'd do anything so stupid." His voice was low and angry, his face blanched with concern. "Don't you know you could've frozen to death out here? If you don't want to consider your own life, then what about Devin away on his honeymoon? If anything happened to you, he'd never forgive himself."

Kate bore up well under Luke's tirade, refusing to cry even though she was trembling with shock and cold and the truth of his words. As for the part about being frozen, she was already halfway there, but he didn't seem to notice that.

"Kate, I don't know what I would've done if you'd left the truck and tried to make it back to the house on foot."

"I knew enough to stay here at least." She'd been a fool not to have taken the danger more seriously. "I'm sorry," she whispered.

He pulled her to him and held her so tight she couldn't move. His face was buried in her hair, one ungloved hand gently stroking her forehead, her cheek, her chin, as if he had to touch her to know he'd found her safe. When he lifted his head, he gazed into her eyes, his own dark and filled with unspoken torment. "Are you all right?"

She nodded and tried to talk, but her teeth began to chatter. Luke shrugged out of his coat and draped it over her shoulders.

"Tell me what happened."

"I swerved to miss a rock and hit…the embankment. It was already snowing and I…the song… I changed stations and that's when it happened… I don't know what I did, but after I turned so sharply, the truck wouldn't start."

"I've got to get you to the house." He half carried her to his truck and placed her in the passenger seat. He climbed into the driver's side and leaned over to wrap a warm blanket around her, then began to rub some warmth back into her hands.

"What about Dad's truck?" Kate asked, shocked by how tired and weak she felt.

"We'll worry about that later. I'll send someone to fix it when the storm's over."

The blast from the heater felt like a tropical wind and Kate finally started to relax. She was terribly cold but dared not let Luke know.

All the way back to the ranch he didn't say a word. Driving was difficult, and she didn't want to disturb his concentration. So she sat beside him, her hands and feet numb despite the almost oppressive warmth, and her eyes heavy with weariness.

Several of the ranch hands ran toward the front porch when Luke pulled into the yard. Kate found the flurry of activity all centered on her disconcerting, but she tried to thank everyone and apologized profusely for the concern she'd caused.

If Luke had been impatient and demanding when he rescued her, it didn't compare to the way he rapped out orders once she was inside the house.

"A bath," he said, pointing toward the bathroom as if she'd never been there before. "Warm water, not hot."

Bill Schmidt, Luke's newly appointed foreman, followed them to the doorway of the tiny room, looking pale and anxious. Kate felt so weak that she simply stood, leaning against the sink, while Luke ran the bathwater, testing it several times to check the temperature.

"It's stopped snowing. Do you think I should contact one of her female friends? Maybe Miz Franklin?" Bill asked, shifting awkwardly from foot to foot. When

Luke nodded, Bill charged out of the house, slamming the door behind him.

Luke turned off the bathwater and straightened. He shook his head, arms limp and at his sides, mouth stern and tight. "Kate, Kate, what could have possessed you to drive in from town during the worst storm of the year? Can you imagine what went through my mind when I was looking for you?"

It took all her strength just to manage a few words. "How'd…you know…where I was?"

"You told me you were going to town to look at an apartment on Saturday. Remember? When you weren't back after the blizzard hit, I called around town until I learned you were renting one of the apartments on Spruce Street. Mrs. Jackson told me she'd warned you herself and that you'd left a few hours earlier. Also that she's fond of April because of all the flowers, whatever the hell that means."

"I'm…sorry I worried you."

His hands gripped her shoulders and the anguish he'd endured during the past few hours was written plainly on his face. The anger and pain in his eyes told her about the panic he'd felt. A rush of emotion crossed his expression and he pulled her close, wrapping his arms around her.

He didn't speak for a long moment. Instead, quietly, gently, he stroked her hair as he dragged in several deep breaths.

Kate's heart pounded wildly in her chest. She longed to look at him, to gaze into his eyes again. She was puzzled by the intensity she'd seen there. Fear, yes, doubt and anger, too, but there was something more, something deeper that she didn't recognize.

She longed to tell him she loved him, just the way he claimed she did, but the thought didn't make it to her lips. Love was a strange, unpredictable emotion, so painful and difficult. Her eyes held his and she tried to smile, but her mouth wouldn't cooperate.

Her fingertips mapped out the lines of his face, as she strove to reassure him with her touch when her words couldn't. He captured her wrist and brought her palm to his lips.

She'd just opened her mouth to speak, when Bill Schmidt came crashing into the room. "Rorie Franklin will be over as soon as she can."

"Thanks, Bill," Luke said without looking away from Kate.

"Uh, I'll be leaving now, if you don't need me."

"Fine. Thanks again for your help."

"No problem. Glad you're all right, Kate." He touched his hat and then was gone.

"Someone should help you out of those clothes," Luke said, half smiling, "and I don't think I should be the one to do it."

"I'm fine. I can undress myself."

Luke didn't seem inclined to challenge her statement. She floated toward the bathroom door and ushered him out, then shut it softly.

Once she started undressing, she discovered that Luke hadn't been too far wrong when he'd suggested she needed help. By the time she sank into the warm water, she was shivering, exhausted and intensely cold again. But the water felt wonderful, although it stung her tender skin. When the prickling sensation left her, she was almost overwhelmed by the sensation of comfort. She sighed deeply, closed her eyes and lay back in the tepid water.

"Kate," Luke called from the other side of the door, "are you okay in there?"

"I'm fine."

"Do you need anything?"

"No," she assured him.

A sudden thought made her bolt upright, gasping. *Luke could have died searching for me.* She closed her eyes and whispered a prayer of thanks that the events of this traumatic afternoon had turned out as they had.

She must have sobbed because Luke called out, "What's wrong? It sounds like you're crying."

"You...could have died trying to find me."

"I didn't."

"I know," she said hoarsely, biting her lip. "I'm glad. I wouldn't want you to die."

"That's encouraging," he answered with a soft laugh.

Dressed in her flannel pyjamas and long robe, her hair hanging wetly against her shoulders, Kate let herself out of the bathroom. She looked like something the cat had proudly dragged onto the porch, but at least she felt better. A thousand times better.

Luke was sitting in the kitchen, nursing a shot glass of whiskey. Kate had very rarely seen Luke drink straight liquor.

"I blame myself," he muttered. "I knew about the storm and didn't warn you."

"Warn me? That wouldn't have made any difference. I would've gone into town anyway. I had to be there before noon if I was going to get the apartment. You couldn't have stopped me, Luke. You know that."

Luke shook his head grimly. "What I can't understand is why moving away from here is so all-fired important that you'd risk your fool neck to do it."

"Mrs. Jackson said she'd have to give the apartment to someone else if I wasn't there."

"She wouldn't have understood if you'd phoned? You had to go look at it in a blizzard?" He urged her into a chair and poured a cup of hot coffee, adding a liberal dose of whiskey before handing her the cup.

"I already told you I couldn't wait. Besides, it wasn't snowing when I drove there," Kate said patiently. "Please don't be angry, Luke." She reached for his hand, needing to touch him.

He clutched her fingers with his own. "Kate, if anything should convince you we ought to get married, this is it. You need me, Princess, can't you see that?" He released her hand to brush the damp curls from her forehead. "How many times do I have to tell you that before you'll believe it?"

"Oh, Luke," she moaned, feeling close to tears.

"I want to take care of you, Kate. What nearly happened today, plus the fiasco with Eric Wilson, should tell you something."

She stared at him, feeling lost and disoriented. "There are women in this community, women my age, who already have children." Even as she spoke, she knew she wasn't making sense.

Luke blinked in confusion. "You want children? Great, so do I. In fact, I'm hoping we'll have several."

"That's not what I meant," Kate said, exasperated. She tried again. "These women don't live with a guardian." Was that clearer? she wondered.

"Of course they don't—they're married," Luke countered sharply.

Kate shut her eyes. "Don't you understand? I'm old enough to be on my own. I don't need someone to protect me."

"We're not discussing your age."

"You don't *love* me," she blurted. "You feel sorry for me, that's all. You think because Clay's married to Rorie and...and Dad married Dorothea that I don't have anyone. But I do! There's Linda and lots of other friends. I've got a good life. I don't need to get married."

Luke sprang from the chair and walked to the sink, pressing both hands against the edge, hunching his shoulders, his back toward her. He said nothing for several minutes and when he finally spoke, his voice was cool, detached. "All I can say is that you must feel a lot more strongly about this than I realized. Apparently you're willing to risk your life to get away from me."

"I didn't go to town knowing I was in any danger," she objected, but he didn't seem to hear.

"Then leave, Kate. I won't try to keep you any longer, despite the fact that I love you and want to marry you. If you want your independence so badly, then take it."

"Luke, please, you don't love me—not the way you should."

"Oh, and what do you know about that? Obviously nothing."

"I know you keep saying you want to take care of me."

"That's so wrong?"

"Yes! A woman needs more. She needs to be an equal. She—"

"My love and my life are all I've got to offer you, Kate," he broke in. "It's a take-it-or-leave-it proposition."

"That's not fair," she said. "You make it sound as

though I'm going to live my life alone if I don't marry you within the next ten minutes."

Slowly he turned to face her. His eyes were piercing and as dark as she'd ever seen them. "Fine. You've made your choice. I'm not going to stand here arguing with you. It's over, Kate. This is the last time we'll talk about marriage."

She tried to say something, but couldn't think coherently. Even if she'd been able to work out her thoughts and give them voice, she doubted Luke was in any mood to listen. He avoided looking at her as he stalked out of the house.

A fire was blazing in the fireplace and Kate stretched out on the nearby sofa, intending to mull over Luke's words. But her eyes felt as heavy as her heart, and almost as soon as she laid her head on the pillow, she was asleep.

Someone working in the kitchen stirred Kate to wakefulness, and when she glanced at her watch she was shocked to see that she'd slept for almost two hours.

Her heart soared when she thought it must be Luke. He'd been so angry with her earlier, although she supposed his anxiety about finding her in the snowstorm explained his attitude. She hoped they could clear the air.

But it wasn't Luke. Instead, Rorie peered into the living room, her eyes concerned.

"I hope you don't mind. Luke let me in."

"You're always welcome here, Rorie, you know that."

"Bill Schmidt called with an incredible story about you being lost in the storm. I could hardly believe it.

Clay drove me over as soon as he could, but to be honest I don't know who was worse off—you or Luke."

At the mention of his name, Kate lowered her gaze to the multicolored quilt spread across her lap. Idly she smoothed the wrinkles, trying not to think about Luke.

"How are you feeling?"

"I'm okay. I just have a headache."

"A bad one from the look of you. I've never seen you this pale."

Kate's hands twisted the edge of the homemade quilt. "Luke was furious with me for going into town— I found an apartment, Rorie. He said it was over between us." She began to cry. "He said he'd be glad when I was gone and that he'd…never bother me again." By the time Kate had finished, her voice was reduced to a hoarse whisper.

"I see," Rorie murmured.

"I don't even recognize Luke anymore. We used to be able to talk to each other and joke together, but lately we can't seem to discuss anything in a rational manner. I've tried, Rorie, I really have, but Luke makes everything so difficult."

"Men have a habit of doing that."

"I wanted to tell Luke about the night I had dinner with you and Clay and—" She stopped abruptly when she realized what she'd almost said.

"What about it?" Rorie coaxed.

"It's just that I'd dreaded the evening because I was afraid of being with Clay again. I'm sorry, I don't want to upset you, Rorie, but I loved Clay for a long time, and getting over him was much harder than I thought it would be. Until the night we were all together." The words came rushing from her. "I saw Clay with you and

I assumed I'd feel all this pain, but instead I felt completely free. You're both so happy, and I knew, then and there, that I never loved Clay the way you do. True, I adored him for years, but it was more of an adolescent infatuation. Clay was part of my youth. When I understood all these things about myself, all these changes, I felt such hope, such excitement."

"Oh, Kate, I'm so pleased to hear that." A shy smile dented Rorie's cheeks.

"I wanted to explain all this to Luke, but I never got the chance, and now it's all so much worse. I don't know if we'll ever be able to talk to each other again."

"Of course you will."

"But he sounded so angry."

"I'm sure that's because of his concern for your safety."

"I can't talk to him," Kate repeated sadly. "At least not yet and maybe not ever…"

"Yes, you will, and it'll be sooner than you think," Rorie said. "You won't be able to break off all those years of friendship, and neither will he. He'll be around in a day or two, ready to apologize for being so harsh. Just you wait and see."

Kate shook her head. "You make it all seem so easy."

"Trust me, I know it isn't. When I think back to the way things went between Clay and me, I empathize all the more with what you're going through now."

Kate remembered the dark days following Clay's visit to California. Neither Rorie nor Clay had ever told her what happened. Clay had gone to San Francisco, intending to bring Rorie back with him, and instead had returned alone.

"Maybe we need to get away from each other for a

while," Kate said. "Maybe if we aren't in such close proximity, we'll be able to sort out what we really feel for each other."

"When are you moving to town?"

"Monday," Kate said, looking at the cardboard boxes stacked against the opposite wall.

"Do you need help? Skip, Clay and I could easily lend a hand."

"That would be wonderful."

The rest of the weekend passed in a blur. Kate didn't see Luke once. So much for Rorie's assurances that he'd come by soon to talk everything out. Apparently he meant what he'd said.

Monday morning, when she was about to leave for school, Kate paused before she got into her car, deciding she should at least say goodbye to Luke before she moved out.

Luke wasn't in the barn, but Bill Schmidt was.

"Good morning, Bill."

"Howdy, Kate," he said with a wide grin. "Glad to see there's no ill effects from your accident."

"None, thanks. Is Luke around?"

Bill settled his hands in the pockets of his bib overalls. "No. Thought you knew. He left yesterday afternoon for New Mexico to look at some new equipment. He won't be back until Thursday."

Ten

Kate was carrying the last of the cardboard boxes to the recycling bins outside the apartment building on Thursday evening when she saw Luke's pickup turn onto Spruce Street. He came to a grinding halt at the curb, vaulted out of the cab and stood there scowling. His features were contorted, but for the life of her Kate couldn't understand why he was so irritated. Didn't he *tell* her to move? Wasn't this what he wanted?

She was about to make her presence known, but before she could act, Luke brought his fist down on the bonnet. She heard the sound from where she was standing. It must have smarted because he rubbed his knuckles, gazing intently at the redbrick building. Then, tucking his hands in the back pockets of his jeans, he squared his shoulders and strode toward it. He stopped abruptly, then retreated to his truck. Opening the door, he balanced one foot on the side rail, as if he was about to leap into the cab.

Kate leaned forward on the tips of her toes and stretched out her hand to stop him. It took everything in her not to rush forward. She was afraid she'd burst

into tears. Viewing Luke's behavior had touched something deep within her.

If Luke had planned to drive away, he apparently
changed his mind, because he slammed the door shut
and resolutely faced the building again.

Knowing that the time to make her move was now,
Kate casually turned the corner.

"Kate."

"Luke," she said, pretending surprise.

For a moment, Luke didn't say a word. "I just got
back to the ranch and discovered that the main house
was empty. I thought you'd be there when I returned."

"Mrs. Jackson said I could have the apartment Monday, and since Rorie, Clay and Skip were able to help
me move, I couldn't see any reason to delay."

"You might've told me."

Kate lowered her eyes, feeling a little guilty, since
they'd parted on such unfriendly terms. "I tried, but
you'd already left for New Mexico."

"Bill did say you wanted to talk to me," he conceded.

"Would you like to come inside?" she asked, opening the door for him.

"All right." He sounded reluctant.

Once in the apartment they stood looking at each other,
and Kate felt suddenly awkward. Luke's eyes were dark and
luminous and his face had never seemed so dear to her—
familiar, yet in some exciting new way, not fully known.
She would've liked nothing better than to walk into his
arms. She wanted to tell him how sorry she was about the
way they'd parted, to tell him she was ready to accept his
proposal on any terms. But her pride made that impossible.

"Nice place," he said when the silence became painful. He tucked his fingers in his back pockets again.

"Can I take your coat?"

"Please." He took it off and gave it to her.

She motioned toward the sofa. "Would you like to sit down?"

He nodded and sat on the edge of the cushion. Leaning forward, he balanced his hands between his knees and rotated his hat with his fingers. Luke had sat on this very same sofa a thousand times, but he'd never looked as uncomfortable as he did now.

"I came to apologize for the last time we spoke."

"Oh, Luke," she whispered, sitting in the overstuffed chair across from him. "I felt bad, too. Why do we argue like that? Some days I feel we're growing further and further apart, and I don't want that."

"I'd like to suggest we put an end to this nonsense, but you've made your views plain enough."

"You still want to take care of me?"

"I don't think that's so wrong."

"I know." She sighed, tired of repeating the same arguments. "But I'm fully capable of doing that myself."

"Right," he said with deadly softness. "You took care of yourself pretty well during that snowstorm, didn't you?"

"Why don't you throw Eric Wilson in my face while you're at it? I thought you came because you regretted our last argument, but it looks to me as if you're trying to start another one."

"All right," he shouted, "I'll stop! You asked me not to bring up the distasteful subject of marriage and I agreed. It's just that—" He clamped his mouth shut. "We're better off dropping the subject entirely," he finished stiffly.

"I hate when we argue," Kate said.

"So do I, Princess."

Although his tone was light, Kate heard the distress in his voice. It filled her with regret, and she longed for something comforting to say, something that would ease this awkwardness between them, and restore a sense of balance to their relationship.

"Do you need anything, Kate?"

"No. I'm fine," she rushed to assure him. She might occasionally date the wrong men and take foolish risks in snowstorms, but she could manage her own life!

Luke glanced around the room, then slowly nodded as if accepting the truth of her words.

"It was kind of you to stop by... I mean, it's good to see you and I really am grateful you wanted to clear the air, too."

"Are you saying you missed me while I was away?"

She had, terribly, but until that moment, Kate hadn't been willing to admit it, even to herself. Unconsciously she'd been waiting for Thursday, hoping to hear from Luke—but not really expecting to. For the past few days, she'd worked frantically to unpack her things and make her apartment presentable. And all along it had been an effort to prove to Luke how efficient and capable she actually was. After falling on her face so many times, she wanted this transition from the ranch house to her first apartment to go off without a hitch. It was a matter of pride.

They were like polite strangers with each other. Kate couldn't think of a single clever remark or probing question to reduce the tension between them.

"Have you eaten?" Luke asked brusquely. "I thought I'd take you to dinner. I realize I'm not giving you much notice and I read somewhere that women don't like a man to take things for granted, so if you don't want to go, I'll understand."

He sounded as though he assumed she'd reject his invitation. "I'd love to have dinner with you," she said, unable to hide a smile.

Luke seemed shocked by her easy acquiescence.

Kate stood up, stretching luxuriously. "If you'll give me a moment, I'll freshen up." She couldn't keep the happiness out of her voice.

Luke rose then, and his presence seemed to dwarf her small living room. Only a few scant inches separated them. With one finger, he tilted up her chin and looked deep into her eyes. "You honestly missed me?" he whispered.

For some reason, her throat squeezed shut and Kate was forced to answer him without words. She cradled his face between both hands and gazed up at him, nodding fervently.

Luke's eyes darkened and she thought he meant to kiss her. Just when she was prepared to slip into his arms and raise her mouth to his, he pulled loose from her light grasp and stepped back. Kate swallowed her disappointment.

"I was thinking about that pizza parlour in Riversdale," he said gruffly.

"Pizza would be wonderful," Kate said.

"Then it's settled."

Kate didn't bother to change clothes, but ran a brush through her hair and refreshed her make-up. A few minutes later, she was ready to leave. Luke stood at the door, and as she approached him, his appreciative look sent small flutters of awareness through her body.

Companionably they drove the thirty miles to Riversdale. By unspoken agreement they avoided any subject that would cause them to disagree.

The restaurant, Pizza Mania, was known throughout the county for its excellent Italian food. The room was dimly lit, and the wooden tables were covered with red-checkered cloths. Since it was a weeknight, the restaurant wasn't especially busy.

Luke guided her to a table in the middle of the homey room. Service was prompt and they quickly placed their order for a large sausage-and-black-olive pizza. Kate also ordered a raw vegetable platter with yogurt-herb dip, and she laughed at the disdainful expression on Luke's face. Then she laughed again.

"What's so funny now?"

"I was remembering the last time I ate pizza from here. It was when Rorie had just arrived, and she and I were making dinner for Clay and Skip. I made a lemon meringue pie and Rorie spent the entire afternoon preparing this fancy seafood dish."

"Where does the pizza come in?"

Kate told Luke about the disastrous dinner, and he smiled slightly, shaking his head. "Rorie must've been devastated."

"Actually she was a pretty good sport about the whole thing. We called Pizza Mania, ordered two large pizzas that Skip offered to pick up, and afterward we sat around the piano for a while."

That night was when she'd realized how hard Clay was fighting not to fall in love with Rorie. All evening he'd tried not to even glance in her direction. Then, later, when he drove Kate home, he'd said barely a word and gently kissed her cheek after he'd walked her to the door. A peck on the cheek, the way he'd kiss a younger sister.

"What's wrong?" Luke asked.

"Nothing." Kate summoned a smile. "What makes you

ask?" She was relieved at the appearance of their vege- table appetizer, immediately reaching for a carrot stick.

"Your eyes looked kind of sad just now."

Kate concentrated on munching her carrot, aston- ished at the way Luke so often seemed to know what she was thinking. But then, sometimes he didn't.... "That night was when I knew I was losing Clay to Rorie. My whole world was about to fall apart and I felt powerless to do anything about it. It didn't mean I stopped trying, of course—it hurt too much to accept without putting up a fight." She paused and helped herself to a zucchini strip. "Enough about me. It seems I'm the only one we ever discuss. How was your trip to New Mexico?" she asked brightly, determined to change the subject.

"Good." He didn't elaborate. His eyes held hers, the mood warm and comfortable. "There are going to be a few changes around the Circle L in the coming months. I don't want you to be surprised when you find out I'm adding a couple of outbuildings and doing some remod- elling on the house."

Although he spoke in a conversational tone, Kate wasn't fooled. "The Circle L belongs to you now. I ex- pect there'll be plenty of changes, but don't worry about offending me or Dad."

He nodded and his eyes brightened with his dreams for the future. "I intend to turn it into one of the top cattle ranches on the West Coast."

"I'm sure you'll do it, Luke." And she was.

He seemed pleased by her confidence in him. Kate couldn't help believing in Luke. In the ten years he'd worked for her father, he'd initiated several success- ful breeding programs. With each passing year, Devin had turned more and more of the ranch business over to Luke. Her father had become a figurehead. Kate had often heard Devin say that he couldn't understand why Luke would continue working for him when he was completely capable of maintaining his own spread. At one time, Kate had thought money was the issue, but that obviously wasn't the case.

"Why'd you delay buying your own ranch for so long?" Kate asked, just as their pizza arrived. Their waitress remained standing at their table and studied them so blatantly that Luke turned to her.

"Is something wrong?" he asked sharply.

"No…not at all. Enjoy your dinner." She backed away from their table and hurried over to the counter, where two other employees were waiting. Almost immediately the three of them huddled together and started whispering.

Luke chose to ignore their waitress's strange behavior and lifted a steaming piece, thick with melted cheese and spicy sausage, onto her plate. Then he served himself.

"Now, where were we?" Luke murmured.

"I asked why you didn't buy your own ranch before now."

"You don't want to know the answer to that, Princess."

"Of course I do. I wouldn't have brought it up otherwise," she insisted.

"Fine." Luke settled back in his chair. He looked at her, eyes thoughtful. "I had a minor problem. I was in love with the boss's daughter and she was crazy about me, only she didn't know it. In fact, she'd gotten herself engaged to someone else. I was afraid that if I moved away she'd never realize how I felt—or how she did—

and frankly, I didn't think I could ever love anyone the way I do her."

Kate focused her attention on her meal. The lump in her throat was almost choking her. "You're right about...me not loving Clay," she told him softly. No matter how hard she tried, she couldn't raise her eyes high enough to meet his.

"What did you say?"

"I... You were right about me and Clay. I could never feel for him the things a wife should feel for her husband. I'd adored him for years, but that love was just a teenage fantasy."

She was well aware of the seriousness of her admission. The room seemed to go still; the music from the juke box faded, the clatter from the kitchen dimmed and the voices from the people around them seemed to disappear altogether.

"I didn't think I'd ever hear you admit that," Luke said, and his face filled with tenderness.

"I tried to tell you the night after I had dinner with Clay and Rorie, but you were so angry with me...because I was moving." She laughed, hoping to break the unexpected tension that had leaped between them.

"Does this also mean you're admitting you love *me*?"

"I've never had a problem with that—"

Kate was interrupted by an elderly man who strolled up to their table. With considerable ceremony, he lifted a violin to his chin and played a bittersweet love song.

"I didn't know they had strolling violinists here," Kate said when the man had finished. Everyone in the restaurant stopped to applaud.

"This next song is dedicated to the two of you," the

man announced, "that the love in your hearts will blossom into a bouquet of *May* flowers."

It wasn't until he'd finished the third song that Kate noticed he didn't go to any of the other tables. He seemed to be playing only for them. Some of the customers had apparently noticed this, too, and gathered behind Luke and Kate in order to get a better view of the musician.

"Thank you," Kate said as the last notes faded.

The man lowered his instrument to his side. "You two have become quite a sensation in Nightingale and beyond. We at Pizza Mania are honored that you've chosen our restaurant for a romantic evening. We want to do our part to bring you together in wedded bliss."

"And you're suggesting the month of May?" Kate asked, referring to his comment about a bouquet of flowers.

"That would be an excellent choice," the violinist said, grinning broadly.

"It's time we left," Luke said, frowning. He pulled out his wallet, but the violinist stopped him. "Please, your pizza's on the house. We are delighted that you chose to dine in our humble establishment."

From the tight set of Luke's mouth, Kate could tell he wanted to argue, but more urgent was his need to escape. He took her by the hand and charged for the door.

"Your leftover pizza!" Their waitress ran after them, handing Luke a large white box as she cast Kate an envious glance.

Luke couldn't seem to get out of the car park fast enough. Kate waited until they were on the road before she spoke. "So this is the first time that's happened to you?"

Luke laughed shortly. "Not really, only I didn't pick up on it as quickly as you did. Several people have made odd comments about certain months, but until now, I didn't get what they were actually saying."

"It's funny when you think about it. Half the county's got money riding on our wedding day, and Fred Garner's making a killing raising and lowering the odds." Suddenly the lottery was the most hilarious thing Kate had ever heard of, and she started to laugh. She slumped against the side of the cab, holding her sides. She was laughing so hard, her stomach hurt. Tears ran down her cheeks and she wiped them away as she tried to regain control. The wedding lottery and everyone's interference wasn't all *that* funny, but Luke's disgruntled reaction was.

"Come on, Luke," she said, still chuckling. "There's a lot of humor in this situation."

He snorted.

"Don't be such a killjoy. I've been getting free advice from the butcher, Sally Daley, the paperboy and just about everyone else in town. It's only fair that you put up with a few of their comments, too."

"One might think you'd take some of that free advice," he muttered.

"What?" she cried. "And ruin their fun?"

Luke was oddly quiet for the remainder of the trip into Nightingale. He stopped at her building, walked her to her door with barely a word, then turned and walked away. No goodnight kiss, no mention of seeing her again.

This was the last thing she'd expected. For the entire drive home, she'd been imagining how good it would feel when Luke kissed her. She'd decided to invite him in for coffee, hoping he'd accept. But this was even worse than Clay's peck on the cheek all those months ago.

"Luke…"

He stopped abruptly at the sound of her voice, then turned back. His eyes seemed to burn into hers as he came toward her, and she stumbled into his arms. His mouth, hot and hungry, sought hers in a kiss that scorched her senses.

His fingers plunged into her hair, releasing the French braid and ploughing through the twisted strands of blond hair.

Instinctively Kate reached up and slid her arms around his shoulders, feeling so much at home in his arms that it frightened her. She trembled with the knowledge, but she didn't have time to analyze her feelings. Not when her world was in chaos. She clung to him as though she were rocketing into a fathomless sky.

Luke broke away from her, his face a study of hope and confusion. "I never know where I stand with you, Kate." With that, he stroked her hair and quickly returned to his truck.

Kate was still reeling from the effects of Luke's kiss. If she hadn't leaned against her door, she might have fallen onto the walkway, so profound was her reaction.

"Luke," she called, shocked by how weak her voice sounded. "Would you like to come inside for coffee? We could talk about…things."

Slowly a smile eased its way across his handsome features. "I don't dare, Princess, because the way I feel right now, I might not leave until morning. If then."

Flustered by his words, Kate unlocked her door and let herself inside.

She gulped a deep breath and stood in the middle of the living room with her hand over her rampaging heart. "You're in love with him, Kate Logan," she told herself. "Head over heels in love with a man and fighting him every step of the way."

Groaning, she buried her face in her hands. She didn't understand *why* she'd been fighting him so hard. She did realize that Luke wouldn't have spent years building up her father's ranch if he hadn't loved her. He could have left anytime, gone anywhere to buy his own ranch, but he'd stayed at the Circle L. He honestly loved her!

Now she knew what she wanted, but she didn't know what to do about it.

She guessed Luke was planning to court her, to use that charming old-fashioned term. If so, one more dinner with him would be enough. They'd be officially engaged by the end of the evening. She'd bet on it!

To her disappointment, Kate didn't hear from him the following day. Fridays were generally busy around the ranch, so she decided the next move would have to come from her.

Early Saturday morning she compiled a grocery list, intent on inviting Luke over for a home-cooked meal. She was reviewing her cookbooks, searching for a special dessert recipe, when she was suddenly distracted by the memory of their kiss. Closing her eyes, she relived the way she'd felt that night. She smiled to herself, admitting how eager she was to feel that way again.

If only she'd been listening to her heart instead of her pride...

She tried phoning Luke, but there was no answer, so she decided to do the shopping first. She put on her coat, hat and gloves, and walked the few blocks to the Safeway store.

It must've been her imagination, but it seemed that everyone stopped to watch her as she pushed her cart down the aisles.

When she'd finished buying her groceries, she headed over to the pharmacy and bought a couple of scented candles. Once again, everyone seemed to stop and stare at her.

"Kate," Sally Daley said, hurrying toward her. The older woman was shaking her head, eyes brimming with sympathy. "How are you doing, dear?"

"Fine," Kate said, puzzled.

Sally's mouth fell open. "You don't know, do you?"

"Know what?"

"Luke Rivers took Beth Hammond to dinner yesterday, and the two of them danced all night at the Red Bull. Why, everyone in town's talking about it. People are saying he's lost patience with you and is going to marry Beth. Really, dear, every woman in town thinks you'd be crazy to let a man like Luke Rivers get away."

Kate was so shocked she could hardly breathe. "I see," she murmured, pretending it didn't matter.

"You poor child," Sally said compassionately. "Don't let your pride get in the way."

"I won't," Kate promised, barely able to find her voice.

"I do worry about you, Kate. I have this terrible feeling that you're going to end up thirty and all alone."

Eleven

Thirty and all alone. The words echoed in Kate's mind as she walked the short distance to her apartment. Tears burned her eyes, but somehow she'd dredged up the courage to smile and assure Sally that Luke was free to date whomever he pleased. In fact, she'd even managed to laugh lightly and say that she hoped Luke's dating Beth would finally put an end to all this wedding-lottery nonsense.

Moving at a fast pace, she kept her head lowered and went directly back to her apartment, clutching her purchases. By the time she let herself in the door, her face was streaked with tears.

No doubt Sally would spread the story of her meeting with Kate all over town by evening. Not that it made much difference. By now, the residents of Nightingale should be accustomed to hearing gossip about her and Luke.

Luke. At the mere thought of him, her heart constricted painfully. He'd given up on her and now she'd lost him. Only it hurt so much more than when Clay had broken their engagement.

Wiping the tears from her eyes, she struggled to take in everything that had happened in the past few weeks. It seemed every time she found her balance and secured her footing, something would send her teetering again. Would it never end? Was her life going to be an endless struggle of one emotional pain after another?

She set her bags on the floor, and without bothering to remove her coat, slumped into the overstuffed chair.

"Okay," she said aloud. "Luke took Beth Hammond out to dinner and dancing. It doesn't have to mean anything."

But it did. In her heart Kate was sure Luke planned to do exactly as Sally suggested. He'd made it plain from the first that he wanted a wife, and like a fool Kate had repeatedly turned him down. He loved her, or so he claimed, and Kate had doubted him. Now she wondered if perhaps he didn't love her enough. But over and over again, Luke had insisted she needed him— and he'd been right.

Closing her eyes, she tried to picture her life without Luke. A chill ran down her spine as an intense wave of loneliness swept over her.

Someone pounded at the door, but before Kate could answer it, Luke strode into the apartment. Having to face him this way, when she was least prepared, put her at a clear disadvantage. Hurriedly she painted on a bright smile.

"Hello, Luke," she said, trying to sound breezy and amused. "What's this about you and Beth Hammond?"

"You heard already?" He looked stunned.

"Good heavens, yes. You don't expect something like that to stay quiet, do you?"

"When…who told you?"

"I went to the grocery store and ran into Sally Daley."

"That explains it," he said, pacing her carpet with abrupt, impatient steps. He stopped suddenly and turned to study her. "It doesn't bother you that I'm seeing Beth?"

"Not at all," she lied. "Should it? Would you like some coffee?"

"No."

Desperate for a chance to escape and compose herself, Kate almost ran into the kitchen and poured herself a cup, keeping her back to him all the while.

"You seem to be downright happy about this," he accused, following her into the small, windowless room.

"Of course I'm pleased. I think it's wonderful when two people fall in love, don't you?"

"I'm not in love with Beth," he said angrily.

"Actually I think dating Beth is a wonderful way to kill all the rumors floating around about us," she said, finally turning toward him. She held her coffee cup close.

Rubbing his neck, Luke continued his pacing in the kitchen. "I thought you might be...jealous."

"Me?" She refused to admit she'd been dying inside from the moment Sally had told her. "Now why would I feel like that?"

"I don't know," Luke barked. "Why would you?"

Before Kate could answer, he stormed out of the apartment, leaving her so frustrated she could have cried.

"You should've told him how you feel," she reprimanded herself. "Why are you such a fool when it comes to Luke Rivers? Why? Why? Why?"

* * *

"I saw Luke yesterday," Rorie said, watching Kate closely as they sat across from each other in a booth at Nellie's.

"That's nice," she said, pretending indifference and doing a good job of it.

"He was with Beth Hammond."

Kate's breath caught in her throat at the unexpected rush of pain. "I...see."

"Do you?" Rorie inquired. "I swear I could shake the pair of you. I've never met two more stubborn people in my life. You look like one of the walking wounded, and Luke's got a chip on his shoulder the size of a California redwood."

"I'm sure you're mistaken." Kate concentrated on stirring her coffee and avoided Rorie's eyes. Her heart felt like a ball of lead.

"When's the last time you two talked?"

"A couple of days ago."

"Honestly, Kate, I can't understand what's wrong with you. Clay and I thought...we hoped everything would fall into place after you moved to the apartment. Now it seems exactly the opposite has happened."

"Luke's free to date whomever he pleases, just the way I am."

"There's only one person you want and that's Luke Rivers and we both know it," Rorie said with an exasperated sigh. "I shouldn't have said that. It's just that I hate the idea of you two being so miserable when you're in love with each other."

"Is love always this painful?" Kate asked, her question barely audible.

Rorie shrugged. "It was with Clay and me, and sometimes I feel it must be for everyone sooner or later. Think about it, Kate. If you really love Luke, why are you fighting the very thing you want most?"

"I don't know," she admitted reluctantly.

When they parted shortly afterward, Kate felt a new sense of certainty and resolve. She *did* love Luke and if she didn't do something soon, she was going to lose him.

She drove to the Circle L, her heart in her throat. Luke's truck was parked behind the house, and she left her car beside it, hurrying through the cold to the back door. Luke didn't respond to her knock, which didn't surprise her, since it was unusual for him to be in at this time of day. But she couldn't find him outside, either, and even Bill didn't know where he was.

Making a rapid decision, she let herself into the house and started preparations for the evening meal. It gave her a way of passing the time. Dinner was in the oven and she was busy making a salad, when the back door opened and Luke walked into the kitchen.

Apparently he hadn't noticed her car because he stopped dead, shock written on every feature, when he saw her standing at the sink.

Kate held her breath for a moment, then dried her hands on the dish towel she'd tucked into her waistband. She struggled to give the impression that she was completely at ease, tried to act as though she made dinner for him every evening.

"Hello, Luke," she said to break the silence that had been growing heavier by the second.

He blinked. "I suppose you're looking for an explanation."

Kate wasn't sure what he meant.

"Taking Beth out on Friday night was a mistake."

"Then why'd you do it?"

"So you'd be jealous. The night you and I went out, I was furious at the way you started laughing, and talking as if you were never going to marry me. I wanted you to know you weren't the only fish in the sea. Only my plan backfired."

"It did?" Not as far as Kate was concerned—she'd been pretty darn worried.

"That wasn't all that went wrong. Beth saw I was in town on Saturday and started following me," he explained. "I swear I had no intention of seeing her again, but before I knew it, her arm was linked with mine and we were strolling through the middle of town together."

"Beth's a nice girl."

He frowned. "Yes, I suppose she is. I'd forgotten it doesn't bother you who I date. You've never been one for jealousy."

"I was so jealous I wanted to die."

"You were? You could've fooled me."

"Believe me, I tried to," Kate murmured.

"So what are you doing here?"

"I made dinner," Kate said sheepishly. She'd admitted how she felt about Luke seeing Beth and she couldn't stop there. "I've got pork chops in the oven, along with scalloped potatoes and an acorn squash," she rattled off without pausing for breath. Then, gathering her resolve, she casually added, "and if you're still asking, I'll marry you."

Luke stared at her. When he finally spoke he sounded strangely calm. "What did you just say?"

"There's pork chops and potatoes and—"

"Not that. The part about marrying me."

She struggled to hold on to what remained of her tattered pride. "If you're still asking me to marry you, the answer is yes."

"I'm still asking."

Kate dropped her gaze. "You've been right about so much. I do need you. I guess I was waiting for you to admit you needed *me,* only you never did."

Luke rubbed a hand over his face. "Not need you?" he repeated, his voice filled with shock and wonder. "I think my life would be an empty shell without you, Kate. I couldn't bear the thought of living one day to the next if you weren't at my side to share everything with me—all the good things that are in store for us. I've waited so long, Kate."

"You do love me, don't you?" she whispered.

For a long, long moment Luke said nothing. "I tried not to. For years I stood by helplessly, watching you break out in hives with excitement every time you saw Clay Franklin. I realized it was a schoolgirl crush, but you never seemed to get over him. Instead of improving, things got worse. How could I let you know how I felt?"

"Couldn't you have said something? Anything?"

A flicker of pain crossed his face. "No. You were so infatuated with Clay I didn't dare. It wouldn't have done any good—although God only knows how you managed not to figure it out yourself. The first day Rorie met me, she guessed."

"Rorie knew all along?"

Luke shook his head in bewildered amusement. "We were quite a pair a few months back—Rorie in love with Clay and me crazy about you. All this time, I thought I'd kept my feelings secret, and then I discovered everyone in town knew."

"Beth Hammond didn't."

"No, but she should have. I've never wanted anyone but you, Kate Logan. I haven't for years. Somehow I always kept hoping you'd see the light."

"Oh, Luke." She took a step toward him, her eyes full of emotion. "Are you going to stand way over there on the other side of the room?"

For every step Kate took, Luke managed three. When they reached each other, she put her arms around his waist, hugging him tight. She felt the beating of his heart and closed her eyes, succumbing to the wave of love that seemed about to overwhelm her.

Luke's hand was gentle on her hair. "Do you love me, Kate?"

She couldn't speak, so she nodded her head wildly. Her hands framed his face and she spread light, eager kisses over his mouth and nose and eyes, letting her lips explain what was in her heart.

"I love you," he whispered. "If you marry me, I promise I'll do everything I can to make you happy." His eyes shone with delight and a kind of humility that touched Kate's very soul. Gone was the remoteness he'd displayed so often these past few weeks.

"Oh, Luke, I can hardly wait to be your wife," she said. "Didn't you say something about a December wedding?"

"Kate, that's only a few weeks from now."

"Yes, I know. But Christmas is such a lovely time of year for a wedding. We'll decorate the church with holly, and all the bridesmaids will wear long red dresses...."

"Kate, you mean it, don't you?" His voice was low and husky.

"I've never meant anything more. I love you, Luke Rivers. We're going to have a wonderful life together."

He kissed her then, with a hunger that spoke of his years of longing. Dragging his mouth from hers, he buried it in the curve of her neck.

"I want children, Kate. I want to fill this home with so much love that the walls threaten to burst with it."

For a breathless moment, they did nothing more than gaze at each other as they shared that dream.

Kate smiled up at him, and as her hands mapped his face, loving each strong feature, she was astonished at how easily this happiness had come to her once she'd let go of her pride.

Luke's mouth settled on hers, his kiss almost reverent, as though he couldn't yet believe she was in his home and eager to be his wife.

As Kate wrapped her arms around his neck, her glance fell on the calendar. She seemed to recall that Pastor Wilkins had placed a sizeable wager on the fifteenth of December. That sounded good to Kate.

Very good indeed.

Epilogue

The sun shone clear and bright in the late-July afternoon, two years after Rorie Campbell's car had broken down near Nightingale. Kate was making a fresh pitcher of iced tea when Rorie knocked on the back door.

"Come on in," Kate called. "The screen door's unlocked."

A moment later Rorie entered the kitchen, looking slightly frazzled. "How did your afternoon at the library go?" Kate asked, as she added ice cubes to the tall pitcher.

"Very well, thanks."

"Katherine's still sleeping," Kate told her.

Rorie's eyes softened as she gazed out at the newly constructed patio where her baby slept under the shade of the huge oak tree.

"It was such a lovely afternoon I kept her outside." Kate wiped her hands dry. She poured them each a glass of iced tea, and carried a tray of tea and cookies onto the patio.

The nine-month-old infant stirred when Rorie stood over the portable crib and protectively placed her hand on the sleeping baby's back. When she turned, her eyes fell on Kate's protruding abdomen. "How are *you* feeling?"

"Like a blimp." Kate's hands rested on her swollen stomach. "The doctor told me it'll probably be another two weeks."

"Two weeks!" Rorie said sympathetically.

"I know, and I was hoping Junior would choose this week to arrive. I swear to you, Rorie, when you were pregnant with Katherine you positively glowed. You made everything seem so easy."

Rorie laughed. "I did?"

"I feel miserable. My legs are swollen, my hands and feet look like they've been inflated. There isn't a single part of my body that's normal-sized anymore."

Rorie laughed again. "The last few weeks are always like that. I think the main difference is that Katherine was born in October, when the weather was much cooler."

With some difficulty Kate crossed her legs. "I only hope our baby will be as good-natured as Katherine. She barely fussed the whole time she was here."

"Her uncle Skip thinks she's going to start walking soon."

"I think he's right." Pressing a hand to her ribs, Kate shifted her position. She was finding it difficult to sit comfortably for longer than a few minutes at a time.

"Oh—" Rorie set her iced tea aside "—I almost forgot." She hurried back to the kitchen and returned with a hardbound children's book. "I received my first copies of *Nightsong's Adventures* in the mail yesterday. Kate, I can't even begin to tell you how thrilled I was when I held this book in my hands."

Kate laid the book on her lap and slowly turned the

pages. "The illustrations are fantastic. They really fit the story."

"The reviews have been excellent. One critic said he expected it to become a children's classic, which I realize is ridiculous, but I couldn't help feeling excited about it."

"It isn't ridiculous, and I'm sure your publisher knows that, otherwise they wouldn't have been so eager to buy your second book."

"You know, the second sale was every bit as exciting as the first," Rorie said with a smile.

"Just think, in a few years our children will be reading your stories and attending school together. They're bound to be the best of friends."

Before Kate could respond, the baby woke and they watched, delighted, as she sat up in the portable crib. When she saw her mother sitting next to Kate, she smiled, her dark eyes twinkling. She raised her chubby arms, reaching for Rorie.

Rorie stood and lifted Katherine out of the crib, kissing the little girl's cheeks. "I'd better get her home. Thanks so much for watching Katherine for me. I promised I'd pinch-hit for the new librarian if she ever needed me, and I didn't think I could refuse her even though it was at the last minute."

"It wasn't any problem, so don't worry. And tell Mary she should visit her sister more often so I get the opportunity to babysit every once in a while."

"Call me later and let me know how you're feeling."

Kate nodded.

Ten minutes after Rorie and Katherine left, Luke drove up and parked behind the house. Standing on the porch, Kate waved to her husband.

Luke joined her, placing an arm around what once had been a trim waist, and led the way into the kitchen. "You okay?" His gaze was tender.

Kate wasn't sure how to answer that. She was miserable. Excited. Frightened. Eager. So many emotions were coming at her, she didn't know which one to mention first.

"Kate?"

"I feel fine." There was no need to list her complaints, but all of a sudden she felt *funny*. She didn't know any other way to describe it. As Rorie had said, there were a dozen different aches and pains the last few weeks of any pregnancy.

Luke kissed her, his mouth soft. "Did you have a busy day with Katherine?"

"She slept almost the entire time, but I think Rorie knew she would." Leaning forward, Kate kissed her husband's jaw. "I made some iced tea. Want some?"

"Please."

When Kate reached inside the cupboard for a glass, a sharp pain split her side. She let out a cry.

"Kate?"

Clutching her swollen abdomen, Kate stared at Luke. "Oh, my goodness. I just felt a pain."

Luke paled. "You're in labor?"

Smiling, wide-eyed, she nodded slowly. "I must be. I didn't expect them to start off so strong."

In an instant, Luke was across the kitchen beside her. "Now what?"

"I think I should call the doctor."

"No." Luke's arm flew out as if that would halt the course of nature. "I'll call. Stay there. Don't move."

"But, Luke—"

"For heaven's sake, Kate, don't argue with me now. We're about to have a baby!"

He said this as if it were a recent discovery. As he reached for the phone, she saw that he'd gone deathly pale. When he finished talking to the doctor, he gave her a panicked look, then announced that Doc Adams wanted them to go straight to the hospital. As soon as the words left his mouth, he shot to the bedroom, then returned with her suitcase. He halted abruptly when he saw she'd picked up the phone.

"Who are you calling?"

"Dad and Dorothea. I promised I would."

"Kate, would you let me do the phoning?"

"All right." She handed him the receiver and started toward the bedroom to collect the rest of her things. If he thought that talking on the phone was too taxing for her, fine. She'd let him do it. The years had taught her that arguing with Luke was fruitless.

"Kate," he yelled. "Don't wander off."

"Luke, I just want to get my things before we leave." A pain began to work its way around her back and she paused, flattening her hands across her abdomen. She raised her head and smiled up at her husband. "Oh, Luke, the baby…"

Luke dropped the receiver and rushed to her side. "Now?"

"No." She laughed and touched his face. "It'll be hours yet. Oh! I just felt another pain—a bad one."

He swallowed hard and gripped both her hands in his own. "I've been looking forward to this moment for nine months, but I swear to you, Kate, I've never been more frightened in my life."

"Don't worry." Her hands caressed his face and she kissed him, offering what reassurance she could.

He exhaled noisily, then gave her a brisk little nod. Without warning, he lifted her in his arms, ignoring her protests, and carried her out the door to the truck. Once he'd settled her in the seat, he returned to the house for her bag.

"Luke," she called after him, "I really would like to talk to Dad and Dorothea."

"I'll phone them from the hospital. No more arguing, Kate. I'm in charge here."

Only another sharp pain—and her regard for Luke's feelings—kept her from breaking out in laughter.

Ten long hours later, Kate lay in the hospital bed, eyes closed in exhaustion. When she opened them, she discovered her father standing over her. Dorothea was next to him, looking as pleased and proud as Kate's father. Devin took his daughter's hand in his own and squeezed it gently. "How do you feel, little mother?"

"Wonderful. Did they let you see him? Oh, Dad, he's so beautiful!"

Her father nodded. For a moment he seemed unable to speak. "Luke's with Matthew now. He looks so big sitting in that rocking chair, holding his son."

"I don't think I've ever seen Luke wear an expression quite like that before," Dorothea murmured. "So tender and loving."

Devin concurred with a nod of his head. "When Luke came into the waiting room to tell us Matthew Devin had been born, there were tears in his eyes. I'll tell you, Kate, that man loves you."

"I know, Dad, and I love him, too."

Devin patted her hand. "You go ahead and rest, Princess. Dorothea and I'll be back tomorrow."

When Kate opened her eyes a second time, Luke was there. She held out her hand to him and smiled dreamily. "I couldn't have done it without you. Thank you for staying with me."

"Staying with you," he echoed, his fingers brushing the tousled curls from her face. "Nothing on earth could have kept me away. I would've done anything to spare you that pain, Kate. Anything." His voice was raw with the memory of those last hours.

Her smile was one of comfort. "It only lasted a little while and we have a beautiful son to show for it."

"All these months when we've talked about the baby," he said, his eyes glazed, "he seemed so unreal to me, and then you were in the delivery room and in so much agony. I felt so helpless. I wanted to help you and there was nothing I could do. Then Matthew was born and, Kate, I looked at him and I swear something happened to my heart. The love I felt for that baby, that tiny person, was so strong, so powerful, I could hardly breathe. I thought I was going to break down right there in front of everyone."

"Oh, Luke."

"There's no way I could ever thank you for all you've given me, Kate Rivers."

"Yes, there is," she said with a smile. "Just love me."

"I do," he whispered, his voice husky with emotion. "And I always will."

* * * * *

Read on for a sneak peek at
One Charmed Christmas,
a heartwarming holiday romance from
USA TODAY *bestselling author Sheila Roberts.*

1

"Your kids are twits," Catherine Pine's friend Denise informed her. "They shouldn't be leaving you at Christmas, not after what you've been through."

"It's been a rough year," Catherine admitted.

Coping with widowhood and then, right after her sixtieth birthday, getting hit with uterine cancer. Not the best year of Catherine's life, for sure. And chemo and radiation awaited her in the new year.

"All the more reason they should be with you," Denise said.

"They have lives of their own," Catherine said in her children's defense.

Denise gave a snort and took a gulp from her latte. "Which they're happy to make you a part of when it suits them."

Catherine frowned. Denise was her best friend and best friends were like sisters. Not that Catherine had a sister—only a brother who'd never bothered to marry—but that was what she'd always thought. Still, there were times when best friends and probably even sisters needed to keep their mouths shut. Morning lattes together at Starbucks and diet accountability didn't give a woman the right to diss her friend's children. Even if they were twits sometimes. Denise's daughter wasn't so perfect. She'd gone through two husbands in twelve years.

Denise pointed an acrylic-nail-tipped finger at Catherine. "They were barely there for you after your surgery."

"They both had to work."

This inspired an eye roll. "And now they're both abandoning you at Christmas? They should be buried up to their necks in lumps of coal."

Catherine had so hoped to have her children with her. "Mom, last year was torture," her daughter, Lila, had informed her when Catherine brought up the subject of the family gathering for Christmas. As if Catherine were planning to give them a repeat performance.

No, their celebration the year before hadn't exactly been a happy gathering. Not a "We Wish You a Merry Christmas" moment anywhere in sight. It had been their first one without Bill, and Catherine had cried through everything, starting with the opening of presents and going clear through Christmas dinner. Her misery had infected her daughter, making Lila cry, as well. William's wife had teared up, too, and poor William had looked miserable and at a loss for what to say or do. Even the grandkids had been miserable. Catherine's youngest grandchild, Mariette, had sat under the tree and sobbed, and Aaron, the oldest grandboy, had muttered, "This sucks."

Yes, it had sucked. Catherine had tried not to turn on the waterworks again when the kids and grandkids gathered their presents and put on their coats to go home, but she'd failed. *Ho, ho, ho.* They'd all left like people anxious to leave a funeral.

But this year Catherine was in a better place, and she'd wanted to make new memories. Still regaining her energy from her hysterectomy, she hadn't felt up to preparing a big meal at Thanksgiving. But now, with the year coming to a close, she'd been feeling more energetic and ready to ring in the holidays. She'd never imagined doing that by herself.

"We're going to Park City with James's parents for Christmas," Lila had said when Catherine called her. Where there would be skiing and spoiling aplenty. James lacked for nothing and, after marrying him, neither did Lila.

Not that she'd lacked for much of anything growing up. Catherine had done her best to make sure of that.

"You'll be fine for a few days, won't you?" Her daughter's tone of voice added, *Of course you will.*

"Yes, but what about your presents?" Presents were always a good lure. Maybe they could get together beforehand.

Sadly, no. Lila had sooo much to do. "You can send them along with us," she'd offered.

William had beaten Catherine to the punch for Christmas plans as well, mentioning when she'd checked in on him that he and Gabrielle were taking the kids to Cabo for the holidays. "We need to get away," he'd said.

So did Catherine. Nobody had offered her the opportunity to get away with them. But then, who liked a tagalong, anyway?

"You spoil the kids," Bill used to say. He'd especially said it whenever Catherine went over to their daughter's house to help with the babies or unpleasant cleaning chores. "Lila can clean her own house. Hell, she can afford to hire someone to clean her house. And she sure can afford to pay a babysitter. It doesn't always have to be you."

Yes, but Catherine had wanted to help her daughter. Wasn't that what you were supposed to do when you got older, help the younger generation? And besides, she liked spending time with the grandkids.

If Bill had been alive to witness her loaning their son that chunk of money for the bathroom remodel six months earlier he'd have had a fit. William now had a new position in his company and was making a boatload of money. So far there had been no mention of paying her back. He would, though. Eventually. Hopefully.

"Why don't you come with me on my cruise?" Denise suggested.

"Oh, I don't know…" Catherine hesitated.

"Come on," Denise urged. "This Christmas cruise is going to be fabulous. We'll hit all those European Christmas markets, drink Glühwein, eat gingerbread…"

"Blow our diets."

Not that Denise needed to worry about that. She never went more than five pounds over svelte. Catherine, on the other hand, rarely made it within twenty pounds over her ideal weight. If only she didn't like to bake…and eat what she baked.

"We can get back on them in the new year." Denise pointed out the coffee shop window at the gray Seattle sky. "Don't you want to get away?"

Catherine did, indeed, want to get away, not just from the Seattle rain but from her life. But you were stuck in the skin you were in, and no matter where she went she'd still be going through what she was going through.

"I don't know," she said with a sigh, and shoved away her to-go cup and the last half of her muffin.

"I really don't want to be in a stateroom all by myself. That darned Janelle, backing out at the last minute." Denise shook her head. "It won't be half as much fun if I have to go by myself."

She wouldn't be by herself for long. Unlike Catherine, Denise instantly made friends wherever she went.

"And who's going to keep me from eating too much kuchen?"

"Kuchen?"

"Cake. German pastries are the best, trust me. Just think, Amsterdam, Heidelberg, men in lederhosen."

Catherine raised an eyebrow. "In December?"

"Okay, maybe not. But who knows who we might meet?"

Denise the merry widow. She'd been on her own for ten years. Carlisle, her dead husband, had been her one true love, but that didn't stop her from enjoying a string of boyfriends or traveling with girlfriends. Denise had adapted well to being on her own. Catherine wasn't sure she ever would.

Denise brought out her brochure with pictures of the towns and cities where the ship would stop. "Isn't it magical?"

It did look magical. The brochure showed her town centers with fountains and cobbled streets, stately ancient churches with their spires piercing the sky, pictures of the Christmas markets all lit up and thronged with happy shoppers. And there was a picture of the boat, all decked out in lights.

It was indeed. And tempting.

"We can split the cost of the room," Denise continued, "and I'm sure my travel agent can work things out with the cruise company to get you on the plane since Janelle only pooped out on me yesterday. Your passport's up-to-date, right?"

"It is." Catherine had been looking forward to using it after Bill retired. She'd never gotten the chance.

"Then dust it off and let's go. After we get back you can have Christmas with me and Carrie and the girls."

A trip down the Rhine River, checking out scenic towns and bustling Christmas markets or sitting home alone, yearning for the past, being miserable in the present and worrying about the future—decisions, decisions.

"All right," said Catherine. Why not? "You talked me into it." Suddenly, the month of December was looking much brighter. Almost merry.

"Should you be traveling?" asked her daughter when she mentioned it during a phone conversation later that night.

Lila had called to see if Mom could come stay with the kids the night of James's office Christmas party and had been shocked to hear her mother wouldn't be around.

"I think I'll be fine. I'm feeling pretty good."

"It's only been three weeks since your surgery."

"I know. But my energy's starting to come back. I'm fine. Anyway, it will have been over a month by the time we go."

"You shouldn't be traveling halfway across the world all by yourself," Lila said firmly.

"I won't be by myself. I'll be with Denise. Anyway, I want to do something fun this December."

There was a long moment of silence. Did Lila think Catherine was guilting her? Hmm. Maybe she was, just a little.

"I still think it's a bad idea, but it's your decision."

No kidding. "Yes, it is."

Lila heaved a sigh. "I'd better start calling around for a babysitter."

"Yes, you had." Because Catherine was going to have a life.

Fifty branded Christmas ornaments successfully ordered online and shipped to the office of Tilly's Timeless Treasures for their annual Christmas party; holiday chocolate sampler boxes found for a wedding planner who needed them for an upcoming wedding; twelve special gifts bought for Harry Davis, Realtor, for his upcoming office party...and a partridge in a pear tree.

Sophie Miles set aside her laptop and stretched. All in a day's work for a professional shopper. She sneezed. Was she coming down with something? This would not be a good time to catch a cold, with the holidays right around the corner. Not that she had any big plans other than hanging out at her parents' house for Christmas.

Of course, hanging out at her parents' was a good thing. Hanging out by herself, well, at this point in her life it wasn't exactly what she'd planned. She'd figured she'd at least have a boyfriend in tow.

Being thirty and single at Christmas, with no hub, no kids, sucked. Being thirty and single sucked, period. She was pretty, she knew that. Blonde, blue-eyed, nice butt. She didn't have the biggest boobs in the world, it they were okay. She had good teeth. She was kind. She liked kids and football and wasn't too bad in the kitchen. Or the bedroom. Yet here she was, still single. Just because she had some health concerns sometimes.

"Sometimes?" her last boyfriend had echoed. "Everything's an emergency with you, Sophie. You've always got something. Or you think you're getting something. Or you're worried you're gonna get something."

That was an exaggeration. And it was only natural to worry. New viruses popped up all the time and people needed to take their health seriously.

"He does have a point," her sister, Sierra, had said when Sophie tried to cry on her shoulder. "You can get a little squirrelly. That's scary to some guys. I mean, I get it, but—"

"I am not a squirrel," Sophie had insisted. "I'm just in touch with my body."

"Right. That's why you thought you had throat cancer last year when all you had was acid reflux. Then there was the time we all stayed at that cabin in the mountains and you were sure you'd been bit by a tick and had Lyme disease, and the time you swallowed that corn nut and—"

"Never mind," Sophie had said, cutting off her sister before the list could grow any longer.

Just because a woman was vigilant about her health, it didn't make her squirrelly or a hypochondriac. Cuts could get infected. So could insect bites. Colds could turn into bronchitis and bronchitis into pneumonia. You could pick up the flu virus simply by touching an elevator button. (Which was why Sophie always pushed those buttons with her knuckle. Or better yet, her elbow.) It was important to be aware of your environment, especially after what people had gone through when COVID-19 hit. That wasn't squirrelly. That was preventive medicine.

Speaking of, she went to the shelf in her kitchen cupboard dedicated to her many bottles of vitamins, minerals and herbs, and took out her chewable vitamin C. Sneezes turned into colds in a heartbeat.

Her work was done for the day and her immune system was now boosted, which meant there was no putting it off any longer. She had to go to Costco and purchase those food supplies for her friend Camilla, the caterer. Camilla almost always did her own shopping but she was swamped and one of her employees was out sick, so she'd begged Sophie to help her out. The big warehouse store would be a zoo, full of people carrying all kinds of germs. This time of year people were walking petri dishes. No one stayed home when they were sick anymore. She'd take more vitamin C before bed.

She was reluctantly moving toward the closet to get her coat when her sister called. "Are you working?" Sierra asked.

She usually worked straight through lunch, eating an apple (an apple a day and all that) and some yogurt (probiotics, good for the digestion) while she surfed the internet on behalf of her clients. Today she'd gotten done early and once she'd braved Costco she was going to curl up on her couch with a cup of rooibos tea and stream a Hallmark movie.

"Just finished," she said. "You on your lunch break?"

"Yeah. Thought you might have a minute to talk."

A minute to talk. Obviously about how Sierra's plans

for the night before had gone. There wasn't any excitement in Sierra's voice. That wasn't a good sign.

"Sure," Sophie said cautiously. "What's up?"

"Murder."

"Oh, no. Mark didn't like his Christmas surprise?" How could he not?

"He can't go."

"Can't go? Why not? Is the Grinch holding him for ransom?"

"He says he doesn't have enough vacation time left and, anyway, he's swamped."

Sophie frowned in disgust. Really, Mark was such a waste of man sometimes. "Why can't he, like, talk to his boss, borrow from next year's vacation time or something?"

Could you do that? Sophie had never been Miss Corporate America. Before she turned her shopping passion into a business, her jobs had been the kind that involved plates of food and tips. So what did she know?

"I don't know. I talked to his boss months ago, told her what I was planning. She said she'd be fine with it."

"Maybe his boss forgot about your conversation and needs him. Maybe he really does have too much work to do."

"Or maybe he just doesn't want to go with me." Sierra's voice was threaded with insecurity.

"What man in his right mind wouldn't be working every angle to go on a glam holiday cruise? With his wife," Sophie hastily added.

"Mine, I guess. I mean, I know things haven't exactly been perfect these last few months, especially with him working so much, but we still love each other."

Correction: they both loved Mark.

This conversation was going to take a while. Sophie took a bottle of juice out of the fridge and settled on her living room couch, put her feet on the coffee table and looked out the window. Her studio apartment had a great view…of the apartment across the street from it. That was what you got when you lived in Seattle and worked not at Amazon.

"I'm sorry, Sissy," she said. *Sorry your man is turning out to be such a subpar husband.*

Mark had a selfish streak that had been widening over the last four years. He was constantly frustrating Sierra by blowing their budget on expensive toys—a new car, that fancy watch he'd just had to have, pricey tickets to football games, which he attended with his buddies, a bigger and better TV. Sierra, the budget-conscious one, had tried to rein him in, but they were now five years into their marriage and the reins were pretty much broken.

Which made it all the more mystifying why he wasn't moving heaven and earth to take this trip. It should have appealed to him, considering his family's German roots and his love of extravagance. Sierra had been paying for the cruise for months.

"I swear if I wasn't such a good wife I'd poison him," Sierra said, the insecurity replaced with anger.

"Well, there you go. He senses danger and he's afraid to be alone with you in a stateroom," Sophie teased in an effort to lighten the moment.

"He's afraid to be alone with me in the bedroom, for sure," Sierra grumbled. "Afraid I'll poke a hole in his condom."

"TMI. Pleeease."

"Sorry," Sierra muttered.

"You guys talked about this stuff before you got married. Didn't he say he wanted kids, or am I misremembering?" Sophie took a drink of her juice. Orange juice. A little extra vitamin C never hurt.

"Yeah, eventually. But I'm thirty-four and he's thirty-five. Eventually is here."

"You still have time. Thirty-four's not that old."

"Yes, it is."

"No, it's not." If thirty-four was old, then thirty was middle-aged, and Sophie wasn't ready for that. "I'm sure you can convince him to change his mind."

"I've been trying, believe me. He thinks we can't afford a baby."

Maybe not, with the way he liked to spend money. Poor Sierra.

"It seems like we've been arguing so much lately. I was really looking forward to us getting away. I thought he was going to love this."

Sophie knew that Sierra had been excited to present her husband with the gift of a Christmas cruise the night before. She'd planned to make a recipe for Rouladen, a German dish she'd found online, and then serve him German chocolate cake for dessert as a warm-up for the big moment. She'd been so sure that this cruise was just what they needed to get back that honeymoon high.

"Not that things are that bad," she insisted. "But we need more time together. We need to get on the same page."

Sophie fumbled around for the right words. "Maybe he was just shocked. He needs time to process, figure out how to make it work." Lame.

"He should have jumped at this." Sierra's voice began to wobble.

"What happened when you gave him the envelope?" Sophie asked.

"He stared at it and asked, 'What's this?' Like I'd given him a raw onion or something."

The rat. "That's all he said?"

"No. He said he was really sorry. We can do something next summer. Blah, blah."

Sierra let out a sigh. "Looks like this wasn't one of my better ideas."

It seemed that, lately, Sierra and Mark spent more time apart than they did together. He did have to work long hours. The price of success.

If you asked Sophie, it was priced too high. She loved her work—what was not to love about shopping for people?—but she also loved hanging out with family and friends. You had to make time for that. She could have understood Mark's long hours better if he owned his own business or was doing something he was passionate about, but from what she could tell he was only a cog in the corporate wheel, working for a paycheck he could blow.

"What are you going to do?" she asked.

"Throw out the leftover Rouladen."

"No, I mean about the trip."

"I'm going. I paid for this and I'm going. I *can* take the time off."

"You're gonna go without him?"

That sure didn't seem like a good idea.

"He said I should since I already spent the money. He felt bad that he can't come with me and he didn't want the trip to be wasted. In fact, he even suggested I take you with me."

Very noble. Except Mark wasn't that noble and his

offer made Sophie suspicious. Did he have some selfish hidden agenda? Did he welcome the idea of a week
away from his wife?

"I'm not sure that's a good idea," she said. "I mean,
you guys are already having problems."

There was a moment of silence. "I know," her sister
said in a small voice. "I thought this would be good for
us. I'd been hoping all morning he'd text me that he got
the time off, after all. I finally texted him."

Having to nag her husband to go on a trip with her.
This was sick and wrong.

"He said he really can't take off. My surprise sure
backfired."

"I'm so sorry, Sissy."

There was a lesson in this somewhere, like never
spend a small fortune on a trip you didn't plan together.
At least, not if you were married to Mark.

There was another moment of silence, then Sierra
said, "Maybe he's seeing someone."

Gaack! "Then you definitely shouldn't go!"

"Like staying home would stop him? A man can always find ways to cheat. Anyway, he's always working.
When would he get the time?"

Sophie thought of the old saying you always find
time for what you really want to do. Mark was selfish,
but surely he wasn't downright evil.

"Maybe we need this time apart," Sierra reasoned.
"Maybe it will make us both realize how much we love
each other."

Or how much he doesn't love you. Sophie frowned
and set aside her juice, which suddenly wasn't sitting
so well on her stomach.

The diagnosis for this tummy trouble was easy. She

worried about her big sister. Sierra was a typical first-born—a real caregiver, watching over everyone, including Sophie.

Sophie still had the card Sierra had made her when she was nine and had to spend the night in the hospital. The angel on the front showed the talent of a young, budding artist. Inside Sierra had written, *I'll watch over you*. She'd kept that promise, telling Sophie stories at night to distract her when she was scared that the invisible monster that had sent her to the hospital would come back and sit on her chest so she couldn't breathe. In high school she'd gotten Sophie through algebra and geometry, shared makeup tips and clothes.

She still watched out for her sister and everyone else, as well. She was always the first to offer to help their grandma decorate the Christmas tree and bullied Sophie and their brother, Drew, into putting up the Christmas lights for their parents every year. When Mark's mom had broken her ankle the year before it had been Sierra who took her to her doctor appointments and physical therapy. She loved with all her heart. Sophie didn't want to see that big heart of hers get stomped on.

"Anyway, I was stupid and didn't get trip insurance."

"You didn't get trip insurance?" Sophie repeated, shocked.

"I know. I should have. I'd just been so sure… Anyway, if I don't go I'll have spent all that money for nothing," Sierra continued. "So I'm going." She might as well have added, *So there*. "Want to come with?"

"On a cruise."

It had all sounded so glamorous and romantic when her sister first told Sophie what she was planning; she'd actually been a little jealous. But not for long, not after she remembered all those poor people quarantined on those cruise ships.

"It'll be fun."

"Yeah, until some disease breaks out."

"Cruise lines are being extra cautious now. You could be safer on a boat than you are here at home. Think of it—quaint German villages, beautiful scenery, sister adventures. Shopping."

The magic word.

"It's all paid for."

More magic words.

"I don't want to go by myself," Sierra confessed. "It'd be too depressing."

"That would be hard. You'd look like the loser of the high seas."

"We won't be at sea. We'll be on a river."

"Oh, yeah. Right."

"It really does look like fun and I know we'd have a good time. So what do you say?"

"Um."

"Come on. The only time you've used your passport was when we did that family trip to Canada. Don't you want another stamp in it?"

Actually, she did. And a weeklong cruise with her sister would be a fabulous way to start the holidays.

Um finally turned to *yes* and Sierra ended the call sounding happy instead of miserable. Sophie, too, was feeling a little swell of excitement. She and her sister always had fun together and she was sure they'd both enjoy this trip. Well, as long as neither of them got sick.

She went to Costco to shop for her friend. While she was there she bought a giant bottle of Airborne gummies. And on her way home she stopped and bought pills to prevent seasickness, several bottles of hand sanitizer (even though she already had three in her bathroom cabinet) and a mask to wear on the plane. Okay, let the fun begin.

One Charmed Christmas *is available to order wherever books are sold.*

From *New York Times* bestselling author

DEBBIE MACOMBER

What would make *your* Christmas perfect?

"Popular romance writer Debbie Macomber has a gift for evoking the emotions that are at the heart of the genre's popularity." —*Publishers Weekly*

Order your copy today!

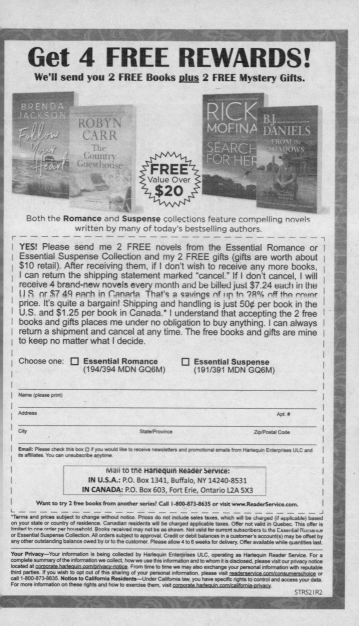